KT-196-548

Bristol Libraries
1804530526

New York Times bestselling author **Christine Feehan** has over 30 novels published and has thrilled legions of fans with her seductive and sensual 'Dark' Carpathian tales. She has received numerous honours throughout her career including being a nominee for the Romance Writers of America RITA, and receiving a Career Achievement Award from *Romantic Times*, and has been published in multiple languages and in many formats, including audio book, e-book, and large print.

For more information about Christine Feehan visit her website: www.christinefeehan.com

***Praise for Christine Feehan*:**

'After Bram Stoker, Anne Rice and Joss Whedon, Feehan is the person most credited with popularizing the neck gripper'
Time magazine

'The queen of paranormal romance'
USA Today

'Feehan has a knack for bringing vampiric Carpathians to vivid, virile life in her Dark Carpathian novels'
Publishers Weekly

Christine Feehan's
'Dark' Carpathian Series:

Dark Prince
Dark Desire
Dark Gold
Dark Magic
Dark Challenge
Dark Fire
Dark Legend
Dark Guardian
Dark Symphony
Dark Melody
Dark Destiny
Dark Secret
Dark Demon
Dark Celebration
Dark Possession
Dark Curse
Dark Slayer
Dark Peril
Dark Predator
Dark Storm
Dark Lycan
Dark Wolf

Dark Nights
Darkest at Dawn (omnibus)

Also by Christine Feehan

Sea Haven Series:
Water Bound
Spirit Bound

GhostWalker Series:
Shadow Game
Mind Game
Night Game
Conspiracy Game
Deadly Game
Predatory Game
Murder Game
Street Game
Ruthless Game
Samurai Game

Drake Sisters Series:
Oceans of Fire
Dangerous Tides
Safe Harbour
Turbulent Sea
Hidden Currents

Magic Before Christmas

Leopard People Series:
Fever
Burning Wild
Wild Fire
Savage Nature
Leopard's Prey

The Scarletti Curse

Lair of the Lion

DARK WOLF

A CARPATHIAN NOVEL

CHRISTINE FEEHAN

PIATKUS

First published in the US in 2014 by The Berkley Publishing Group
A division of the Penguin Group USA (Inc.),
First published in Great Britain in 2014 by Piatkus
Reprinted 2014

A CIP catalogue record for this book
is available from the British Library.

Hardback ISBN: 978-0-349-40216-1
Trade paperback ISBN: 978-0-349-40191-1

Printed and bound in Great Britain by
Clays Ltd, St Ives plc

Papers used by Piatkus are from well-managed forests
and other responsible sources.

MIX
Paper from
responsible sources
FSC® C104740

Piatkus
An imprint of
Little, Brown Book Group
100 Victoria Embankment
London EC4Y 0DY

An Hachette UK Company
www.hachette.co.uk

www.piatkus.co.uk

For my Skyler, with much love

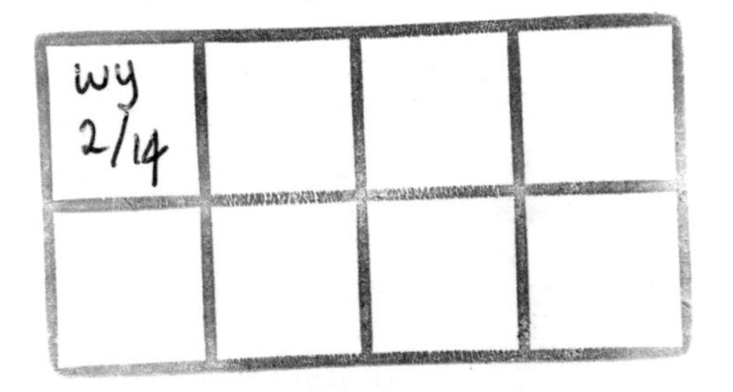

For My Readers

Be sure to go to christinefeehan.com/members/ to sign up for my PRIVATE book announcement list and download the *free* ebook of *Dark Desserts.* Join my community and get firsthand news, enter the book discussions, ask your questions and chat with me. Please feel free to email me at Christine@christinefeehan.com. I would love to hear from you.

Acknowledgments

Many thanks to my sister Anita Toste who always answers my call and has such fun with me writing mage spells.

Thank you to my wonderful daughter Cecilia who also helped with mage spells; rhyming is not my forte, and she only laughed at me a little bit! We certainly had fun.

I have to give a special shout out to C. L. Wilson and Sheila English, who were gracious enough to include me in our power writing sessions. We rocked it, didn't we?

As always, thanks to Brian Feehan and Domini Stottsberry. They worked long hours to help me with everything from brainstorming ideas and doing research to edits. There are no words to describe my gratitude or love for them. Thank you all so very much!

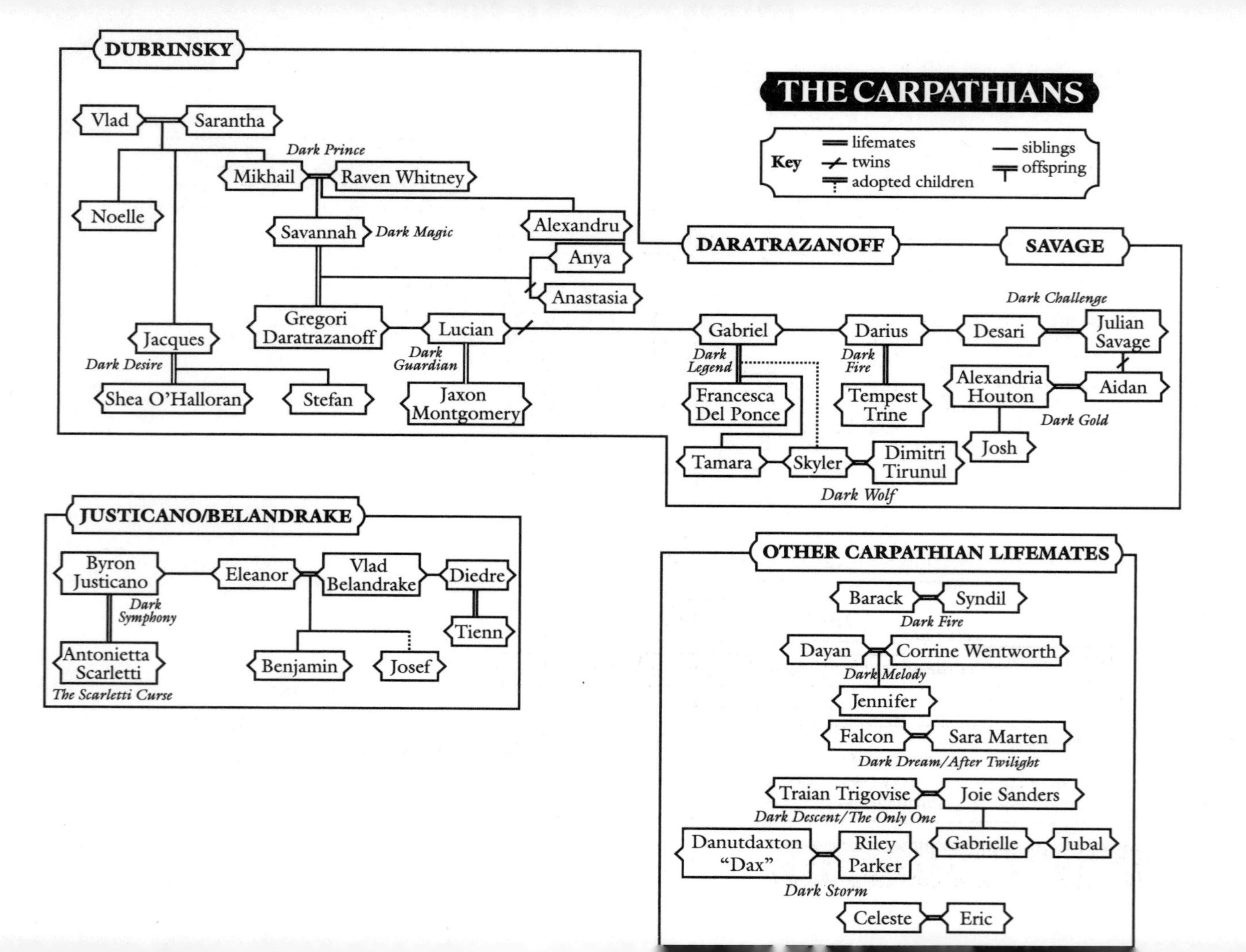

THE CARPATHIANS
Key
lifemates
twins
adopted children
siblings
offspring
DUBRINSKY
Vlad
Sarantha
Dark Prince
Mikhail
Raven Whitney
Noelle
Savannah
Dark Magic
Alexandru
Anya
Anastasia
Gregori Daratrazanoff
Lucian
Dark Guardian
Jaxon Montgomery
Jacques
Dark Desire
Shea O'Halloran
Stefan
DARATRAZANOFF
SAVAGE
Gabriel
Dark Legend
Francesca Del Ponce
Tamara
Skyler
Dimitri Tirunul
Dark Wolf
Darius
Dark Fire
Tempest Trine
Desari
Dark Challenge
Julian Savage
Alexandria Houton
Aidan
Dark Gold
Josh
JUSTICANO/BELANDRAKE
Byron Justicano
Dark Symphony
Antonietta Scarletti
The Scarletti Curse
Eleanor
Vlad Belandrake
Diedre
Tienn
Benjamin
Josef
OTHER CARPATHIAN LIFEMATES
Barack
Syndil
Dark Fire
Dayan
Corrine Wentworth
Dark Melody
Jennifer
Falcon
Sara Marten
Dark Dream/After Twilight
Traian Trigovise
Joie Sanders
Dark Descent/The Only One
Gabrielle
Jubal
Danutdaxton "Dax"
Riley Parker
Dark Storm
Celeste
Eric

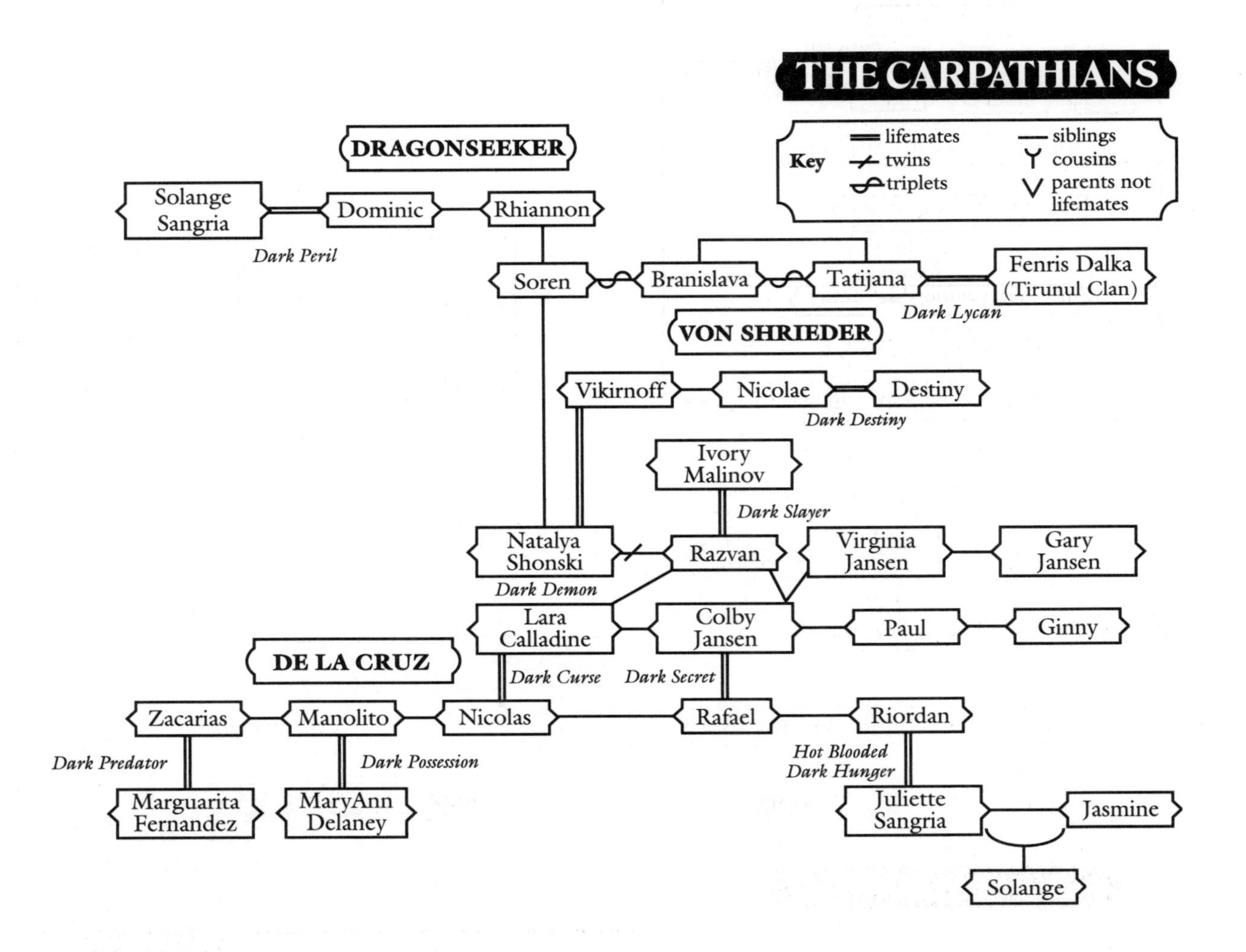
THE CARPATHIANS
Key
lifemates
twins
triplets
siblings
cousins
parents not lifemates
DRAGONSEEKER
Solange Sangria
Dominic
Rhiannon
Dark Peril
Soren
Branislava
Tatijana
Fenris Dalka (Tirunul Clan)
Dark Lycan
VON SHRIEDER
Vikirnoff
Nicolae
Destiny
Dark Destiny
Ivory Malinov
Dark Slayer
Natalya Shonski
Razvan
Virginia Jansen
Gary Jansen
Dark Demon
Lara Calladine
Colby Jansen
Paul
Ginny
DE LA CRUZ
Dark Curse
Dark Secret
Zacarias
Manolito
Nicolas
Rafael
Riordan
Dark Predator
Dark Possession
Hot Blooded
Dark Hunger
Marguarita Fernandez
MaryAnn Delaney
Juliette Sangria
Jasmine
Solange

Dark Wolf

I

Skyler Daratrazanoff pulled the long black shawl closer, making certain her hair was covered and there was little to see of her face. Her heart beat so hard she was afraid anyone close would hear. Everything hinged on making the official believe her. Josef had forged the papers, and he was the best. He could hack any computer, provide information or get it. She didn't doubt for a minute that the papers he created would be in order and pass close scrutiny, but she still had to make the official believe her.

The tin building was rusted and looked as if it might fall apart at any moment. A man came forward to meet her, looking solemn as the casket was wheeled ahead of her into the shade of the building. Fortunately the sun was setting and shadows fell around her, helping to make it more difficult to see her clearly.

"Your papers?" he said. His voice was kind. The name on his badge identified him as Erno Varga.

She glanced back toward the small plane she'd flown to the airport and then handed her papers to the official, making certain her eyes were downcast and she looked weepy. She had taken care to use drops to make her eyes red and watery, just in case she couldn't pull off acting on her own.

Varga looked over her papers and then up at her several times with sharp, disbelieving eyes. "You're young to be bringing home your brother's body alone. No one else is traveling with you?"

She shook her head, trying to look more tragic than ever. "My father is dead, and now my brother." She choked back a sob worthy, she was certain, of an Oscar performance. "There is no one else to bring him home to our mother."

The official looked at her again and studied her papers closer. "He died of a broken heart?" There was skepticism in his voice.

Skyler nearly choked. *When I get my hands on you, Josef, you're going to die of more than a broken heart.* She used her telepathic connection with Josef to let him know he was in huge trouble.

A terrible tragedy. Josef was unrepentant as always. There was amusement in his tone. No matter how serious a situation, he didn't mind in the least being mischievous.

She managed to keep a straight face and gave Varga a solemn nod. "He just wasted away when his girl left him. He refused to eat." She had no choice but to go with it, even if it meant twisting her fingers together hard in order to prevent the official from seeing she was shaking. "It's a terrible tragedy. Nothing could save him."

Okay, even to her ears, that sounded totally lame. But a broken heart? Only Josef would come up with something so dramatic and unbelievable. How else could she explain he'd died of a broken heart? There was *definitely* going to be another cause of death after they opened the casket.

She could feel Josef's laughter. *Of course you're laughing. You're safe in the coffin, the tragically dead brother, while I'm lying my ass off to this man who could put me in prison for the rest of my life.*

She knew Josef would never let that happen. If necessary he'd give the official a "push" to believe her. Right now, he was having too much fun listening to her squirm—and she supposed she deserved it. She was making him do something highly dangerous, and he would be blamed more than she would be if anything went wrong. Her father would probably just kill him on sight.

He will, too, Josef said. *He'll rip me from limb to limb.*

You should be worrying about me ripping you from limb to limb, she threatened.

"How old are you?" The official stared at her passport and papers and then back up to her face. "Did you pilot that plane?"

She lifted her chin, trying for older and much sterner. She knew she looked young, but not her eyes. If he looked her directly in the eye, he would believe what those forged papers said. And they were great forgeries. Josef had many talents, although making up stories was clearly not one of them.

"I'm much older than I look," Skyler replied. It was partially the truth. She felt older, and that should count for something. She'd been through more than most women—okay, teens.

"Twenty-five?" he said skeptically.

Josef had insisted she be twenty-five if she was going to pilot the plane. Piloting planes had come easy to her and it was something she especially loved, so her adopted father, Gabriel, had allowed her to learn.

"I have to open the coffin," the official added, watching her closely.

Skyler managed a little sob and covered her mouth, nodding slightly. "I'm sorry. Yes, of course. They said you would. I was expecting you to." She straightened her shoulders and spine courageously.

He looked at her much more kindly. "You don't need to watch. Stand over there." He nodded to a corner of the building just a few feet away.

She felt a little sorry for him. If she knew anything at all about Josef, she knew he would put on some kind of show.

Don't you dare blow this by scaring him, she warned. *I mean it, Josef.*

You're no fun. I can always remove his memories. Wouldn't it be so delicious to do an impression of Count Dracula? I've watched the movie a million times. I've got the look and accent down perfectly.

He sounded far too eager. It took a lot of discipline to keep amusement from her mind where he could read it. She didn't doubt for a moment that Josef could do a perfect Dracula impression.

Resist the urge. We aren't out of the woods and we can't afford to take any chances. We're in Carpathian territory. Or at least close enough that someone might be near us to sense the use of energy. Restrain yourself, Josef.

He heaved a sigh. *No matter what the outcome, your father is going to kill me, a slow and painful death, too. I should be able to have a little fun.*

That was hitting very close to the truth. Gabriel was going to murder all of them, but if their plan worked, it would be well worth it.

She gave Varga a small, grateful smile and moved away from the coffin. Standing in the open door, her arms wrapped around her middle for comfort, she stared outside into the gathering darkness, holding herself very still. Their plan *had* to work.

Behave Josef, or else. Gabriel's in London and I'm here. She had never been on the receiving end of Gabriel's wrath, but he and her uncle Lucian were legendary vampire hunters. The Carpathian people, most extremely powerful, whispered their names in awe.

You've got a point. Laughter bubbled over in Josef's voice. *What a sorry waste of a good coffin.* Now there was disgust in his tone.

Skyler couldn't tell if he was going to behave or not. It was impossible with Josef. He marched to his own drum. She sent up a silent prayer, hoping for the best.

Right now, Francesca and Gabriel were probably awake and would soon be preparing to fly to the Carpathian Mountains. They thought she was a continent away, safe with her human college friend Maria, using her vacation to help build homes and run irrigation to farmers in South America. She had never lied to them before. Not once. And it hurt her to do it now, but there was no other way.

She knew her parents had been summoned to the huge meeting between Lycan and Carpathian to discuss an alliance between the two species. Most of the Carpathians had been called home. Gabriel and Francesca had been more than happy to receive a call from her from school asking to go with Maria. They didn't want her anywhere near the Carpathian Mountains.

She would never think of repaying their extraordinary kindness, the love they had given her from the moment she'd been taken into their home, with lies and betrayal—not for anything or anyone except Dimitri. Dimitri Tirunul was her unexpected miracle. A man beyond any she'd ever dreamt of. She was human. He was Carpathian—nearly immortal. She was nineteen years old. He was an ancient, centuries old. She held the other half of his soul, the light to his darkness. Without her, he would not survive. She was his lifemate—his savior. Yet she knew just the opposite was true—Dimitri was the one saving her.

He knew she was his lifemate when she was just a child, and he had given her time. Space. Unconditional love. He never demanded anything of her. He never told her how difficult it was for him—that she was his salvation—just out of his reach. He had always been there for her, in the middle of the night, when her violent past was too close and she couldn't sleep, when nightmares haunted her to the point she couldn't breathe. He was there, in her mind, holding all those terrifying memories at bay. Dimitri. Her Dimitri.

Dimitri was caught in the middle between the two species. The Lycans had taken him and planned to kill him. No one had gone after him to save him. He had spent centuries hunting the undead to keep his people as well as humans safe. He had survived honorably when others had chosen to give up their souls. Yet there was no rescue party. No hunters were rushing to save him. He was badly injured. She felt that much before he cut himself off from her to protect her from his pain—or his death.

Dimitri was stoic about life or death. He was a Carpathian hunter and he'd been around for centuries, protecting innocents from vampires. Her lineage was complicated, but for all intents and purposes, she was human. The Lycans would never expect a teenage, human girl to mount a rescue operation for a Carpathian. She had the element of surprise on her side. That, as well as good, trustworthy friends and her very powerful but untested abilities.

Skyler had faith in herself. She knew her every strength and every weakness. Like Josef, she was extremely intelligent and most of the time underestimated. She believed the Lycans would underestimate her—she was counting on it.

No one would start a war over a Carpathian hunter it seemed, but she knew her father would come after her, and if anyone harmed one hair on her head, the Lycan world would be in for a nightmare it couldn't possibly conceive. Not only would Gabriel come after her, but so would her uncle Lucian. She was fairly certain her biological father, Razvan, and his lifemate, Ivory, would join the hunt for her. They were extremely lethal as well. There was satisfaction in knowing if she was injured or killed, she would be avenged. No one, not even Mikhail Dubrinsky, the prince of the Carpathian people, would be able to stop a war if the Lycans harmed her.

She lifted her chin. Dimitri would never leave her in danger. He would rush to her side the moment he knew there was trouble; he had—more than once—just to soothe bad dreams when she had too many in a row. She couldn't do less for him.

Holding her breath, she turned back to watch the official gingerly open the coffin. It creaked ominously. Hideously. Just like in the movies. The sound sent a chill down her spine. The lid rose slowly and darn Josef anyway, it looked as if it was lifting all by itself. Varga stepped back, one hand going up defensively.

There was silence as the lid came to a stop. Nothing moved. She could hear the sound of a clock ticking loudly. Varga coughed nervously. He glanced at her. Skyler put her hand over her mouth and lowered her eyes.

Josef! Behave yourself. Skyler was somewhere between laughing and crying with nervous tension.

Varga stepped back to the coffin and peered in, beads of sweat visible on his forehead. He cleared his throat. "He certainly looks robust for a man who starved himself to death."

The least you could have done was make yourself look emaciated if you wanted him to believe your preposterous story, she scolded.

Skyler pressed a handkerchief to her mouth. "They did such a good job at the funeral home. I particularly asked them to make certain he looked good for our mother."

Varga pressed his lips together and studied the body. He was suspicious, but she wasn't certain of what. Clearly there was a dead body in the coffin. Did he suspect her of running drugs? Guns? If so, that didn't bode well for what she had planned. She needed to look like a naïve, young teenager who might be slightly ditzy.

She held her breath as he reached for the lid of the coffin and slowly closed it.

"Is someone coming for you?" Varga asked as he locked the coffin lid and glanced at his watch. "I can't stay. You were the last plane coming in."

"My brother's friend arranged for a truck to pick us up. He'll be here any minute," Skyler assured him solemnly. "Thank you so much for all your help."

"You can wait in here," Varga said in a kind voice. "I'll come back in a couple of hours and lock up." He looked around the dilapidated building. It was nothing more than four metal walls, mostly rusted, some so badly there were holes. "Not that there's much to lock up." He glanced again at his watch. "I would wait with you, but I have another job to go to."

She sent him a wan smile. "It's all right. Really. He'll be here any minute."

Varga gave her one last look and exited the rickety building, leaving her there alone with the locked coffin. Skyler waited until she saw his car drive off and the lights disappear completely down the road. She took a careful look around. She appeared to be alone.

"Josef, you can quit playing dead," Skyler said, her voice dripping with sarcasm. She banged on the coffin lid with her fist. "Died of a broken heart? Really? You couldn't think of anything else, anything, say, more realistic?"

The lid of the coffin opened with the same series of ominous, horror film creaks he'd used when Varga had opened the lid. There was silence. Skyler's heart beat steadily. She leaned over the coffin and glared at the young man who lay as if dead, his arms crossed over his chest and his eyes closed. His skin was pale porcelain and his black spiky hair with the dyed blue tips stood out starkly against the white backdrop.

"You look amazingly robust for a man who starved himself to death," she said sarcastically, mimicking the official. "You could have blown everything with your absurd story."

Josef's eyes snapped open dramatically. He faked an accent as he slowly sat up. "I could use a drop of blood or two, my dear."

She smacked him over the head with her papers. "The customs official didn't believe I was twenty-five."

Josef flashed a cocky grin. "You're not. You're barely nineteen, and when Gabriel and Lucian find out what we've done, we're both going to be in more trouble than either of us has ever known." He paused, the smile fading from his mouth. "And I've been in a lot of trouble."

"We have no choice," Skyler said.

"Don't kid yourself, Sky, there's always a choice. And you aren't the one they're going to kill. I'm going to be their prime target. When Gabriel and Lucian come looking for you—and they will," Josef said, "they'll find you. They have a reputation for a reason. If we really do this, every Carpathian hunter will be out looking."

Her father, Gabriel, was extremely powerful, a legendary Carpathian hunter. Her uncle Lucian, Gabriel's twin, had helped to create that legend among the Carpathian people, and when they discovered her gone, *of course* they would come after her.

"Isn't that the point?" Skyler replied with a small shrug. "By the time they wake and realize we're gone, we'll have a good head start. We should be able to find Dimitri."

"You do realize," Josef said, floating out of the coffin, "this could very well cause an international incident. Or worse, war. All-out war."

"You agreed to help me," Skyler said. "Have you changed your mind?"

"No. You're my best friend, Sky. Dimitri probably despises me and wishes I was dead, but he's your lifemate and he's been literally thrown to the wolves." Josef sent her a little grin, pleased with his pun. "Of course I'm going to help you. I helped you come up with this plan, didn't I? And it will work."

"Dimitri doesn't despise you; in fact, he's glad you're my friend. We've talked about it. He isn't like that." Skyler made a face at him. "You know very well he knows I think of you like a brother. He'd defend you with his life."

Josef grinned at her. "Forgive *me* for despising *him* just a little bit. He's good-looking, intelligent, an ancient hunter, and your lifemate. He destroyed all my dreams and fantasies about you. I don't dare even think along those lines or he'd know."

Skyler rolled her eyes. "As if. Even I know you don't think of me that way, Josef. You can hide a lot of things, but not that. There's no fantasy and no destroyed dreams. Your lifemate is either not born or"—she smirked at him mischievously—"she's probably one of Gregori's daughters."

He groaned and slapped his forehead with his palm. "A curse on you forever for uttering those words, for putting that thought out into the universe. Don't even think that, let alone say it aloud. Can you imagine Gregori Daratrazanoff as a father-in-law? Sheesh, Skyler, you really do want me dead."

She laughed. "It would serve you right, Josef. Especially after putting you died of a broken heart on those papers!"

"It could happen. I'm a romantic, you know. Dimitri thinks I'm a little kid, just like they all do, which is probably just as well, because otherwise he'd see me as a rival."

"You take great pains to keep them all thinking you're a kid," Skyler pointed out with a small smile. "You like them to underestimate you. You're a genius, Josef, and you don't let any of them see the real you. You deliberately provoke them."

His grin widened until he looked positively mischievous. He blew on his fingertips. "That is very true. I don't deny it." His smile faded. "But this is very different than the pranks I pull on them. This is big, Skyler. I just want you to understand what's at stake."

"Of course I know what's at stake."

"Your family is one of the most powerful families of our people." He frowned. "Which reminds me, why don't you ever refer to Gregori as your uncle? He's a brother to Lucian and Gabriel, so technically, he is your uncle."

"I guess I never thought about it. I don't know him. We're in London, and he's here in the Carpathian Mountains and he's never shown a tremendous amount of interest in me."

"He's a Daratrazanoff, believe me, Sky, he's interested in you. If you disappear, your family is going to come looking and they'll be on the warpath. *All* of your family, especially Gabriel."

"Are you afraid of my father?" Skyler asked.

"I've got news for you, honey, *everyone* is afraid of your father, and if they aren't they should be, especially when it comes to you. Haven't you noticed how protective he is of you? Your uncle Lucian is just as bad if not worse, and if anyone messes with one of those men or anyone they love, they answer to both of them."

Skyler bit her lip. "I'm sorry, Josef, for putting you in this position. I can't turn back. I have to find Dimitri. I know I can do this. This plan is flawless. And we both knew—and counted on Gabriel and Lucian coming after me. I can go from here by myself, I really can."

Josef burst out laughing. "Now you really have lost your mind. If I let you do this alone, they'd *really* kill me. No, we're here and we have to see it through. I think you're the only one who could pull this off. But, Skyler, if you get into trouble, this really will start a war. Lucian and Gabriel are not going to back off if someone hurts you, or if you're captured. They won't care what the prince says. They'll go after you and no one will stand in their way. You'd better go into this knowing that. You have to know the consequences and be willing to face them."

Skyler pressed her lips together. She'd thought about little else since she and Josef had come up with the plan. "Dimitri is a good man. He could have claimed me, taken me away from my home and the only stability I'd ever known. I wouldn't have been able to resist him, the pull of lifemates is just too strong. But he didn't, Josef, no matter the terrible cost to him. He didn't insist on claiming me or binding us together. He wasn't afraid of Gabriel. He was never afraid of Gabriel."

Josef waved his hand at the coffin and the lid creaked closed. "I know," he admitted softly.

"He knew I wasn't ready, that I needed time to find myself and overcome . . . everything in my past." Skyler ducked her head, so that her wealth of silky hair covered her expression.

"Don't, Sky," Josef said. "We're best friends. What happened to you wasn't your fault, and you should never feel ashamed."

"I'm not ashamed, well, not like you think. I believe Dimitri is a great man and he deserves a lifemate who can match him in everything. I'm not that woman yet. I want to be with him, I feel that need nearly as strongly as he does. It grows in me every single day."

"Do you think he would hold your past against you?" Josef asked.

Skyler shook her head. "No, he often is close enough to talk to me at night when I can't sleep. We talk a lot at night. I love his voice. He's very gentle with me, never demanding. I know it's difficult for him. I can feel his struggle, although he hid it from me at first. You can't be in someone else's head without eventually seeing everything. Darkness threatened to swallow him all the time, yet he never said anything to me, he never tried to hurry me. He certainly didn't condemn me because I was too young—and afraid. Dimitri doesn't judge me."

"No one does, hon," Josef pointed out. "You're the one so hard on yourself. I especially loved the stage when you dyed your hair constantly. It took a little while to find yourself and be comfortable with who you really are."

Skyler's eyebrow shot up. She stared pointedly at Josef's black, spiked hair tipped with blue.

His grin was contagious, revealing twin dents near his mouth. "This is who I am. I found that out a long time ago. I like my hair with blue tips."

"Because no one will ever guess just how smart you are. They're too busy looking at your hair and the piercings you occasionally put in just to bug them all," she accused, laughing softly. "I love you, Josef, you know that, don't you?"

"Yep. That's why I'm here, Sky. I don't have all that many people who care about me. If you say you need me, I'll come." He looked away from her.

Skyler put her hand on his arm. "There are many people who care about you, Josef, you just don't let them get close. If you gave Dimitri a chance, he would be a good friend to you. I know he would. I've talked to him many times about you."

"I thought you hadn't seen him since you'd been to the Carpathian Mountains."

"He thought it best if we stayed away from one another. I knew it would be too difficult for him with me being physically close to him, but he came to London on and off when he needed to hear my voice."

"Did Gabriel know?" Josef asked.

"Probably. He didn't ask me, but I noticed when Dimitri was close, Gabriel stayed closer and when he wasn't with me, Francesca was close by. There were times when Uncle Lucian and Auntie Jaxon hung around. They're busy, so I knew it was because they were afraid Dimitri would come and claim me."

"But he didn't."

"Of course not. He's a man of honor. I'm not old enough in the Carpathian culture, which is funny, because in the human culture I could marry easily. No one would think twice about it."

"Did you want him to claim you?" Josef asked curiously.

Skyler shrugged. "Sometimes. I dream about him. I don't ever think about other men, or even look at them. It's always Dimitri. He calls to me and isn't even aware of it. When we're talking, mind to mind, I see things. How alone he is. How dark his world is. How hard it is to struggle against the constant pull of the darkness. He endures so much for me. So much for all of us. When he hunts, it has become harder for him. Every time he has to kill. I see all that, and the terrible sacrifices he makes for me."

"He wouldn't want you to see those things, Sky," Josef said gently. "You know that, don't you? Carpathian males, especially the hunters, they're like stone, total warriors, and if he thought he wasn't protecting you from that creeping shadow, he'd be very upset."

Skyler smiled at Josef. "I can't help what I see, Josef. I'm not exactly like everyone else. What kind of a concoction am I? Psychic. Mage. Partly Carpathian. Daughter of the earth. Dragonseeker. I see things I'm not meant to see. I feel things I shouldn't. I know he was nearly taken from me. I felt him. I called to him. Sang the healing chants I've heard Francesca sing. I lit candles, and I cried for days when he was so far away I couldn't reach him."

She looked into his eyes, letting him see her grief. Josef was definitely underestimated by most people, but she saw his genius, and she valued their close friendship. She could talk to him, tell him anything, and he never betrayed her confidence.

"I need him," she admitted simply. "And I have to find him."

Josef slung his arm around her shoulders. "Well, little sister, that's exactly what we're going to do. Paul should be here any minute. He texted me and said he had everything ready."

"Did he cover his tracks? Didn't he tell you once that Nicolas took his blood? If he did, he can track Paul."

"Baby, any of them can track us, and they'll be hot on our trail the moment they realize you're missing."

"I know that. I'm just saying it can't happen until we're ready." Skyler glanced again at her watch. "He's late."

"His cover is perfect," Josef assured. "He flew over with the De La Cruz families, and he told them we were going to go exploring the mountains on the Ukraine side. We're camping for a couple of weeks. Of course they were happy to get rid of us, and no one is going to question that we'd want to do something together. We talked about it endlessly for the last couple of years. This would be the perfect opportunity for us to get together so they bought our story easily."

Skyler gave a little sniff. "Of course they don't mind if you two go off camping in the wilds together. Remember when I wanted to go on one of your camping trips? The world almost came to an end."

Josef laughed and leaned one hip lazily against the coffin. "Gabriel turned into the big bad wolf and nearly ate Paul and me for dinner just at the suggestion. I was surprised he allowed you to go off to college. You were so far ahead of your age group in school."

Skyler shrugged. "I went home at night the first year. I needed to. That had nothing to do with Gabriel and Francesca. I don't know what I would have done without them. I needed them so much in the early days. And they really came through for me." Tears shimmered in her eyes. "I hate to repay their love and kindness with lies, but they left me no choice."

"You tried talking to them about Dimitri?" Josef asked.

Skyler nodded. "I knew something was wrong, that Dimitri was troubled the last time we talked. He left abruptly for the Carpathian Mountains a few weeks ago and then he was in a terrible battle. I felt him slipping away from me. He was so far away, and I almost couldn't reach him. By the time I did, he was nearly gone. I could feel his life force fading." She looked up at him. "You remember that night? I called you to come and help me."

"You were in the college library and fortunately I'd come to visit you, so I wasn't far away," Josef said, "but you didn't tell me what happened. Only that Dimitri needed you. You were wiped out."

The memory of that night shook her. Dimitri had been badly wounded. Mortally wounded. She was far from him, studying in the college library—so mundane—the distance dimming their connection. She'd reached for him, knowing he was in trouble, and it was his brother she found. When she touched Dimitri, he had grown so cold, ice-cold. She shivered, the coldness still in her bones. Sometimes she didn't think she'd ever get it out.

"His brother was there, fighting for him, following after his fading light and trying to bring him back. I called to Dimitri and begged him not to leave me. I did my best, even across such a great distance, to help his brother bring him back to the land of the living. I just couldn't let him go."

She caught her lower lip between her teeth, biting down hard. Even now her heart ached. She pressed her palm tightly over the pain. "I can't lose him, Josef. He has always been there for me, as long as I've needed him, any way that I've needed him. It's my turn now. I won't let him down. I'm going to find him, and I'm going to help him escape."

"Before, when he was dying, you could reach him," Josef ventured carefully, knowing full well he was walking through a minefield. "Why do you think you can't now?"

"I know what you're getting at, Josef," she snapped, "and it isn't true. Dimitri is alive. I know he's alive."

Josef nodded. "I hear you, Sky, but that doesn't answer my question.

Maybe we'd better figure out why you can't reach him when the two of you have always been able to communicate telepathically. You're extraordinarily powerful. More so than some Carpathians. Many of us can't cover the kinds of distances you've been able to. So what's different now?"

She frowned at him. Josef was incredibly brilliant and even if she didn't want to hear it, she needed to listen to him. He had a point. She'd been able to cross great distances to connect with Dimitri—and him with her. She had known when he was in trouble, when he had fought in a battle with a rogue pack and took the brunt of the attack in order to give his brother the opportunity to destroy a very dangerous vampire/wolf cross.

She had felt Dimitri's pain, so terrible she could barely breathe. Right there, in the college library she had nearly fallen to the floor, with that flash of pain that wasn't hers. She had followed that trail back to him unerringly despite his fading light. Over the years of talking telepathically, the connection between them had grown strong, and she found him even as his life force was fading away, traveling to another realm. If she could do that, Josef was right, why couldn't she find him now? It didn't make sense—and she should have figured that out on her own.

"You're too close to the problem," Josef said, proving he was so tuned to her he could practically read her thoughts.

"I don't like it when I'm not thinking straight," Skyler said. "He needs me to be one hundred percent on this."

"I think it's called love, Sky, as much as I don't want to admit you could love anyone but me." Josef winked at her.

"Something's really wrong, Josef. I know it is. How could I find him when he was already technically dead, but I can't do it now?"

"Perhaps he's unconscious," he ventured.

She shook her head. "I thought of that. I could still find him. I know I could. There's something about our connection. It's so strong, I can follow him anywhere. I could touch him when he was underground, rejuvenating in the soil."

Josef's eyes widened. "No way, Sky. No one can do that. We stop our hearts and lungs and we can't move. That's our most vulnerable time. How could he be aware?"

"I don't know, but whenever I reach for him, day or night, he's always been there for me. Always. I can't remember a single time that I couldn't find him. Mother Earth always sang to me, a vibration I could feel, and I would know where he was."

"Did you tell Gabriel and Francesca you could do that? Could you do it with them? With me?"

Skyler paced across the floor, looking once more at her watch a little impatiently. "I never thought to tell anyone, not even Dimitri, the *how* of it. But no, I never tried to wake anyone else. Francesca and Gabriel get very little time alone together these days, so I never considered waking them. It seemed natural to turn to Dimitri. I knew that he needed me as much as I needed him."

"All this time I thought you were afraid of a relationship with him," Josef said.

Skyler's smile held little humor. "I was never afraid of a relationship with him. How could I be? We have a wonderful relationship. He treats me like I'm the greatest, most desirable woman in the world. He's intelligent, we can talk about anything together for hours. He's kind and gentle. He's everything a woman could want in a partner."

"I'm hearing a 'but' in there."

"I am not certain I can be the lifemate he truly deserves. I'm great at the emotional relationship and the intellectual relationship, but I have no idea if I can ever be what he needs physically. That's an entirely different matter."

Josef shook his head. "Skyler, don't get all psycho about that. It will happen when it's supposed to. Dimitri will never want another woman. Not ever. He'll give you all the time you need."

"I know. I do. Dimitri would never push me and he never has. It isn't him that's worried. I just get anxious thinking about it. I want to be the best lifemate possible to him, but my mind just can't go to a physical relationship yet."

She glanced again at her watch. "Paul had better get here soon. Are you certain he got away without anyone being suspicious?"

"Yeah, he's on his way. Only a few minutes out. You said Dimitri was alive. If he is, we'll find him."

Skyler let her breath out slowly. "I don't like any of this. I detest the fact that the prince, along with everyone else, has abandoned him."

Josef slung his arm around her and hugged her tight. The smile faded. “We'll find him. We will.”

Skyler clung to him for a moment and then nodded, straightening her shoulders and stepping away from him. “I don't like the only explanation I can think of for not being able to connect with him.”

“What is it?” Josef asked.

“He's blocking me.” There was hurt in her voice. “He has to be. There's no other explanation that makes sense.”

2

Paul Jansen gathered Skyler into his arms and hugged her hard. He was taller than she remembered, his shoulders wide and chest deep. He'd filled out and looked more of a man than a boy. He worked hard on his family's ranch and it showed in his deep tan, strong build, defined arms, and confidence. He looked older than his twenty years, responsibility weighing on him.

Skyler hugged him back just as hard. "Thank you for coming. I wouldn't have asked you if I wasn't so desperate."

He held her at arm's length, looking her over carefully, a small, affectionate grin on his face. "I wouldn't miss this for the world. We made a pact a long time ago, the three of us, if any one of us was in trouble, we'd come running. I'm glad you called me."

Josef caught his forearms in the traditional Carpathian greeting between warriors, shocking Skyler a little. There was nothing traditional about Josef, and when he used any of the ancient rituals it always surprised her.

"Good to see you, brother. It's been too long. They don't let you get off work very often, do they?" Josef said.

Paul hugged him in the more traditional human way. "I look after my sisters, especially Ginny. The De La Cruz brothers and their lifemates have enemies, and there's a ranch to run and Ginny to look after during the day."

"You always did work too hard," Josef commented, hugging him back. "It's good to see you. Talking online doesn't cut it. How is your sister? She's growing up fast."

"Ginny is amazing with horses, just like Colby always has been. She's beautiful, too, which means I have to watch all those ranch hands and make sure they don't get any ideas." Paul grinned, but there was no amusement in his eyes.

Skyler had to smile. Most Carpathian hunters were tough as nails and then some, but Paul's sister Colby had married into one of the roughest families of all. She was a lifemate to Rafael De La Cruz. There were five brothers and all of them were considered extremely lethal, some of the most feared predators on the planet. Clearly, Paul had already learned a lot from them. She had no doubt that he'd learned to defend himself as well. He fought vampires and did a man's work on the ranch, running things while the Carpathians slept during the day.

"Josef, load your coffin into the truck, please," Skyler told him. "We've got to keep moving. We need to be on the road just in case someone comes looking for one of us."

Paul looked over the ornate coffin and then burst out laughing. "Look at that thing. Josef, you've been having fun, haven't you?"

Skyler rolled her eyes. "Don't encourage him. You have no idea. He actually put the cause of death as a broken heart in the official documents. Can you believe that?"

Paul laughed harder. "I would expect nothing less." He ruffled Skyler's hair. "You grew up beautiful. Who knew?"

Josef scowled at him. "You see her nearly every day on FaceTime or Skype. She looks the same way she always looks. You, on the other hand, have grown your hair out. You're even beginning to look like the De La Cruz brothers. Are you crazy?"

Paul shrugged and pushed his cowboy hat back on his head with one thumb. "Everyone is a little afraid of the De La Cruz brothers. I don't mind in the least being associated with them. It automatically makes me a badass."

Skyler found herself laughing—and relaxing—for the first time in days.

She'd forgotten the easy camaraderie she shared with Paul and Josef when they were together like this. She loved them both and knew they felt the same way about her. Both might tease her about Dimitri, but they held him in great respect. They wanted to find him every bit as much as she did.

Josef was worried that she might not know the consequences of their actions, but she knew all too well. How could she not? She was lying to the people she loved. And she knew, without a shadow of a doubt that the De La Cruz family would protect Paul just as Gabriel and Lucian would her. The De La Cruz brothers had been a long time away from the Carpathian Mountains, and they were a law unto themselves. They were loyal to the prince, but at the same time, it was the eldest, Zacarias, who governed their actions. He would never, under any circumstances, allow one of his family members to be in jeopardy without coming to his aid.

She had thought a lot about what she was doing. Paul was important to her and he knew it. They had discussed openly what the De La Cruz brothers would do should the plan fail and they all get in trouble. The De La Cruz family had more to lose than any other. MaryAnn and Manolito De La Cruz would be hunted and killed, just as Dimitri would be, if the Lycans had their way at the summit taking place soon in the Carpathian Mountains. They were considered the dreaded *Sange rau*—literally bad blood—a mix of Lycan and Carpathian.

She watched Josef float his coffin into the back of the truck. He was astonishingly adept at moving objects. She could do it, but not as easily as he did. Josef had gone through an awkward phase, but he had certainly come out of it and was smooth and adept at using his Carpathian gifts. He was considered a child in the eyes of the centuries-old Carpathian males. Carpathian children weren't considered adults until they hit their fiftieth year.

The Carpathians were just beginning to understand his genius with technology, especially computers. There was little he couldn't do, nothing he couldn't hack, and no program he couldn't write. She was fairly certain they still didn't recognize the enormity of his abilities and what it meant for their people. Carpathians were very intellectual, but she knew Josef was a true genius, miles ahead of most people in any species.

Paul and Josef were outsiders in their own world, just as she was, to a much lesser extent. She lived with Carpathian parents who treated her lovingly, but she wasn't Carpathian. Paul also was surrounded by Carpathians, but he had to live in a human world, even if he didn't fit there anymore. He'd seen vampires, had even been possessed by one. And then there was Josef. Her gaze fell on him. Flamboyant. A rebel. Yes, he was both of these things, but he was also loyal, brilliant and someone who could always be counted on.

Her heart had always gone out to him. She couldn't deny that she loved him, so of course Dimitri knew. He knew everything about her. Long ago she'd opened her mind to her lifemate. At first she'd allowed Dimitri entrance into her mind with the vague idea he'd see, after her terrible childhood, that she could never be what he wanted her to be. He had been then what he was now. Absolute. Calm. Implacable. Certain. Loving.

He was a man nearly impossible to resist. Well. Okay. Her resistance to the idea of being his lifemate had faded completely. She just needed a little time to build confidence in herself that when the time came she would be able to be a full partner to him.

Skyler bit down hard on her lip, wincing a little when it hurt. She wasn't there yet, not the physical part, but that didn't matter, nor would it ever if he didn't survive.

Josef's teasing nudge nearly sent her flying. He groaned. "There she goes again, off to la-la land. She's taken to doing that lately, Paul. You'll be talking to her and she seems like a normal person and then she gets that hokey, moon face, all gooey-eyed and goofy and she drifts off somewhere. I think before we do anything else we need to get her to a doctor and fast."

"Oh, you're going to need a doctor." Skyler retaliated with a swift kick to his shins, and as he turned to flee, she leapt up on his back, pretending to punch his ribs.

"Help, help, she's gone mad." Josef spun in circles as if trying to get her off his back, all the while holding her safely to him.

"Come on, you goofballs. We can't be certain someone hasn't figured out yet that Sky is not where she said she'd be," Paul cautioned. "All either Francesca or Gabriel has to do is try to touch base with her."

Josef stopped his wild spinning and bent his knees to ease Skyler to the ground. He glanced around him, suddenly wary.

"I don't think they'll find us this fast, bro," Paul said.

"No. Not Francesca and Gabriel," Josef said, stepping in front of Skyler and sweeping her behind him with one arm. "But something has."

"I can help," Skyler hissed. "I'm very adept at all kinds of defense." She peeked around Josef. She had met and faced all kinds of monsters and they scared the hell out of her, but she wasn't about to show fear to either of her friends—not when they were risking their lives in her rather desperate plan to take Dimitri back from his captors.

Paul closed in on the other side. "Pipe down, lunatic, at least let us see what's coming at us."

"The coffin's in the truck, do you want to try to just drive away?" Skyler suggested hopefully.

"I'd rather meet them out in the open," Paul said. "Josef?"

Josef held up his hand, fingers spread wide. "Five of them. Punks. They saw the customs guy close up shop and they like to come see what might have been left behind. Two of them are pretty high. All of them have been drinking. No vampires."

Skyler caught Josef's arm. "Let's just go then. Five humans with knives and chains and maybe guns can still slow us down. Let's get out of here."

"I don't think they have any intention of letting us take the truck, Sky," Josef said. "They've got their eyes on our ride."

Skyler sighed. Josef and Paul were spoiling for a fight. They both had pent-up energy as well as suppressed anger toward their prince and the other hunters. If she was being entirely truthful, she did as well. She was angry. Furious. Dimitri deserved so much more loyalty than his people were showing him. All three of them had been kept out of the loop, too young to count, when the very person who was her other half was in danger. It wasn't right. She was Dimitri's lifemate and at the very least, she should be kept informed at all times, not dismissed as if she were a child and wouldn't understand.

She took a deep breath, knowing that the only one of the three of them who looked as if they could handle themselves was Paul. Josef, they would dismiss. He was tall and lanky, but hadn't developed the outward muscle that might impress a group of toughs like the ones posturing. Josef, of course, was the one that everyone should be afraid of, but he looked like the techie he was.

She listened to the trash talk and gave a little sigh. The world sometimes seemed the same everywhere she went. London, South America, the United States, even her beloved Romania had the same types that would much rather rob than earn.

You're too soft, Sky, Josef said. *They'd kill you for those chic boots you're wearing.*

The worst part of it was Josef was probably right. He could read their thoughts. She could, too, if she chose, which she didn't. Sometimes she just wanted to pretend that most people were really good, like Gabriel and Francesca, not the monsters she'd known as a child. Living in a world where she knew vampires and monsters existed didn't help her fantasy.

The smell of the five approaching them reached her first. Two were definitely on drugs. The reek of alcohol was strong, not a good sign. Her experience with alcohol wasn't the best. Men who were drunk definitely had an enlarged sense of bravado and very impaired judgment. Most likely, these five would think they could do anything.

She watched them come close, noting the two hanging back were clearly drunk. They couldn't walk a straight line, but one had a gun. She could see him stroking the barrel, and to her, he appeared the most dangerous. She kept her gaze glued to him.

"Well, look what we found?" the self-appointed leader said. He pointed to Skyler and crooked his little finger. "Come here."

Josef smiled at them, deliberately showing his longer, sharper teeth. "You'd better leave while you have the chance."

"No one's talking to you," the leader snapped. "Get over here," he added, his hand on his knife.

"She's not going anywhere," Josef said, his eyes taking on a red glow. "I'm giving you one last warning, although I am a little hungry. I just woke up, but you all reek of alcohol and I'm opposed to drinking on so many levels."

"Look at that ride, Gustoff." The one directly to the right of the leader indicated the truck. "And a cool coffin. I want that."

"That's my bedroom," Josef said. "And I didn't invite you in."

Gustoff had had enough of dealing with Josef. He drew his knife and immediately the others followed suit. Skyler wasn't so much worried about the knives as she was the gun the drunken man pulled. He pointed it straight at Josef. She concentrated on the object. The gun seemed to take on a life of its own. Slowly the smirk faded from the drunk's face as the gun began to turn on him. No matter how hard he tried to turn his hand back, the gun kept coming around until it was pointed at him.

"Gustoff!" he exclaimed.

Gustoff glanced over his shoulder. "Stop messing around."

"I'm not," the drunken man insisted. His hand shook. He tried to open it, but his palm was firmly latched around the gun, his finger locked on the trigger. "It's going to shoot me. Do something."

Gustoff scowled. "Petr, help that idiot."

Petr sprang into action, grabbing at the gun. He couldn't budge it, nor could he remove the drunk's hand from it.

Alarmed, Gustoff turned back to Josef, his knife in front of him, blade up.

"Hey, don't look at me, that's all her," Josef said, indicating Skyler. "She's got a mean streak. Me, I'm the nice one." As he spoke buttons began popping off of Gustoff's shirt. The seams of his jeans split.

Paul snickered as the pants fell down around Gustoff's ankles. "Nice one, Josef."

"Get them!" Gustoff shouted, furious.

The others rushed them, knives drawn. One swung a heavy metal chain. Skyler stepped back behind Paul and Josef, extending her concentration to the other weapons. This time she changed the temperature so that even as the drunken fools wielded them, the knives and chain began to grow warm and then hot.

Paul slammed his hand down hard on the wrist of the one coming at him, gripping the knife hand and turning it up and to the side as he stepped forward. The man went down hard, an audible crack signaling a broken wrist. Paul kicked the knife away and delivered another kick to the man's head.

Two rushed Josef. He dissolved just as they reached him, leaving them standing looking at one another. One of the two had been swinging his chain, but now the metal links glowed red in the night, a bizarre streak of fire spinning over his head. The chain was suddenly wrenched away from behind and just as fast looped around the man's body. He screamed as the burning hot links touched his skin.

The remaining man spun around, trying to find Josef, nearly hysterical with fear. The metal of his knife began to glow as the temperature rose. He opened his hand fast and the knife fell to the ground.

Paul was on him immediately, smashing his fist into the man's mouth, driving him backward. He followed up his advantage with a front kick to the stomach, using his steel-toed boots.

Josef emerged out of thin air directly in front of Gustoff. The leader stabbed at him, but Josef caught his wrist in a deadly grip and spun him around, so that his arm was locked around Gustoff's throat. He was enormously strong, his grip unbreakable. He bent his head to Gustoff's pounding pulse.

"I haven't eaten in a while," he whispered. "And I need blood to survive. Too bad you came along and didn't heed my warning."

He sank his teeth deep into that drumming beat, allowing Gustoff to feel burning pain. Fear laced his blood with adrenaline, helping to wipe out the bitter, disgusting taste of alcohol. Gustoff screamed and screamed, horrified at the vampire draining him of his life force.

His band of toughs went rigid, just watching in absolute terror.

You're always so good at theatrics, Skyler said, trying not laugh. *You're putting on quite the show for them.*

Josef's eyes were all red now, glowing like twin embers in the dark. He enhanced Gustoff's looks, making him grow paler with each passing moment. His body appeared to begin to convulse. Josef dropped him to the ground. Two thin trickles of blood ran from his mouth to his chin.

Skyler rolled her eyes. *I can't keep this gun pointed at him forever.*

Josef suddenly turned his head toward the drunk who held the gun. His gaze fell on the man. "You look tasty."

"I'm not. I'm not." The drunk shook his head and tried to stagger back.

Josef waved his hand, and the drunk couldn't move. Josef floated to him, taking his time, making little swimming motions with his hands.

Oh for heaven's sake. Must you? Skyler demanded.

Paul bent over laughing. When one of the men on the ground moved, he delivered another kick, but even that didn't deter his amusement over Josef's antics.

Yes, my little dove. I must. What's the fun in being Carpathian if you can never actually scare the crap out of someone?

Josef, you have a mean streak in you.

Josef reached the drunk. He held out his hand for the gun. The drunk extended his arm and to his shock, the gun dropped into Josef's palm.

"Thank you," Josef said with a little formal bow. He removed the bullets and then crushed the gun in his fist.

Paul slipped into the driver's seat. "Come on, Skyler, let's get out of here."

She took the little jump seat in the back. Josef was tall and would need the legroom to stretch out. Paul started the truck and drove around the five men, leaned his head out the window, and called to Josef.

"Come on, man, let's go."

Josef waved him away and turned back to gather up the weapons. One by one he destroyed them. Next he waved his hands toward the men and their clothing disappeared, leaving them naked on the ground.

"It's a little hard to rob and kill when you're bare-butt naked, now isn't it? I'll be watching you. You don't want me coming back." Laughing, he took to the air, streaking after the truck.

He was still laughing when he materialized in the front passenger seat.

Skyler smacked the back of his head. "You took their clothes, didn't you?" she said for Paul's benefit. Paul was becoming more adept at telepathic communication, but he couldn't merge his mind and read thoughts as she could do with Josef, although he was learning very fast.

Paul snickered and held up his hand to give Josef a high five. "Oh, yeah, I'd like to see them slinking home in their birthday suits."

Both men erupted into laughter.

Skyler rolled her eyes, trying hard not to laugh with them. "You're impossible, Josef. Those men are going to have to make it through their neighborhood without a stitch on." She pressed her palm against her mouth, but laughter spilled out anyway.

Paul's eyes met hers in the rearview mirror and Josef turned in his seat, his eyes sparkling with amusement. All three of them burst out laughing.

Skyler had forgotten what it was like being with them. At college, she'd made a few friends, but she was guarded with them at all times—she had to be. At home, Gabriel and Francesca were loving and wonderful parents. Her baby sister, Tamara, was the most adorable child in the world and she couldn't imagine life without her, but she couldn't be honest with them about her relationship with Dimitri.

She wasn't Carpathian and she couldn't wait until she was fifty years of age to be with her lifemate. She was human. Without Dimitri, she might not have gotten through many of the long nights where she woke with sweat covering her body and the memories of men pawing at her, hurting her, beating and using her. She'd been a child, but that hadn't mattered to them.

She'd learned to keep her screams silent, internal, and when she had nightmares, she did the same thing. Dimitri always heard her. *Always.* He came to her in the dark of the night, at her worst moments, surrounding her with unconditional love. He never asked her for anything. He never demanded his rights or threw it in her face that he suffered because she wasn't able to fully be his lifemate.

And he did suffer. As the years had gone by, Skyler was more adept at accessing his mind and memories. She saw clearly the terrible darkness crouched like a monster, whispering in temptation, trying to destroy him.

Dimitri. Beloved. I'm so afraid for you. I'm holding you close to me, pretending that I'm certain you're alive, lying to my closest, dearest friends, but in reality I can barely breathe. The terror of being without you feels so close—so real.

She waited there in the darkness, grateful for the backseat in the truck, grateful that Paul and Josef fought over the music and thought her asleep. She kept her eyes closed and her breathing even, but her heart pounded too hard, raced too fast and surely, at least, Josef could detect that. If so, he was polite enough not to call her on her pretense.

The silence stretched. There was no answer. Dimitri, even in his worst moments, once even during a battle with a vampire, had always sent her reassurance if she reached for him, however brief it might be. The silence was cold and lonely and absolutely terrifying to her. She'd lived too long in a nightmare with no way to escape until Francesca had found her. But still, her nights had always been spent trapped in those earlier years, repeating and repeating until she thought she might go insane.

Francesca had done everything she could think of to help alleviate the nightmares, including giving Skyler Carpathian blood. She took turns with

Gabriel sitting by Skyler's bed when the nightmares were so bad Skyler could only scream, recognizing no one. They'd called in healers. Nothing worked—until Dimitri. There was only Dimitri to stand between her and her past. Now that shield was gone and as hard as she tried, she could not reach him.

Terror gripped her. Sorrow. Despair. There was no way to go on if Dimitri wasn't in the world. Her knight. Her other half. She took a breath and reached again, pouring everything she felt, everything she was into her urgent plea.

My love. If you think to protect me from something terrible, it cannot be worse than thinking you're dead. I need you. Your touch. Even if it's just for one moment. I can't breathe without you. I need to know you live and there is hope for us.

The burst of pain was sheer agony. Her body went rigid. Convulsed. The air was driven from her lungs in one long scream that abruptly ended when her air supply did. She couldn't think, the pain turning every nerve ending to fire. Her fingernails tore at her skin, trying to ease the burn.

She was barely aware of the truck stopping, of Josef lifting her out of the backseat to lay her in the grass. Paul held her hands down to prevent her from tearing her skin open.

"Breathe," Paul demanded. "Right now, Skyler. Take a breath."

She had asked for this, and if it was this bad for her, so far from him, what must it be like for Dimitri? She forced air into her lungs. There was no way to push away the pain. Her connection to Dimitri ran too deep.

She looked to Josef. He was Carpathian and he was strong when he wanted to be. She knew what she was asking, pleading with her eyes for aid.

"Paul," Josef said softly, "she's found Dimitri and it's bad. I have to help her. That leaves you to guard us, get us back in the truck when it's over and give me blood."

Paul nodded. "I've got this, just help her."

Josef didn't waste time. "I'm all yours, Skyler, take my strength and energy freely. Wherever he is, help him."

Skyler didn't dare take a break and then try to overcome that mind-numbing pain again. It took nearly everything she had to stay conscious while she followed the thread back to Dimitri. If Josef hadn't been with her, it would have been impossible. He was a great distance away. The Lycans who had taken Dimitri had managed to move him very quickly out of the country. They left no trail behind; Josef had managed to get that information for her.

She knew that the agony she was feeling was nothing in comparison to what Dimitri was going through. He would shield her, trying to block as much pain as he could when he reached for her to let her know he was alive. She felt him retreating from her, breaking the merge to stop her from feeling pain.

Skyler used every ounce of strength and discipline she possessed. She had been forged in the fires of hell as an infant. Honed in those same fires as a young girl. She was Dragonseeker. A daughter of Mother Earth. In her own right she was a powerful psychic. She refused to lose the thread leading to her lifemate. He wasn't going to last long, not with that kind of torture—and they *were* torturing him. Skyler set her mind on one thing only—staying with Dimitri, following that faint trail back to him.

The path was broken, fading away, very faint, but she could follow it, those psychic footprints she was so familiar with. Pain ripped through her until every nerve ending was inflamed and burning. She had to turn her head to vomit, the pain excruciating.

She tugged at her hands, silently telling Josef she was under control and to let go. The moment he did, she pushed her fingers into the soil. That act alone gave her more strength. More determined than ever, Skyler reached again for the fading trail leading back to Dimitri.

She saw the way in colors as she always did, long silver streaks like a comet, only this time those streaks were edged bloodred. Dimitri had once told her he knew of no one else who could see a psychic trail in the same way she did. Bitter cold slipped into her mind. Her body continually shook. She drew on Josef, all that wonderful strong psychic energy he possessed and so freely and generously gave to her.

Csitri. Little one. You cannot be here.

She nearly sobbed. Tears collected in her throat until the lump threatened to choke her. His beloved voice was ravaged and raw.

There is no other place for me. There is only you. Be still and let me examine you. She found it more of an effort to speak to him; the pain, so close to him, was overwhelming.

I don't want this for you.

She knew that already. He would protect her from any hurt if he could. The biggest threat to her would be to lose him—and that was *not* going to happen. She took a deep breath, her fists curled tightly in the soil as an anchor, and she sent her spirit into his ravaged body.

Dimitri was being attacked from so many directions it was difficult to find a starting point. Long thin streaks of silver inched through his body like deadly worms, tracer bullets, she thought at first. Had he been shot numerous times with silver bullets? She followed the path of one of those lines back to the source.

Her heart stuttered in her chest. For the first time she faltered. Hooks. He had hooks of silver in his body, great terrible claws shooting out their deadly poison into his system. The silver inched its way through his veins and muscle, spread along his bones, threading its way to every organ, always seeking his heart. The slow spread of silver throughout his body was deadly to the Lycan in his blood.

She chose the line closest to his heart. The silver seemed to be liquid, tiny beads of it stretching through his body. Very small, the threads appearing as veins. She experimented with bringing her spirit close to the end of it. The silver trail flinched back. She didn't dare melt it because it could run through his body even faster. There were so many hooks. The problem seemed impossible.

She pushed aside anxiety and near panic as the emotions rose so sharp and ugly. She was thinking as a Carpathian, but what of that other side of her? Razvan was her father, and he had mage blood. His father was the most powerful mage ever known. Surely she had mage blood as well. That was the very reason her grandfather had rejected her and sold her to another man. He believed she didn't have the Carpathian blood he needed to be immortal. It was possible she could use that other side, often ignored because she didn't want to remember it was part of her heritage.

Tiny silver threads, so deadly and bright,
I call upon the earth to steal your might,
As you were created, I shall undo.
I call on your makers and take on your hue.

Skyler moved forward, closer to the silver threads, concentrating on the end as she stretched her spirit, extending her white light to touch the fine end.

That which was created shall now become mine,
Chlorine, sulfur, antimony and arsenic I bind.
Chlorine that holds the color of green and gold,
I take on your energy and now so do I hold.

She called on the things of the earth. She was a daughter of the earth, bound to its properties. Mother Earth had always come to her aid when she had need. She felt that connection now and drew on it.

Sulfur, oh brimstone with life-giving gifts,
I breathe in your essence and take of your gifts,
Antimony, sweet metal, I take on your shine,
And weave now a barrier that none may unbind,

She was the granddaughter of the most powerful mage the world had ever known, and his blood, whether she liked it or not, ran in her veins. Right now, in this moment of terrible crisis, she used whatever gifts had been given to her gratefully.

Arsenic sweet arsenic so lethal and gray,
I call on your power to shift poison away.
Silver I touch, silver I wind,
Silver I release back to your source.

To her utter astonishment the silver vein began to actually move backward.

It's seeping out my pores. Dimitri gave a gasp, desperate to suppress the pain, to block it so Skyler couldn't feel the burn as the silver seemed to eat through his entire body, flame through his very skin, to drop away onto the ground below him.

She followed that thin line of silver back to the source. The hooks the Lycans had placed in his body were actually tubes of silver beads. The tiny beads at the tip of the hook where it was inserted into the body eventually heated from body temperature, turning the bead to a liquid form. The bead dropped into the body and began to stretch out, reaching for the heart. It took thousands of those beads to form the network of deadly veins. It was an ugly way for anyone to die.

Skyler focused on the hook, searching her mind for a way to stop the flow of venomous silver into Dimitri's body.

Hooks of silver, curved and sharp,
Inserted in flesh to poison the heart,
Iced brimstone and fire I call you now forth.
Come out and heat this evil source.

Skyler focused completely on the tips of the hooks, determined to close the hollowed, opened end so that there was no way for that terrible silver to continue poisoning Dimitri's body.

Take what is open and seal it now closed,
So no more that is poison can seek what is exposed.
Take what is liquid and give it a form,
Sealing away all, so it no more can harm.

Skyler knew she couldn't hold the bridge between them for long. There was no way to remove all the silver spreading through his body in the time she had before she collapsed. She had chosen the longest lines, the ones most threatening, and meticulously pushed them back to their source and then through Dimitri's pores. One by one she removed those thin, deadly threads as fast as she could.

Skyler. Come back. You have to come back now! Dimitri, send her back to us now! She's lost. She's too far away and stretched too thin.

She heard the call as if from a great distance. Josef, she recognized, and his voice was filled with fear.

Sívamet.

Dimitri's tone was tender, gentle. Filled with love. Surrounding her with warmth when she was so cold. Icy cold.

You must go back. Now, csitri, I cannot lose you. When you are strong enough, come back and finish what you've started.

She had removed a lot of the silver, at least half, but that didn't lessen the agony he was in. The thought of abandoning him when he needed her was absolutely abhorrent. She told herself one more thread—just get one more out of him.

She felt Dimitri's spirit brush up against hers and then he thrust her away. The momentum pushed her from his body, back onto that ice-cold psychic path. The path itself was so broken and torn she felt very confused. She looked around her somewhat helplessly, not understanding what was happening to her.

I swear if you don't come back, Sky, I'm going to throttle you.

Josef sounded desperate. She felt lost and alone there in that cold stream. She reached for his familiar voice, using it as a guide.

She found herself back in her own body, so cold she couldn't stop shaking. Josef bent over her, hissing his anger, pressing his wrist to her mouth, glaring at her. His skin was paler than ever, almost stark white. If she could have lifted her hand to his face she would have been able to trace each line of fear stamped into it. She tried to turn her head away from his wrist, but he clamped it over her mouth and stroked her throat, forcing her to swallow.

Paul brushed back her hair with gentle fingers. Her hair was damp, as if she'd just stepped out of the shower. She couldn't stop shaking, although Paul's coat lay over her. The Carpathian blood Josef pushed into her system was hot inside her, beginning to thaw out her body after that terrible cold. Josef closed the laceration on his wrist and flopped down beside her there in the grass. He slipped his arms around her, trying to heat her with his body.

Paul lay down beside her as well, using his body to help warm her. "Look at me, Skyler," Paul instructed. There was fear in his voice as well. "Are you back with us?"

"He's somewhere in Russia," she managed. Her voice was hoarse and sounded far away. "In the forest. It's worse than I ever imagined."

3

Skyler woke in a panic, gasping for breath, her heart pounding, the echo of her nightmare filling her with dread. How could she have ever dreamt up such a brutal, ugly way to kill another being? What was wrong with her that she had such a vivid, disgusting imagination?

It took tremendous effort to sit up. Her head exploded with pain and she felt dizzy, so faint she was afraid she might collapse again. Drawing in a deep breath, she looked around her. She was in an unfamiliar room. It was very neat; traditional quilts lay across the bed, piled on her. Paul lay on the floor a few feet away, sleeping soundly. He looked exhausted.

She felt thin and stretched out, so utterly tired. She wanted to curl up in the fetal position under the warm covers and go back to sleep. But that nightmare . . . Dimitri. Silver threading through his body . . .

She couldn't breathe. All the air was gone from the room. *Dimitri.* She hadn't dreamt it. The Lycans were killing him slowly with silver. The hooks tearing through his body were bad enough, but the silver snaking its way through him was pure agony. *She hadn't stopped it.* She'd failed him. Completely failed him. She covered her face with her hands, weeping.

"Skyler." Paul leapt up instantly.

He wrapped his arm around her while she rocked back and forth, her face buried against his shoulder. "I didn't stop it," she sobbed. "I didn't have enough time."

Paul didn't say a word, just held her, letting her cry while he rocked her, patted her back and stroked her hair.

Exhaustion more than anything else stopped the tears. She reached a point where she couldn't cry anymore. She couldn't do anything but cling to Paul.

"I just left him there," she whispered, lifting her head to look at Paul while she made the confession. "He's in so much pain, and I just left him there."

Paul frowned. "Josef couldn't say anything at all last night. I gave him blood and he immediately tried to bring you back. He didn't say why, but I assumed you were still trying to heal Dimitri."

"He's being poisoned, and I couldn't get it all." She gasped and let out another little sob.

"You had no choice," Paul assured her. "If you'd stayed any longer, we couldn't have brought you back. You'd be dead, or wandering in the spirit world and then where would Dimitri be? No one else can find him. At least this way, when you're strong enough, you can go back and help him."

"In the meantime he's suffering horribly. That pain is worse than anything you can imagine," she said. "At least when I was there, he knew someone was looking for him, someone cared enough to come after him. But the pain . . ." She trailed off with another choking sob.

"During the day, he'll be in a Carpathian sleep and won't be able to feel anything," Paul reminded.

She shook her head. "His Lycan blood will keep him awake most of the time. I doubt with that kind of pain he'll be able to sleep at all." Her head nearly exploded again and she pressed both hands to her temples. "Is Josef all right? Are you? You must have had to give him blood a couple of times."

"He was in bad shape," Paul admitted. "He couldn't move a muscle. I think you used up every bit of energy both of you had, but I knew if I gave him blood it would help him." He showed her his wrist where he'd slashed his vein open and pressed the wound to Josef's mouth.

Paul was human and didn't heal the way Carpathians did. The laceration looked ugly and raw. She took his hand gently and turned it over to examine the clean cut his knife had made.

"Don't try to heal me, Sky," Paul admonished. "I'm healthy, I can heal on my own. You need to conserve your energy to get well yourself." He hesitated, clearly afraid of upsetting her more.

"What?" she asked, pulling back and taking in great gulps of air. "I'm okay, really. I just feel weak and my head is pounding." And guilty. So terribly guilty. Fearful beyond any description. There was no way to express to Paul or anyone else the endless agony Dimitri was in. She felt some of the pain, but he'd attempted to block out most of it from her. She couldn't imagine how much worse it was for him.

"Josef couldn't tell me anything last night. What exactly is going on with Dimitri? What have they done to him? How can they hold someone so powerful a prisoner? That doesn't make sense to me."

"They have him wrapped in silver chains," she explained. "I know this because they burn right through his skin in the way acid does ours. They're torturing him. He has these silver hooks in his body, his chest, ribs, his hips and thighs, even his shoulders and calves. The hooks allow tiny silver beads to break off and drop into him when his body temperature heats them, one by one. It's a slow, torturous death."

Paul shook his head. "A Carpathian should be able to get rid of any silver if it really poisoned him."

"Dimitri is both Lycan and Carpathian. His Lycan blood reacts to the silver, and he can't free himself. The silver works its way through his body until it pierces his heart. Once it threads through the heart, it will kill him." She forced herself to look at Paul, her lashes wet, her throat trying to close on her. "It's a brutal, ugly way to die."

Paul put his hand over hers. "We aren't going to let that happen. Josef thinks he can take us both over the mountain. We'll abandon the truck and coffin as soon as he wakes and feeds. We can't take the time to drive and go through all the borders of each country. Josef can cover a lot of territory flying us all night."

"*Both* of us? Can he do that? One maybe, but two?"

Paul shrugged. "He says so and I have to believe him. Josef will be up anytime. I think that he's aging at a faster rate because he isn't kept away from society like most Carpathian children are. He's in human society and learning modern technology, probably ripping it off from everyone around him that he comes in contact with, but still, he understands it all. He has to grow up faster. In human years he's no teen and he's treated like a man."

Skyler rubbed her temples again. She didn't have the strength to heal her own headache. "I thought with Josef giving me blood last night, I'd heal faster. It's not like I don't have some Carpathian blood in my system already."

"He said you wouldn't. He said to get you somewhere safe and have you sleep as much as possible. He said psychic healing takes longer than a mere body healing, and you were pretty far gone." Paul took a deep breath. He looked shaken. "I honestly thought you weren't going to make it, Sky. I know you'll go back to Dimitri and try again to rid him of the silver . . ."

"I *have* to find a way to rid him of the silver. He won't last until we find him. He's dying, Paul. I hate letting him suffer just so I can heal but I know you're right. I can't go to him like this and do any good at all. He's hanging in there, and now he knows I can find him, that should give him hope. He knows I'll come back."

"I'll get you something to eat. There's a restaurant across the street."

"Soup, maybe," Skyler said reluctantly. She couldn't imagine keeping food down, her stomach rebelled at the thought of it. "You know I'm a vegetarian."

She had been given two blood exchanges by her parents, just in case of an emergency. It took three to convert her completely and bring her fully into the Carpathian world. Since then, she hadn't been able to look at meat. Sometimes it was difficult to force herself to eat fruit or vegetables.

"Don't worry."

"And knock, please, before you come in. I'm going to take a quick shower." The bathroom looked a good distance away—at least ten whole steps. She was that shaky.

Paul glanced from her to the bathroom door as if he might be reading her thoughts. He never talked about his psychic gifts, but he had jaguar blood in him and he had to have something. He couldn't *actually* read thoughts—he would have said so. He just knew her really well.

"I can carry you in. Maybe put a chair in the shower for you."

"I can make it," she reassured him. "I'm not going to do anything stupid." She was crawling into the freakin' bathroom on her hands and knees if she had to. Paul was *not* carrying her. She was already feeling like a little bit of a burden to Paul and Josef. They both had to take care of her last night. Not only had she failed Dimitri, but she'd put both of them—especially Josef—in danger.

Paul pushed off the bed. "I trust you, Sky. Josef will beat the crap out of me if anything happens to you."

That made her laugh, she couldn't help it. Even her exploding head didn't matter in that moment. There was something very beautiful about their friendship, Paul, Josef and her, which made her happy.

"Boys are so violent," she observed, blinking back a fresh flood of tears. She was lucky to have the two of them as friends.

"Girls are so mushy," Paul countered, leaning down to drop a kiss on top of her head. "Don't go all sobby on me. Can you imagine what will happen if Josef comes in and finds you crying? Sheesh, I'll be dead meat."

She made a face at him and gave him a little push, her stomach churning at the reference to meat. "Ugh. Go away before I throw up all over you."

"You already did that," he pointed out.

"I did not," she denied, uncertain if it was true, but adamant all the same. "I carefully *and* politely turned my face away from you." She gave him a little huff of disdain, just to emphasize that he must have remembered the sequence of events incorrectly.

"Then why did I have to spend half the day in the laundry room?" he asked with a smirk.

Now she knew he was teasing her. This little room was not in a hotel. She could tell it was a private residence renting out rooms. No hotel was this cozy or had the detailed quilts, obviously handmade, in them. There wouldn't be a laundry room.

"Go away, mean boy," she said. "If I don't take my shower soon, Josef will show up before I'm out."

"Lock him out," Paul said as he crossed to the door.

She laughed again. "You try locking him out."

"He can't come in if the doors and windows are closed and locked, not without an invitation," Paul said.

"Really?" She arched an eyebrow. "This is Josef we're talking about. He's very adept at picking locks, as you well know. You both have studied enough to be criminals."

Paul put his hand over his heart. "Ouch. Such a hurtful woman."

He hurried out the door laughing, slamming it quickly so that the pillow she threw hit the door instead of him.

Skyler sat for a long moment, the smile fading from her face. Paul had allowed her to cry, something she clearly needed to do. He had done his best to assure her leaving Dimitri had been her only recourse. Now she had to heal so she could get back to her lifemate. How much time did she have? She doubted if it was very much. One night. Maybe two.

She staggered to the bathroom, appalled at her weakness. Maybe a chair in the shower would have been a good thing, but she did have some pride. Paul had given blood to Josef twice. He'd carried her to the truck and probably had done the same for Josef after he'd collapsed a second time beside her. Then Paul had driven through the rest of the night to find a place for them to stay during the day. He had to be exhausted.

The hot water felt good on her skin, reviving her a bit. Some of the tension eased out of her neck and shoulders enough to keep her head from shattering into a million pieces. Twice she had to stop washing her hair and just stay very still to keep from getting sick. Both times she held on to her head, pressing her palms hard on either side of her temples.

"Hey! Sky! You in there?" Josef demanded.

"No!" she shouted back. "I'm not."

"Yeah, that's what I thought. You left your brain somewhere in the cold zone."

Leaning against the shower stall, she finished rinsing her hair, taking her time. Josef wasn't going to be quite as nice about what happened as Paul. She'd be lucky if he didn't shake her until her teeth rattled. She could already feel his anger, and she certainly heard it in his voice.

"Stop stalling," he snapped. "You don't want me coming in there after you."

"Sheesh, Josef, you just got here. Give me a minute. I'm moving a little slow."

"That isn't surprising."

She sighed. She was *not* going to shout back and forth through the bathroom door. She understood his anger. It came out of fear for her. She would certainly feel the same if the roles were reversed. *But* . . . she was Dimitri's lifemate. Seeing him that way, feeling his pain, she doubted if too many other lifemates—man or woman—would have been completely rational in the same situation. Still, Josef deserved to be heard.

She dressed carefully, brushed her teeth and walked out of the bathroom drying her hair with a towel. Josef had his back to her, but spun around as she emerged. He looked thin and tired, his face still very pale, although she was certain he'd already fed. He held himself very tightly.

"You almost died last night." He made it a statement. An accusation.

Skyler tossed the towel aside, walked right up to him and circled his neck with both arms, leaning close to hold him. "I know. I'm so sorry," she said sincerely. "I almost took you with me."

For a moment he held himself very stiff, then his arms came up and he hugged her so hard she feared she might break in half. "I don't care about me, you goofball," Josef said, "but I can't lose you. Dimitri can't lose you. Gabriel and Francesca can't lose you. You can't take chances like that. If you're going to travel over a thousand miles and attempt a healing, you know you're on a time limit. You *know* that. I don't know how I got you back."

Skyler pulled back to look up at him. "He booted me out of him."

He blinked. The tension eased out of him a slow inch at a time. "He did?"

"Yes. And don't sound so happy."

"Thank God that man can boss you, because no one else seems to be able to."

"I don't need bossing," she pointed out. "Josef, I really am sorry. I'll be far more careful next time. We know what we're facing now."

Josef took a deep breath and nodded. "I caught glimpses in your mind, Skyler. You're one tough chick."

Skyler flinched. "I wouldn't call me a tough chick in front of my parents or someone say . . . like the prince. They wouldn't appreciate the modern jargon."

For the first time Josef smiled. It was more of a self-satisfied smirk, but she'd take it. At least he was finding his sense of humor again.

"They need to lighten up and become a little more modern, especially Gregori. He's still living in the caveman days."

"We don't have to be around him much," Skyler pointed out. "Think of poor Paul, living with the De La Cruz family—especially the eldest brother. I've never met him but I've heard the rumors."

Josef gave a little shudder. "I'm totally avoiding Paul's family. It's the only safe, intelligent thing to do. When this is over, I'm making myself scarce for a century or two."

A knock on the door heralded Paul's arrival. Josef waved his hand and the door opened. Outside, Skyler could see night falling fast. The weather was overcast, clouds drifting across the sky, but there was no rain.

Paul set her soup on the small table. "Come eat, Sky. I wolfed down a sandwich while I was waiting for your order."

That was code for telling her he ate a meat sandwich and didn't want her to smell it and feel nauseated. "Thanks, Paul. I appreciate it." She looked at the bowl of soup and shook her head, her stomach already rebelling.

"It's not the enemy," Josef told her. "It's sustenance—the very thing you need to build your strength again so you can heal Dimitri."

She didn't dare take a deep breath, but she nodded. Josef made sense. She had to get strong fast and that required eating. She touched her tongue to her lower lip, tracing it, finding her skin quite dry. In spite of the hot shower, she was still shivering, unable to maintain her body temperature.

"Staring at it isn't going to get it down," Josef said. "We want to get moving. We've got a lot of territory to cover, and the faster we reach Dimitri, the sooner he's safe."

She approached the table and the bowl of steaming soup warily. The aroma, instead of making her hungrier, made her feel more nauseated than ever. Pressing the back of her hand to her mouth she gingerly took the chair facing the bowl of soup. Who knew it would be so difficult to take a few spoonfuls of vegetable soup?

"Skyler." Josef used his sternest voice. "You're wasting time."

She spun around, glaring at him. "Don't you think I know that? You're not helping, Josef." Just the act of moving so fast set her head pounding. She fought down the bile in her lurching stomach.

The stirring in her mind was faint, but her heart leapt and began to stutter with anticipation. She reached out, and immediately pain exploded through her head. Paul made a sound of distress.

"You're bleeding, Skyler." He rushed to the bathroom to get a wet cloth.

Let Josef aid you, beloved. I cannot, and we need you strong.

Skyler closed her eyes, tears burning behind her eyelids. Dimitri had found the way to her in spite of the agony he suffered. She couldn't make it easier for him by bridging the distance for him. Her psychic abilities had been depleted after her night of trying to heal him. She felt surrounded by his warmth, his enduring love, by his indomitable spirit.

Dimitri didn't give up—for her. He suffered the agonies of hell for a chance to get back to her. She wrapped herself up in him, knowing he needed to help her, and had to be distraught that he couldn't.

I love you, Dimitri. Don't let go. I'll be there as soon as I can.

He was in far too much pain to realize she meant literally. He knew she would return to heal him and he didn't try to delve further into her mind. She felt a burst of agonizing pain and then he was gone. She had no memory of shooting out of the chair and reaching toward the sky after that faint psychic trail, but she heard her own cry of sorrow as Dimitri faded away.

The pain drove the breath from her body, but it steadied her as well. She had to pull herself together and heal fast. Paul thrust a washcloth into her shaking hands, and she carefully dabbed at the blood trickling from her nose.

"I'm sorry I snapped at you, Josef," she said. "I should have just asked for your help."

"I should have just offered," Josef answered, slinging his arm around her. "We'll get him out of there, Sky. We will. I can't believe he managed to come to you even for a moment when he's in such pain. I tease you about him, but you know I think of him as a brother. Few Carpathian males would tolerate a relationship like ours—the three of us—but Dimitri encourages it."

Skyler hugged him gratefully. "He knows I love both of you."

"How do you want to do this?"

"Just have me eat it. And then, if you're strong enough, give me a small amount of blood again. It will speed up the healing process, but I don't want to experience anything."

"You got it."

Skyler blinked and found herself sitting at the table, an empty bowl of soup in front of her. Her stomach protested a little, but she found the soup nourishing. Or perhaps that was the Carpathian blood Josef gave her as well.

"Thanks."

She was still cold, and they had a long night ahead of them. She didn't look forward to streaking through the night sky.

"I'm going to shift to a dragon form. I've been practicing ever since they found Tatijana and Branislava. My dragon can carry you both on his back comfortably," Josef said.

"Skyler still hasn't stopped shivering. All day she's been so cold I couldn't pile enough blankets on her," Paul said.

Skyler glanced at the spot on the floor where Paul had been sleeping. For the first time she realized there were no blankets—they were all on the bed where she had been.

Josef did what all Carpathians did—he simply made the clothes for her. Skyler donned the fur vest and slipped on the long fur coat. It fell to the ground and had a hood. He handed her fur-lined boots and gloves as well.

"You're stylin', Sky," Paul said with a laugh. "The next thing we know, Josef is going to go into fashion design."

Josef shrugged. "I always look good. I've considered a career in that field." He looked and sounded very serious.

Skyler punched his arm. "You would do that just to really tweak the powers, wouldn't you?"

Josef sent her a little grin. "Of course. Where's the fun in conforming?"

She followed the two men outside. "You do realize karma is going to catch up with you. You probably really are lifemate to one of Gregori's daughters."

"Or both," Paul said. "As a nonconformist, you could be the first Carpathian to have two lifemates. Twins. Not bad, Josef."

"Ha. Ha. Ha. You two really do want me dead, don't you? Gregori would cut off my head and other very precious parts of my anatomy and feed them to the wolves."

"Slowly. He'd slowly feed them to the wolves while your head sat next to him watching," Paul informed him.

"Eww. That's just gross." Skyler made a face at them. Already the fur coat helped to control the continual shivering. Even the pain in her head seemed to lessen.

"That's why you love us so much," Paul pointed out.

"How long do you think it will take us to get there?" Skyler asked.

"I can't fly as fast as an airplane, but I think I can make it to the outskirts of the Russian forest by dawn," Josef said.

Skyler was surprised. "I thought it could take us a couple of nights."

"So did I," Paul said.

"I felt Dimitri's pain through you, Sky," Josef replied. "I feel a sense of urgency, and that means we need to get there as fast as possible. I'm going to try it. I honestly don't know if I'm that strong. All we can do is try. You'll have to rest as much as possible, Skyler. Sleep if you can. Paul won't let you go flying off, but we need you in shape as soon as possible."

Skyler nodded. "Thanks, Josef. I know tonight isn't going to be easy on you."

"We're in this together," Paul said. "Dimitri is our friend, too, Sky. We *want* to do this. We're not just going after him for you. Now, more than ever, we have to get to him. If he's suffering the way the two of you say, we might be his only chance."

The thought of that poisonous silver inching its way slowly, torturously, through Dimitri's body sickened her.

"Hang on, my love," she whispered to the night. "I'm coming to you as fast as I can."

Josef moved a distance away, scanning quickly to ensure they were alone. Paul had found the perfect place to spend the night. The little house was tucked back into the woods, a distance from the road. A widowed woman rented out a room for extra money to those traveling. There were no close neighbors and that allowed for Josef to have the privacy needed to shift into the form of a dragon.

He extended his wing, and Paul helped Skyler climb up onto the dragon's back. He'd provided a double saddle to make the night's travel more comfortable. She slipped into the saddle, her feet in the stirrups while Paul climbed up behind her, doing the same. His arms came around her.

"If you need to sleep," Paul said, "just lean back against me."

"Thanks," Skyler said. "I'm certain I'll take you up on that."

She had traveled through the air many times with Carpathians. Gabriel took her flying all the time, using various forms. She'd always enjoyed it. That was the start of her love of flying and her need to get her pilot's license.

Flying had become almost an obsession, but Josef was young for a Carpathian and inexperienced in comparison to the ancients. She wasn't certain if he had the strength it took to keep the form of a dragon as long as he'd need to, as well as keeping Paul and her safe.

If you get tired, Josef, don't push it. We can find a place to rest.

Don't worry, Sky. I lectured you about pushing your strength too far. I'm not going to make the same mistake and give you a chance to say I told you so.

The cheery amusement in Josef's voice made her smile as the dragon lurched a couple of times, wings flapping as it stood on two legs. She held on tight as it began hopping along the ground, gaining more air with each hop. The dragon's great wings beat hard as he struggled to get off the ground. When they finally went airborne, Paul cheered and Skyler let out the breath she'd been holding.

Not particularly graceful, Josef commented, *but we made it. I think the two of you need to lose a little weight.*

Hey, now I'm totally offended. Skyler gave him her haughtiest, snippiest tone. *It's all Paul.*

Josef snorted.

To her shock, Paul dug his fingers into her rib cage, making her squeal. *Thought you were safe, didn't you? Josef hooked me up with this telepathy thing. It's working rather well.*

We should have done that a long time ago.

Well, of course my family and I can speak together, Paul admitted. *It's weird that we never thought about it. It's just blood.*

Skyler laughed. *Isn't that funny how we both just say, "It's just blood"? We're human and that's such a taboo in our culture, but we've obviously been around the Carpathians far too long. I actually asked Josef to give me blood this morning, didn't I?*

Yes, you did, but it did help you. Paul tightened his hold on her as the dragon's wings beat hard to take them higher over the mountain peak.

Are you cold? Maybe Josef should have provided warmer clothes for you as well.

I've got my jacket. If I get too cold, I'll call a halt and ask him then.

She knew immediately that Paul had deliberately not asked for warmer clothes. If he felt the dragon tiring, he planned to ask Josef to drop down to earth on the pretense that he was cold.

You're a good friend, Paul, Skyler said. *Have you checked out this dragon? It's the coolest dragon I've ever seen.* She included Josef in that comment.

The dragon was black but every scale was tipped a deep blue, just like Josef's hair. The body of the dragon was good-sized, the tail long and spiked. Each spike was tipped in blue.

Even your dragon is stylin', Paul said.

Your dragon is totally rockin' the look, Skyler added, admiringly.

He is very cool, isn't he? Josef sounded pleased.

Absolutely cool, Skyler agreed.

You should see my owl, Josef said. *Feathers look ultra-cool tipped in blue. Sometimes I spike the owl's head with blue feathers as well.*

Skyler looked at the wedge-shaped head. Sure enough there were blue tipped spikes protruding from the dragon's head. Laughing, she patted the dragon's neck. *You're so wonderful, Josef. I love everything about you.*

Josef had such an air of fun about him. In the worst situations—such as this one—he could still make her laugh.

Have you worked out how we're going to find Dimitri? Paul asked. *I imagine he's being held in an isolated place surrounded by some very tough Lycans, who, by the way, are pack hunters. Just saying.*

They had to take him somewhere they believe they have the upper hand, Josef said. *Carpathians must not be too close or they wouldn't be using that forest to hold him. He could send for help.*

Skyler shook her head, although seated as she was on the dragon's back, Josef couldn't see the movement. *I'm not certain he could. He blocked me, and maybe he has blocked everyone else as well, but our connection is . . . different—stronger. Neither of us knows why, but together we seem to be able to span distances that others can't.*

So are you just going to go walking through the woods like Little Red Riding Hood? Paul asked.

Skyler tilted her head back against his shoulder to see him. *That's exactly what I'm going to do.*

I'm actually going to give her a red cape with a hood, Josef said. *We want to make it easy for the big bad wolf to spot her.*

Paul was silent for a moment, frowning, clearly not liking the idea. *And if they just kill her? You're taking a huge chance with her life, Josef. It might sound funny to give her a red cape and hood and send her off walking alone through that forest, but it won't be so funny if she turns up dead.*

Lycans don't kill humans, Skyler said. *We researched very carefully. Only the rogues do, and they're treated by Lycans the same way Carpathians treat vampires. Dimitri wasn't taken by the rogues. The Lycans have him.*

How does anyone know that? Were they wearing shirts proclaiming the difference? Paul's voice dripped with sarcasm.

There was a brief silence. *I never considered that it could be members of a rogue pack who took him,* Josef said. *Everyone assumed it was members of an elite Lycan special commando-type team, because two of them disappeared at the same time as Dimitri did, but Paul's right, Sky. No one really knows for certain. Maybe we need to rethink our plan.*

If they were rogues, Skyler argued, *they would have killed him right there. They would have no reason to take him out of the country and then keep him alive just to torture him. Rogues kill and eat their prey. They're werewolves craving raw meat and fresh blood.*

Are you willing to bet your life on that? Paul asked.

It wasn't her life she was concerned with. It was Dimitri's. Clearly, if they didn't find him in time, even should she be able to stop every silver tracer bullet crawling through his body, eventually the Lycans would find another way to kill him. They *had* to find him. *She* had to find him.

Yes, Paul. I'm going to walk through the forest and pray a Lycan finds me. That's the plan. I wandered away from our campsite and got lost. You and I are part of a student group studying wolves in the wild. The papers are in perfect order, the site is up on the Internet looking extremely legit, and when they find me, the hope is that they will return me to my camp, not eat me for dinner.

I always knew you were a little crazy, Sky, Paul said. *You could get killed.*

Skyler accepted that she might get killed—but she wasn't going to have much of a life without Dimitri in it. She might not be Carpathian, but she was his lifemate, claimed or unclaimed. She knew her emotions were not the crush of a young girl, or the romantic fantasies she knew her college friends thought she indulged in. Dimitri was a special man. She would never find another man like him, one totally focused on her. She was the only woman he would ever look at. She was his world. His other half. There was no explaining to anyone how that felt. None of her college friends would ever be able to conceive of that kind of devotion.

The thing Paul didn't yet understand—and perhaps Josef didn't either—he was far too young—she was equally as devoted to Dimitri. She would walk through fire to get to him, so a trip through the deep woods might be terrifying, but it would never stop her.

Whoever found her. And she had sent up many prayers that it would be the elite hunter Josef had heard everyone talking about—Zev—to come to her rescue. He sounded like a decent Lycan who definitely could protect her from anyone or anything else threatening her.

Here's the reality of the situation, Paul, Skyler said. *I might get killed. If I don't find him, Dimitri will die. He doesn't have much time left. Even if the Carpathians had launched a rescue mission to find him, they won't get there in time. They don't know about the silver hooks.*

Unexpectedly her stomach lurched again. *They put hooks in his body and strung him up in the trees like a piece of meat.* She couldn't help the tears or the horror so stark in her voice. She didn't bother to try.

Paul tightened his arms around her, nudging her shoulder with his chin. *We'll find him, little sister, and when we do, we'll get him out of there.*

The wind tore the tears from her face. She shrank down into the warmth of the fur, so grateful to have two friends who loved her enough to risk everything for her lifemate. Behind her, she could feel Paul begin to shiver.

Maybe we should find a place for Josef to set down and get you some warmer clothes.

Not yet. He's still flying strong and we're covering kilometers fast. When he tires, I'll get warmer clothes. Go to sleep. Talking this way probably isn't the best thing for you.

She hadn't thought of that. She was so used to communicating telepathically she hadn't considered that it took psychic energy to do so even so close to the one she was speaking with.

She didn't answer him. She was tired. Paul would never let her fall. She closed her eyes and willed herself to fall asleep.

4

Skyler, what are you doing? I can feel you close to me.

The pain in Dimitri's voice tore at her. At least she was on the right track if he could feel her close. The forest was very dark, the trees large and ancient. She could almost hear them whispering to one another.

Skyler followed the psychic footprints directly back to her lifemate. Again, the path was stretched thin and ice-cold, but it wasn't long. Triumph swept through her. She wouldn't have to hold a bridge over a horrendous distance in order to heal him.

You are supposed to be healing.

The pain took her breath as she connected fully with him. She had thought herself prepared—after all, she knew what to expect—but there was no real way to remember the agonizing pain so clearly until one touched on it. She let it burn through her in an effort to acclimatize herself to it.

Josef was totally exhausted. They had made it to the forest in one evening of flight, but it had seriously depleted his energy. Paul had given him a tremendous amount of blood, which in turn had weakened him. She would have to be careful and not take this healing session as far as she had the last one, but she could not be so close to Dimitri and not try to get the worst of those silver threads away from his heart. She'd slept most of the way and felt more energized just because Dimitri was somewhere in the vicinity.

I'll be more careful this time, Dimitri, she promised. *I have to do this. You know I have no choice.*

The entire time she'd been asleep she'd dreamt of poisonous silver piercing his heart. His beautiful blue eyes had grown ice-cold as they stared lifelessly at her. Accusingly at her.

"You're too late. Why were you late?" he'd asked her.

It was a dream, sívamet. A nightmare only. You eased the pain for me.

There can be no untruths between lifemates, she quoted him. *It would be impossible to lessen your pain. The threads of silver remaining are still in your body burning just as severely as the ones I removed.*

Perhaps that is so, but it felt less. Your love kept me safe from the Moarta de argint—death by silver.

Is that what they call this torture?

It absolves the Lycan council from all guilt. They didn't kill me. Essentially, I kill myself by moving my body constantly to try to get away from the pain and the silver works its way deeper. They can go to Mikhail with a clear conscience.

That made her furious. How could the Lycan council sentence Dimitri to such a torturous death and then go to a meeting with the Carpathians discussing becoming allies with them?

I'm going to remove more threads, Dimitri, but I won't be able to get them all. I'm going for the ones closest to your heart.

She didn't wait for his reply. She entered his body as pure spirit. The hooks she'd tampered with had remained closed off. No new silver had dripped into his body, but the ones she'd left had made progress. She knew what to do now. Calling on her mage heritage, she again used her gifts to push the silver from his body.

Silver, silver, so deadly, so bright,
I summon earth's power to stay your blight,
As you were created and formed deep within,
I command you, silver, to remove and ascend.

Silver threads that twine and harm,
I release your hold of snaking charm.
I call to you, silver, harken my call,
Retrace the path from which you fall.

Harken to me, silver, hear my command,
Remove yourself doing no further harm.

This time she added a new element in order to lessen the pain of the burn for him. She'd been so exhausted and she'd just *left* him the night before. She'd been unconscious when she'd returned to her body, but she'd had plenty of time to think about how he was suffering.

Corydalis, Valerian, Meadowsweet all,
Cloak the pain that does now fall.

The silver responded with the same reluctance, almost as if it was alive, moving backward, away from his heart, the tiny silver beads burning his skin as they pushed through pores to drop to the ground below him.

Elation swept through her. The silver responded to her commands. She could see it moving backward away from his heart, as on the other end, it pushed through his pores and dropped to the ground in tiny little deadly beads. However, everywhere the silver touched burned him, both inside and out. This time she wouldn't leave him until she was certain she had healed every possible wound on his body that she could reach before her strength gave out.

Aloe sweet aloe, green and bright,
I call to your essence, seeking what is held hidden inside.
That which is sticky and filled with balm,
I seek of your essence to heal what is burned.
Kathalai, ancient name,
I call forth your power to steal away pain.

The elements were removing themselves at her command and the pain was lessened with the herbs. She managed to remove three more threads before exhaustion took hold of her. There were still several others, coming from his calves and his thighs, two from the hooks in his hips, but the silver from those hooks hadn't progressed nearly as close to his heart as it had from the ones she'd removed.

Can you manage this pain a while longer? I would take it from you if I could.

You have kept me alive, csitri, and just touching minds with you has made me stronger. Where are you? This is a dangerous place.

Those holding you, are they rogues?

No. Lycans. You cannot possibly understand the danger they represent. They will not hesitate to fight any Carpathian rescue party. You must relay that message to whoever travels with you. My brother. Any of the other warriors with you.

Skyler had to move away from him, backing down that psychic trail. She needed to rest. *I am human, not Carpathian and no such rescue party accompanies me.*

There was silence. She found herself back in her own body, lying in the hammock Paul had slung between two trees for her. She stared up at the canopy overhead. The wind gently moved through the branches, setting them swaying. She loved the sound of the breeze as it rustled the leaves and the feel of it on her face. She was ice-cold, but the fur coat lay over her. Somehow, even in his weakened state, Paul had managed to take care of her.

Skyler. In spite of the pain in his voice, Dimitri sounded commanding. He'd only used that voice on her a couple of times. *Did you come after me on your own? Is Josef with you?*

She had known this moment would come. She had hoped it would come much later. Pressing her lips together she nodded, even though he couldn't see the gesture.

We have a good plan. Once we free you, none of them can possibly harm us. She infused absolute confidence into her voice. She believed they could rescue him or she wouldn't have had Josef and Paul come with her. She would have come, but she *wouldn't* have involved them.

It's only getting those hooks closed off and the silver out of your body and then we're home free, she added. *You know the Lycans can't defeat you.*

Skyler, I want you to turn around and get out of here. I mean it. I'm not asking.

Even if you did ask, it wouldn't happen, Dimitri. I'm coming for you. I'm not the child everyone thinks, and you, better than most, know that. You're mine and these Lycans have no business trying to kill you.

Dimitri, in spite of the pain, and exhaustion, couldn't help the burst of amusement at Skyler's furious rant against the Lycans. She was unique. Special. His own personal miracle. So many people underestimated her. He loved the fire in her. He loved everything about her.

He was proud of her courage and tenacity, in spite of the fact that he wanted her out of danger. He didn't want her anywhere near the Lycans. He didn't trust what the wolves might do if they discovered she was working to free him. Still . . . how could he not feel elated and overwhelmed with her love, that she had dared such dangers to come for him?

He was a Carpathian male, an ancient hunter and his first instinct—his duty—was to protect his woman. Skyler was his other half, and to know that he had put her in danger was far worse to him than the seemingly endless pain he had endured.

You must leave. I cannot have you in danger and survive this.

There was that moment of silence that made his heart stutter. Had she spent too long trying to stop the silver from poisoning his system? Was she unconscious? Even though he knew she was much closer, the distance was still difficult. She had to use so much energy to bridge the void and then twice that to heal him.

He was well aware he couldn't push that poisoned silver from his body the way she had done it. She'd been meticulous, and more, everywhere the silver had burned through him, she'd soothed the terrible burns.

You cannot survive this without me and you know it.

Relief swept through him. She was weak. He could feel her energy level was very low, but she wasn't anywhere near the state she'd been in the last time.

I am grateful that you are removing the silver from my body. Once it is done, I can escape myself. You cannot come any closer.

She made a little sound in his mind, a *hmph* of annoyance. *You cannot unwrap the chains that bind you. If you could, my love, you would have done so weeks ago.*

Dimitri was beginning to feel a little desperate. She couldn't stay. He was helpless to aid her if she got into trouble. She was correct about the chains wrapped so tightly around his body. Had it not been for the unusually strong connection between them, he could never have reached out to Skyler. He had tried reaching his brother, Fen, but to no avail.

Sadly, I'm all you've got right now, Dimitri. The three of us. Josef and Paul will do whatever is necessary to help me set you free.

He loved her friends. He'd come to know them through her, and her love of them. The two boys were brothers to her, family, but they were boys, not men, not in the sense of warriors who were experienced in battle. They had no idea what they were facing, and how in the world could they possibly protect Skyler from a pack of Lycans?

He took a deep breath to try to keep still. The burn twisting through his body set him on fire. He could barely force his body to stay under his control, instead of moving continually in an effort to ease the never-ending agony bent on destroying him. He had to admit it was a medieval torture worthy of a Machiavellian punishment.

Skyler, I love you more than life itself. He told her the stark truth in a low, compelling tone. Compulsion wouldn't work on her, but he could use his best, loving persuasive voice. *My brother, Fen, will come. He is already on his way.* He spoke with absolute confidence. He *knew* Fen would come for him. *I need to know you're safe. More than anything else, I need that. Stay where you are and continue to drive the silver from my body. That will buy the time my brother needs to find me. You can reach him and know the time it will take for him to reach me.*

Skyler took her time mulling that over while his heart accelerated with fear for her. She gave a little sigh. *The idea is to get in and get out without anyone knowing we are here. If I call to your brother, he will have no choice but to let my father know. Gabriel will come. With him will be Lucian. Maybe others. There could be a war just when Mikhail is trying to make peace with these cretins.*

He knew she was right. Her family would come and there would be hell to pay. Worse, if the De La Cruz family found out Paul was with her, they would come, and there would be no stopping Zacarias if one hair was harmed on his nephew's head.

Skyler wasn't going to back down. Desperation set in. He was helpless, chained by silver, hanging in a tree with hooks in his body to slowly poison him. *Moarta de argint.* He couldn't save her if she was attacked.

How could he stop her? He didn't want her in the hands of the Lycans. Despair swept through him when even in his worst moments he hadn't considered, not for one moment, helping the silver to move through his body faster. He had known he could get the suffering over, but he would never leave Skyler alone, not if there was a chance. But to save her life . . .

Don't you dare even think about leaving me! Pure fury edged the trembling fear in her voice. *If you choose to go, I will follow. I won't be understanding about it either, Dimitri. We have a pact, you and I, we made it a long time ago when everyone else wanted to decide our fate. We decide together. You. Me. Together.*

I cannot stand the thought of you in danger.

It is only because you suffer . . .

Suffering does not matter. The silver does not matter. Death does not matter. You have no concept of what drives me. I cannot have you in danger.

Her voice changed completely. The fear and anger disappeared. Her tone was musical. Soft. Red velvet brushing over every inflamed nerve ending with a soothing touch. *My love, no one, not even an ancient so courageous and strong as you could withstand the lack of sustenance. You need to feed. You have been chained for over two weeks, and you've suffered agonies no one else could have endured. The combination would drive anyone mad.*

At times he *had* felt mad. His mind wandered. Before Skyler had come, he sometimes couldn't think clearly, but . . .

You have to trust me. I am your lifemate and I hold you close in my heart. You're the other half of my soul. Trust me to do this right.

The sad truth was—Skyler had a point. Days and nights ran together. He was left outside and at times he was helpless, caught in the Carpathian paralysis, yet unable to sleep. The sun beat down through the trees, nearly blinding him, burning his skin until he was blistered, but fortunately, the thick canopy—and his Lycan blood—kept him from the death most Carpathians feared.

The silver burned continuously, his insides on fire, his skin and bones feeling as though he was being scalded and scorched endlessly. Hunger beat at him, until he didn't know which was worse—the need for blood, or the ceaseless agony in his body. Now, all that meant little when he knew Skyler was in danger.

Dimitri. The way you feel about me . . . That is the way I feel about you. We belong together and I cannot go away and leave you alone like this. It would break my heart. I would rather risk everything on the chance of getting you back than know you are suffering and I did nothing.

Call Fen. He will come and I'll know you're safe.

He felt her sigh. She was worn. The edges of her mind were stretched thin. She was shivering with cold. He couldn't see where she was, but he could feel that much.

My love, you and I both know he will not get here in time. The silver was inches from your heart. Even now, I fear resting, afraid something will go wrong. Let me do this. For you. For us. Let me do this, Dimitri. I can do this.

There was no denying Skyler. He knew he was fighting a losing battle. Both of them needed to conserve strength.

Tell me your plan, sívamet.

He felt her love surrounding him. He tried to keep his body as still as possible, but the silver twisted through, burning along every nerve ending until he thought he might go mad. Before, in the darkness surrounding him during the endless days and nights, he had wanted to end it all, but the thought of what that would do to his lifemate kept him trying to be still to keep the poison from finding his heart. Now, with her love, with her courage, he felt lifted up. How could he not stay alive when he had a woman like Skyler fighting for him?

He felt her hesitation and found himself scowling. Skyler was no "yes" woman, and he loved that about her, but more than anything, he wanted her to be safe. His heart contracted painfully. She was going to do something she knew he would never approve of.

Josef has provided us with the best papers possible, three students conducting a study on wolves in the wild. He used your organization and we look very legitimate. The boys are setting up camp now. It should pass any inspection.

That tells me nothing.

It tells you we have planned this carefully. We don't want a war, we just want you safe and back with us. Tomorrow I'll go walking in the woods and get lost. I'm human. Someone will find me. One of the Lycans. I'll have a turned ankle, Josef is quite good at providing such things. The Lycan will escort me back to the camp if for no other reason than just to check out my story. I will plant a tracking device on him. That will lead us straight back to you.

Dimitri closed his eyes. It sounded so simple. Sometimes the best plans were the simplest, but Skyler would be in the deep forest, far from civilization, where real wolves and Lycans both inhabited the woods. Not all men were good—Lycan or human. Of all people, Skyler should know that.

He kept silent, knowing she did know. She had nightmares often. She was risking her life, along with her hard-won peace of mind and she had to be terrified, but she was doing it for him. The thought made him feel humble.

You would do the same for me.

He was an ancient warrior, she was so young and vulnerable. He could feel how exhausted she was. Under any circumstances, healing was difficult. Given the distance and the fact that she'd been drained of all energy the preceding night, he was surprised she could function at all. There was no use in arguing with her.

If anything goes wrong and you get in trouble, swear to me you will call for Gabriel. He capitulated, but his heart pounded and the silver twisted through his body that much faster. He could feel the burn worming its way through his rib cage.

Have no worries, my love, I will be shouting at the top of my lungs.

Skyler reassured her lifemate, honesty ringing in her voice.

I love you and that doesn't begin to describe what I feel for you. There were no words, Dimitri decided, that had ever been invented that could ever express the all-consuming love he felt for Skyler.

Please be safe, Dimitri. Stay very still. I'm with you, she whispered, tears burning in her eyes as the connection between them abruptly ended.

Skyler hated letting that thread between them go. He was so alone, in such bad shape, far worse than she could have ever imagined. Her Dimitri was so strong, so very powerful, it didn't seem possible that he could be a prisoner, tortured and near his life's end.

She felt tears on her face. She couldn't move, she was just too exhausted, but staring up at the canopy overhead as the branches swayed and danced to the music of the wind, she realized how lucky she was. Dimitri was alive. He was close enough that she could reach him and he could connect to her. They would find a way together.

"Sky, I'm going to give you a few minutes," Josef said, "and then you're going to have to try to eat something. We've got a lot of work ahead of us and you have to be in shape."

She nodded, content to lie in her hammock and listen to the sounds of the forest. The continual drone of the insects seemed familiar to her and yet not at all. Wings fluttered overhead as birds flitted from one tree to the next. Marmots scampered and mice infiltrated the vegetation on the forest floor. The forest was alive with life.

She turned her head to watch as Paul set up a safety zone. There were predators in the forest and, although they had Josef with them, they needed to prepare just in case. She lay in her hammock, thinking about their last line of defense, should everything go wrong. If they were discovered and the Lycans attacked them, it was up to her to provide a safe shelter for them all. Dimitri would be weak. If there was no time to give him blood and heal him, they would be tasked with finding a safe place they could defend while he went to ground to recover.

Paul strode over to her, holding a water bottle. "Here. Can you sit up?" He already had his arm around her back, helping her. "Drink this. We're nearly set up here. Josef has everything in order. Even our findings will stand up under scrutiny. I can't imagine that the Lycans won't buy our cover."

"Josef said the simplest plan was the best, and I think he's right," Skyler admitted. She had to lean against Paul to sit up enough to drink the water. "I'm so tired, all I want to do is sleep." She looked up at him, frowning. "He can't go to ground or get out of the sun. The last time, the distance was so great I couldn't see anything around him or even get a sense of what was happening to him. The pain was so awful, but this time . . ." She trailed off.

"He's strong," Paul assured her. "He'll survive."

"I know how very fortunate I am that he loves me. Knowing he didn't deliberately move and squirm to allow the silver to pierce his heart when he's been tortured all this time just to stay alive for me, is an amazing feeling. I don't know that I could have withstood that kind of agony as long as he has."

Skyler took another long, slow drink. The water felt good on her parched throat. Dimitri hadn't fed for over two weeks. What would that do to him? She looked around for Josef. He was busy with the fire pit. He'd always had a thing about fire.

"If Dimitri hasn't fed in a long while, Josef, what does that do?"

Josef turned slowly, the flames from the fire pit casting eerie shadows. "That's not good, Sky. He'll be starved. It's best that, when we rescue him, I give him my blood first, not you."

She didn't like the sound of that. Josef could be quite adult at times, and he sounded very serious—and concerned.

"Can you get up, Skyler?" Paul asked. "We've got a chair for you and the fire is warm."

"I don't know." That was dishonest. If she tried to stand, she'd fall on her face.

Paul scooped her up without asking, carrying her straight over to the fire and placing her in a chair facing it. "Josef remembered the marshmallows and chocolate," he added.

"Sounds fun," she replied.

Josef came up behind her and wrapped his arms around her shoulders, putting his chin on the top of her head. "Do you think you're up for this tomorrow? Should we give it another day so that you can recoup?"

He was reluctant to wait, she heard it in his voice. She knew the chances of their plan succeeding went down the longer they waited. If a Lycan discovered their camp before she was "lost" their ploy wouldn't work. She doubted she could get close enough to plant a tracking device without their knowledge if she wasn't injured and needing help. They would have to find another way to track Dimitri back to his prison. She knew she could find him now, with the psychic trail becoming stronger, but it would take time and energy they clearly didn't have. And then there was Dimitri. Anything could happen on his end—and none of it was good.

"I'll be ready," she said. She took the mug of hot chocolate more to appease both of her friends than because she thought she'd drink it. "What I need is to let Mother Earth help heal me. Can you open the soil here for me to stretch out in?"

"Baby, you can't sleep in the ground," Josef said. "I can't cover you and you'd be vulnerable to any attack. Crazy woman, you aren't Carpathian yet."

She found herself laughing. "Crazy man, I meant just a few layers. I didn't plan to sleep there. The insect population alone would stop me."

"Worms," Paul added. "They crawl in and out of bodies . . ."

"The worms crawl in, the worms crawl out . . ." Josef quoted an old song children had sung to one another in play yards the world over.

"Stop," Skyler commanded. Just being in the company of her two best friends made her feel lighter. Safer. More grounded. "Eventually I'll be sleeping in the dirt, and I don't want to think about worms or any other bugs crawling over me."

She needed to feel her connection with Mother Earth if her fail-safe plan had any chance of success at all. She didn't want to talk about it yet, not until she was certain she could do it. Everything depended on what she learned there in that ancient forest soil.

Josef kissed the top of her head. "You really are a squeamish little baby sometimes, Sky. *Dirt* is *not* a dirty word. You said it with such distaste. Like a girl."

"I am a girl, you goof," Skyler pointed out. She looked down at the chocolate in the mug. Her stomach rebelled again. She was going to need Josef's aid again. "And no girl likes the idea of sleeping in the ground with insects. I am human, after all."

"You aren't *exactly* human," Josef said, letting go of her. "More like a trippy little alien. By the way, I forgot to tell you, I've really gotten far in that database of human psychics Dominic found in South America. I've gotten past the encryptions and I've figured out the code they were using for each person entered. I'm close to cracking the entire thing. If I do, I can give the names to Mikhail and those women can be protected from the human society trying to kill us, vampires, and anyone else hunting them."

Skyler's stomach lurched. An ugly knot had formed. She looked down and the mug was empty. "Thanks, Josef."

"For the chocolate or the 'trippy little alien' compliment?"

Paul snorted. "Is that what that was? A compliment? You're never going to make it with the ladies, Josef, if you don't get better at talking to them."

"I'm not wasting my swag on my sister here," Josef nudged her foot with his. "I do just fine with the ladies."

Paul shook his head. "I was your wingman at the last little party we went to together, and I'm pretty sure you struck out once you began talking." He winked at Skyler. "They all thought he was pretty cute until he opened his mouth and began spouting some kind of number theory."

"Oh, Josef," Skyler said, covering her smile with one hand. "You didn't really, did you?"

Josef took the empty mug from her hand, glaring at Paul. "The girl was beautiful, you know, not all skinny and blond and cloned like most of them. I mean she had a real figure and her hair was dark and shiny and when she smiled, my heart sort of exploded and took my brain with it. When I short-circuit, I fall back on the numbers in my head."

"He sees in numbers," Paul said. "Can you believe that?"

Josef thrust another mug into her hand. She recognized the aroma of vegetable soup. Her stomach knotted even more. She closed her eyes, wanting to get it over with. Whether the food stayed down or not was another matter. She knew, before she slept, Josef would give her more of his healing blood. She couldn't be converted without a true blood exchange, but that didn't mean she wouldn't feel the effects.

When she opened her eyes, she was grateful that not only the soup was gone, but the mug as well. Paul handed her the water bottle again while she concentrated on keeping the food in her stomach.

"Josef is amazing," she said, meaning it. "So are you, Paul. I couldn't be any luckier. Thank you both for coming with me."

"Don't go getting all girly on us," Josef reprimanded. "The next thing you know, we'll be sitting around the fire sobbing and some Lycan will catch us and figure it would be best to put us out of our misery."

"Fine, open a patch of earth for me—take it down to where the soil is rich with minerals."

Josef looked around the forest floor. "Anywhere should be good. This is ancient land and has been regenerating for thousands of years."

He peeled back the vegetation and topsoil to expose the richness hidden beneath. Paul lifted Skyler again and gently deposited her in the two-foot-deep opening. Skyler handed him back the water bottle and turned her attention completely to the soil.

She lay back, uncaring that the dirt would get into her hair. Josef could take care of that easily. All that mattered was her connection to Mother Earth.

Great Mother Earth, who gave us all birth,
Hear my call.

Help me, great one, show me the path that I must walk,
I place myself in your arms, hear the beat of my heart,
Hear my call.

Sounds came first. The deep booming beat of a drum. Steady. Coming from the earth's very core and spreading throughout the land to give life to the plants and trees, all the flora and fauna. The trickle of water came next, so soft at first, but when she listened, the sound was powerful, the flow of earth's blood reaching out like arteries and veins to nourish.

Great one, I am of your making,
I ask for your healing balm,
I have need of you and your gifts,
My body is worn and tired.

She had never felt so stretched thin, afraid if she asked Paul and Josef they would tell her they could see where she was frayed, or holes torn in her very skin. Without Josef's blood, she knew she would never have the strength to help free Dimitri from such a terrible weapon.

Help me, Mother, bring forth your healing energies to give me strength.
My need is great. Hear me. See me. Be of me. Wrap me in the warmth of your arms.

Rich soil poured around her body, over it, a thin layer, but almost up to her neck. She should have felt claustrophobic, but instead, she felt warm and safe. As if from a great distance, she heard a gasp from Paul, but her mind was connected to the steady drumming beat of the earth's heart. Her own heart matched that strong rhythm. She felt the new growth, long twisting vines, pushing out of the soil beneath and beside her to wind around her body, a cover of forest green.

Skyler felt as if she was in the very cradle of life, held by loving arms. Small hairs from the roots reaching toward her brushed along her legs and arms. Little shoots of greenery reached for her, to snuggle in close to her body, beginning to weave together into a thin, fine blanket over her body.

I need you, great one, my soul mate burns,
He is hung on hooks, their tips delivering silver poison into his body,
Threads of silver burn their way toward his heart.

His life runs out through my fingers like fine grains of sand.
Hear me, great one, bring forth your healing energies,
Give me your strength, heed my call, heal me, Mother.

Already she could feel strength flowing back into her. The small cracks she felt fragmenting her mind slowly closed and the continuous pounding in her head faded away. Her legs and arms felt stronger than ever. The chaos in her mind stilled, and she found herself calm and determined.

Tell me, great one,
Those of the Lycan breed were born of this place,
What was their making?
How can they be subdued?

Show me their path,
Reveal to me their weaknesses,
Show me the way to diminish them.
Give me the power to release their hold.

She had to feel the Lycans when they came near. They were pack hunters and gave off little or no energy. They were somehow able to contain it, so that even the Carpathians couldn't feel their presence before an attack. She would need to know where every single wolf was, why they were there and what their plan of action would be.

Mother Earth had seen it all played out on her surface. Centuries had gone by and the Lycan species had taken on the mantle of civilization, but like the Carpathians, they were predators first. They were wolves. They hunted in packs, rather than as single hunters like the Carpathians. Packs generally had an alpha pair and they used the tried and true attacks that had worked for centuries.

They had evolved, strong, fast, very lethal, and they were smart. They had integrated into human society, looking civilized, but deep under their skin, they were always Lycan. They still hunted the same way they had been successful so long ago.

Skyler absorbed the information stamped into the very ground by the Lycans who had used this forest for so many years. She took her time, grateful to be a daughter of the earth, grateful the offering was so detailed. It was important to learn about Lycans as pack hunters in order to figure out the best way to elude—or defeat them.

When she was certain she knew how the inner workings of the pack were managed, she gave thanks and then asked for help with Dimitri. His weakness beat at her. His hunger. He was starved, and no Carpathian could go days or weeks without going to ground.

Great Mother, my beloved is of your making,
He is your own son, a son of Mother Earth.
You have judged him, you know him. You know his worth.

Spare him, Mother,
Bring forth your healing power,
Aid me in his healing,
Use me, bring forth your power through me.

Skyler hadn't realized how truly shaken she was after connecting so often with Dimitri and seeing, no matter what she'd done to help him, that his suffering continued. There was little she could do about the silver chains binding him so tightly from neck to ankle, not from so great a distance. She had barely allowed herself to acknowledge those evil chains.

She knew it was the thin loops wrapped so tightly around his body, a mummy suit of silver, that kept Dimitri contained. He couldn't reach out to his kind for aid. He couldn't free himself, or fight his enemies. She had to find the best way to remove the silver and make certain she could heal the burns in his body at least enough to allow him to travel fast.

She really didn't want to start a war. It would be so much better if they could rescue Dimitri without being detected.

If their plan worked, she would take the information Mother Earth provided on the Lycans, their strengths, weaknesses and habits, their nature and the very characteristics unique to them, and she would use those things against them.

Their last fail-safe depended on her. If they were wounded, or Dimitri was too weak, they needed that last safety zone. She would need to call on every ounce of her mage blood, of her connection to Mother Earth, of her Dragonseeker lineage, to provide a protection spell strong enough to allow anything human or Carpathian to enter, but hold all Lycans out. If she succeeded, they would have a place to run to, a place to defend if the Lycans attacked them. If not, they would all certainly die.

5

Pain was endless, slowing time so that each individual second crawled by. Dimitri could barely breathe, his breath coming in ragged, shuddering gasps, signaling he was nearly at the end of his endurance. His body shivered continuously of its own accord. Try as he might, he couldn't stop that automatic reflex, much like a wounded animal alone and cornered. His mind was in chaos, the sound of his stuttering heart thundering in his ears.

Hunger beat at him with every slow second that passed. He was aware of every living creature with blood running in its veins that came near him. He could hear that throbbing beat deep in their veins like a drum summoning him. Even the twisting, agonizing pain couldn't stop the need rising like a tsunami that couldn't be denied.

His teeth were lengthened and sharp. It took every ounce of discipline he possessed to keep from fighting the silver chains encircling his body. Even with the hooks in him he could have called prey, but the chains prevented him.

He smelled the Lycans approaching long before he heard them coming. In his weakened state, he thought the tremendous gifts of a mixed blood—the Lycan's dreaded *Sange rau*—would lessen, not strengthen, but his every sense stretched and grew until he was aware even of the insects crawling on the ground and up the tree trunks.

Sometimes he thought he could actually see and hear the plants growing around him. A few minutes earlier, the grasses surrounding him had been a few feet away from where he hung, but now they covered the ground beneath him like a thick mat. Bunches of flowers seemed to be springing up, fully formed with stalks and petals within minutes. He fastened his gaze to the ground, surprised to see ferns pushing through the earth in a dozen spots surrounding him.

"You don't look so tough hanging there," Gunnolf sneered as he came up on Dimitri.

Dimitri didn't deign to respond, what was the point? Gunnolf wanted to elicit some response out of him, and he wasn't about to give him the satisfaction. It wouldn't lessen his pain, and he couldn't get to him to take his blood, so really, retreating into his own mind was a far better option.

"Your friends haven't exactly come running to save you," Gunnolf continued, idly kicking at Dimitri's leg. He laughed when Dimitri's body swayed and the hooks dug in deeper, ripping at his flesh. "They must have realized what a dirty, disgusting monster you are and left us to kill you. They weren't all that good in a fight anyway."

Dimitri remained silent, his eyes on the ground. He could see dirt pushing up in places around the ferns and the mystery of it fascinated him. Some of the grass in spots directly beneath him had grown high enough that the blades brushed his legs. The grass wound around his ankle and slid beneath the tattered hem of his trousers. Slowly he could feel it traveling up along his skin until it found that exact spot where the Lycan hunter had kicked him. Tiny droplets of something cool and wet fell from the leaf to find the bruise. At once that pain was gone.

"I will say, you've lasted longer than anyone else ever sentenced to death by silver." This time there was a hint of apprehension in Gunnolf's voice. "No one has lasted past three days. They say it's impossible to hold still and the silver reaches your heart faster. If you want to end the misery, just dance around a little bit more."

He caught Dimitri's shoulders and shook his body hard, laughing again as the fresh blood poured from each of the wounds where the hooks held him prisoner.

"Gunnolf! What are you doing?" Zev snapped sharply.

Gunnolf sobered instantly. He leaned close to Dimitri's ear. "Die already, you monster, so I can get out of here." He released him and stepped away from the dangling body.

Zev shoved him away from Dimitri. "You have no right to put your hands on him. The man is suffering. Isn't that enough for you? If you weren't one of my pack, I would think you've gone rogue and enjoy the suffering of others."

"He's *Sange rau*, a monster beyond compare." Gunnolf spit on the ground to show his contempt. "He would kill every man, woman and child we have and never look back."

"He is not vampire as the others were," Zev argued.

His tone had gone thoughtful. Dimitri's gaze jumped up, and he found Zev was now looking at the ground. His rugged features were expressionless, but his piercing eyes saw far too much. Dimitri's heart gave a jolt in his chest as Zev glided forward, a fluid, easy move that was nearly impossible for Gunnolf to follow, but so very easy for Dimitri.

There, on the ground beneath his swaying body, mostly buried in the thick mat of grass and the ferns and flowers, were a few telling beads of silver glittering, drawing the eye. The sole of Zev's boot slipped over the silver, mashing it further into the ground. When he moved his boot, stepping forward, grass sprang up as if he'd never taken a step. The silver beads were completely hidden from view.

Zev raised his gaze to Dimitri's. "You had better get out of here, Gunnolf. You've challenged me one too many times and my patience has grown thin. The next time, you had better come prepared to defeat me in battle."

Gunnolf snarled, baring his teeth, but he turned abruptly and strode away. Zev sighed, shaking his head. "That one and I will tangle in the near future, and it will be a fight to the death."

"He will not fight fair," Dimitri predicted. "In fact, I doubt he will come at you face-to-face. He will try to kill you when your back is turned and there is no one to see his treachery."

"I am truly sorry," Zev said. "I sent word to the council to try to get this sentence retracted, but there has been no word. I cannot go against my people, but I would help in whatever way I can."

"You have been kind to bring me water," Dimitri said.

"No one has ever been able to remove silver from their system," Zev said, looking down at the ground beneath Dimitri.

Using the toe of his boot, Zev pushed aside the grass and ferns. No trace of silver remained. Frowning, he dug into the soil. "It's gone."

Dimitri said nothing. He could feel the grass blades winding their way around his ankle and slipping over his calf to the point of entry where the hooks were embedded in his muscle. Those tiny beads of salve dropped onto his raw wounds. The grass seemed to massage the soothing gel into lesions and then began moving up toward the gashes on his thighs.

Skyler. His woman. His lifemate. Who would have ever thought she could have so much power packed into that little frame of hers? She had a core of pure steel. He had no doubt in his mind that she had made some pact with Mother Earth and this form of healing was her doing. Healing and hiding evidence.

Zev came closer. "I cannot free you, but I can aid you. There is no law that says I cannot provide nutrients for you. Allow me to give you blood."

Dimitri's heart jumped and then began to pound. He had never considered that a Lycan would make such an offer. The temptation was overwhelming. He could feel saliva forming in his mouth. His teeth were sharp and terrible.

"I am weak. Far too weak to trust myself. I am uncertain if I could stop." He forced the truth out, respecting the man, not wanting to take any chances. He would have drained Gunnolf dry, but Zev had integrity and the sentence of the council had clearly come as a shock to him.

"You are wrapped in chains," Zev pointed out. "I can control your intake."

Dimitri lifted his head to look around him. The forest was thick with trees and brush, but he felt and heard the life force of other Lycans close by. He could feel eyes on them. "The more you aid me, the more suspect you become in the eyes of the others. The one you call Gunnolf is poisoning the minds of the others against you. By aiding me, you help his cause."

"What is his cause?" Zev asked. "Why is it so important for you to die before the summit reaches its conclusion? It makes no sense. Key members of our council are meeting right now with your prince and his people to settle the issue of the *Sange rau*—the Bad Blood, and the *Hän ku pesäk kaikak*, or *Paznicii de toate*—Guardian of all. Doesn't it make sense to see that outcome before sentencing you to death?"

Dimitri tried a smile, exposing his lengthened canines. "I'm the one sentenced to death, so obviously it makes perfect sense to me."

"I see you've retained your sense of humor."

"I try." The soothing grass had reached his thighs now, moving up both legs to find those terrible, burning wounds in an effort to ease the pain.

Hunger reached a new high. He could count each individual beat of Zev's steady, strong pulse. A strange roaring in his head consumed his mind with the urgency to feed. He saw red, the color banding in his vision.

"Maybe you should step back, put a safe distance between us," Dimitri cautioned. His voice had become more of a growl than an actual vocalization.

Unafraid, Zev stepped closer, his own teeth tearing a hole in his wrist. He was careful to avoid the silver chains encompassing Dimitri's body as he lifted his wrist, dripping with life-giving blood, to Dimitri's mouth.

Blood surged to every starved cell, every withered organ, moved over the many burned paths the silver had taken, to revitalize and rejuvenate. Dimitri tried to be polite, tried to hold on to awareness. Zev risked his life by giving him blood. His pack could turn on him at any moment. Dimitri was certain Gunnolf had his own agenda. He wanted more power and Zev was standing in his way. This act of kindness could very well be Zev's downfall.

Yet Dimitri couldn't make himself stop. All he had to do was sweep his tongue across that wound in Zev's wrist to close the gash, but hunger was so raw, so terrible, such a monster gaining control of him, that he couldn't quite manage on his own.

You must stop me. He pushed the words out from his mind onto a path, any path, hoping Zev would pick it up. They'd used telepathic communication on a hunt of a rogue pack before, although the path had not been between them. Telepathic communication grew easier once it was established, but there was usually a blood path between a Carpathian and the one he reached out to. His heart sank. He'd never given Zev blood.

Zev pulled his wrist from Dimitri, wincing as those strong teeth jerked out of his skin. Dimitri closed his eyes, trying to breathe deep, desperate for more, but grateful for what had been given.

"I heard you. How is that possible?"

Dimitri shook his head. Even that slight movement sent his head spinning. He had grown dizzy with pain and lack of sustenance. "I have no idea. Maybe desperation on my part."

Zev wrapped a strip of cloth around his wrist and knotted it tight. "Stay alive, at least until I hear personally from the council. Like I said before, none of this makes any sense, and the council is all about logic." He glanced in the direction Gunnolf had gone. "I don't like this set-up at all."

Dimitri raised an eyebrow. Tiny beads of blood dotted his forehead as he worked at keeping very still. The grass continued to move up his thighs to his hips, curling around the hooks and dropping the small droplets of salve over the wounds there. Nevertheless, the silver in his body burned like a raging inferno ceaselessly until at times he forgot even the basic mechanics of breathing.

"There are too many of us here," Zev said, his voice pitched very low. "This forest is an outpost, one reserved for the wolves in the wild and basically used for extremely sensitive meetings or private camping when one can't take civilization one more moment. We don't keep large packs here. There are no women or children. This is the base camp of an army."

Dimitri went still inside. Skyler had no idea of the size of the camp or the trouble she would be walking into. He kept his features absolutely expressionless. It was imperative that no one know she was even in the forest. She might be a few hundred kilometers away, but for the Lycans, that would be considered too close.

He liked Zev. Even respected him. But he didn't trust anyone with Skyler's life. "Perhaps your council has decided on treachery and plans to attack the prince."

"That would be suicide and you know it. They went to that meeting in good faith."

Dimitri sighed. It was becoming difficult to talk. The sun was rising, filtering through the canopy. This time of day was manageable, but it signaled hell was coming.

"I suppose my sentence, after giving their word that they wouldn't kill me, was also a sign of their good faith."

Zev frowned. He rubbed the bridge of his nose and let out a soft sigh. "I think the entire world's gone mad."

"Just so you know, the only one likely to come after me is my brother. He will have his lifemate and some of his friends along, but he probably won't have the prince's approval."

Zev stiffened. "Fen. Fenris Dalka is your brother. He's *Sange rau*, too. He must have been Carpathian before he was Lycan."

"An ancient warrior, and not *Sange rau*. He is *Hän ku pesäk kaikak*. His skills have always been the thing of legends." Dimitri tried a faint smile but it came out more of a grimace. "You've seen him in action. He isn't going to be happy about this."

"He was badly injured," Zev said. "I don't want to take away your hope. Something has kept you alive this long, but when I left the Carpathian Mountains, your brother was nearly dead." He shook his head. "I'm sorry, Dimitri, but there is little chance he lived through those injuries."

Dimitri closed his eyes and allowed air to move through his lungs. It was so hard to keep his body still when the silver persisted in snaking its way up his legs, through his thighs, over his hips and into his abdomen, turning his gut into a fireball that ate him from the inside out.

"You met Tatijana." He made it a statement.

"Of course. What does she have to do with it?"

This time Dimitri did manage a brief smile. He opened his eyes and looked directly at Zev. "Everything. He's going to come. Not today. Not tonight, but sometime soon, and when he does, all these Lycans packed into this forest just waiting their opportunity aren't going to be enough. I'm going to still be alive, no matter how badly Gunnolf wants me dead."

Zev swore under his breath and turned away.

"And Zev," Dimitri added, his voice hoarse and edged with pain. "He won't come alone." He put the idea in the elite hunter's head deliberately. If it was too late to stop Skyler from carrying out the first part of her plan, he wanted Zev to be out in the forest, scouting for the enemy, and not for some other Lycan to find her.

Dimitri watched Zev walk away. He stayed very still, letting time pass, concentrating on the grass moving from his hip to spread across his burning belly. *Skyler.* He used his remaining strength to reach for her. The moment he felt her response, that instant pouring of love into his mind, filling every dark place that so many kills and so many empty centuries had left scarred, hope was renewed.

You're such a miracle. How did you get Mother Earth to agree to aid me?

You are her son. She wanted to help. I just added a few touches to help her. I'm going to work on the threads reaching toward your heart from your hips. When I've rested enough, I'll set out and hope to find a Lycan. Paul's scouting for tracks. He's very good at it. We're leaving our tracks everywhere, following the wild wolf pack and recording every sound as well as putting up cameras. The cover is very solid.

Just the sound of her voice turned him inside out. She was indomitable. He knew her human frailties, yet she didn't swerve from her intended path.

Skyler. Sívamet. I have learned from one of the better men here that this place is harboring an army of Lycans. He was obviously worried. I threw him off by telling him Fen would come. He knew Fen was wounded and thought he might even be dead, but he'll go search for signs that a rescue party is coming for me. He won't expect you.

Skyler searched his memories. She sent another wave of warmth into his mind. With it came strength. *He gave you his blood.*

Yes. I need far more to try to heal, and to be at full strength, but I can last until Fen comes. You should pack up and go. I think they're preparing for war.

Skyler stretched across the telepathic path leading to him. He could feel the approach of her healing spirit. She was white light. Pure unconditional love. She moved inside him, entering easily, already knowing what she would find. She was stronger now. Josef had clearly given her blood again. He couldn't find it in his heart to be jealous of another male helping her, he could only be grateful.

The moment she began to work, he felt the difference in her. She seemed powerful. Mage. She had come to terms with that part of her and she welcomed it now. Drew on her heritage, her bloodline, where before she had tried to forget she was related to Xavier, the hated and feared criminal who had nearly single-handedly brought down the Carpathian race.

I call upon my blood.
I am born of mage and dragon, no more shall I hide.
I call to you, Mother, bring forth to me the records of encoded light.
Show me the past, as I live in the present.
Let me view the future as you aid me in the now.

I know your words,
I hear your thoughts,
I feel your heart,
I know your intent.
You cannot hide.
I am both mage and Dragonseeker.

The silver obeyed her as it had done on two previous occasions, but this time much faster, as if now it recognized a master of elements and minerals. She finished with the silver tracers, driving them from his burning belly back to the hooks in his hips. She closed those off and moved downward, following the thin, deadly silver to his thighs, pushing it back so that he felt it burning through his pores, and down his leg as it rolled off of him to the ground below.

I call to you, Mother, absorb that which is deadly,
Aid me in this time of healing,
I call to comfrey, knitbone,
I use your power to sedate, to soothe, that which burns,

I call upon you, Mother, to assist in the healing of internal damage,
Seek out the path from which this poison has come,
Cauterize it and close it,
So that which is open and causing pain, cannot be open again.

Dimitri sensed she was tiring. There was still a great distance between them. She had used telepathy too many times not to feel the effects. *You need to stop.*

I'm almost done. I only have the hooks in your calves left. If I can manage to stop the flow of silver altogether, it will give you relief through the day. I'll come for you at night.

She began the work of pushing back the last two snakelike threads of silver toward his calves. Not once did she falter, although Dimitri could feel that white light fading with the length of time and the drain on her energy. Again she made certain the tips of the hooks were closed so no new silver could enter his body.

I call upon you once again, aloe and comfrey,
I seek and use your healing salve to stop this raging pain,
Seek deep into his flesh where burns run deep and raw,

Seek out the damage that is done deep within,
Use your gifts to repair cell and skin.

The relief was nearly instantaneous. Dimitri had been writhing in agony for so long, for a few moments he almost didn't realize the pain in his body had dimmed to a very tolerable level. He could actually push it aside entirely. The outside chains were another matter, but compared to that silver moving through his body, forming its own veins and arteries, the damage to his skin seemed minimal.

Mother, I call upon you to take into your arms,
That which is doing no harm.
Take on the poison. Eat it, drink it,
Remake it into something of the earth.

May the green of the great Mother be seen,
And used to hide that which would do evil.
May her beauty bloom, showing all the colors of her heart,
May her beauty shade and hide us from all harm.

Skyler didn't leave loose ends, not when she was fully aware as she was now. He felt real hope for the first time. As long as no other Lycan discovered the hooks were no longer injecting beads of fluid silver into his body, he would have a chance to gain strength. Fen would come.

You have to leave this place. The Lycans preparing for battle changes everything.

She was already fading away. *I don't care what they prepare for.*

Send Josef then. He can slip in and release me.

He cannot. His energy would tip the Lycans off immediately and he'd stir up a hornet's nest. Paul and I are human. They won't see us as threats.

Skyler heard him swearing in his ancient language as she found herself back in her hammock. Birds sang loudly, calling to one another as they flitted from tree to tree. The forest was alive as the early morning rays of the sun poured through the canopy. There was such beauty in nature, and now that she knew Dimitri would stay alive long enough for her to get him out of the enemy's camp, she could truly enjoy where she was.

She didn't want to argue with him anymore. He was a dominant male, like most of the Carpathian men, and she didn't blame him for worrying about her. She worried. She knew, because she often merged minds with Dimitri, that safety and health was placed above all else for their females. The species was too close to extinction. Women were too important to risk. There was also the fact that only one woman could be their lifemate. If she was to die, or the male Carpathian missed finding his lifemate, the warrior had no choice but to meet the dawn or choose to give up his soul.

She hadn't just impetuously jumped into the rescue without thinking it through. She wasn't an impulsive person. Her earlier life had made her very cautious. Dimitri was severely injured and felt helpless, she understood that. She was human and vulnerable in his eyes, and she understood that as well.

Csitri, I am not in any way reprimanding you. You saved my life. You've given me hope and surrounded me with love. I cannot bear the idea of you hurt or injured.

Dimitri, I'm your best chance at escape right now. The longer you're there, the more likely something goes wrong. I'm not willing to take that chance. I'm just not. If what you say is true, and they are preparing for a war, then they need you dead. And just for the record, I know it's difficult for you to think of me hurt or injured. Can you imagine what it's like for me to know you're hurt? To know they tortured you? That the first night I finally found you I wasn't capable of removing all the silver? Or stopping the terrible burn?

She brushed at the tears running down her face. She hadn't been able to hold the connection long enough, but that didn't make it any easier to bear. *Why do men always think they suffer more when their partner is in danger? Women love as much, they suffer as much. You aren't alone in this, Dimitri.* She couldn't help the edge to her voice.

There was a small flash of amusement, and then he poured love into her mind. It was impossible to stay angry with him when he merged his mind so deeply with hers.

I stand corrected, päläfertiilam—my lifemate. I had no idea I had such a fierce warrior woman for a partner. Just make certain you're protected. I trust that Josef and Paul will watch out for you while you do this.

Relief swept through her. *I promise to be careful, my love. If I get into any trouble, you'll know. So will the world. I'll send for Gabriel immediately. Rest now.*

One more thing, Skyler. I'm up in a tree, wrapped in silver chain. I cannot free myself. You will need to find a way to remove the chain as well as the hooks.

I am prepared. She had absolutely no idea yet what she was going to do to get him free.

He laughed softly in her mind, as if he knew she was struggling to figure that piece of his escape out. His laughter wrapped her up in his love, and then the connection between them slowly faded as if he were exhausted.

Skyler took a deep breath and let it out. She might be afraid to walk out in the forest, seeking a Lycan, but still, she looked forward to it. That would bring her one step closer to freeing Dimitri. She sat up gingerly, feeling faint and dizzy.

Josef looked up immediately from his conversation with Paul. "Are you okay?"

She shook her head. "I'll need your help again."

"You're going to have more Carpathian blood in you than Josef does," Paul said with a little grin. "You should see the weapons Josef managed to get for me."

Skyler rolled her eyes. "Men. You just couldn't wait for me to know all about your cool weapons, could you?"

"I almost came over to your hammock and dumped you out," he teased.

She closed her eyes and let Josef give her blood, grateful he was adept enough to keep her unaware when she consented to his aid. She took the water bottle Paul offered and drank, more to make certain there was no aftertaste in her mouth than because she was thirsty.

"You don't think the Lycans will sense the Carpathian blood in her do you, Josef?" Paul asked, suddenly anxious.

"They can't tell we're Carpathian until we use our energy to manipulate the elements," Josef said. "I read the emails between Gregori and Gabriel."

Skyler scowled at him. "You *hacked* my father's email?"

Josef shrugged, completely unrepentant. "He made it easy. I told him his password needed to be a lot better, but he didn't listen. They never do. I hacked the prince as well." He held up his hand to stop her when she opened her mouth to give him a lecture on privacy. "Better yet, I managed to find and hack two of the Lycan council members."

Skyler closed her mouth. Somehow hacking the Lycans' email didn't seem nearly as bad as hacking her father's email or the prince's.

"Did you find anything out about what's going on?" Paul asked.

"Only that they seemed to want to work things out with the Carpathians. They want them as allies. They obviously are terrified of the ones they call the *Sange rau*, but they're certain they can convince Mikhail of the danger."

Skyler frowned, shaking her head again. "Josef, Dimitri says he's being held in a war camp. The Lycans are preparing for a battle. It has to be with Mikhail. Did any of the emails mention Dimitri?"

"No, which I thought was a little odd."

A small fox trotted into their camp, and then came to an abrupt halt as if confused by the presence of the three of them. He was beautiful, his fur coat thick and bright. He shook his tail, gave an indignant bark and retraced his footsteps back into the brush.

Skyler laughed softly. "Life just goes on no matter what's happening, doesn't it?"

"That fox was a little annoyed with us," Paul said.

"For a moment I thought it was Gabriel and my heart nearly stopped," Josef said. "I've thought a lot about where I want you to scatter my ashes after he kills me," he added.

Paul and Skyler looked at Josef's sorrowful expression, the dramatic hand over his heart, and both burst out laughing simultaneously.

"He's not going to kill you, Josef," Skyler soothed. "He'll just . . . you know . . . do his Gabriel thing."

"He's going to kill you," Paul assured. "Dead. For certain. But he'll make you suffer first."

"Don't look so happy about it, bro," Josef said. "He's going to kill you, too."

Paul shrugged. "Better him than Zacarias. I've got like five of the craziest Carpathians known that are going to be eager to strangle me; you've only got a couple."

"We'll get in and get out with no one the wiser," Skyler said. "That way no one will get killed."

"Sky, I'm going to be in the ground when you go wandering in the woods," Josef said, worry taking the laughter from his voice. "You'll be very vulnerable. Paul won't be able to be too close to you, so you have to make certain that there is as clear a line of sight as possible from Paul to you at all times. He's your only protection until sunset."

"I honestly don't think the Lycans are going to worry about me rescuing Dimitri. Our papers are in order. We've set the camp up perfectly to be a working environment, and they must know of Dimitri's organization to save the wolves. He's set up preserves all over the world. Of course they have no idea it's that Dimitri they've wrapped in silver."

"There are other things in this forest to worry about than just the Lycans," Josef pointed out. "Wild predators live here."

"I know, but most of them come out at night. Really, I feel like between you and Dimitri, I could use a little encouragement."

"I think the plan is solid," Josef said. "I think your presence will draw a Lycan to you. Just make noise. I want you aware, that's all."

She heard the reluctance, the concern in his voice. He would be in the ground, unable to aid her if she got into trouble. She knew, like Dimitri, being helpless would be the most difficult thing of all. "I'll be hypervigilant," she promised.

"Were you able to remove the silver from his body?" Paul asked. "All of it?"

Skyler nodded, relief sweeping through her. She hadn't realized how tense she was until that moment. "Yes. And one of the Lycans gave him blood. He's been starving for over two weeks, so it wasn't nearly enough to bring him to full strength, but it should be enough that he can get out on his own after I remove the hooks and chains."

"There is no way you, or either of us, could ever carry Dimitri. He's too big of a man," Paul said.

"Excuse me." Josef blew air on his fingernails and polished them on his shirt. "You're forgetting my mad skills. I could float him out of there."

Skyler rolled her eyes at his blatant bragging. "And every Lycan in the forest will feel that rift in the energy field and come running."

"I just wanted you to be very aware of my talents," Josef said. "I *could* do it if it was necessary, that's all."

"Could you carry him out of the forest on your dragon's back?" Skyler asked, suddenly very serious.

The smirk disappeared from Josef's face. "If it was just him, sure, but not with the both of you as well."

Skyler reached out her hand to him. "It won't be necessary. You can give him blood. Paul and I will as well. He'll be fine. Even if he has to go to ground for a night or two, we can hide. And if we can't do that, we'll have our fall back plan." She spoke with far more confidence than she felt.

"So the silver is out of his body and a Lycan gave him blood," Paul said, his tone speculative. "Maybe all of them aren't bad."

"Dimitri knows I'll be coming for him tonight and he'll be ready. I just have to figure out how to get the hooks from his body and the chain from around him. It's burned into his flesh. Literally burned into it. His arms, his chest, all down his legs. They wrapped him up like a mummy in silver." There was disgust and anguish mixed together in her voice.

Paul slung his arm around her shoulders. "He's alive and he's waiting for you. We're getting him out."

"So we laid a trail for you," Josef said. "I'll take the two of you deeper into the woods. There's no sign of Paul anywhere, leading in that direction. Our tracks will go in two opposite directions, clearly searching for you. If a Lycan stumbles across, or goes looking for tracks, we've done a good job of making it look as if you've been gone several hours."

"I'll need a sprained ankle," Skyler pointed out.

Josef frowned. "That's the one part of the plan I'm not wild about. You can't run with a sprained ankle."

Paul burst out laughing. "*Hello*, you idiot. Have you forgotten who she is? She can heal anything, including a sprained ankle."

"I just am squeamish about giving myself any injury," Skyler admitted.

"Cause she's such a girlie girl," Paul teased.

Skyler made a face at him. "I don't giggle."

"You giggle," Josef said, flicking her chin with his finger. "I'll help you with your sprained ankle, but you'll be hobbling around until someone comes. Groan a lot."

"*If* someone comes," Paul emphasized. "It's a big forest." He suddenly grinned. "This is your big chance to really show your girly side. Weep and look beautiful while you're doing it, like they do on television."

Josef snickered. "Her face turns red when she cries."

"So does the end of her nose," Paul contributed.

"Way to make a girl feel beautiful. Neither of you are ever going to find a woman who will put up with you."

Paul shook his head. "Zacarias has a woman doting on him. Seriously, Skyler, if that man, as mean and as scary as he is, can get a woman, anyone can. It gives a man hope."

Josef smirked. "I'll have a lifemate. She'll have no choice," he added.

"Poor woman," Skyler said. "I'll befriend her and teach her how to box your ears when you get obnoxious."

"What makes you think I'll get obnoxious?" Josef demanded.

"You will never give up playing pranks. She'll be afraid to go around a corner in case you fly at her in the form of a giant bat or something worse."

Paul punched Josef in the shoulder. "She's got you there, bro."

The smile faded from Skyler's face. "I have to figure out how to get the silver chains off of Dimitri. I know I can remove the hooks. I was able to get the silver to back up to their point of origin, and I could melt the hooks if I had to, but that chain. It's actually in his skin. Any ideas that don't include triggering the Lycans' ability to feel a spike in energy?"

The two men looked at one another.

"Can you cut it off?" Paul said. "Josef can provide the tools you would need."

"That depends how deep it's embedded in his skin," Skyler said. "I guess I'll have to see it before I can make a decision. I haven't really taken a look around him. I've been so busy concentrating on getting that silver out of his body that I didn't think to see what his surroundings were."

"Don't sound so disgusted with yourself," Paul chastised. "The truth is, his surroundings wouldn't matter if he'd been dead. If you hadn't worked so hard to save him, there would be no point in any of this. We have a plan. Let's just stick to it and go one step at a time. If this works today, and you plant that tracking device in our Lycan, then we'll figure everything else out quickly."

"Agreed," Josef said.

6

Skyler glanced around her. The trees towered above her, branches swaying and dancing in the wind. She'd been hobbling around for several hours, and no one had come to rescue her. It had been a long shot, they all knew that, but they had to try. She could follow the psychic trail, knowing it would eventually lead to Dimitri. Truthfully, that's what she'd been doing, mile after mile, but wandering as if she was trying to find her way. Several times she took care to turn in different directions, starting out, going a distance and then turning back as if confused.

Her ankle was throbbing. Josef had ensured that it wasn't just a little sprain. He wanted her to appear as no threat to anyone at all. It would be dark in a few hours and Josef would come for her. She followed the sound of water, struggling over the uneven ground and exposed roots. Little animals scurried in the vegetation, rushing for the shelter of brush and leaves in an effort to avoid her.

Twice she thought she saw that little fox. Intellectually she knew it couldn't be the same one, but she told herself he was her guardian, watching out for her. That would be something Dimitri might do for her. Her heart seemed to always melt a little when she thought of him. He had watched over her for years, so selflessly, and hobbling around on a sore ankle, terrified she might really come in contact with a strange man, seemed a small price to pay for his steadfast loyalty and love.

She made her way to the small ribbon of a stream and found a large enough rock to sit down on. It was close to the running water as it bubbled over the smaller pebbles, making its way down a slight slope.

The moment she sank down onto the rock and leaned down to remove her boot, she knew she wasn't alone. A chill went down her spine and she lifted her head and carefully looked around. *Paul, can you see me?* She made certain that her telepathic path to Paul had clean lines so that no Lycan could discern it or feel the psychic energy. She let her gaze move from tree to tree, a woman lost and alone and scared there in the forest. Unfortunately, the emotion was all too real.

I'm here, honey, I've got you covered.

Do you see anyone?

No. Do you?

He's here. I can feel him. Which was strange, because according to Josef, no Carpathian could sense a Lycan. She wasn't even Carpathian—she was human—and yet she knew with a certainty that someone was there. The only explanation could be that Mother Earth had passed her so much information that she was tuned to the rhythm of nature.

Maybe it wasn't a Lycan watching. Maybe it was a real wolf pack hunting her. Or worse. Was there worse? Her imagination was getting the better of her. Paul had a gun and he would protect her. She just had to hold on to that.

She unzipped her boot and pulled it off, playing the part of the lost intern, her foot swollen and bruised and hurting. A human would be nervous, but would never know someone was out there watching every move. She could feel those eyes burning through her. Her heart began to pound and her mouth went dry.

She knew terror. Real terror, and right now, she had to fight it off. She was no longer a child to be abused sexually or physically or even emotionally. She was a grown woman with power of her own. With friends. With an ancient hunter for a lifemate, and he needed her. Dimitri needed her to be strong. She took several deep breaths, fighting off the need to put her head between her legs to keep from feeling so light-headed. Her body shivered continuously, and there seemed little she could do to prevent it.

As a child she had retreated to a place in her mind where no one could harm her. She didn't have that luxury now, no matter how frightened she was. If the fear became too great, Dimitri would know. She didn't want him any more upset than he already was. Skyler forced herself under control. She could do this. She'd planned every move out carefully. She had been a helpless child when evil men had dominated her life, but she was no child—and she sure wasn't helpless. She straightened her shoulders, determination settling deep.

A twig snapped and she spun around to see a tall, broad-shouldered man striding out of the forest. He had to be Lycan to move with that easy fluid grace and absolute confidence. His eyes were the color of mercury with a glittering, piercing, very focused stare that seemed to look right through her. Her mouth went a little dry. He was rough-looking—and tough. Clearly he'd seen many battles.

He wore a long coat that fell to his ankles, but flared out, giving him plenty of room to fight. She could see the trousers and shirt were loose enough to move, but tight enough not to get caught on anything. His chest was thick and rippled with muscles beneath the thin shirt. His arms could have been those of a bodybuilder, but she would bet everything she had that he'd never been anywhere near a gym. When he moved she caught the glitter of silver from the many weapons he carried inside his coat and around his belt.

She tried to rise, clutching her boot like a weapon. He held up both hands as if to show he didn't mean her harm, that he'd come in peace. He halted a small distance from her.

"I came across your tracks about an hour ago. What are you doing out here alone?" he asked in Russian.

Skyler pressed her lips together as if wondering if she could trust him or not. "I'm an intern, working for the All Things Wolf Foundation." She spoke in halting Russian, although she spoke the language fluently. "I was setting up a camera and I got turned around."

"Are you English?" He spoke in English, moving a little closer to her.

Skyler lifted her boot in a reflex action. It seemed a little silly since she was certain he was Lycan and could move far faster than she could, but still, she couldn't help herself.

She nodded, switching to English as well. "I twisted my ankle. I thought if I put it in the cold of the stream it would give me a little relief."

"You're far from your camp."

Her face brightened. "Do you know where it is? Which direction? I know I could find it if I wasn't so turned around. Everything starts looking the same after a while."

"Didn't they tell you not to go wandering off by yourself?" the Lycan asked. "My name is Zev Hunter. What's yours?"

He sounded friendly enough. He didn't appear particularly hungry, as if he had been searching for a meal. "Skyler," she answered, suddenly remembering she couldn't provide a surname. He would recognize Daratrazanoff.

"I'd like to take a look at your ankle, but I'd rather not get clobbered over the head by that wicked-looking boot."

She forced herself to lower her boot to her side. "I'm sorry. You startled me. It never occurred to me that anyone would be out in these woods. The others are probably out looking for me right now. There are only three of us at the moment, but more will be bringing in supplies in a few days. We came early to set up camp." She talked fast, a woman still nervous and chatting too much.

He crouched low, one hand reaching for her ankle. Around his wrist was a strip of cloth, bloodied as if he'd been seriously wounded. Relief swept through her. Dimitri told her one of the Lycans had shown compassion and had given him blood. This had to be that same one. Dimitri had definitely put the idea in his head to go looking for Fen and a rescue party.

She couldn't help herself. She inhaled deeply, reaching for Dimitri's woodsy scent. It was faint, but she caught it, still lingering on the Lycan's wrist. She took that familiar scent into her lungs and just held it there, suddenly desperate to see him.

"Your ankle is very swollen. This must hurt."

"I walked more than I should have on it," Skyler admitted, putting one hand on his shoulder to steady herself. Deliberately she wobbled and clutched his arm a little lower to keep from falling.

Her heart began to beat hard again. In her fist was the tiny little tracking device Josef had made. She just needed an opportunity to sweep her hand down that coat to one of the side pockets. She had a feeling this particular man would be tough to fool.

"The cold stream will be good for it," Zev told her. "We'll give it a few minutes, and then I'll take you back to your camp. It isn't safe in these woods. The forest is home to many predators and you're just about snack size for some of them. The very wolf pack you're trying to study would be happy to give you a firsthand experience."

Skyler managed a small smile. "I have a very vivid imagination. Believe me, I thought of that many times."

She sank down onto the rock, allowing her hand to naturally brush down his coat as if she was still unsteady and afraid of falling. The flap was over the pocket but she was well versed in making small objects obey her. The flap lifted and the transfer was smooth and complete.

Josef had told her many times that he couldn't feel her energy when she used her art on objects, but still, she held her breath, afraid this very savvy Lycan would pick it up.

"You can't be very old; why would your parents allow you to come to such a remote area where it's so dangerous?" His concern was genuine.

Skyler smiled again, this time more naturally. "I just look very young. I'm actually twenty-five. I've got my degree and am working toward my master's. I volunteer at the various wildlife research centers as a way to travel. I mean, I'm genuinely interested in the work, but I've gotten to go to so many countries and see many amazing places, as well as meet some very cool people."

Zev raised his eyebrow. "In a million years I wouldn't have guessed your age. If anything, I thought maybe fourteen or fifteen."

Skyler shrugged. "I get that all the time. At least I've reached the fourteen or fifteen mark instead of the ten or twelve."

He laughed, suddenly relaxing. The tension completely eased from his body and he sank down into the grass beside her while she bathed her swollen ankle in the icy stream.

"That must be annoying, having everyone tell you you look so young."

"In some ways. Especially when I'm traveling. There are a lot of creeps in the world and having some man who preys on children . . ." She trailed off, realizing genuine anger had crept into her voice.

Zev was quick. She saw knowledge in his eyes and knew she'd given away too much information. Cursing silently to herself, she idly picked up a pebble and tossed it downstream.

"The forest is oppressive at times, isn't it?" she asked. "I find it so beautiful, all the colors, but sometimes it's hard to breathe when you're deep in the middle of it."

His eyes focused on her, all that piercing intelligence. She had to fight to stay relaxed. He looked as if he could see right into her soul. "You're very sensitive."

"That's what my mother always says," Skyler said. That much was true. Francesca said it all the time. She indicated his hand. Let him fish around for something plausible. "What happened to you?"

Zev didn't so much as flinch. He lifted his wrist for her inspection. "I was working and got a little careless. I tore my wrist on a nail. It's not a big deal but it was deep enough to bleed a lot. I put this cloth around it and it stopped."

"There's a first-aid kit at the camp. When we get there, I could put some antibiotic cream on it so the laceration doesn't get infected."

He nodded. "If we don't run out of time. We should get moving soon or night will fall. Here in the forest it tends to get dark fast."

She was happy to get moving. The faster they made camp, the faster she could heal her ankle and set out to follow the Lycan back to Dimitri.

"Do you live close by?"

"I'm camping with some friends a few kilometers from here," Zev explained. "Although I've been coming to these woods since I was a boy, so I'm very familiar with them."

She frowned at him as she pulled her throbbing foot from the stream. Her wince was very genuine. She was going to have to throttle Josef for making her injury so real. "You don't hunt here, do you? The wolves are protected in this preserve." She managed her most schoolmarmish voice, the one that always made Josef sit up and take notice—or topple over in gales of laughter.

"Sometimes with a camera, although when we were kids, we hunted for food. Not wolves, but other creatures, mostly wild fowl, partridge, things we could manage when we were pretty small. If we killed it, we had to carry it."

He was telling the absolute truth, which was why he was so good at intrigue. He mixed truth with implication—not outright lies. She tried to pull her boot back over her swollen ankle. It hurt like hell.

"I'll carry you."

"You will not," Skyler said. "I can walk. Just give me a minute to get my boot back on." Who knew what a Lycan might discern that close? "How far away is the camp? Have I been walking in circles? Sometimes I was pretty certain I'd been to the same place more than once."

"I thought all you researchers always carried a GPS with you."

She called on her mad nonexistent acting skills to blush, her long lashes sweeping down deliberately. "We're supposed to. It's my first time with this group and my partners are both . . ." She trailed off, doing her best to look ashamed and guilty.

"Men," he finished for her. Zev took the boot from her hands and gently eased it over her ankle.

"I know I don't have anything to prove, and this isn't going to get me off to a good start, but I guess I wanted to look good. I got up early and set up the cameras. In my haste to be helpful, I completely forgot the GPS. It's probably still clipped to my hammock."

He stood up and reached down to lift her easily into his arms, ignoring her protest. "I'm sorry, young Skyler, but it's getting late. I need to be somewhere and I've got to get you back to your camp."

She had no choice but to be gracious. In any case, she hadn't been looking forward to walking on her swollen ankle. "Thanks, Zev, I appreciate it, although I feel a little silly."

"Walking around alone in these woods is silly," he said sternly.

Skyler was used to being around physically strong men. Gabriel, her adopted father, was extremely strong, being Carpathian. Dimitri certainly was. Even Josef, as young as he was, had the Carpathian strength, but Zev was amazing. He moved through the forest absolutely sure-footed. He was graceful even. He didn't breathe hard and he never once acted as if he needed a rest. He was born and bred for the forest, and he was every bit as strong as a Carpathian.

She closed her eyes and breathed evenly, opening her mind a little at a time to try to take in, to absorb the feel of a Lycan through every sense she had. She recognized the way he moved from what Mother Earth had revealed to her earlier. He barely made a sound, a soft whisper, no more, as his clothing occasionally brushed against leaves. He was so quiet they startled wildlife they came upon.

She felt the mechanics of him, the steel-like but flexible framework and the muscles moving beneath his civilized clothing. She even began to absorb the field around him that protected his energy from leaking out and giving him away in a hunt—or battle.

He was a good man. She got that much from him, but he was lethal and wouldn't hesitate to kill if necessary. She wouldn't want him coming after her. That thought was frightening and she couldn't help the little shiver that went down her spine. Of course he noticed instantly.

"We're nearly there. There's nothing to fear. I'm not going to let anything happen to you," he assured. His voice was kind, even compassionate.

"I'm sorry I'm so much trouble," Skyler said. That was the truth. She didn't like using a good person. He clearly wasn't the demon she'd conjured up in her mind. The Lycans had taken Dimitri prisoner when he'd been defending not only his prince, but also the Lycans. They tortured him and would have killed him if she hadn't intervened. She'd developed a dislike of them. Still, she would much rather have had Zev find her than some really awful Lycan who might kill her.

"You don't weigh much," Zev observed. "A good wind might blow you away."

A bubble of nervous laughter welled up. "My father says that."

"Your father is right." He frowned. "He should be watching out for you. Coming here was not a good idea."

She couldn't very well tell him her father didn't know and the world as she knew it would probably be over once he found out. "My ankle agrees with you."

He found their base camp unerringly, as if he already knew it was there. He hadn't cast around for signs looking for the site, but seemed to follow a direct—and the shortest—route straight to it.

He came to an abrupt halt. "Where is everyone?"

"Out looking for me, I suppose," Skyler replied in a small voice. Her ankle really was hurting and she was grateful when he put her into a chair. He had been smooth, walking through the forest, but still, movement jarred the injury. "There's only Paul and Josef. The others haven't arrived yet."

Paul strode into camp, a mixture of concern and aggravation on his face. He held a rifle in his hands. She knew it carried tranquilizers. "What the hell happened, Skyler?" he demanded. "We've been searching for you for most of the day. I was about to call for help."

Zev's entire demeanor changed. He ate up the distance between Paul and him with long, fluid strides, nearly gliding. He was on Paul before he had a chance to even bring his weapon up.

"I'm a cop," Zev announced, with a small apologetic glance over his shoulder at Skyler. "I'd like to see your papers *now*. No one should have authorized work in this area. We closed it off a few weeks ago."

It was the last thing Skyler expected, but she realized his revelation and demands made perfect sense. The Lycans had to have a way to keep everyone away from them while they prepared for war, or tortured and killed their prisoners. Zev probably really did have a rank of some kind in law enforcement.

Paul kept possession of his weapon but went to the locked box and removed the papers giving them permission to set up cameras in this area of the forest. Zev studied their passports and the official documents carefully, taking his time. This was no cursory glance.

Skyler's mouth went dry. Her heart began to pound. Josef was the best, she reminded herself. His paperwork was always impeccable.

Zev looked up suddenly, pinning Paul with his piercing, focused stare. "Who's in charge?"

"He's not here at the moment," Paul said. "He went out searching for Skyler, but we come back to the camp every two hours." He glanced at his watch. "He should be coming back soon."

Zev handed the papers back to Paul. "Everything appears to be in order, but there's been a mistake. I want you to break camp tomorrow morning and get out of here. This girl cannot be wandering the forest alone, nor should you or whoever is in charge. It's too dangerous."

"We're aware there is an active pack of wolves here," Paul said. "That's why we're here. We just study their environment. We don't try to interact. If we're lucky we'll have the cameras in the right places and we'll get a glimpse of them."

Zev shook his head. "There have been several killings. Mutilations. Not the wolves, someone human. This area is closed at the moment. You need to pack up immediately and leave."

"Are you saying a serial killer is on the loose?" Paul asked.

"We don't acknowledge such things. We've chased a criminal into these woods, and he knows his way around. I am officially telling you and your party to leave. I'll be back tomorrow to ensure you've obeyed."

Paul scowled and tried to protest. Skyler ducked her head, twisting her fingers together, looking guilty, as if she knew Paul would take his anger out on her. After all, she'd set this all in motion by getting lost.

"She has a sprained ankle and needs care," Zev added. "And in case you think to chastise her, I was already aware of your camp and was coming to tell you to leave when I ran across her."

That made sense, too. He was Lycan. He belonged in the forest. It would talk to him the way Mother Earth spoke to her. She had no doubt that he had known—that he'd heard foreign footsteps or smelled their scents on the wind.

Zev dropped a hand on her shoulder. "I hope you feel better very quickly. I'm sorry we met under such circumstances. Please persuade whoever is in charge to take me seriously. You can always come back once we've found the killer."

It was a perfect cover—a police manhunt. Skyler nodded. "Thank you for your kindness."

Zev left them, striding away, disappearing into the trees. Skyler wrapped her arms around herself and rocked back and forth. She hadn't been aware that she'd been scared, but now she felt a little sick, but definitely triumphant. She'd done it. She'd slipped that tiny little bug into Zev's pocket, and he hadn't even known.

Paul hurried over to her, wrapping his arm around her shoulders. "Are you all right?"

She nodded. "He's a very scary man, but he was really nice to me. I was terrified the papers wouldn't hold up."

"I was more worried he'd take out one of his weapons and annihilate us both," Paul said. "My little tranq gun didn't seem so great when I could see weapons in his belt, hanging from a million loops on the inside of that coat, and even inside his boots. But, he looked and felt human."

"He was Lycan," Skyler assured. "I could tell the difference. He smelled wild. Part of the forest. It was in the way he moved as well. He's a wolf."

She slowly unzipped her boot and straightened her leg, holding out her injured foot toward Paul. "Can you get this thing off of me? Josef did a great job on my cover, that's all I'm going to say on the matter."

"You mean until he gets here. You've got that look on your face." Paul did his best to remove the boot without hurting her further. He whistled when he saw her swollen, bruised ankle. "Well, one thing about Josef—he's thorough."

"I think I'll lie down and rest until the sun goes down," Skyler said.

She needed to touch Dimitri's mind. He might be in the Carpathian paralysis, but he hadn't been able to sleep the sleep needed for rejuvenation and his mind was still active. She found that the more she merged her mind with his, the more she needed to do so.

She'd fallen in love with Dimitri, his gentle, tender ways and his absolute, unfaltering love for her. Now she knew the pull between lifemates. That link had grown stronger between them. She could feel the need to touch him, to just know he was alive somewhere, rising in her more and more as every hour slipped by. Perhaps it was because she was older now, or because she'd made that final commitment to him.

Paul helped her hobble to her hammock and she lay down, stretching out, trying to relax. She knew the worst would be this night. Their plan would either work or they would all be in trouble. Most of it depended on her.

She opened her mind and stretched herself along that now familiar path. *Dimitri. It is done and I am safe.* She knew he would need to hear her voice just as much as she needed to hear his.

Dimitri, caught in the Carpathian midday paralysis, would have closed his eyes had he been capable of moving. Relief was so raw it was tinged with madness. He hadn't been able to move, but he could think—imagine—every bad scenario that could possibly happen with Skyler alone in the forest. He poured himself into her mind, needing to touch her, to feel that closeness with her.

Skyler could feel Dimitri's relief flowing into her mind along with his warmth, the heat that always drove the cold of her nightmares away.

I was worried. It was nothing less than an understatement.

She found herself smiling. He felt different. He knew, like she did, that tonight was their night. Her plan had to work, there was no other choice.

She took a deep breath and let it out. She had committed to him. She knew she loved him. There was no other. They could both die this night.

Dimitri, I love you with all my heart. I know you feel that. I have never hesitated to come to you as your lifemate from lack of love.

I am aware you love me, Skyler, he said, his voice a little perplexed. *Did you think I would doubt you? I feel your love surround me every time we touch.*

I have always told you the truth, that I fear I will not be able to satisfy you on a physical level. They had talked so much that she was no longer embarrassed to bring the subject up, although she still felt inadequate when they did discuss sex.

Sívamet. Dimitri spoke the Carpathian endearment tenderly. His heart always seemed to grow bigger and fuller when she was near. *Sex is not making love. There is a difference. I will show you the difference and you will no longer fear us coming together in a physical way. There is no need to worry. When you're ready . . .*

I am ready. That's the point. I want you to claim me. Right now. Please claim me right now. Her heart pounded in her chest. She wanted him in that moment. Not just in her head. Or her heart. She wanted their souls to be woven back together as they were meant to be.

Dimitri's entire body reacted. For one moment all pain was gone and there was only Skyler—his lifemate—reaching for him. Offering herself to him in his weakest moment. How could he possibly resist her? She was everything to him. Yet here he was, hanging from the branch of a tree, pierced with silver, wrapped in silver chains, helpless to even aid his lifemate should she run into trouble. What did he have to offer her? Even if they managed to get him free, they would be hunted for all time by the Lycans.

He had no idea what his mixed blood would do to her during a conversion. He didn't know if children were possible, or if so, what they would become. He loved her with everything he was or would ever be, but what right did he have to tie her so closely, an unbreakable bond . . .

Dimitri's silence frightened Skyler. Surely he felt the same way. She knew the drive to claim one's lifemate was primal, strong, nearly impossible to ignore—and Dimitri had managed to ignore it for years. Was he as worried about her inability to commit to a physical relationship as she was? That stood to reason.

He was rejecting her. Pain sliced through her like a knife. She pulled her knees into her chest, drawn into the fetal position. She'd waited too long. She had made him wait forever, thinking he would always be there for her.

Dimitri felt her instant fear, the pain of rejection, and cursed himself for such clumsy handling of her tremendous gift. And it was a gift, a treasure beyond anything else she could ever offer him. His mind felt slow and sluggish. He could barely breathe, his lungs laboring, and the agonizing burn of the silver hadn't allowed his brain to function in the way he needed.

Sívamet, you are my heart. You are, Hän ku vigyáz sívamet és sielamet—keeper of my heart and soul. Above all else, I want to bind our souls together. It is my greatest wish. But, Skyler, you cannot tempt me this way. I'm weak and you're vulnerable. We've both been through so much. You cannot tempt me, he reiterated again, hoping she understood what she meant to him, but that it was his duty to protect her.

She heard the urgent need in his voice, every bit as strong as it was in her, maybe stronger. Her heart settled. Fluttered. Filled with joy. She took in the fresh air. *I know it's the right time. Our time. We need to be strong together. Bind me to you, my love. This is what I want.*

How could he possibly explain to her the peril his life choices would put her in? He wanted her to be permanently his, bound so that no other could ever take her from his side, but they weren't in a safe place where he could surround her with his love and hold her close to him, reassure her if she became fearful. He didn't know if he would even live out the night. He couldn't even give her that reassurance.

I can't hold you in my arms and do it properly. Once this is done, it can't be undone.

Skyler found herself smiling. More than anything else she was certain of what she wanted, and she wanted to be Dimitri's lifemate in every sense of the word. She was merged with him and him with her. The connection between them was so strong. It had been growing since their first encounter. How could she not fall in love with him? How could she possibly want anyone else in her life?

Once we met, my love, we both knew our connection could never be undone. I want this with all my heart. I want you with all my heart. I know I'm ready. I would follow you anywhere, Dimitri. I would walk on fire to get to you.

How can you be so certain?

Skyler crossed her arms over her chest and stared up at the branches above her head. The forest was preparing for nightfall and the birds were returning to their roosts. She was fully prepared to take the next step in her life—her biggest step.

Today I met a stranger in the forest. I was alone with a man I didn't know. He was big and strong and looked very tough. Before I actually saw him, I felt his presence and knew he watched me. For a moment, I was that terrified child again, helpless and hopeless and wanting to slip deep into my mind where no one could harm me.

Sívamet, I am so sorry. Dimitri wanted to shake down the very trees holding him prisoner to get to her. His Skyler. She deserved to always feel safe.

No, it was a good thing. I knew who I was. I'm Skyler, lifemate to Dimitri. I knew then that I could brave anything—even my past—in order to get to you. I am your lifemate, and I will be all things you need as you already are to me.

She knew she was committing to a physical relationship with him—that was part of being a lifemate. She meant what she said, she would brave anything for him, learn anything for him. He was already part of her. She had found on this journey of awakening that she was beginning to know the signs of physical attraction.

When he spoke to her, his voice was like thick molasses moving slowly through her body, touching nerve endings she'd never known she had. That attraction had been building over time. Sometimes she found she just waited for that one note in his voice her entire body reacted to.

Dimitri turned her argument over and over in is mind. Everything she said was true. They were already connected. No other pair of Carpathians could span the distances they could. They already needed to touch one another's minds continually. He tried to block out the pain, to think clearly, so in this, he could do the right thing. Explain everything to her. Let her see the truth of what their life together could be before she made the ultimate decision.

You have to be certain, and before you make up your mind, there are other things you need to know, reasons the Lycans have condemned me. Those reasons will affect you as my lifemate. I am no longer Carpathian. I have become more. Something different.

Whatever you are, I will be.

That is your loyalty to me as well as your youth talking. You need to know the consequences. You need to have all the facts before you make up your mind. Please. Listen to me and then really give it thought.

Skyler watched a leaf floating to the ground. A journey. The leaf had lived out its existence one way and now was free-falling, trusting the next journey would be the right one. *I am listening, my love, with an open mind. Please keep your mind open as well.*

The Lycans call what I am the Sange rau. The literal translation is "bad blood." One such as me is very difficult to stop—or kill. The thing about this transition, Skyler, is that it continues to mutate. I don't know what will happen if I try to convert you. I doubt I will take that chance. Someone else may have to bring you fully into my world.

Skyler frowned, her fingers idly drumming on her thigh as she turned the information he'd given her over and over in her mind. She could see why Dimitri would be reluctant. He had no idea of the future or what he was offering her. Male Carpathians didn't like other males around their women much, but their relationship was different and had been different almost from the beginning. Dimitri accepted her friends, Josef and Paul, treating them as younger brothers. He knew how she felt about them; she held nothing away from him when she opened her mind to his.

I know many Carpathians, Dimitri. I've been given two blood exchanges. One more will be enough for a conversion. Gabriel and Francesca feared, because our presence drew the vampire, that I would need to be saved in an emergency. I'm not afraid of the conversion, she assured him with absolute confidence.

Lifemates exchange blood. It is part of our physical relationship and one we cannot deny. Eventually, over time, you would become as I am.

Do you really think that frightens me?

No, because you do not yet know what can happen. The Lycans all believe that the Sange rau must be destroyed. They very well could be planning a war right now over this issue. You will be hunted and hated. The Carpathians call us Hän ku pesäk kaikak. The actual translation is "Guardian of all." That distinguishes the Carpathian/Lycan from the vampire/wolf. The Lycans refuse to acknowledge a difference. They believe that no chances should be taken and anyone with mixed blood should be destroyed.

Why?

A single Sange rau nearly wiped out their entire species, centuries ago.

Skyler studied the leaf as the wind gusted, taking it first one direction and then spinning it in a different one. The leaf appeared to be dancing. She lifted her hand idly and began to direct the dance rather absently, the sound of the breeze playing through the leaves creating music.

Xavier, the most hated and yet powerful of all mages, nearly did the same to the Carpathian species, she reminded him. *And yet, do you know what I found out, Dimitri? I feared that side of me. I often tried to deny that he was related to me in any way. In fact, so much so that I have avoided any real relationship with my birth father, Razvan, because I couldn't bear the knowledge that mage blood ran in my veins. But I found, through this entire event, that being mage is a good thing. Having those gifts to be used for good is a gift. What you are is a gift to the entire world.*

It is my Lycan blood that allows them to torture me.

It is your mixed blood that has kept you alive when no one else could have possibly survived this long. They expected you to die long ago, Dimitri, you know that's the truth. They would have done better to kill you outright. What you are is a testimony to what can be used for good.

There is uncertainty of the future.

Skyler laughed softly, sharing her amusement with him. The leaf still continued on its journey, its brief dance only delaying the inevitable—as Dimitri was simply delaying the inevitable.

The future is always uncertain, my love. Especially now. I want this, Dimitri, now, before whatever happens tonight, whether we succeed or not. I will follow you wherever you go. We cannot be undone. Please make me yours. She meant every single word. She was certain. Absolutely certain that this was the right time for her—for him. And if they were killed in this rescue attempt, their souls would be bound.

Dimitri had envisioned an entirely different scenario. He would have held her in his arms, in front of her parents and best friends. He wanted a celebration for her, a moment in her life that transcended every traumatic event. He wanted elegant clothes and her favorite flowers, a party of dancing and laughter, their joy shared with their families. It was more of the human tradition, but she talked of such things with her school friends.

He didn't want to be hanging in some tree like a criminal, his body torn and starved. God only knew what he looked like—or would look like if she managed to get the chains off of him. He would never again be that elegant, handsome man she had grown so used to. He didn't want to be far away from her with Lycans surrounding him or have her in danger while sneaking through the woods in a rescue attempt, certainly not when he bound them together.

He searched her mind. There were no doubts there. No regrets. She was different—a grown woman—and she was coming to him as a woman. This was her choice. He had promised her long ago that it would always be her choice.

Skyler knew the exact moment he capitulated. She felt his heart race. Swell with love and pride. The warmth of his love surrounded her, swamped her, filled even that dark space in her mind where she hid when she couldn't stop what was being done to her body. He was there, seeing it all, healing her. Sharing her worst moments and holding her in his arms while he did. He was Dimitri, her private phenomenon.

You have always been mine, Skyler Rose. Always. Te avio päläfertiilam. He translated the ancient words for her. *You are my lifemate. Éntölam kuulua, avio päläfertiilam. I claim you as my lifemate.*

Her heart gave a leap of joy. She placed her hand over her chest, directly over her heart. *Did you feel that, Dimitri? Even my heart is aware of you.* She knew those ancient words were the words she had pleaded for. She felt them, tiny little threads weaving her soul to his.

Ted kuuluak, kacad, kojed. I belong to you. I do belong to you, Skyler. From the moment I saw you, you were not simply the lifemate I had waited centuries to find, but you became my world as well. I love and respect you.

She felt the truth of that each time his mind merged with hers. Even now, when he was so tortured, his first thoughts were always of her and her well-being.

Élidamet andam. I offer my life for you.

She loved that part of the vow, because she would offer her life for his. She knew each word to be the absolute truth.

Pesämet andam. I give you my protection. His amusement was warm in her mind. *At this very moment, csitri, I think you are giving me protection rather than the other way around.*

Isn't that how the whole thing works? she asked. *We love and protect one another.* Because she knew he felt a fierce desire to ensure her health and safety and she felt that same tigress-like need to take care of him.

Uskolfertiilamet andam. I give you my allegiance. You have always had my allegiance, but we're making it official.

She had known she had his loyalty and faithfulness from the moment their eyes met. She couldn't imagine her life without him.

Sívamet andam. I give you my heart. Her heart changed rhythm, matching his. A steady, strong beat in spite of the fact that he was still nearly starving.

Sielamet andam. I give you my soul.

There it was, that tie she had been waiting for. He had her heart. He gave her his. Now he tied his soul to hers.

Ainamet andam. I give you my body. Sívamet kuuluak kaik että a ted. I take into my keeping the same that is yours.

She took a deep breath and let it out. There was that, his body. So strong. So much stronger than she was. She would never be able to stop him if anything he did frightened her. For a moment, one terrible moment, she felt her heart go out of rhythm and her breath exploded from her lungs. He waited as he held his breath, but he said nothing, letting her absorb what he said, what that commitment actually meant. It was a vow, like all the others.

She let her breath out. Felt her heart settle. Dimitri was a man of honor. He loved her, and she always had to trust in that love, just as this night, he would be trusting in her love.

I have no doubts, Dimitri. You are my other half and together we'll get through anything.

Again there was that burst of heat, bathing her mind in his love. It surrounded her and lifted her up as nothing else could.

Ainaak olenszal sívambin. Your life will be cherished by me for all my time. Skyler, you know I have cherished you always, but this means so much more. Te élidet ainaak pide minan. Your life will be placed above my own for all time. I would never hurt you, or frighten you or ask you to do something you are uncomfortable with. Do you understand?

Of course she understood. She'd always known, on some level, that

Dimitri was a man above men. He allowed her to work her way to him on her own. He never once had tried to make her feel guilty or to push her toward him faster. He gave her room, and yet he was always there when she needed him. How often had she leaned on him in the middle of the night when the nightmares were too close? He'd never asked for anything in return.

I understand. His loyalty to her, his complete regard for her past and her feelings made her want to be what he needed all the more.

Te avio päläfertiilam. You are my lifemate.

She loved that word. This binding ritual was the equivalent of a human marriage, but more. The vows could not be broken.

Ainaak sívamet jutta oleny. You are bound to me for all eternity.

They could follow one another from one life to the next. They were bound, heart and soul. She felt even closer to him. She knew those threads weaving their souls together had done their job.

Ainaak terád vigyázak. You are always in my care.

It was done; they were tied together for all eternity. Dimitri sent her one last burst of love before he allowed the connection to fade. *I love you, Skyler, with all my heart. Be safe for me.*

Stay alive no matter what, Dimitri, she responded. *I am coming for you.*

7

Skyler had done everything she could to prepare for the night, other than the most important one—their fall back plan. Josef was definitely a strategist. He believed in backup plans. His backup plans had backup plans. She and Paul liked to tease him about it, but it was the meticulous care he paid to detail that always made everything work—like the swelling and bruising on her ankle. A Lycan such as Zev would never have bought her story if she hadn't been truly injured.

"It's almost time, Sky," Josef pointed out. "It's now or never. Can you do it? We need a safe place to retreat to, one the Lycans can't enter. This is their territory. They know every cave, every rock. I can go to ground, so could Dimitri, but you and Paul can't, so in the event of an emergency, we have to have a safety zone."

"I know." Of course she knew. They'd discussed it a million times. She was 75 percent certain she could do it. Okay, maybe it was more like 50 percent now that she actually had to produce something.

"If we're caught and given the opportunity to run, some—or all—could be wounded. We won't be able to outrun a pack, not with the shape Dimitri is in."

Skyler glared at him. “You’re not making this any easier. Just give me a minute.”

She’d thought about this moment a long time. She had to completely embrace who and what she was. She was Dragonseeker. Her birth father was from a powerful Carpathian lineage, one with great honor. Not a single Dragonseeker had ever turned vampire. Her father had been tortured for centuries, and still he refused to give in to the darkness that would have freed him from Xavier’s terrible prison. That blood ran in her veins.

Her birth father was also mage, grandson to the most powerful mage the world had ever known. She was Xavier’s great-granddaughter. That blood also ran in her veins. The more she’d used her abilities, the stronger they had become. That power was there, running beneath the surface, calling to her. It didn’t have to be evil. Evil was a choice—like the giving up of one’s soul. She could use her gifts for good as they were meant to be.

Her birth mother had been a very powerful psychic. Her ability to cross such long distances telepathically had come not from Dragonseeker or mage, but from her human mother. More, her mother had been the one to have a connection with Mother Earth. She could grow any plant, and sometimes, plants responded just to the sound of her voice.

Skyler knew her strongest connection was with Mother Earth both from Dragonseeker blood and her human mother. She would need everything she was in order to create a safety zone where no Lycan could cross—unless, like Dimitri, he had Carpathian blood as well.

She had chosen her spot well. Just a few miles from where they set up camp was a clearing. They could see anything coming at them from any direction. The soil was rich so Dimitri and Josef could go to ground and no harm could come to them. Paul and she would be exposed to the sight of the Lycans, but the wolves wouldn’t be able to get to them. If they reached that safety zone—and it worked—they could simply wait the arrival of her father and uncle.

She winced, thinking about facing her father. He would be very angry, which she could take, but he’d also be hurt and that was far worse.

“I picked up the exact location from the tracking bug you dropped in the Lycan’s pocket,” Josef said. “We’re good to go. Get our fail-safe up and running and I can take you close to the camp. Paul and I will be waiting to cover your retreat."

Fortunately, her chosen clearing brought them a few miles closer to Dimitri. Paul and Josef walked with her to the spot, neither trying to hurry her, both sensing this was a difficult task. Each part of that shield, above them, below them, surrounding them, had to be sealed.

She stood in the middle of the clearing for a moment, feeling the welcoming earth beneath her feet. She was surrounded on four sides by the cool of the forest. Slowly, she began to walk clockwise. As she moved, she sent out a brilliant stream of light ahead of her, to clear and cleanse the clearing.

I call upon you, powers of air, bring forth your breath to guard this circle.
I call upon you, powers of fire, witness this rite, bring forth your flame.
I call upon you, powers of water, hold and align your healing waters.
I call upon you, powers of earth, sustain me by holding me close.

Air that is my breath,
Fire that is my heart's blood,
Water that is the blood of my veins,
Earth that is my mother,

I call to thee,
I summon thee,
See my need, hear my voice, answer my call,
Guide me, protect me, and avail me of your powers.

Skyler took out a small dagger, one of her very few treasured possessions. It had been passed down through generations from mother to daughter. The dagger was intricately carved, etched with the tree of life on its hilt and with runic symbols running down its blade. Holding her hand sideways, she made a quick cut across her palm so that the blood dripped down onto the earth where she stood.

I call to my birthright
I am Dragonseeker,
Born of dragons,
Dracaena, Draco—dragon's blood.

I am Mage,
Born of those who wield power—magic makers,
Time benders,
Portal makers.

I summon thee, earth,
Open your arms, create a space that is safe, protected.
I call on light to surround,
Let your bright protective light circle and protect.
I command thee, fire, wrap this place like a cocoon that cannot be penetrated.
Mother, allow this space only to us,
Allowing no other entry,
Water, supply us with your life-giving sustenance.

As above, so below,
So mote it be.

The ground below her rippled in response to her command. The air shimmered with fire, and then settled into a nearly transparent wall barely seen. Letting out her breath slowly, Skyler looked at Josef. "It's done."

Josef looked at her with awe. "I never actually thought you could do it."

"You didn't? Why did you agree to all of this if you didn't think we'd have a fail-safe?" She punched his arm. "I thought I could do it because you thought I could."

Paul laughed. "You ought to know Josef by now." He put his arm around Skyler's shoulders. "You're awesome, you know that? I think you could do anything."

"I hope you're right," she said. "I know I can get those hooks out of

Dimitri's body, but the chain has burned so deeply into his body that I'm not certain . . ."

"Don't start doubting yourself at this late stage of the game," Josef cautioned. "Now is when you need confidence. You just did what no one believed possible. Paul is right, you can do anything, including getting the chain off Dimitri. Once that's done, I don't care how bad a shape he's in, he'll get you out of there."

"Have you considered that he won't look the same?" Paul touched the small crescent-shaped scar on her temple. "He'll have scars."

"Carpathians don't scar," Josef said.

Paul shook his head. "That's not true. I've seen plenty of them with scars. If the wound could be fatal and it's there too long without care, they'll scar."

"Do you really think that would matter to me?" Skyler asked in a low tone. "I couldn't care less what Dimitri looks like to other people. He's beautiful to me. He always will be."

Paul smiled down at her. "I knew you'd say that. The cool thing, Sky, is you mean it."

"I'll take Paul first, and get him in position to protect your retreat," Josef said. "Will you be all right here by yourself until I come back for you?"

"Of course, but, Josef, the Lycans can sense your energy. Don't get too close to that camp, or any of the guards."

"I'll be careful," he promised.

Paul hugged her hard. "Good journey, little sister."

"Good journey, my brother," she murmured, holding him close for a moment. She closed her eyes briefly as she returned his hug. He had come there for her, and he very well could get killed if the Lycans discovered their prisoner gone before she managed to get them all to safety.

Reluctantly she dropped her arms, releasing him. Paul raised her chin, looking into her eyes. "Always remember I wanted to come. I *chose* to help my friends. Dimitri is a good man and I consider him family, just as you are to me. With or without you, I would have chosen to rescue him, or at least try."

She felt the burn of tears, but she managed a smile, nodding her head. Intellectually, she knew Paul spoke the truth, but still, she felt responsible.

If anything happened to him she would always carry that with her. She watched them go, Josef taking to the air with Paul, before she sat down right there in the vegetation, ignoring the drone of insects.

We're ready, Dimitri. I will be coming for you. Can you look around? Can you see a likely route to get in and out without detection?

She didn't want him balking at the last moment. This would be hardest on him. A Carpathian male did not ever want to feel helpless, especially when his lifemate was in danger. She knew he would want to fight his restraints, and now, more than ever, he had to be still and conserve his energy.

There is no one around me at the moment, but usually they stay a few meters away, hidden in the trees, watching me. I believe I am the entertainment for the bored. From my vantage point I can't see much. Without these chains, I could . . . He broke off in frustration.

She sent him instant warmth, surrounded him with her confidence and her love. *We have a great ally in Mother Earth. She'll come to our aid when we have need,* she promised. *Give me a minute.*

She plunged her hands deep into the soil and instantly felt the connection with earth itself. Her heart found that steady deep boom that came from below. Sounds of water, the wind, the sap ebbing and flowing in the trees all came to her as if they were part of her very life force.

I call upon thee, Mother,
Hear my voice.
Feel my need,

Send me the creatures that dwell within your darkness,
Cloak our energies so we are not seen, heard or felt.

The flow of information was strong, as if that connection with the earth was growing with each touch. Even the insects spoke to her. She was no longer bothered by them, but understood exactly why they were needed and what part in the ecological system they played.

Earth Mother,
I give thanks to you and your minions.

May there always be peace and harmony between us,
I release you now, go in peace.

She was grateful for the guidance and murmured her thanks.

Dimitri, I am certain of the way. Just hold on a little longer. As soon as I get the chains off, I'll give you blood. Then it will be up to both of us to run like hell. She tried to push a little amusement into her voice, feeling his tension.

Dimitri was a man who rarely was tense. In the worst situations he was always calm and cool, but knowing she was putting herself in danger for him bothered him on an entirely new level. He probably had never known what the word *tense* actually meant until he found her.

She had to struggle to understand his nature. She saw his needs in his mind, but she hadn't lived for centuries. She didn't have his experiences. She wasn't Carpathian and didn't fully understand the driving need of the male to protect his lifemate.

I cannot aid you until these chains have been removed, he reiterated. *I am weak, starved. I won't be able to move fast.*

Dimitri tried to make her understand his condition. He'd been mortally wounded numerous times over the centuries, but he'd never felt so helpless. The silver chains prevented the most basic of Carpathian abilities. He couldn't reach out to his brother—something that he'd been doing all of his life. His brother couldn't reach him. Josef was close, and he'd tried to touch him on the common Carpathian path, but that was closed to him—because of the terrible chains wrapped from his forehead to his ankles.

The burning in his skin was endless, but now his fear for Skyler's safety even overrode that horrendous agony. He could only hang helplessly, terrified for her, waiting for the night's work to play out.

We have to do this as silently and as stealthily as possible, Skyler reminded him. *Lycans are sensitive to all energy used. We don't want them to feel us.*

Dimitri suppressed a groan of frustration. *I am Sange rau. They cannot feel me, which is why they hate me. They fear me.*

You are a Guardian of all, Dimitri, not the dreaded Sange rau. You will have to think of yourself as a Guardian always.

Clearly, Skyler didn't understand his desire, his *need* to be *Sange rau*, even if just for a moment, to rip out the throats of his tormenters, the ones who came around when Zev wasn't near. They kicked him, spit on him, and some even dared to get close enough to use their fists on him. They deliberately shook and jarred his body in the hopes that the hooks would tear at his flesh and the silver race for his heart.

Their hatred was tangible. Facing them, being in their midst, he knew Mikhail Dubrinsky, the prince of his people, could never change the minds of such fanatics. Their hatred ran deep, taught to them by generations of hatred. He had done nothing to them. In fact, he had come to the aid of their kind. Gunnolf and Convel, the two he had saved, were the worst of his tormenters and seemed to take it personally that he hadn't died quickly.

Dimitri had never known such a thing as hatred. He hunted the vampire, but he was completely emotionless when he did so. It was a matter of honor, of duty, never personal. A vampire was evil and he murdered innocent men, women and children. He had to be brought to justice. There was no joy in the taking of a life, any life. This experience taught him what hatred was. Had it not been for Zev's compassion, he might have decided the Lycan species was not worth saving and he would have been just as bad as they were.

Josef is back. He'll bring me close to the camp and leave me to make my way. I have a path to take and I can sense the presence of the Lycans, Skyler informed him. *And, my beloved, lest you think you really would form these narrow opinions, I can assure you, that is your pain and your fear for me talking to you, the lack of sustenance and your weakness. I see into your mind and there are no such true feelings. You can't hold evil in your heart or mind, Dimitri, that is not who you are.*

Dimitri let out his breath. Skyler always brought comfort. She was a young woman, yet her soul was old, and matched his perfectly. She could play and tease, but there was always that distance in her, that part of her that knew monsters lived in the world. Human monsters, vampires and wolves. She already had experiences no young girl should ever have had and now she was facing brutal wolves—the ones declared to be good.

The Lycans surrounding him were no rogues. They didn't hunt and kill humans for food. They lived among them. They even protected them. Yet . . . None of it made sense. Dimitri could tell it didn't make sense to Zev either.

Be safe, sívamet. Without you . . . Would he stay the man she believed him to be? The one she saw and had such faith in?

If they killed her, would he become the very thing they detested to give himself a chance to kill them all? Or would he follow her to the next life and go to her clean and with honor? He wished he knew the answer. He was weary beyond endurance. Sometimes, his mind played tricks on him. He knew he was close to the end. If she didn't succeed, he honestly didn't know how much longer he could hold on without going mad.

Skyler felt Dimitri's despair. She had known all along that the brutal torture had sapped his strength. With his lack of sustenance for over two weeks and no rejuvenating sleep, it was only Dimitri's will of iron keeping him going.

The night breeze felt good on her face. Her nerves had been all over the place, but once Josef had returned for her and she was on her way, all she could think about was reaching Dimitri, freeing him, and holding him close to her. Nerves were gone. They would live or die this night—but they would do it together. If they didn't make it, Dimitri would know she loved him enough to risk everything for him, and she would know she'd done her absolute best. She couldn't ask for anything more.

Josef put her down in the middle of a thick stand of trees, exactly where she directed him. He kept his arms around her, holding her tight against his body, saying without words how much she meant to him, the family he didn't really have. She hugged him just as hard, conveying her love. Neither risked telepathic or verbal communication. She didn't feel any Lycan close, but all the same, they preferred their silent exchange. Josef dropped a kiss on the top of her head and left her abruptly.

Skyler let her breath out. She was on her own now. Dimitri's escape depended solely on her. This was her time. When a woman tied herself to a man like Dimitri, she knew he would be a dominant, no matter how gently or tenderly he treated you. She might never be able to give of herself the way she could in this moment. She was his equal here. She could fight with him. She could save him.

She let her senses stretch out, slowly, a quiet stealth, reaching into the night, searching for the markers that were Lycan. She knew their origins. She knew their birthplace. Like Mother Earth she could discern their heart-beats and their primal needs. She knew how the pack thought and worked.

Skyler lifted her hand, palm facing down, and moved it slowly just above the ground. Like a magnet, the pull went to her right. She put her booted foot on the untraveled grass. At once she felt the grasses urging her to move forward. She jogged, the soil cushioning her footfalls, preventing sound from traveling through the night.

She knew the Lycans so well now. Their sense of hearing and their sense of smell were so acute that it was important to remain absolutely silent. As she jogged, she used a small spell to mask the sound of the air moving in and out of her lungs.

That which is my breath
Now may not be heard.
That which is my body,
Now must be silent.

She trusted Mother Earth to keep her footsteps silent. The Lycans actually could feel the footsteps of those they hunted through the vibrations. They had so many gifts, but they had a few weaknesses, just like every species, and she intended to exploit each one.

The pack hunted together and few were comfortable without their pack-mates. Even among the elite hunters, those who chased down rogue packs, the members rarely were without their companions. Only a few, like Zev, were able to rise above that driving force to be safe and comfortable within their group.

Lycan packs had a tendency to position their guards in a way that best protected the center of their group, mainly to protect their children. Like the Carpathians, children were a rarity, and guarded closely. Although there were no women or children in this camp, the formation had worked for centuries and had become instinctive. She knew the approximate location of every guard surrounding the encampment. In this case, with no children, Dimitri had been placed in the center of the camp. The Lycans had set up around him and the guards were on those outer boundaries.

She knew how many meters out each guard would go before they considered it too far. The very footprints of the Lycans were etched into the land and the land shared information with Skyler. She jogged, careful to keep her clothes from brushing branches, moving toward Dimitri. She could feel him now, and her heart sang. Adrenaline flooded her body and she wanted to weep with joy. This had been a long, arduous journey. She'd been so afraid for him. Now, she was close to freeing him.

As she approached the quadrant of the first guard, she slowed her pace. The ears and nose of a Lycan were so much better than her own. She knew if a vampire was near—her Dragonseeker blood assured that—but wolves were different. Now it was Mother Earth she relied on, and the hints were subtle.

She felt the slight check of the ground beneath her feet, almost as if the surface switched from a carpet of soft grass to sand. She halted immediately and drew in long, slow breaths. She'd tied her hair back and slipped the braid inside the dark, mottled clothing Josef had provided for her. The weapons she'd requested were in the pockets of her cargo pants. She had come prepared to fight Lycans and she knew every weapon she would need. She also had brought along the tools necessary to protect the Lycan in Dimitri.

The back of her neck tingled, another subtle alarm. She sank down behind a shrub and went very still. The guard patrolled but clearly he didn't really think he was going to find anything. He relied exclusively on his sense of smell and his hearing. They were expecting Carpathians to attempt to rescue Dimitri and they believed they would feel aggressive energy coming at them before the Carpathians arrived.

She circled around in the opposite direction of the guard's movements in order to get in front of him. Behind her trotted a curious little fox. This time he followed exactly in Skyler's footsteps, marking his territory quite thoroughly, masking any scent she might have left behind. She noticed the moment the sandy soil turned back to a welcoming grass carpet and she picked up her pace again. The next circle would be closer, but she was inside.

She felt a burst of triumph and had to tamp down the desire to share her success with Dimitri. So far the Lycans hadn't detected their strange brand of telepathy or become suspicious, but after meeting Zev, Skyler didn't want to take any chances. She hurried along the faint trail, winding in and out of the trees. She walked fast, resisting the urge to jog. The inside guards were always stationed in a vee formation from the outside guards, to better keep out the enemy.

The path veered to her left. She slowed down even more, moving cautiously along the cushion of grass, dark now in the thick of the trees. Her feet felt the way more than her eyes saw, but still she trusted the way Mother Earth had provided.

A twig snapped off to her right and she held her breath. The guard had changed direction and was moving toward her, not away. The little fox trotted off in his direction. She heard the little creature bark a warning and the Lycan gave an explosive burst of laughter. Almost immediately the guard turned back, certain he had come close to a fox den and the male had given him notification that he'd better go away.

Lycans were essentially wolves, children of the forest, and they guarded the wildlife as carefully as Dimitri always had. She found it ironic that he had cared for wolves and given them sanctuary for most of his life, and yet the Lycans had turned on him.

She inched past the second guard's quadrant and now she was deep in the inner circle. This was where the main pack would be scattered, camping, perhaps using the few cabins, but any could be out for a walk.

She felt the pull of her lifemate now. Strong. So strong. His agony burst through her like an inferno out of control. She crouched low and fought down the need to vomit. She hadn't counted on feeling his pain just because they were in close proximity. She should have thought of that possibility. There was no way she could get closer without some sort of protection. Again, she called on her mage blood to aid her.

Mother of my blood,
I call upon you,
Surround me, cloak me,
Abolish this pain,
So that I may continue.

Drawing several deep breaths, Skyler continued to follow the path. Twice, it veered away from where the pull to Dimitri was the strongest, but she trusted the earth to guide her and she kept to the path. Both times, she caught a glimpse of a small cabin sheltered beneath trees.

Then she saw him. She hadn't prepared for that sight either. Nothing could have prepared her. He was still a distance from her, hanging by hooks and nothing else from a thick tree branch. The sight was sickening. His body was blackened, burned from the silver chain that literally ate into his flesh. His neck had at least three loops around it, his forehead one. But his body was chained all the way down so that he appeared to wear a robe of silver.

His face was so ravaged with pain, she wanted to cry. There were dark circles under his eyes. His skin was pulled tight around his skull, his cheeks hollow. Clearly they had been afraid to unwrap the chain long enough to cut away his clothing, so they'd just slipped a knife inside and along each winding wrap slashed at the material in an effort to keep the silver in contact with his skin. They hadn't cared whether or not the blade of the silver knife had cut open his flesh. She could see where he had bled in hundreds of places onto the chain.

She wanted to drop to her knees, cover her face and sob. How could one living being do such a thing to another? How much would you have to hate? Shaken, she pressed her hand to her mouth and forced herself to study him.

She could see where the hooks tore into his body and held him prisoner. Twelve of them, six down each side. She knew each location because blood welled from beneath those chains and smeared over them. Tiny beads of blood dotted his forehead and ran down his face. He stayed as still as possible, but the pain had to be excruciating, even without the silver traveling through his body toward his heart.

My love. Her voice wobbled. She choked on the lump in her throat. She knew it was bad, yet she hadn't imagined—this.

He didn't move or give away that she was so close. He kept his eyes closed. His head down. But she felt his love.

I shouldn't have waited. The moment I heard, I should have set out after you.

You are here now. Can you feel them watching me? He meant it as a warning. *There is someone always watching.*

I feel them. I have come prepared for that. In all our conversations over these last years, I did pick up a few things from you. And Josef is a mini-general. He is very good at planning a battle, even one such as this, where we hope to escape unnoticed.

He didn't ask her how. He knew she had a plan and he gave her the trust she deserved. She'd gotten to him against impossible odds.

She stayed in the shadow of the brush, a few meters from Dimitri. This night, she would be the very thing she'd always despised in herself. This night, she had to rely on the mage—the hated mage—that she now found she embraced with all of her heart. It was the mage in her that would save Dimitri.

Digging her feet deeper into the soil, she raised her hands in front of her, keeping movements small and called on the four elements.

I call upon Air, breathe forth a tempest of might.
I call upon Earth, bring forth your trembling might.
I call upon Fire, bring forth your flames.
I call upon Water, wash away that which remains.

At once the wind increased, short little microbursts that shook the tallest of the trees. An ominous crack was loud in the silence of the night. The top of a very heavy tree came crashing down, right on a cabin some distance away. Branches and trunks plunged through the thin roof and landed in the small confines, one of the branches landing directly in the fireplace. Flames shot up the branch, and reached the trunk just as another burst of wind fanned the blaze.

Shouts came from every direction. The earth beneath her shook with footsteps as the Lycans converged on the conflagration. The cabin went up fast, and they had to hurry to keep the fire from spreading to the neighboring trees and other huts. Many of the little structures used dried branches and needles and mud for a roof.

When she was certain every Lycan was engaged in saving their camp, she turned her attention to the hooks. She had to get him down first.

That which is hooked and made to hold,
I unmake your properties so you release and unfold.
Air, I call upon you, float him gently down.
Keep us safe from all sight and sound.

I call upon Earth, take him into your arms,
Surround him, protect him, keep him from harm.

Fire I call you, cauterize his wound.
Burn that which is bleeding, so it may not seal our doom.

Water, I call thee forth, your healing might,
Wash away that which is blood
So there is no scent,
No sight.

Dimitri's body nearly dropped to the ground, but she was able to send a cushion of air beneath him to float him down. Skyler didn't let the joy sweeping through her take control. Removing the hooks from his body had been the easy part. Now there was that terrible chain embedded in his very skin. He lay helpless in the thick grass, the chains wrapped tight, biting into flesh and in some spots, bone.

She pressed her lips together hard. She needed to draw on her courage, not think about what would happen after she removed the chains. She wasn't positive Dimitri would even be able to walk, let alone help if they ran into trouble.

She took a deep breath, let it out and made her try.

Chains of silver bedded within,
Chains of silver under tissue and skin,
Chains of silver connected to bone,
Chains of silver now may you be undone.

Skyler felt her heart begin to accelerate into panic. The chains were so deeply embedded in his flesh they'd become a part of him. Nothing happened. What if she couldn't do this?

They loosened.

The calmness in Dimitri's voice steadied her. He sounded the same. Her Dimitri. Cool under fire. A rock. Skyler nodded her head, took another deep breath and tried again.

Chain of silver buried deep within,
Chain of silver wrapped like a serpent's skin.

Chain of silver that cuts to the bone,
I seek out your making so that you will now be known.

I trace your pattern and follow your path,
Removing your roots as I seal and cast.
In each valley and burn I insert a balm,
So that your poison is ceased and can do no more harm.

Skyler forced herself to go slow, to plan every movement methodically. She couldn't afford to draw any attention their way. The wind fanned the flames, but she hadn't wanted to risk a forest fire, so the Lycans were putting it out fairly quickly. She glanced at the flames and waved her hands so that the fire jumped to a second cabin, the roof exploding into orange-yellow flames as the chains fell away from Dimitri's body, revealing the horrible extent of his burns.

Kneeling beside Dimitri, she put her wrist over his mouth. *Now, right here, take my blood. We only have a few minutes. I need you to do this.*

He was so weak. She felt his fear beating at him. Hunger was terrible, dominating his every thought now, beating in his veins, through his starving heart. Her blood was potent for him, the blood of his lifemate. It would tempt him as no other. He feared loss of control. His mind was already wandering, the pain mixing with the hunger until sometimes he wasn't certain where he was or what was happening around him.

Dimitri, feed now. If they find us, they will kill me. Skyler used the one thing she knew would get through to him.

He took her wrist gently. His thumb brushed over her pulse, the movement so light, but she felt that soft touch through her entire body. His lips, cracked and dry, feathered over her skin, right where her pulse leapt. She had expected his teeth to sink in and tear at her, but there was love in his touch—seduction even.

Dimitri lay there on the ground, his burned body nearly paralyzed after hanging in the tree so long and his mind barely comprehending that he was free of the hated silver. He was starving, yet he took great care not to frighten her—or hurt her. She framed one side of his face with her free hand, her palm against those terrible burn marks, trying to soothe away the pain.

His teeth sank into her wrist. For one moment there was blazing pain and then the sting was gone, instantly giving way to something else. Something she hadn't expected. Josef had taken her blood, and it was purely a necessary function. Neither felt anything when he'd done it. This was so different—and unexpected.

Skyler smoothed back hair from his tortured face and then leaned down to brush kisses over the burned and blackened skin where the chain had dug into his forehead. She had never voluntarily kissed him. Not once in all the years they'd been talking together. He'd kissed the top of her head, and sometimes the corner of her mouth or her chin, but she'd never made a single move to do something she considered intimate.

She thought her kisses would feel healing. She thought she would give him comfort and it would feel that way to her. It was kiss him or cry. Her beautiful Dimitri, so ravaged by hatred when he was capable of so much love. When she brushed those kisses along the line where the silver chain had been, she felt more than just comforting, more than healing. She felt an overwhelming love that seemed, for the first time, to transcend the physical.

She didn't understand the need that began right there in their worst moment, but it didn't matter. That was part of who they were together. She would have let him take every drop of blood she had in her body if he wanted—or needed it. It was Dimitri who found the strength to stop, running his tongue over the two holes in her wrist to stop the bleeding and then pressing a kiss over the mark to ease any ache.

He opened his eyes and looked up at her. She saw him there, in his glacier-blue eyes. That smile that didn't reach his lips, but was there just for her.

We have to go, Dimitri. Can you stand? That was her biggest fear. She couldn't teleport him out of there, and she doubted if she could even get him on his feet by herself.

I can do whatever it takes. I can't believe you did it, sívamet, you actually got the chains off. That was a miracle right there. They'd become part of him, eating through his skin and finding muscle until the silver had adhered to every cell it touched, driving him mad.

Dimitri sat up slowly, tentatively, stretching out his arms, finding movement painful, but wonderful at the same time. He didn't try to stand, his feet and legs were still numb, but he rolled onto his hands and knees, testing his strength. Hunger still was uppermost, thundering in his ears and pounding a demand in his veins, but he could get past it now. Skyler's blood was a powerful mixture, nearly intoxicating. Still, he was weak, even with what she'd given him.

He was grateful she didn't panic, or try to force him to his feet. He had to know he could get up and run and then do it, all in one motion. The trees she'd emerged from looked far away. He felt her hand on his back, rubbing, massaging. Healing.

You go first and I'll follow. Don't argue with me. Just do it, he told her.

He would bring up the rear and protect her as best he could. They would come after him with silver, and he knew there would be no mercy in him if they got close enough for him to get his hands on them.

Skyler nodded and turned toward the trees she'd used for cover. Dimitri stopped her with a hand on her shoulder. She looked back at him. She was beautiful, crouched there, determination in the set of her chin and shoulders. Love in her eyes. He needed to see that. He needed to see reality. He nodded, and she took off, staying low, Dimitri right behind her.

They gained the protection of the heavy stand of trees. Brush had grown up everywhere, unusual in a forest so dense, where the canopy kept the sun from hitting the forest floor. In the very center of the brush, a thick green carpet stretched out before them. The strip of grass was narrow and Dimitri realized with every step he took, behind him, the grass sank into the ground so that only dried leaves and brush remained, covering their tracks.

Skyler indicated the need for stealth. *A guard directly ahead of us.*

He already knew that. His senses were coming back, acute, the senses of the *Sange rau*, or *Hän ku pesäk kaikak*, whatever he had become. Whatever his mixed blood and the silver had made him. He knew exactly where the Lycan was. They would forever be a stench in his nostrils. He knew each individual. This one had stayed away from him. Several times Dimitri had noticed him speaking with Zev.

They have a pattern they follow when they guard their pack. This man will move to the right while the guards in the outer circle will move to the left to cover where he has been.

He shouldn't be surprised anymore with any information Skyler had, but the inner workings of a Lycan pack?

The moment the guard shifted direction, she was on the move. How had she known the precise moment the Lycan had changed his position? Dimitri found he was just a little in awe of his lifemate. They edged past the first guard and picked up the pace, moving quickly along the little strip of grass that wound through the trees and kept them covered by heavy brush.

8

Dimitri found he was getting his legs back as they hurried along. At first he'd been stiff, walking like a marionette with someone jerking the strings to his arms and legs. Blood flowed back with movement, and he found he could easily block the painful pins and needles. After the burn of the silver, the prickly sensation was more annoying and troublesome and easily manageable. Skyler picked up the pace, but in deference to his state, she wasn't moving very fast. His longer strides kept up with her easily.

There will be another guard a few meters ahead. We have to wait for him to circle back around, she cautioned.

He hadn't believed that they could just walk out of the Lycan camp. Hanging from a tree with silver wrapping him from head to toe, he'd had plenty of time to study the pack and the way they operated. A lot of the day-to-day operations were instinctual, probably imprinted on them before birth.

His own wolf had fed him information on the species, giving him the data necessary to be Lycan, but this was different. His wolf told him how to fight in pack formation, but Skyler had gleaned much more. She knew movements, times, how the pack guarded camps. He kept his mind merged with hers, learning the information, and how Mother Earth had shared with her.

He found his heart swelling with pride and respect. There should be no more surprises with his lifemate, yet she astonished him at every turn. Her abilities continued to grow along with her confidence. Was it the combination of her bloodlines? But there were others with her specific bloodlines, and they didn't exhibit the extreme power she displayed. Her mother? What did they really know of her mother and her gifts? Clearly he needed to learn more about her.

The path shifted to the left and then cut back sharply to the right. He could smell the other guard. The Lycan was much closer than Skyler had expected, which meant he had deviated from his normal routine. Dimitri put a hand on her shoulder, halting her progress. They crouched together on the narrow path, Dimitri sheltering her body as best he could, making certain he completely covered her in the event bullets started their way. The pack preferred hunting without guns, but he'd seen plenty of weapons in the camp. If they were preparing for a war, they would be using modern weapons.

Every breath he drew was difficult, and he had to prevent the wheezing from being heard. His lungs were shot. He needed blood. His close proximity to Skyler made his mouth water and his teeth stay lengthened. He could move, and he could endure pain, but he couldn't stop the ever-present hunger that crawled through his body demanding he feed starving cells.

His hand remained on Skyler's shoulder and he felt her tremble. She had gone to her hands and knees, sitting back a little on her heels, but she kept her hands in contact with the mat of grass. Through her, he felt the silent footfalls of the Lycan guard approaching. The earth gave off the smallest of vibrations. Skyler was so sensitive she felt it.

He stayed relaxed, but deep inside, he coiled, ready and more than willing to strike to protect his lifemate. He might be weak, but there was no silver chain to stop him. Skyler held her breath as the guard came even closer. The man moved first to their right and then to their left. Was he searching for them? The brush surrounding them was thick enough that the Lycan avoided going through it, and he wasn't aware of the thin strip of forest green carpet leading them to safety.

Dimitri allowed his enhanced senses free rein. Being a mixed blood gave him all the gifts of a Carpathian as well as a Lycan. As time went on, he would evolve even more. He already was gaining the speed of the mixed blood, and he had the acute vision and sense of smell as well as hearing.

The stench of the fire, the burned tree and cabins permeated the forest. The Lycan guard continued to move back and forth in an effort to see what was happening back at camp. He couldn't abandon his position, but he was clearly worried.

A sense of relief swept through Dimitri. He wasn't anywhere near full strength and he doubted if he could fight off a pack of Lycans. He wanted to get away without any of them realizing he was gone until it was too late to stop them.

They waited, counting the seconds ticking by, both knowing any moment someone would discover Dimitri had escaped. After what seemed an eternity, the guard gave up and resumed his normal patrol. Dimitri squeezed Skyler's shoulder. She looked back at him, her eyes changing color, like a kaleidoscope, a signature of her Dragonseeker blood. He knew the color change indicated nervousness.

You're amazing. He breathed the words into her mind, accompanied by his deep respect and love for her. *I honestly didn't think you could possibly get me out of that tree, let alone remove the silver chain from my body, but you did it. And now we're moving through the second circle of their guards.*

It's a long way until we're really free, she reminded. *From here on out, you would have a much better chance without me. I can't go to ground or take to the air.*

He leaned close, his mouth moving against her ear, although he spoke in her mind. *I can't do those things at the moment either, csitri. I am far too weak.*

Josef is waiting just ahead. We couldn't risk his being too close in case the Lycans sensed his energy. But he'll give you more blood—Carpathian blood. Paul's here as well. He's just a few kilometers from Josef. And you can feed again there.

He should have known she would even have prepared for feeding him, attempting to get him into good enough shape for a fast escape.

Skyler shook her head, obviously reading his mind. *Josef was the one who remembered you would need more blood than just mine. All I could think about was taking away the pain and trying to heal you.* Her lashes swept down, hiding the shame and guilt in her eyes. *I should have thought of it, though. I'm sorry.*

Dimitri took her chin between his finger and thumb, raising her head until her lashes lifted and her gaze met his. *We have good friends in Josef and Paul. I'm certain between all three of you, every detail of my rescue and escape has been attended to. Thank you for coming for me. You have such courage, Skyler. I tried to shield you from what was happening to me . . .*

She shook her head. *You were wrong to do that. I don't want you to keep anything from me—good or bad. We're a team—partners. We're lifemates, and I want to be that in every sense of the word.*

He nodded his chin toward the path, indicating they could start out again. The guard had completely moved away.

I think you've more than proved your abilities to be my lifemate, Skyler. We are tied together, bound, soul to soul. Before she could rise, he wrapped his arm around her and just held her for a long moment. She felt warm and soft, her body fitting into his burned and battered one, bringing a soothing balm to him.

Skyler rubbed her cheek gently over his burned chest, taking care to keep the gesture featherlight, but he felt it through his entire body, a gossamer touch that reached deep inside and sent his heart soaring.

I love you, Dimitri. We'll make it out of here and start our life together.

He brushed a kiss along her temple. He would give anything to have her anywhere else but where she was right then. Somewhere safe. He nodded, and she rose and began to walk along the narrow, inviting path between the two rows of thick brush.

He struggled into a standing position, shocked at how weak he was. As a Carpathian he'd always had strength, and as his blood had mixed with the Lycan blood over the centuries, he had become even stronger. His body needed healing inside and out. He also desperately needed the rejuvenating sleep of his kind, deep beneath the earth in the richest of soil.

Skyler picked up the pace, jogging slightly, just enough that he had to extend his strides to keep up with her. He had a difficult time keeping his feet on the carpet of grass. He concentrated on staying to that small strip.

I didn't want you in danger, but I can see that you're a woman who will stand with me through anything. I'm not so old, sívamet, that I can't learn. In spite of the dire situation, his ravaged body and weakness, Dimitri still managed to laugh at himself.

Skyler had always been drawn to his gentle ways and his sense of humor. She knew he was a predator and that any Carpathian male who had fought off the temptation of darkness for centuries was a strong, dangerous man. Still, with her, there was always tenderness and his humor.

She could barely look at his burned body. Had he been able, she knew he would have changed his appearance, but he was too weak. The damage done to him only served as a reminder to her that she'd waited too long. She'd been too concerned about hurting others, lying to her parents, getting in trouble. That seemed so trivial in comparison to what he suffered.

I didn't know how much I loved you until I nearly lost you, she admitted. *I've always known there was no one else for me, that I was your lifemate, but it's so much more, it's everything, Dimitri.*

She had loved him, but almost with a teenage crush, an infatuation that seemed obsessive at times. She'd leaned on him, counted on his strength, and she'd been selfish without even realizing it. She knew it was difficult for him to wait to claim her, but she hadn't really considered the consequences to his soul. To his honor. She'd been a child, playing at being an adult.

Why do you insist on being so hard on yourself, Skyler? I would not have claimed you when you were sixteen. Even in terms of human years, you deserved time to find out who you were and what you wanted.

His response to her thoughts only made her love him more.

A gun went off, four shots in rapid succession, the sound loud in the stillness of the night.

We're blown, csecsemõ, just run. The pack will be coming after us hard. They're fast, faster than you can possibly conceive.

Skyler knew the moment she heard the shots ring out that the pack was signaling to the guards. They'd found their prisoner gone and were hot on their trail. She sprinted along the grass carpet.

Dimitri, try to stay on the grass. Mother Earth will hide our scent. We can make a few more kilometers before they discover us. Both Paul and Josef are armed.

They can't hope to fight them. We have to find a place for all of you to give me blood. If I'm near full strength, I might be able to hold them off until help arrives.

She heard the doubt in his voice. He was severely wounded, starving, weak. She couldn't imagine, any more than he could, that he would be able to fight off an entire Lycan pack in his present condition.

If they catch up with us, I don't want you to try to fight them. If we can't escape, you and Josef must leave us. Paul and I are human. They probably won't harm us. Their stupid silver won't do the damage to us that it has to you. If you and Josef escape and you get to full strength, you can come back for us.

No.

Skyler sighed. That was an absolute. Dimitri rarely gave her that tone, but he meant business when he used it. No one dared disobey him when he spoke like that, including her. He would never harm her, but he would use whatever means available to him to ensure obedience—and he had quite a few options.

She ran along the path, determined not to get caught—to put as much distance as possible between the pack and them. If they managed to reach her safety zone in the clearing, the pack wouldn't be able to touch them.

We can't start a war, Dimitri said. *Make certain Josef and Paul don't shoot unless we have no other alternative.*

He wouldn't mind killing a few of the Lycans. Some were unnecessarily cruel. He had his suspicions about them and their motives. But there were others who clearly were uneasy about the council sentencing him to *Moarta de argint.* They had avoided him, averting their eyes. A few brought him water and shook their heads, but didn't speak. Only Zev talked to him and encouraged him. He seemed to be actively trying to reach the council members who were in the Carpathian Mountains with Mikhail, the prince of the Carpathian people. Cell phones weren't working very well where they were, and he had been unable to reach any of the people in power who could reverse the death sentence.

Twice Dimitri had heard Gunnolf talking with a group of Lycans, and he referred to Dimitri as Zev's pet. He was deliberately undermining Zev's position with the Lycans. Some seemed to agree with him, but many did not and they walked away in disgust.

He didn't want to be the cause of a war between Carpathians and Lycans, but if it came down to protecting Skyler, war it would be.

Skyler glanced at him over her shoulder. Her face was very pale. *We're coming up on Josef, and the Lycans are on our trail. I feel their footfalls as they run toward us.*

Tell him to get moving. Not to wait.

You need blood. Fear crept into her voice, even as she tried to hide it.

Have him run with us. If we get the opportunity, then he can give me blood.

Dimitri felt calm the way he did before any battle. This was his life and even as weak as he was, he was a dangerous man in a fight. He ran, not for himself, but for his lifemate. Had he been alone he would have eluded them, gone to ground and waited until he was at full strength. Still, he had no doubt that even now, should they attack, he could take a few of them down.

Josef. Skyler sent the call ahead of them.

Merged as he was with her, Dimitri heard every word.

They're coming up on you fast, Josef warned.

Don't fire at them. Dimitri wants you to run with us so if it's possible you can still give him blood.

There was a questioning note in her voice, and Dimitri realized her plan had been for Josef to take Paul and get away if anything went wrong.

If we get into trouble, csitri, he will still be able to get away, Dimitri assured.

Josef leapt out of a tree, landing lightly, just behind Dimitri, matching their pace. *We're in this together by choice, Sky, I'm not going anywhere. We just have to make the clearing and we're home free.*

She ran as fast as she dared, Dimitri, for all his weakness, matching her pace with no problem. She tried not to panic, knowing that would make things worse, but they were still some distance from their safety zone. The ground beneath her vibrated with the footfalls of the Lycans. They were incredibly fast, streaking toward them from different directions.

She had heard they were fast, but hadn't conceived of such a pace. Already they had fanned out in hunting formation. They were attempting to circle around and get in front of them. If they managed to do that, they would have to fight their way through that line in order to gain entrance to the sacred spot waiting to protect them.

She was tiring. She didn't have the physical stamina the other two did. Even with Dimitri in such bad shape, he wasn't faltering. Her lungs were already screaming.

Paul's just ahead, Josef said. *In those trees.*

Call him down, Dimitri instructed. *I need to know exactly where the clearing is, what's there and how far away it is.*

Skyler showed him the information in her memory, but she was trying to puzzle out how the Lycans knew which direction they'd taken. They ran silently, Mother Earth making certain there was no scent to follow. Their footsteps were muffled. There had to be something she was missing.

Wait. Wait. Skyler breathed the words. *Just for a moment, we have to stop. While we do, Josef, give Dimitri blood. Not too much, you have to be at full strength.*

Dimitri put his hand on her shoulder, urging her forward as she began to slow down. *Not yet, Skyler. We can't be caught out here on the trail.*

That's the point, they already know exactly where we are. How?

They're Lycan. Hunters.

There shouldn't be a trail for them to follow, yet they know our location, Skyler insisted. She halted abruptly and turned to face Dimitri.

"Clever, clever Lycans," Josef said aloud, extending his wrist to Dimitri. "I offer freely," he added the formality. He tried not to stare at Dimitri's burned body, but it was difficult to look away. He took a deep breath, let it out and got back to the business at hand. "They must have put a tracking device on their prisoner, and it's been activated."

Dimitri took the offering, knowing they had very little time. He bit down and allowed the rich Carpathian blood to flow into his starved body.

"We have to find it, Josef. You can take it in another direction and buy us time. The moment they get close to you, drop it and take to the air. Don't let them see you," Skyler cautioned.

While Dimitri drank, Skyler searched through the rags of his clothing and came up with a tiny bug that had been placed in the pocket of his trousers.

Josef reached for it with his free hand. "I'll bring Paul down from the tree and get moving, and then see if I can lead the pack away from you." He winked at her, his grin wide.

"Be careful, Josef," Skyler cautioned. "Don't play hero. This isn't a game."

Dimitri closed the wound on his wrist, but retained possession. He looked Josef in the eye, his gaze icy. "You will not take any chances, do you understand me? You're not expendable, not matter what you think. You are our family and we stick together."

Josef swallowed hard and nodded. "I'll be careful."

"Get back to us the moment you can," Dimitri said. "We'll need you." Reluctantly, he released Josef. The boy did think himself expendable. Skyler hadn't come to that realization yet, but Dimitri saw it in his eyes.

"I'll get Paul. You start running." Josef took to the air before either of them could say anything else.

Skyler set the pace again, a steady, but fast speed, Dimitri on her heels. She tried not to think about what she'd gotten her friends into. If they hadn't found Dimitri when they had, he would be dead. She knew that with certainty, but she didn't want to sacrifice Josef or Paul for her own happiness.

Josef set Paul down directly behind Dimitri on the narrow path that muffled their footsteps. Without another word, he veered away, moving fast, taking the tracking device with him.

At first, Skyler was certain the ruse wasn't going to work. The pack seemed to stay on course. Her heart accelerated and she felt her mouth go dry. She wasn't going to be able to get Dimitri and Paul to their safe haven. She'd chosen the meadow for the richness of soil. Nothing had disturbed it in centuries. The earth was rich with minerals and healing agents, everything Dimitri would need when he went to ground.

Ordinarily, it might take weeks to heal his terrible burns, both inside and outside his body, but they didn't have weeks. Mother Earth would see to it that her son was in the best shape possible for fight—or flight—if Skyler could just get him there.

Abruptly, she felt the shift of the pack, moving away from them, circling around, following the tracking device they'd placed on Dimitri. Josef was leading them away. He'd veered closer to the Lycan pack then she would have liked, obviously to make certain he had their attention, but now he was in full flight, giving them the opportunity to make better time and reach their goal.

Do you know how many there are? Paul asked.

Dimitri glanced at the boy over his shoulder. No, not a boy. Paul had turned into a man. He was family to the De La Cruz brothers, some of the most lethal of Carpathian hunters. They swore fidelity to the prince and Dimitri didn't have any doubts that all five brothers would defend him with their lives, but they answered to the eldest, Zacarias. His reputation was well deserved. He was a dangerous predator, untouched by civilization, a hunter renowned for his skill and relentless pursuit. These were the men mentoring Paul.

Too many, Dimitri said.

So basically an entire army. There was a faint note of humor in Paul's voice.

You could put it that way, Dimitri agreed. *I didn't realize you were telepathic.*

Josef exchanged blood with me. He enabled me to speak to Skyler and him. Otherwise, I'm not really, Paul admitted.

But you do have psychic gifts after all. Dimitri made it a statement. Paul might have exchanged blood with Josef to start the process, but he was too good at telepathy not to have some natural talent. *I knew you and your little sister had some jaguar in you, which can pass on psychic abilities, but I was told you didn't have them.*

Ginny is a lot like Colby, Paul said, sidestepping the issue. *She has a gift with animals, not just the horses, but all animals. She can talk to them. At first I just thought she was a horse whisperer, but it's much more. She can communicate with animals, and they understand her just as much as she understands them.*

When did you first start noticing the ability in her? Dimitri did his best to keep Paul's attention away from the fact that they were running for their lives, and Skyler from thinking too much about Josef's safety.

Still, Dimitri was genuinely intrigued. Gifts expanded or showed up as human children got older. Was that why Skyler was becoming so powerful? Was it her age? Or her acceptance of who she was and the acknowledgment of what gifts she actually wielded?

She always had a way with horses, Paul said. *But since we've been in South America, she's really thrived. This last year we all started noticing her abilities.*

Dimitri suddenly became aware of another heartbeat. He caught Skyler just as she paused. Paul ran into him, nearly knocking them all off the path. He signaled Paul to crouch low and go still. He slipped his arm around Skyler's shoulders.

There is only one heart beating that I can hear ahead of us, he said. *Probably a sentry left behind to warn the pack if he came across your trail. They know someone had to aid me.*

Skyler let out her breath, her hand on the path, pushed into the soil to gather more information. *Just one in our way. He's nearly directly in our path. Even if we're super stealthy I don't see how we can get past him without detection.*

Dimitri could, but even if Skyler cloaked her breathing and muffled her footsteps, the Lycan was on high alert and he would feel them. Skyler tried to think of a spell, anything at all to misdirect the wolf.

Dimitri's fingers went to the nape of her neck, massaging, easing the tension out of her. *Give me a minute. I'll be back.*

Skyler caught his hand, shaking her head. *No, the pack will know the moment he's down. They communicate through some kind of psychic network. Not telepathy, but when they hunt like this, they have some kind of ability to know where each member of the pack is. The formation is crucial to them. Give me a minute to figure this out.*

We don't have a minute. Josef can't run against them for long. Once the pack catches up to him, he's going to have to get out of there fast. Even if he takes to the sky, they leap impressive distances.

Skyler bit her lip hard. *Can you give him a sense of how high? Josef takes chances. I know you told him not to, but he always is proving something to himself.*

He doesn't yet have a sense of self-worth, Dimitri said. *I can send him the information and caution him again that we need him.*

Skyler turned her attention to the task at hand. Creating a diversion to move the guard was the safest way.

I call to the heart of a hunter,
I call to the scent of blood,
I call to the fox that is trickster,
Use your cunning to lead them astray.

They waited, crouched on the path. Skyler could hear the guard's heart now, through her connection with Dimitri. She was astonished at how acute his senses were. With her hands in the soil, she felt the movement of the fox, trotting out just a little way from the wolf, out of sight, but brushing his fur along a thorny bush.

Instantly, the Lycan responded to the furtive noise the fox made. He moved with far more stealth, picking his way through the brush.

Now, we've got to go now, Skyler said. Suiting action to words, she was up and hurrying along the green carpet, sending up silent prayers that the guard wouldn't return to the same exact location, but pick a spot away from their path.

Josef, hear me, Dimitri said. *You cannot allow the pack to come too close to you. You've given us a lead. They jump tremendous heights.* He did his best to give an example in imagery, showing the elite hunters in battle. *We need you with us as soon as you can come back.*

Josef knew the Lycans were gaining on him. He was a fast runner, and in truth, he wasn't setting his feet on the ground, but rather skimming just above it, because he didn't want the Lycans catching his scent. They hadn't been able to follow Dimitri's scent, but they had known where he was from the device they'd planted on him.

Still, for all his speed, they were breathing down his neck. It was time to abandon his subterfuge and get out of there. He'd led them several kilometers from Skyler, Paul and Dimitri, and that had been his goal. He threw the tiny tracking device into the thick layer of vegetation on the forest floor and launched himself skyward. As he did, a Lycan burst from the brush, half man, half wolf and leapt after him.

Claws hooked into his legs, terrible curved nails that ripped and tore his flesh. The Lycan refused to let go, trying to claw his way up Josef's body to his belly. Josef couldn't shift with the claws in him. The sheer weight of the Lycan pulled him back toward the ground where more of the pack waited eagerly. They jumped and snarled. One pointed a weapon his way.

Desperate, Josef changed tactics. He couldn't shift his body, but he could his hands. He lifted his arm and brought his clenched fist, now made of solid iron, straight down on the Lycan's head. The crunch was sickening. Josef's stomach lurched, but the wolf dropped away from him, landing on top of two of the pack.

Josef reversed direction, shifting as he did so, making his body too small for them to grab, the bird spreading its wings and taking off, making it to the safety of the canopy. Small droplets of blood streamed after him like a comet. He circled away from the pack and back toward Skyler and Dimitri.

Get ahead of us, to the clearing, Dimitri directed. *We're coming in fast.*

The pack knows, Josef warned. *They're already spreading out and heading your way, trying to get in front of you and around behind you. I can see them from up above. They're fast, Dimitri, too fast.*

The pack knew the woods, and they were used to running flat out for kilometers without breathing hard. Now they were in a frenzy to reach Dimitri.

I might have killed one of them, Josef confessed. *I'm sorry. They're really stirred up.*

Dimitri dropped all pretense. "Run. As fast as you can. Don't look back, just go for the meadow. Don't follow the path anymore, Skyler, take the shortest possible route."

What did it matter to hide their scent? The pack knew their direction and would use every means to cut them off. They couldn't know about Skyler's safe haven smack in the middle of the clearing, but they knew they were making for a specific destination and the pack was determined they wouldn't make it.

Skyler picked up the pace, running hard. She couldn't imagine what this type of exertion would do to Dimitri. She already had a major stitch in her side and her lungs were burning. The trees began to thin, giving them less cover.

Wolves leapt out of the forest just behind them—the guards left behind, converging together to make their attempt at stopping the escaping party.

One raised a weapon. Dimitri dropped directly behind her, his larger body shielding hers. Skyler, undaunted, sent her plea once more.

I call to thee, Mother, hear my call,
Send that which is silver to stop their footfall.
Bring forth that which is silver, now let it block,
Use that which was hidden to protect and to stop.

Beads of silver bubbled up from the soil and began to liquefy and extend across the ground behind and around them in a semicircle. Dimitri glanced back and down at the silver spreading so fast. His body gave an involuntary shudder.

Lycans wear boots. This cannot stop them.

Lycans wore thin gloves in order to handle the necessary silver weapons when going after rogue packs, and they almost always wore boots to protect their legs in the thick forest. The silver on the ground would not be a deterrent.

It won't stop them, but it will slow them down. We just need time, Skyler assured.

The silver began to rise in columns, much like dust devils or mini tornadoes, spinning rapidly as they rose and fell, always surrounding the fleeing escape party.

The moment a Lycan came too close, the tiny beads shot out of the whirling twisters, peppering the wolves coming up behind them. Curses, growls and snarls rose, someone shot at them, the bullet whining through the rotating beads.

Dimitri spun around as if he might attack them, but Skyler caught at him, jerking at his arm. *No, no, we can't take a chance on starting a war, not if we have a chance to make it to the clearing. My blood was spilled there. The spell is strong. They won't be able to penetrate through the shield.*

He ran, but he didn't like it. Twice he tried to drop back and cover Paul as well, but Paul just slowed with him.

Take care of Sky, Paul admonished. *I'll be fine. If they keep shooting at us, I'm going to shoot back, war or no war. This sucks.*

Dimitri had to agree with him. He wasn't used to running or being so weak. He prepared himself for battle, knowing that even Skyler's clever wall of silver twisters wasn't going to keep the Lycans back for long. Even as the thought entered his head, the wolves took to the trees, leaping high to catch branches, working their way around the twirling silver walls.

He caught glimpses of void spaces as if in the distance the trees were much thinner.

We're close, Skyler said. *But I can feel the main pack gaining on us. I'm sorry, Dimitri, I know I'm the one slowing you both down.*

He had always known the pack would catch up with them. His worry was the safe haven Skyler had created wouldn't be there and they'd be caught out in the open in a place nearly impossible to defend.

My body is still shaky, csitri, he told her, *I'm not altogether certain I would be any faster on my own.* But he would turn around and pick them off one by one. The hell with not going to war, not when they were going to kill his lifemate and Paul.

I'm with you, bro, Paul said.

Did I think that out loud? Dimitri asked. It was a sign of his weakness that he had.

Skyler answered him. *Loud and clear. I heard it, too. All this time I thought you were the cool, peaceful, Zen-like warrior.*

Dimitri saw that both Skyler and Paul found his little gaffe amusing in spite of the danger they were in, and he was grateful he'd made the mistake. They were running flat out now, uncaring of their burning lungs and cramping muscles. They knew they were running for their lives.

Paul gave an inelegant snort. *Yeah, cool and Zen-like, that's Dimitri. I say let him loose on these bozos.*

Just ahead, Dimitri could see the clearing. Skyler broke into the open first, running fast, heading for the very center. Josef waited, his hands in the air, ready to do whatever it took to protect them, but having no real idea how.

Dimitri paced himself just behind Skyler, always making certain his body blocked hers from the line to the Lycans. Behind him, he heard Paul grunt and the boy's pace changed. He glanced over his shoulder but Paul continued to run, not quite as fast, but he was into the clearing.

Shots rang out. He scented blood. Dimitri whirled around while Skyler skidded to a halt. Behind them, Paul was down, writhing on the very edge of the meadow. Just as Dimitri began to backtrack, Paul staggered to his feet, waving him off.

Paul picked up his pace again, sometimes hopping, but gamely coming toward them. Dimitri could see the shield shimmering, translucent, but definitely warping in the night air. Something was there waiting for them. He was reluctant to remove his body from where he blocked the Lycans' line of fire from his lifemate.

Get inside, Skyler. Get to safety. I'm going back for Paul.

Paul went down again, hard. Anyone could see the boy was in trouble. There was blood on his shoulder, clearly a through and through, and more blood on his leg.

Let me get him, Josef said, rushing past Skyler and Dimitri.

Another volley of shots rang out, and Josef hit the ground, his body rolling. Skyler let out a frightened cry and would have run past Dimitri, but he blocked her way.

"I'll get them. You get inside." Dimitri used his firmest voice, a command.

He sprinted toward the two boys. Both boys were game, Paul pushing himself up enough to drag his body forward as Josef rolled over and came to his feet, staying low and zigzagging as he ran toward Paul.

"It's a trap," Skyler yelled, suddenly seeing the pack of Lycans emerging from the forest, all with guns trained on Dimitri. "They're using Josef and Paul as bait."

Dimitri had already been certain that was exactly what the Lycans were doing. They would have been far more accurate in their marksmanship had they wanted the boys dead. He sprinted past Josef and reached Paul, bending down to lift him.

A volley of shots rang out, so many guns firing silver bullets straight at him. He heard Skyler's scream of raw fear for him, and then, somehow she was there, flinging her body in front of his, her arms completely outstretched to give him as much protection as possible. She even leapt into the air to protect his head.

Her body was flung hard back into him and he caught her, the burn of silver smashing through both his arms and legs. He turned and ran flat out for the safety of her shield. Behind him, Josef scooped up Paul and raced after him.

The Lycans fired over and over, the sound like claps of thunder, one volley running into the next. Dimitri leapt through the shimmering wall, feeling the wrench on his body, a terrible, disorienting twist, pulling his body nearly apart, almost as if their safe haven rejected him. Once he was through, the strange sensation disappeared, leaving behind the realization that not only had Skyler been shot numerous times, but so had he.

Josef yelled as he came through, Paul slung over his shoulder. Splashes of red dotted both bodies.

Dimitri put his lifemate on the ground, his fingers looking for a pulse. She was bleeding from half a dozen wounds, any one of which would kill her. Finding not even a faint heartbeat, he threw his head back and roared his rage and grief.

9

Mikhail Dubrinsky, prince of the Carpathian people, sat across from the four members of the Lycan council who had come to negotiate an alliance with him. They had brought a full regiment of guards to protect them. He couldn't blame them for that—he'd called in his warriors as well. It made for an interesting combination.

Gregori Daratrazanoff liked none of it, but then he was tasked with Mikhail's personal protection, and he basically glued himself to Mikhail's side. The main topic on the table, and the biggest bone of contention between the two species, was the subject of mixed blood. The Lycans had avoided the Carpathians for centuries, to ensure such a mix between their two species would not occur.

The Lycans referred to any mix between Lycan and Carpathian as *Sange rau*—bad blood. They believed anyone who had such a mixture must be hunted down and killed. Since it didn't happen very often, none of their hunters were well versed in killing one of such a mixture.

Mikhail had seen the *Sange rau* in action and he could well understand the danger, not only to the Lycans, but to all species. They were almost unstoppable—unless you had another of mixed blood to bring them to justice. That was the key in this meeting. He had to convince the Lycan council that there was a difference between a wolf/vampire cross and a Lycan/Carpathian cross. The wolf/vampire murdered everything and everyone without discrimination, sometimes simply for the joy of killing—just as a vampire would do. The Lycan/Carpathian was called *Hän ku pesäk kaikak*—Guardian of all. Carpathians had given that name to the mixed blood because it was true: they fought for all species against the *Sange rau*.

He liked all four of the council members. They were each quite different. Lyall was soft-spoken, listened attentively and appeared extremely intelligent. Randall was a bear of a man, shaggy and bulky, with a booming voice, a grip like a vise, yet he was definitely the most reasonable. He weighed what he said thoughtfully. Arno had the best sense of humor, was more open and friendly than the others, but he was also the one most outspoken on the *Sange rau*. Rolf rarely spoke, but when he did, the other Lycans immediately fell silent and listened to every word. If there was a single alpha among the council members—and Mikhail was certain there was—Rolf would be the leader.

Francesca Daratrazanoff moved gracefully over by the tables. Lycans ate food, and she laid out the meals the local inn had delivered for them. She was an asset with her gentle, calming ways, and more than once, when the debate between Lycan and Carpathians became heated, she chose her moment to insert some small comment in her soft voice, bringing them all back under control.

Still, the level of tension was extremely high in the room, given that the De La Cruz brothers were present. All had brought their lifemates to Romania, although none of the women were at the meeting, which didn't surprise Mikhail at all. Manolito De La Cruz and his lifemate, MaryAnn, would be considered *Sange rau* by the Lycans as they had mixed blood. Fortunately, the Lycans could only detect such a thing during a full moon, so they had no idea, but keeping the very lethal brothers from wanting to leap up and slay the Lycans each time they insisted the *Sange rau* must be killed was definitely becoming a problem.

Lucian and Gabriel Daratrazanoff said little. Neither joined in the arguments, but stayed in the background watching the proceeds of the meetings with interest. Gabriel's daughter, Skyler, was lifemate to Dimitri, and the Lycans held Dimitri captive. Mikhail had been assured by the council members that Dimitri was safe and would remain that way until the summit between the two species came to a decision.

Mikhail rubbed the back of his neck. His people would never accept the Lycans' view of mixed blood—and neither would he. All the discussions and heated arguing were really a waste of time. He would never change his position on the subject, or agree to pass a death sentence on innocent men just on the off chance that they might turn criminal.

Mikhail stood up, a fixed smile on his face, calling a halt to the meeting as the debate was once again becoming extremely heated. "I'm certain you're all hungry, and Francesca is signaling your food has arrived. She has made it very clear to me that you must eat it while it's hot. Shall we adjourn and give this subject a rest?"

Give it a rest?

He glanced across the room to Gregori. Their eyes met. Amusement showed in Gregori's eyes briefly, although he hadn't changed expression.

Zacarias hasn't said a word, but the women aren't here this evening. Marguarita, Colby, Juliette, Lara and MaryAnn have all been tucked away somewhere safe, Mikhail pointed out. *This meeting is going to deteriorate fast if we don't think of some way to get the Lycans to understand the difference between vampire and Carpathian. Manolito and Rafael are total hotheads.*

Does that surprise you? Something really catastrophic would have to happen to trigger Zacarias to make any kind of move without your permission, Gregori assured.

The Lycan council members rose and drifted toward the tables. Their guards fell into step behind them, flanking them, a solid wall of large men. Mikhail was very aware of how fast the Lycans moved in battle. All were armed, just as his men were.

Somewhere, in the distance, he heard a woman cry out. Colby De La Cruz, Rafael's lifemate. The sound was high, keening, a wail of fear and sorrow. Nicolas De La Cruz leapt to his feet, his brothers following suit. There was instant silence in the room, the Lycans swinging around to face what appeared to be a very lethal threat.

Mikhail stepped between the two factions, holding up his hand, facing the brothers. Francesca screamed, covered her face with both hands and would have fallen to the floor had Gabriel not caught her around her waist and held her, pressing her face to his shoulder, his eyes cold and hard as he, too, stared with lethal intent at the Lycans.

There was no way to stop the instantaneous ripple of knowledge, of treachery. Mikhail spun around to face the council members. The grief in the room was overwhelming, pressing down on all of them.

"They're *children*," Francesca accused. "You killed our child." She began to sob. "She's dead, Gabriel. Oh, God, how could this happen? How could they kill her?"

"You come into my home, sit at my table and all this time, you have been committing such treachery?" Mikhail said, his voice very low, a whip, striking hard at the four council members.

They winced at his tone, looking at one another. The Lycan guards reached for their weapons. Gregori caught Mikhail and all but shoved him back. Lucian stepped up beside him so they presented a solid wall between the Lycans and their prince.

It was Rolf who pushed past his own guards and stood without any weapon, facing his accusers. "I have no knowledge of what is happening. Clearly, you are aware of something tragic taking place. We came here in good faith. We have not committed any crime against your people, and we certainly do not kill children."

Mikhail moved past his own bodyguards, although both stepped up beside him, prepared, he was certain, to kill everyone in the room if they made a move toward him. He could barely stand the look of such grief carved deeply in Gabriel's face. Francesca's weeping broke his heart, yet there was the ring of truth in Rolf's voice.

"Skyler, Gabriel and Francesca's daughter, is lifemate to Dimitri," he explained.

"I heard her," Francesca said, lifting her face from Gabriel's shoulder. She pushed back her long dark hair and took a step toward Rolf—a very aggressive step.

Like all Carpathians, man or woman, she held great power. Mikhail might be able to keep the men under control long enough to get to the truth, but a grieving woman who had lost a child was something else altogether.

"I *saw*. Dimitri hung in a tree by hooks, silver winding its way to his heart. You lied to us. You told us he was safe, but even while you sat here charming us all, you were killing him, torturing him, death by silver you call it," Francesca accused.

She took another step toward the Lycan. Gabriel put a gentle hand on her arm, but she shook it off. "She set him free, and your army chased her."

"Paul was with her," Nicolas said. "He's been shot as well."

"With silver," Francesca said. "They riddled her body with silver."

Rolf frowned, shaking his head. "They wouldn't. I'm telling you no sentence was ever passed on Dimitri. He was to be held safely."

The other council members looked at one another, expressions puzzled or alarmed.

Francesca took another step toward Rolf. "She was nineteen years old. *Nineteen.*"

The door burst open and a couple stood together in the doorway. Mikhail's heart sank. How could he possibly prevent a war between Lycan and Carpathian? Razvan of the Dragonseekers, birth father to Skyler, and his lifemate, Ivory, stood shoulder to shoulder. Paul was a De La Cruz. Skyler was Daratrazanoff *and* Dragonseeker. To harm either of them would set lethal predators relentlessly pursuing the perpetrators of the crime. There would be no stopping the families.

"We did not do this," Rolf said again, this time looking directly at Francesca. "I swear to you, give you my word of honor, we did not do this."

"She's not dead," Josef yelled. "She can't be dead. Go after her, Dimitri. You have to go after her." He scrambled on all fours to get to Dimitri's side. "She's Dragonseeker. She's strong. Go after her."

Paul dragged himself to the other side of Skyler and Dimitri, one leg useless to him. He nodded his head. "She'll fight for life with the same determination she fought for you."

Skyler lay lifeless in her lifemate's arms. Dimitri took a deep breath. He was bleeding from several wounds himself, the silver twisting through his body, burning with terrible intensity, but nothing could rival the grief and rage rising like a firestorm out of control. The madness was close—too close. He could feel darkness swirling inside him, the edges turning a fiery red.

He took another breath, fighting back the emotions that threatened to dishonor him.

"If I can get her spirit and bring her close, you have to convert her, Josef. I cannot do both," Dimitri instructed. His voice was raspy, hoarse, fear for Skyler choking him.

He shed his body fast, becoming pure spirit, a white light that entered her body and rushed down the tree of life after her fading spirit. He knew her so well. Every expression. The sound of her laughter. The way her eyes changed color and her hair banded with color, even when she dyed it. He knew her heart and soul. That steel spine that made her so formidable. Most of all he knew her love.

I cannot lose you. Your soul is tied to mine. We are one, csitri. Where you go, I will follow. Stay where you are, hold on and let me come get you.

There in the darkness he felt her. There was no light to guide him, but he would know the feel of her anywhere. That soft, gentle nature, the one that surrounded him and held him to her when all else was lost. She had come for him in his darkest hour. His lady. His Skyler.

His spirit moved downward along the trunk of the tree of life, passed the upper branches. Once below them, he couldn't feel her anymore. For a moment panic nearly threw him back into his own body, but then he settled, calling on centuries of discipline. Hunting her in the cold and dark required calm, not panic, and he refused to lose her when he knew she was still there—somewhere.

Dimitri rose slowly, this time allowing the sense of the Guardian to emerge. The instant he did he became aware of everything there in the dark. Souls crying out. Those without souls crouched in the dark waiting for an unsuspecting traveler who knew them. The bitter cold coming from deep below, rising to infuse everything in its path with ice.

Yet above him and just to his left, there was a pocket of warmth between two branches, almost as if something had been caught there, or had clung there. He moved fast, surrounding that warmth with his light, holding it captive, recognizing the feel and strength of her unconditional love for him.

Päläfertiilam. Lifemate. Hän ku vigyáz sívamet és sielamet—keeper of my heart and soul. Give yourself into my keeping. Let me hold you close while Josef brings you fully into my world. To do this, you must have absolute trust in me. I will need to possess your body.

She was too far gone. She would never be able to take Josef's blood even with his aid. He wasn't even certain if the conversion could be done. Possession was forbidden, a tool of the mage world or the vampire, but he could see no other way.

Skyler could not respond. He couldn't even see a faint flickering light, but her warmth increased to the point of true heat. He took that as a yes. He divided his spirit, a dangerous move when his own body was burning from the inside out. Nothing mattered to him but saving his lifemate.

He came back into his body disoriented and shaking. A part of him had remained in the nether world. "Paul, she is a daughter of the earth. We can't heal these wounds in time, but Mother Earth may do so. Get the richest soil and press it into each of the bullet holes. Josef, take her blood, enough for an exchange."

"But . . ." Josef and Paul exchanged a look of disbelief.

"Just do it. Then give her your blood."

Dimitri didn't wait for them to agree with his plan. He took possession of Skyler's lifeless body. The fit was strange and wrong. Her eyes snapped open and she looked at Josef.

Josef fell back away from Skyler. He recognized those ice-cold blue eyes, and they weren't Skyler's. If he did as Dimitri asked, would she rise a puppet? The undead? He shook his head at the idea. There was no darkness in Skyler, not even with her powerful mage blood. He knew her.

He leaned down and sank his teeth into her neck, taking in the powerful combination of her lineage. He had taken her blood many times before when he was caught out away from others and needed to feed, but she was different now. More potent. There was even a different taste to her. He didn't know if he was feeding from Skyler or Dimitri or a combination of both.

When he was certain he had taken enough for an exchange, he tore at his own wrist and pressed the laceration to Skyler's mouth. Her movements were jerky, stiff even, as if she had little control over her own body. Her tongue tentatively swiped over the wound and then she began to drink, a small movement, barely there, increasing in strength.

Shocked, Josef gave her as much blood as he dared, not understanding what Dimitri was doing. He knew healers could retrieve spirits that hadn't gone too far into the other world, but he'd never seen this done. Conversion was hard on a body. One species didn't easily allow another to take over. But possession? Such an abomination was forbidden. One did not take over the body of another.

At this stage, Skyler was still human. Pressing dirt, no matter how rich, into her wounds couldn't possibly heal her. Still, Paul did as Dimitri instructed and so did Josef. What else could they do?

Around them, the Lycans had gone wild, desperate to get through the transparent shield Skyler had erected. They tore at it with bare claws. They bit at it, fired bullets into it, and even hacked at it with swords. The shield held. Lycans climbed the trees surrounding the clearing and the strongest of them made large leaps in an effort to get over the shield. Most dropped to the ground, but two landed above their heads, slamming their bodies hard into the transparent ceiling. More dug at the ground in a feverish, frenzied effort to tunnel beneath the shield to gain entry.

Razvan sent Gabriel and Lucian one silent look, turned on his heel and abruptly left the doorway, striding away, the set of his shoulders the only thing that gave away his absolute rage. There was no doubt in anyone's mind that he intended to go find those who had murdered his daughter.

Ivory stepped inside the door and walked straight up to the Lycans, fearless. Her back was covered with tattoos of wolves. The wolves stared at the Lycans with lifelike eyes as she moved through their ranks. No one said a word. No one moved, not even when she emerged from the pack of Lycans to go up to Rolf and look him in the eye.

"He does not lie," she announced. "It appears as if none of the members of the high council were aware of this betrayal, but I cannot tell if all of those who guard them were unaware of this treachery. There is the smell of conspiracy here. Which ones are guilty, I cannot say."

Ivory stepped back from Rolf. "You do not know me, but I am wolf as well, not in the sense of blood, but I have had my own pack for centuries. I can tell you, someone wants a war between Carpathian and Lycan. I do not know who would benefit from such a war, but there are those of your kind working against you."

Rolf frowned at her. "I hear the ring of truth in your voice, but there has been no hint of such a treachery. It would be difficult to hide from us."

Ivory gestured around the room. "Whoever is behind this now has the perfect weapon available to them. These warriors will go to get their children. None will stand down. None will stop. They will hunt every Lycan who took part in the killing of their children. No one will be safe. No one. You and Mikhail must find a way to stop this."

Abruptly she turned and walked out, following her lifemate.

"Rolf." One of the guards, a man by the name of Lowell, pushed forward. "We should get all of you out of here, before this escalates."

Another guard, Varg, nodded in agreement. "We have no confirmation that any of this is true. This could be *their* conspiracy to kill all of us and throw the Lycan world into chaos."

Several guards pulled swords so that the light struck the silver, making it gleam as if in eagerness. More than one began to shift from their human form to Lycan, half wolf, half man.

Two of the elite hunters Mikhail recognized moved into position to defend Rolf. Daciana and Makoce, two of Zev's elite pack, exchanged uneasy glances. They were aware, more than the others, of the danger all the Lycans were in. There would be a bloodbath here, if the tension continued to escalate between the two species.

The De La Cruz brothers spread out immediately, a clear sign of aggression. Jacques Dubrinsky, Mikhail's brother, and several other Carpathian males moved into the spaces around Mikhail. The two species faced one another, moving warily to give themselves fighting room, yet careful not to trigger an attack.

Rolf did not take his eyes from Francesca's grief-stricken face. "We did not know. When we heard that a *Sange rau* had been taken . . ."

"Dimitri is not *Sange rau*," Mikhail reiterated, ignoring Gregori's warning hand and emerging from the line of fierce protectors that had placed their bodies between his and danger. "He is *Hän ku pesäk kaikak*, Guardian of all. He saved the lives of your Lycans, and they repaid him with treachery. Would the *Sange rau* have risked his own life to save two of your people?"

Rolf shook his head. "Most of the others have never had to experience the complete destruction such a combination causes. We forbade contact with Carpathians in order to prevent such a mixed blood from rising."

"If you know Dimitri couldn't possibly be *Sange rau*, a rogue vampire/wolf mix, why would you hold him at all?" Mikhail asked.

In spite of the low, cool tones of both leaders, the tension in the room continued to escalate. Mikhail pinned Zacarias with piercing eyes. Zacarias was the leader among his brothers, a fierce, wild predator who remained untamed and uncivilized in spite of finding his lifemate. He was the most lethal man in the room, and the most unpredictable, a throwback to the old days when Carpathians hunted without fear of discovery.

He knew Zacarias was a law unto himself. He had been too long in the wilds, an ancient hunter on his own, far from home, with darkness always tearing at him, yet he had stayed an honorable man.

We will not be the ones to start the war, Zacarias. Keep your brothers, especially Rafael, under control while I sort this out. Rafael was lifemate to Colby, Paul's sister. He loved the boy and no doubt was furious that the Lycans had dared to attack him.

"We have not interviewed Dimitri as of yet," Rolf said. "None of us have ever laid eyes on him. We sent word to treat him with respect and care as we were away. One phone call to Zev Hunter, and I will have a much clearer understanding of what is transpiring."

"Zev is a good man," Mikhail said. "One we have trusted. He was not a part of the taking of Dimitri and left soon after to track those who had taken him."

Rolf shook his head. "Zev is the leader of the elite team. They would not have acted without Zev's authority. It would be . . ." He frowned, looking from Daciana to Makoce, two of the four members of Zev's elite hunter pack that were there to guard them. "Treachery."

Daciana and Makoce both nodded their heads. "We were fighting the rogue pack with the Carpathians here," Daciana explained. "Zev was with us. The *Sange rau* projected an image, an illusion of himself, and we all believed there was an imminent threat to the prince. While we fought here, two members of our team, Gunnolf and Convel, slipped away, and somehow this incident occurred with Dimitri."

"How do we get from two of your elite hunters fighting with us, to betraying us, kidnapping the very man who saved their lives, torturing him and murdering our children?" Francesca demanded.

Rolf looked around the room at the posturing warriors and shook his head. "I do not have an answer for you. I can only reiterate we did not come here to start a war. We came in peace to build an alliance with you. An alliance between us would benefit not only your species, but ours and humans as well. Allow me to step outside and make a call to Zev. I'll get to the bottom of this."

"Why do you need permission for anything from those who harbor the *Sange rau*?" Lowell, the guard who had insisted there was no proof of the attack on the children, demanded. His raised his voice, a belligerent sneer adding fuel to the fire. "Look at them, living in the mountains, hiding from the world. They think they have the power to dictate to us, but they are nothing at all. We don't need them. No Lycan would kill a child." He looked around at his fellow guards. "They have contrived this story in order to have reason to kill us all."

A murmur of agreement nearly ignited Rafael into action. He made a move, his hands coming up, but Zacarias glanced at him, his face set in stone and Rafael subsided.

"Lowell," Rolf said, his voice firming. "You will remain silent."

"It is my duty to keep you and all council members safe," Lowell insisted. "I have a job to do, and while I respect your authority, in this instance, I believe that it is important to save you from yourself."

The majority of the guards seemed to agree, nodding their heads, or simply drawing more weapons.

Mikhail, you must leave now, Gregori insisted. *This is getting out of hand. Lowell is deliberately turning the other Lycans against us. He wants to start a fight. Your safety is too important to risk you.*

Perhaps that is so, Mikhail agreed, *but once I leave the room, a fight will start. I don't want to give up yet. Rolf is an honorable man. Not only do I sense that, but Ivory confirmed my belief, and you know she is extraordinary.*

Gabriel moved up to Francesca's side. Lucian, his twin, slipped through the ranks of the De La Cruz brothers to join his brother in protecting Francesca.

"You will stand down, Lowell," Rolf ordered. "All of you. We are not going to escalate this without knowing all the facts." He returned his attention to Francesca. "I am so sorry for your loss. I cannot imagine what you must be feeling, but I promise you, I will get answers."

Francesca looked into his eyes for what seemed an eternity before she nodded her head and turned to bury her grief-stricken face against Gabriel's shoulder. As Gabriel turned away from the Lycans, his arm around his lifemate, Lowell lifted his sword, executing a fast, fluid sweep at the two Carpathians.

Lucian was faster. The legendary Carpathian met sword with sword, parrying away the blow so that Gabriel and Francesca were unharmed. The sound of metal clashing ignited the room.

Josef sank back on his heels, trying not to sob. He had no idea how Dimitri thought to save Skyler, but there was no real life in her body. She lay as if dead, her eyes open and staring, yet they were not her eyes. Not her spirit. Paul had packed each bullet entry with rich soil in an effort to stop the bleeding. The bullets were silver, designed to kill a rogue wolf or the *Sange rau*. Josef had a mad desire to cut the silver out of Skyler's body. Even that seemed an abomination to him.

He looked at Paul's grief-stricken face and then down at his body. "You've been shot," he announced, as if it was news. He realized he was in shock. Of course he knew Paul had been shot. *He* had been shot. Dimitri and Skyler had been shot. The Lycans were out for business. He looked around him, feeling dazed and a little dizzy. "They've surrounded us."

"Yeah, I noticed," Paul said. "I think they intend to bring in a nuke." He took Skyler's limp hand in his and stretched out beside her. "Go to ground, Josef. You can heal yourself in the ground. Skyler would want that."

"I'm not going to ground until I fix your wounds as best I can and see if Skyler comes back."

Josef choked several times, clearing his throat repeatedly, determined not to break down and cry. He wanted Paul to believe there was still a chance to save Skyler. He didn't believe for a moment that Skyler could come back from the dead and judging by Dimitri's crazy choices, he feared the

Carpathian would turn from Guardian to *Sange rau* and everyone would be in trouble. The thought terrified him. He could never defeat Dimitri in battle, not even a weak, starved, tortured Dimitri, but he couldn't leave Paul to face him alone—or face Skyler's death alone.

Skyler's body jerked so unexpectedly both men nearly jumped out of their skin. Josef caught her hand. It was ice-cold—cold enough to make him shiver. Wherever she was, she didn't inhabit the body lying between them.

See to Paul's wounds.

Dimitri's voice in his head made him jump nearly as much as Skyler's awkward jerk. He sounded far away and strained as if whatever he was doing was costing him dearly.

What are you doing? Josef demanded. *Dimitri, possessing Skyler's body won't bring her back.*

I have found her spirit. It is still warm. If her human body undergoes the conversion, I have a chance to thrust her spirit back into her body. She has consented, given me her complete trust.

Josef's breath caught in his lungs. Dimitri was going to undergo the conversion with Skyler's body. He was wounded. Silver burned through his body. Already weakened and starved, the chances of him dying with Skyler were enormous.

You can't be in two places at one time, holding Skyler to this world and undergoing the conversion, Josef warned. He took a deep breath, terrified, but willing. *Is there a way I can take your place in either Skyler's body*—the thought of which totally creeped him out—*or holding her spirit to this world?*

Skyler's body jerked again. Her eyes went wild, glacier-blue, but swirling with other colors beneath the blue—a beautiful dove gray Josef recognized. Skyler's eyes, when she was completely calm and relaxed often went that amazing shade of gray. When she was happy, her startling blue shone through. Now, there seemed to be a mixture and for the first time, Josef felt hope that she hadn't completely departed from their world.

"Fight, Skyler," he whispered. "I don't have anyone but you and Paul. Fight to come back. You're strong."

Thank you, Josef, for your offer, Dimitri said. This time his voice was edged with pain. *You have always been the brother she has loved. You and Paul. She's glad you're here with her, both of you. You give her added courage to see this thing through. You cannot take my place. She is too far gone from us, and I'm holding her by our connection more than anything else. You cannot undergo the conversion with her.*

Dimitri's voice strained now. Turned hoarse and raspy. Josef could see ripples beneath Skyler's skin as if her body had come to life, yet only her eyes showed real signs of life. Her body was icy cold, her skin tone nearly gray.

I count on you to see to Paul and then open the ground for us. Find some way to keep Paul as safe and comfortable as possible. Fen and the others are drawing closer, but they, too, will need to go to ground. I've told him of this . . . Dimitri broke off abruptly.

Josef felt a flash of blinding pain. Skyler's body convulsed.

Paul gasped and rolled to face her, pulling her hand to his chest. "What should we do? We have to do something."

Josef shook his head. "There isn't anything we can do. She's undergoing the conversion, her organs reshaping. Her human body must die in a sense, in order for the conversion to work. All toxins will be removed from her body and she'll be remade as Carpathian. The process is extremely difficult."

He made his way around Skyler to kneel beside Paul. "The wound in your leg seems to be the worst. You're bleeding pretty badly."

"*Don't* put dirt in the wound," Paul said. "I'm not Carpathian or about to be, and I'd end up with gangrene or something equally as awful." His gaze kept straying to Skyler's body even though he tried his best not to look at what was happening to her.

Josef wanted to distract him, knowing the worst was to come. He didn't want to tell Paul it was Dimitri possessing Skyler's body with her, because even for their world, that was bizarre—and wrong.

"A little dirt never hurt anyone. Hold still for a moment. You can't move or distract me, even if Skyler starts convulsing. Be prepared for anything, Paul. I'm counting on you not to move while I'm trying to heal you from the inside out."

He shed his own body and entered Paul's. He had deliberately given Paul the task of concentrating on him, rather than what was happening to Skyler. Skyler was completely in Dimitri's hands. Josef had never heard of anyone attempting what Dimitri was trying to do. As much as he wanted it to work, he feared Skyler could not be recovered and Dimitri would be pushed over the edge into madness. He was very pleased that Fen was drawing closer, and he sent up a silent prayer that Dimitri's older brother—a Guardian himself—would get there in time to destroy Dimitri if he became the *Sange rau.*

Dimitri was well aware of Josef's thoughts. He feared those very same things. He was weak, and right now, his only focus could be on saving Skyler. Once he had taken possession of her body, he was certain a spark of light, very faint, but there nonetheless, had appeared in that warm mass he held to him in that other world.

He felt her, their connection transcending space and time now. In that other world one could easily get lost. During the worst of the conversion, Skyler might want to be lost. He feared she might try to pull away from him once the pain took hold. He did his best to warn her.

Feel me, sívamet. Feel me holding you close to me. This will be pain unlike any you can imagine. The fire will burn through your body, cleansing it, preparing it for the full conversion. I will be with you every step of the way.

He felt the smallest of answers. Warmth in his mind. His heart jerked in his chest. Stuttered with joy. She was there, clinging to life, relying on him, trusting him.

The Lycans put me through the very fires of hell, but I am thankful now. I can guide us through this. You felt the burn of silver twisting through my body. You were able to withstand that torment. We can do this together.

He had no idea just how bad a conversion actually was, but even in his weakened state, he knew with absolute certainty that he could face anything, take the brunt of it and remain honorable—for her.

Stay with me. Stay, Skyler. I know you're weary and in pain, but I'm asking you to stay for me. She had said similar words to him when he had been mortally wounded, eviscerated by the rogue wolves he had fought. She had come to him, across an impossible distance and she had helped to heal him. *Stay, csitri, I cannot bear to be without you. We're so close to our life together.*

Again there was that small spread of warmth. This time he was certain of that small light in the midst of the warmth. Skyler had an indomitable spirit. She would not desert him. She had fought for him, dared to cross into Lycan lands to rescue him. She would not leave him now. He had to believe that.

Pain welled up, a wave sharp and terrible, burning through his/her insides, raking and clawing at their stomach. He turned Skyler's head just in time as her human stomach rebelled, emptying the contents over and over, a wretched action he couldn't stop. Something more powerful than him consumed them. Wave after wave crashed through them, lasting long minutes that could have been hours. He lost track of time.

Abruptly, the pain faded, and they panted together, desperate to draw air into their lungs. He felt dizzy and weak. He couldn't leave Skyler's spirit alone in the other world. She would never make it back to him. Possessing her body took a tremendous amount of energy. He was still bleeding from multiple wounds and silver burned through his own body, yet he didn't dare take the time to try to push it out. Already another wave of fire rose in Skyler's body, lifting her up and slamming her back to earth.

The strength and intensity of the convulsion knocked the very breath from his body. His/her eyes widened in shock. He had suffered endless days and nights when the silver burned and twisted relentlessly through him, but this pain was different, a long wave that roared through them, building so fast it was next to impossible to get above it or on top of it.

He forced Skyler's body to relax, relying on centuries of discipline. There was no blocking the pain, no way to stop the convulsions, or the way their body lifted, went rigid and slammed back to earth. As the wave subsided, she vomited again and again, a horrible retching sound that seemed to reverberate through the clearing.

Dimitri became aware of two things. Skyler's spirit, rather than diminishing and retreating from the pain, seemed to grow a little brighter right in the center of the warmth he had surrounded. The earth sank around them, drawing them deeper into the richness of her soil almost with every wave or convulsion. Both things gave him hope that he might actually pull her back from the land of the dead.

10

Fenris Dalka cursed in every language he knew, streaking through the sky, furious that he hadn't been able to track his younger brother. He was *Hän ku pesäk kaikak*—Guardian of all, yet he hadn't kept his brother safe. Dimitri had saved his life on more than one occasion, had fought the rogue pack and the *Sange rau* valiantly, saved the lives of Lycans and Carpathians alike, and yet he'd been betrayed, held prisoner and tortured.

Fen, we're close to him and he's still alive, Tatijana, his lifemate whispered into his mind, trying to soothe him.

Skyler has been murdered. He will either follow her or choose the path of revenge. Should he do that, he will be lost to us for all time—lost to her. This is my fault. I should have taken far more care over the centuries with him, with just how much blood I gave him when he was wounded.

He could smell the Lycans now. The wind brought him the overpowering scent of blood, of war. The Lycans were in pack formation, surrounding prey, most likely his brother and the two men who had aided Skyler in trying to rescue Dimitri.

He was not alone. The four Carpathian warriors who had started out with him to find and rescue Dimitri had been abruptly called back to the

Carpathian Mountains. Two others had joined him, and he hadn't been surprised. Byron Justicano and Vlad Belendrake, Josef's only family, had come the moment they were aware he was in trouble. Both had been much closer to the area, and once they knew the exact location of Josef they had set out fast to find him. Byron's lifemate, Antonietta, was blind and his sister, Eleanor, Vlad's lifemate, had never been in a battle her entire life, so neither had come, although both had apparently argued to do so.

Fen couldn't blame them. Had Josef been his son or nephew, he would have raced into the fight as well. As they streaked across the sky, he imparted to both men as much as he could about the way a Lycan pack fought, cautioning them about their speed and ability to leap, how they favored weapons and to stay out of their range whenever possible.

Fen, Tatijana tried to be the voice of reason, *we have to actually see what's happening before we go in and start a war.*

They tortured my brother after giving us their word that he would be safe. They sentenced him to death. He called out to me when Skyler was lying in his arms, the breath gone from her body, and showed me everything that had taken place.

Fen had considered Zev Hunter his friend. He liked and respected the elite Lycan hunter. They had fought together and were wounded together. He was angry with the Lycans, but it was Zev he felt a cold, dangerous fury at. It mattered little to him that Zev had been the one to cover for his brother or even that he'd given blood when he could see Dimitri was slowly starving. He hadn't taken him down from those terrible meat hooks made of silver. He'd allowed Dimitri to be tortured.

The truth was, had not Skyler, Josef and Paul set out to rescue Dimitri on their own, his brother would have died. The silver would have found its way to his heart. Skyler, in his opinion, had been magnificent, worthy of being Dimitri's lifemate, no matter how young she was. Josef, for all his reputation, had earned Fen's respect. And young Paul, a human, had been courageous. None of them deserved the treatment the Lycans had shown them.

The forest thinned, and through those trees, he saw the clearing. He had no idea how many Lycans surrounded the meadow, but they seemed to be attacking a transparent wall on all four sides, using axes. The blades simply bounced back at them. He could see where Lycans had tried to dig their way under that rippling transparency, and where a few had hacked at the top.

Skyler created that safe haven right in the middle of Lycan territory. There was pride in Tatijana's voice. *In spite of their best efforts, they haven't been able to get through.*

Fen took his time studying the transparent haven. Josef, splotches of red staining his clothes in several places, appeared to be trying to stop the flow of blood from Paul's wounds. Dimitri's body lay beside him, seemingly lifeless, but he was bleeding from several wounds. Skyler's body lay beside his, one hand outstretched toward Paul.

As he watched, Skyler's body convulsed. His heart jumped. *Tatijana, did you see that?*

She's undergoing the conversion. There was excitement in her voice.

Can you feel her life force? She was gone. I couldn't touch her. I felt the ripple through our connection with all our people, with the prince himself. She was lost to us. Fen saw the body lift up and slam down again, and yet even witnessing it with his own eyes, he couldn't believe what he was seeing. *How is this possible?*

Tatijana was Dragonseeker, Skyler her kin. She reached through their connection, eager to find the girl alive. She reached and reached, but there was only cold space, empty darkness.

She is too far away for me to touch, she admitted reluctantly. *Her body would not be undergoing the conversion if she were dead, Fen. I don't understand what's going on here, but Dimitri and Skyler have such a powerful connection, perhaps he was able to find her when no other could.*

Fen knew they didn't have a lot of time before the Lycans detected the Carpathians. They would feel energy coming at them—although not Fen's. He was of mixed blood, condemned by them, but they weren't aware of it. As far as they all knew, he was Lycan, one of them. They had no knowledge that he was Dimitri's brother, and that would get him close to Zev.

No. No, Fen. You can't throw away your life, our lives on revenge. We don't yet know if Skyler is dead . . .

You cannot feel her and she's your own kin. The prince cannot feel her and he is the vessel for all our people. He would know if her life force was gone. Even while he argued with her, his gaze searched relentlessly for Zev in the pack of frenzied wolves trying to tear down Skyler's safe haven and get at the four people inside to finish what they'd started.

Skyler's body had settled again. Around Dimitri and Skyler the earth seemed to sink so that their bodies were partially in the soil. He could see that someone had pushed rich, black loam into Skyler's wounds. Even as he watched, Josef turned away from Paul and dragged himself over to Dimitri.

Watching the boy's determination and his selfless act of courage, Fen's heart swelled with pride. Josef might be young, but he was a Carpathian warrior through and through. He could have gone to ground to heal his own wounds. No one would have blamed him. He was clearly severely wounded, but he had taken care of his friend and now turned to try to aid Dimitri.

Relief poured into him. Dimitri wasn't dead or Josef wouldn't be bothering. If Dimitri hadn't gone to ground in an effort to heal himself, he must have a good reason, and the only good reason would be to try to save his lifemate's life.

From his position, he couldn't get a good look at his brother, but Josef worked diligently. Fen saw the exact moment when the boy shed his body and went into Dimitri's.

He's adept at healing, Tatijana said. *Did you have any idea he could do that?* she asked Vlad, Josef's adopted father.

Vlad and Byron exchanged a long look. Vlad shook his head. *He continually surprises us. The boy is . . . different. He follows his own path. I'm not surprised, however, to see him with Skyler or Paul. They're very close.*

Fen signaled the others to stay where they were, while he allowed the wind to take him closer. The Lycans couldn't sense his energy and they would never know he was there. He shifted into the form of vapor, sending small fingers drifting out of the trees toward the clearing. He drifted with them. He wanted to get a good look at the occupants of the safe haven and a number count on the Lycans.

Fighting a Lycan pack was ludicrous with only three men. They would have to pick them off, one at a time. Tatijana's dragon could unleash the fires of hell on them right there in the clearing, and he contemplated whether or not that would be the best move to make, just to drive them back. He and the others could gain access to the haven and help the wounded.

He was directly over the transparent force field. No matter how hard the Lycans hacked and chopped at the shield, not a single scratch appeared that he could see. How could it be so strong to withstand such an assault, especially when Skyler lay nearly dead—or dead?

He dropped lower, forcing himself to be patient, to allow the wind to take him naturally. He caught Skyler's scent. Dragonseeker blood. Mage blood. She had used her own blood to build this safe place for the others. Her very essence was woven into the spell. He even smelled the scent of potent, rich soil. Daughter of the earth.

If he could catch her scent, so could the Lycans. They would know Skyler had been the one powerful enough to create such a fortress they could not enter. She had been the one to rescue Dimitri and find a way for them all to flee, avoiding the Lycans until they were nearly to safety. They wouldn't understand the kind of power she had—and that would make her suspect in their eyes. The *Sange rau* was hated and feared. Skyler very well could have just put herself in the same category with that condemned abomination.

Fen allowed himself to drift to the roof to peer down at Dimitri and Skyler. His heart nearly stuttered to a halt. He barely recognized his brother. Dimitri had always been extraordinarily handsome, tall, broad-shouldered and muscular. Blackened swirls of linked chain were now burned into the flesh of his forehead and over his entire body. He looked emaciated, his skin gray between the burned circles covering his body. His clothes, always elegant, were shredded, in tatters. Bright red splotches soaked into what was left of his shirt and trousers, and into the ground beneath him.

Josef valiantly fought to stem the blood, but clearly his focus was on pushing silver liquid from Dimitri's body through the pores. Everywhere the silver had touched Dimitri's skin were burn marks and blisters.

Fen found himself cursing again. He was furious that the Lycans had tortured Dimitri. Torture was so uncivilized, and yet the wolves were supposed to be far more civilized than Carpathians. They had integrated into human society and, in spite of their longevity and predatory instincts, had become quite adept at hiding their identities' from other species.

You lived among the Lycans for this last century and even at times before that, Tatijana said. *Does this seem like normal behavior to you?*

Fen had too many years as a vampire hunter, too many years existing in the endless, emotionless void not to be able to call upon self-discipline when he needed it. Tatijana's comment struck a chord with him. He had never seen Lycans armed in the way these were, or so many. They did look more of a military force than an organized pack.

He pulled his gaze away from his brother's burned body and began to assess the Lycans surrounding the haven Skyler had constructed. At first glance, every wolf seemed to be trying to tear down the walls, but after a few moments of study, he realized there were three factions. The first—and they appeared to be the strongest and most numerous—were the aggressive, determined Lycans actively using weapons and instruments to get at the four wounded inside.

He recognized Gunnolf and Convel in the front, driving the others to greater effort. He sent a silent snarl their way. Dimitri had virtually risked his life to save theirs and they had repaid him with betrayal and torture. They would not live out the night if Fen had anything to say about it.

We need to get inside in order to help them, Tatijana reminded. *I will shift to my dragon. Vlad and Byron will follow suit. We can drive them back from this fortress that Skyler has created and get inside. Our blood very well may be what turns the tide.*

Fen couldn't argue with her. Dimitri definitely was in starvation mode. He had no idea if Skyler was dead or hanging on by a thread, but his mixed blood and Tatijana's ancient blood would definitely help.

Give me another minute here. I have to figure out what's going on.

Something wasn't right. The second faction appeared to be arguing with the first, trying to stop them, separating themselves from the frenzied activities of the first group. There was a conflict, a definite division between the Lycans. He spotted Zev in the second group, clearly furious, throwing Lycans to the ground as he waded toward Gunnolf and Convel.

The third group of Lycans seemed uncertain. They were the smallest in number, and they didn't want to join either side, confused about what they should be doing. Where was the decisive leadership always present in a pack? In all the centuries Fen had been around the Lycans, the alpha always called the shots and settled all differences—there was a clear hierarchy. Yet this enormous pack seemed fragmented, a huge schism dividing them.

He had begun to return to the others, ready to call in the dragons to burn the hell out of the Lycans, when he heard a roar that sent chills up his spine and stopped every Lycan in their tracks. Below him, Zev rushed at Gunnolf in his Lycan form, accepting the challenge for leadership.

Lycans fought for supremacy bare-handed. They didn't kill one another as a rule. It happened in the heat of battle, but very rarely. Gunnolf swung around to meet Zev, lunging forward, but not before Fen saw the signal he gave to Convel.

The Lycans formed a circle around the two combatants, abandoning their efforts to enter the haven harboring the four escapees.

Convel inched his way around behind Zev, his hand on his sword. Fen made his decision. He'd been angry with Zev, certain the Lycan had betrayed them all, yet Zev clearly was trying to stop the assault on those already wounded.

Fen made the decision to trust him. They had fought together in battles before and Fen wasn't about to let him get cut down from behind. As far as they all knew, Fenris was Lycan.

If you get the chance, if the distraction is enough, the three of you slip inside and help the others. I'm going to remain on the outside and do what I can to figure out what is happening. I still believe there is someone at work, someone behind this trying to start a war between Lycan and Carpathian.

Whoever it was, if such a person existed, was very close to their goal. Fen came striding out of the forest, moving fast, a graceful flow of muscle and sinew, dressed in trousers with a belt holding an array of weapons, his boots with loops inside holding silver stakes as well as two knives, and his long coat concealing even more weapons. His long hair was pulled back severely from his face, flowing down his back, caught at the nape with a cord wrapped around the length to keep it from getting caught on anything as he fought.

He came up behind Convel just as the Lycan drew his sword and made his slash at Zev's unprotected back. Fen's sword seemed to come out of nowhere, parrying the blow and following it around in a semicircle, sparks showering down in the night. A collective gasp went through the Lycan ranks at such treachery. Even those Gunnolf led seemed to be shocked.

Zev threw Gunnolf off of him, following up his advantage, leaping onto the Lycan and driving him to the ground with such enormous strength the ground shook. Zev spared one quick glance behind him to see Fen and Convel battling with swords.

Tatijana, Vlad and Byron took advantage of the moment when all the Lycans were occupied watching the four combatants. Energy was flashing through the clearing almost as bright as the two swords clashing. The ring of metal against metal was loud in the stillness.

Gunnolf rolled free and leapt to his feet, gasping for air. He tore his shirt away, showing a mouthful of teeth as he circled Zev. Twice he wiped the blood from his muzzle and licked it from his claw-tipped hands.

"You disobeyed the council," Zev accused, loud enough for all Lycans to hear. "You went directly against their orders. You lied to us all, and you put the lives of the council members in jeopardy along with those of everyone here."

Gunnolf charged, rushing Zev. At the last moment, his clawed hands returned to those of a man's, enabling him to pull a silver dagger from his belt and slice viciously across Zev's arm. Blood sprayed over the treacherous Lycan. Zev let out a string of curse words, leaping back away from the man who had followed him for so many years—a man who had been his friend. No Lycan ever drew silver on another—not unless they were rogue. Another collective gasp went up in the Lycan circle.

Fen had his hands full keeping Convel from working his way around him in order to take a slice at Zev. He was faster and stronger than the Lycan, but he couldn't accidently give himself away as a mixed blood. He had to toe a fine line, fighting just well enough to appear nearly evenly matched.

"Clearly you're supposed to kill your alpha," Fen said, in a mild, but carrying voice. He wanted the other Lycans to be aware of the true nature of both challengers. "You and Gunnolf obviously planned to kill Zev during your raid on wounded people. Was that the true goal? Getting rid of the man who had the true ear of the council?"

Convel drove at him hard and fast with his sword, moving easily over the uneven ground, clearly an accomplished swordsman. To be an elite hunter he would have to be. He had confidence. He had experience, and he expected to cut Fen down quickly.

Gunnolf grinned at Zev, once again licking at the drops of blood catching in the fur along the back of his hand and arm. "Your time is over."

"You don't have the brains to come up with this plot on your own," Zev said. He ignored the wide slice on his arm, although blood was pouring from the wound. "Who gave the order for Dimitri to be sentenced to the *Moarta de argint*?"

"Dimitri," Gunnolf snarled. He spat on the ground in disgust, circling Zev, looking for an opening for the attack. "You mean the *Sange rau*? Why do you champion him? I have noticed you have become very friendly with Carpathians. Is it possible you are mixed blood and you seek to save your own kind?"

Another collective gasp went up, and the Lycans closest to the two combatants moved back, putting distance between them and a possible *Sange rau*.

Zev shrugged his shoulders, his gaze fixed on his opponent. "You have betrayed our council, Gunnolf. You put them all in jeopardy. You've disobeyed nearly every law we have. Even now, you do not fight fair, challenging me for leadership, yet not following the rules of the pack. Calling me a hated and feared name seems a desperate tactic. If that's all you have left, put down your weapons and allow me to take you into custody."

"There is no fairness when fighting a *Sange rau*," Gunnolf countered. "We kill them—exterminate them where we find them."

He rushed Zev again, feinting to his right and then striking left, the dagger still gripped in his hand. Zev was ready this time, avoiding the razor-sharp blade and catching Gunnolf's wrist in his unbreakable grip, bending it back and away from Gunnolf so that the wolf fell to the ground. Zev retained possession of the wrist, extracting the dagger and tossing it away.

Gunnolf rolled, howling as an audible snap signaled that his wrist was broken. He kicked out at Zev, driving him back just enough to leap back to his feet. The two bodies came together with a loud crash.

Fen parried Convel's sword, over and over, but never once gave ground, guarding Zev's back from the Lycan determined to cut his pack leader from behind. The swordplay was fast and ferocious. Convel tried to drive Fen from his position, but Fen fought him back, increasing the strength of each cut minutely, ratcheting up the speed so skillfully that at first Convel didn't notice the difference.

Convel obviously recognized that Fen was every bit as skilled as he was with a sword. His expression changed from pure confidence to anger and then desperation. He was now on the defensive, frantically meeting each cut of Fen's sword. His movements were just that little bit too slow. His footwork began to suffer as time after time the heavy metal jarred his arms and sent shockwaves through his entire body.

He tried to retreat, but the blows kept coming relentlessly, so hard, so fast, he couldn't begin to keep up with Fen.

"Throw your sword down," Fen advised. "And face the council."

Convel couldn't if he wanted to. His grip was so tight, adrenaline and fear gluing his fingers to the hilt. Fen feinted toward him and triumph burst through the Lycan. At last, Fen had made a terrible mistake. He thrust hard straight at his opponent's body, putting everything he had into that attack, determined to kill him.

Fen wasn't there, he'd glided to the other side, and Convel never saw the sword coming at him. He heard it, that betraying whisper as the sword, seemingly alive, cut through the air straight at him. He felt the energy, so aggressive and deadly, rushing toward him. The blade was so sharp he actually didn't feel the cut as it sliced through flesh and bone. He was dead before he hit the ground, his sword slipping through lifeless fingers.

Dimitri, this is one of your enemies gone, Fen whispered into his brother's mind.

He took the opportunity to glance into the haven Skyler had created there in the meadow. Tatijana was inside.

Do they live? he asked his lifemate.

Tatijana smoothed back Dimitri's hair from his forehead. She had never seen a body so torn and battered, not even in the ice caves of her father's torture chamber. The burns were deep and vicious. Healing the wounds, if even possible, would take time.

He is fighting to save her. Take care of business out there, and I'll see to the wounded.

She didn't tell him what she suspected—that Dimitri had possessed Skyler's body and was undergoing the conversion with her. The idea was distasteful and wrong. No one should ever possess another's body. For her especially, and for Skyler herself, it was such a crime, an abomination.

Tatijana's father, Xavier, had made a practice of possessing his son's body, seducing women and getting them pregnant. He wanted Carpathian blood for immortality. Skyler had been born of such an unholy unity. Possession was taboo in any species. Her stomach churned, but she forced herself to get past her aversion and examine Skyler's body.

She'd been shot multiple times. Someone had packed rich loam in the wounds in anticipation of her conversion. She sent herself outside her own body to become pure healing spirit. Entering Skyler's body confirmed her worst fears, Skyler was not alone; if anything, there was more Dimitri than Skyler.

The idea was so repugnant to her that Tatijana found herself back in her own body, thrown there by a force outside herself.

"What is it?" Byron asked. "Is she dead?"

Tatijana took a deep breath. She felt oily, dirty even. Wrong. "I don't know. How's Josef doing?"

Josef lifted a hand and waved at her, still feeding from his uncle's wrist.

Vlad smoothed a hand over Josef's blue-tipped spiky hair. "He'll be fine once he's in the ground," he assured.

Josef closed the pinpricks on Byron's wrist and looked from one man to the other. Twice he opened his mouth and closed it, blinking rapidly. "You came," was all he managed to get out, choking a little and turning his face away.

"Of course we came," Vlad said. "You're my son, Josef. Our world. Our pride and joy. How could you ever think we *wouldn't* come?"

Tears burned in Josef's eyes and he quickly averted his eyes. "I'm different. I give you a lot of trouble."

Byron laughed. "You're *supposed* to give us trouble. You keep us from being old men."

"Eleanor and I have always been proud of your ability to do things most of us can't do," Vlad said. "I had to handcuff her to the bedpost to keep her from coming," he added.

Josef laughed, but even that familiar sound was a little watery and choked. "That's just wrong, Vlad. I'm going to tell her you said that."

Byron slung his arm around the boy's shoulders. "You kept them all alive, Josef."

Josef shook his head, looking down at Skyler's body. Another ripple of pain across her face signaled a convulsion coming. "I don't know if I did. She's . . . gone."

Vlad shook his head. "Dimitri's fighting for her. He's a powerful ancient."

Tatijana pressed her lips together tightly. Her eyes met Josef's across the two bodies. He knew. He knew exactly what Dimitri was doing. Her brother-kin must not have had any other choice. It was a desperate move, and one few would try.

She took another deep breath as Skyler's body convulsed, pushing the last of the toxins from her system. Dimitri lay lifeless beside her, but his fingers were tightly threaded through Skyler's. They both looked so battered and far gone from the world. Tears welled up. She pressed a hand to her mouth, pushing back a sob of despair. How could either survive?

She sat quietly beside the two bodies, undecided how best to help. She couldn't attempt to heal Skyler as long as her body continued to go through the conversion. Dimitri's spirit was gone from his body, but he was definitely alive, and more than anyone else, his body had taken a terrible beating.

With each convulsion that shook Skyler's body, the earth beneath her trembled slightly and the two bodies sank a little deeper into the soil. She judged the movements were no more than a quarter of an inch each time, but the numbers were beginning to add up. Soil trickled from the edges of the sinking hole, pushing against the two bodies, working its way up their hips and legs in an effort to blanket them.

Tatijana wasn't altogether surprised that Mother Earth was aware of Skyler's plight and had reached out in the only way she could to try to aid her daughter and son. She couldn't help herself, so she brushed her hand soothingly over Skyler's hair, pushing the strands from her forehead.

"Hang on, little sister," she whispered aloud. "Stay with him. Trust him to keep you safe." It was all she could think to say. Dimitri had gone to great lengths to ensure Skyler didn't die this night.

Skyler's eyes suddenly opened as her body quieted. Tatijana felt a chill go down her spine. Both Skyler and Dimitri stared back at her, glacier-blue eyes swirling with color, sending an eerie, creepy feeling through her entire body.

"If you can hear me, we're with you now," she whispered. "I go now to heal Dimitri's body as best I can. When he is successful and your body has finished the conversion, I'll do my best to heal you as well, although Mother Earth is already standing in line to do just that."

Tatijana sent her spirit seeking outside her own body and into Dimitri's. She could see where Josef had made his attempt to push the silver from the Guardian's body. He'd done a fairly good job for one so young and inexperienced. She made a mental note to herself to watch the boy. He had a gift to be able to accomplish so much when he was untrained.

There were traces of silver burning long thin lines along the bones, as if that precious metal had attached itself where it could hurt the most as well as do the most damage. Meticulously, taking her time when everything in her wanted to move fast, she began to work.

Tatijana, my brother? He has not moved. A conversion does not take this long.

Fen's anxiety crept into her mind in spite of focusing completely on her task. *Be patient, wolf man,* she said. *I'm healing Dimitri's body and I need to concentrate.*

Fen let out his breath. He should have known not to disturb her. He couldn't keep risking glances through the transparent wall when the Lycans' attention was so focused on the life or death battle between Gunnolf and Zev.

Convel's body lay at his feet, cut in two by the precise silver sword. His task wasn't finished, it rarely was, unless you knew how to kill a Lycan. Their bodies could regenerate given the opportunity. He slammed home a silver stake, driving it through the Lycan's heart, and then severed the head.

Fen stared down at the body for a moment before wiping the blood from his blade on the traitor's shirt and then replacing the sword back in the scabbard. Lycans moved out of his way as he strode through the thick circle to the inside where he could keep an eye out for others who thought to aid Gunnolf.

There had to be more of them—supporters of Gunnolf's rebellion. Gunnolf would never have made his move against Zev unless he thought he had the advantage. If Zev was right, and Gunnolf had deliberately gone against the word of the council, then he had done so with enough followers right here in this camp to challenge Zev's authority.

Two Lycans caught Fen's eye. They would have blended with the large crowd but for the fact that their movements seemed furtive while everyone else shouted encouragement to Zev or Gunnolf, all fully focused on the fight.

Those shouting encouragement to Gunnolf growled warningly at any of the Lycans who grumbled about Gunnolf's methods.

It had gotten very brutal as fights between Lycans often did. Both men were bloody, shirts stripped off, muscles streaked with lacerations and dirt. Gunnolf's left eye was nearly closed and he favored his left side, as if protecting a cracked rib. His wrist was broken for certain, although he used the hand, tough enough to get past pain.

The slice that had opened Zev's arm worried Fen. It was bleeding too much, as if Gunnolf might have treated the blade on the dagger with an anticoagulant. Fen sniffed the air, allowing his mixed blood senses to flare out into the night. The scent of blood was strong. So was fear and treachery. And yes . . . there it was . . . that faint odor confirming his belief that Gunnolf had rigged even his blades against his opponent. There was no doubt that Gunnolf had come prepared to kill Zev.

Once again he started to move, making his way through the crowds of Lycans to intercept the two who were acting so shifty. One, a darker wolf with a square muzzle, pushed his way through the other Lycans, skirting around again and again, in order to come up behind Zev. The other was much stealthier, and he moved *away* from the Lycans. *Away* from the combatants.

Fen swore under his breath. He had to choose one of them to stay on, he couldn't guard both. *Get it over already, Zev,* he snapped through gritted teeth. They had established a line of communication through Tatijana's sister, Branislava. He followed that path now, trying to push his warning into Zev's mind.

I'm a little busy here, Fen.

The ability to communicate gave them a bit of an advantage the other side wouldn't see coming. Gunnolf couldn't violate the code of Lycans without angering and bringing about retaliation from the Lycans not yet joined with him. If he succeeded in defeating Zev, he would be the top alpha over the pack and the others wouldn't question his authority—his methods maybe—but not his authority.

You look like you're playing with the bastard. Get it done. You've got about a hundred others waiting to kill you. Big oaf, dark fur, square jaw, working his way behind you.

Take care of it. I've got my hands full with this one. He isn't the ringleader and I'd like to find a way to extract the information from him without his knowledge.

Kill him and keep his head intact. I'll see what information I can get out of him. Fen kept his attention on the Lycan slipping away from the crowd and heading toward the edge of the forest.

That's a dangerous practice. Zev caught Gunnolf and threw him to one side as the Lycan attacked, snarling, raging, beginning to lose control.

Zev moved with fluid grace, a ballet of lethal intent. He seemed not to move his feet, yet he was everywhere, flowing around Gunnolf, striking with punches, kicks and openhanded slaps. The fight was brutal, but the alpha managed to make it look more like a dance or a martial arts exhibition, than a fight to the death.

There's a second threat, moving into the forest. I believe he has a sniper rifle on him. I'm just guessing here, but someone wants you dead. Don't cut off Gunnolf's head until I can get back.

Sniper rifle?

Fen heard the shock in Zev's voice, even felt it in his mind. The elite hunter had told himself Gunnolf and Convel wanted to take over the pack for power. Perhaps in the back of his mind he believed the two had gone rogue and were recruiting followers, but a sniper rifle was a serious threat—one that smacked of a larger conspiracy.

Fen was on the move, fast, fading into the crowd but making his way quickly to the nearest point of the tree line. At the edge of the clearing there were fewer Lycans, and the stealthy one climbing the tree might be able to spot him. He blurred his image just enough to make it into the forest without detection.

There was always a fine line to walk when he was around the Lycans, but he'd been doing it for centuries and had a lot of practice. He couldn't use the speed or senses of his mixed blood or his abilities as a Carpathian in front of them. At all times they had to believe he was fully Lycan. At times like this he felt handicapped.

He glanced at the sky, pulling in the storm clouds, building them fast so that they rose into the air like dark towers. Thunder rumbled in the distance and lightning veined the darker clouds. Sinking deeper into the trees, and using the darker sky as a cover, he streaked to the bottom of the tree he had seen the Lycan climb.

Knowing he was hidden from view and his mixed blood hid his energy from the Lycans, he shifted, going to pure vapor, racing up through the branches until he was behind the Lycan. This one had military training. He set up his rifle and scope with meticulous care. He'd tied a bit of cloth to an outside branch across the clearing to get a feel for the wind. Already he had his eye to the scope.

Fen abruptly commanded the wind, sending a capricious blast that sent the little flag in all directions. The Lycan lifted his head and waited. He had the patience of a marksman, Fen noted, his gut tightening.

From his vantage point in the tree, Fen got a better look at what was happening in the clearing. The Lycans were no longer paying any attention to the Carpathians trapped inside the safety structure. They barely glanced at the dead Lycan whose head remained separated from his body so close to the edge of the ring. The Lycans surrounded the two combatants, and they had gone wild. Fen had seen the behavior before, a frenzied madness that swept through a pack during a challenge for leadership.

Gunnolf and Convel had counted on that trait in their fellow wolves. The animal came out when they were in combat with one another, especially during a challenge. Few thought clearly. They cheered and yelled and paced back and forth, their adrenaline and untamed nature taking over their more civilized half.

Fen could see the recruits to Gunnolf's army surrounding the others, a subtle move that no one would notice inside that circle. They shifted from one spot to another, closing ranks so that Zev's supporters were entirely ringed. A massacre? Or did Gunnolf believe that if he defeated Zev by any means, the pack would accept him?

We're in trouble, Zev. He's got an army surrounding your fighters, Fen announced.

II

I think we're nearly in the clear, Skyler, Dimitri whispered softly into her mind. *You're so amazing. Thank you for giving me your trust.*

That light right in the center of the warmth he had surrounded and protected so diligently there in the nether world glowed just a bit brighter. She hadn't retreated. She'd fought to stay with him. She just had to hang on a little bit longer.

He sensed how weary she was. She had accepted the pain, allowing it to flow through her, not once trying to fight or resist. They were bound together, intertwined tightly, both feeling the pain rising like a wave and crashing over them. He concentrated on breathing for both of them, pushing air through her lungs, through his lungs.

If this lasted much longer he would lose her. *Fen has arrived. He is somewhere close. I know, because Tatijana—your sister-kin—heals my body even as I am with you in yours.*

The pain was worse than ever, robbing him of breath, of the ability to think for a long moment. He couldn't compartmentalize it for her. He couldn't distance either one of them from it. The agony really was as bad or worse than the silver snaking its way through his system, burning him from the inside out. Her body shuddered with the memory of it.

Strangely, instead of dimming, the light in the very center of her warmth stretched out, spreading through the darkness there in the icy cold world, reaching for his light. Comforting him? Only Skyler, on the very edge of death, already in another world, would think to reach out to him. She had come for him when he thought there was no hope. Against all odds, she had stayed for him, when he doubted any other would have done so under the circumstances.

The wave subsided, and he sensed that it was the right time to attempt to reunite body and spirit. Dimitri surrounded Skyler's warmth and began to move very slowly away from the icy darkness.

Come with me now, csitri. Your spirit cannot be away from your body for too long. I must take you back.

His light moved, but that small warm consciousness that was Skyler didn't. She stayed hovering in the limbs of the tree of life. The moment his spirit ceased to touch hers, the light in the very center of her warmth dimmed and then flickered on and off as if she couldn't keep the spark going without him.

His heart jerked. He had nearly lost her. He forced calm. He needed to be confident and sure. Skyler needed to know she could rely on him through anything. Once again he surrounded her with his light, stopping to examine what held her in the nether world.

Just a few more minutes in the dark and cold, Skyler. I'm with you. You aren't alone, he assured her. She never would be again. If she couldn't make it out of the darkness with him, back into her own body, he would go with her to light her way to wherever the next life was.

Her spirit seemed caught in the branches and he had to pause to figure out how to get her free. It was only then that he realized Skyler had somehow attached herself to the branches. She was a daughter of the earth and the tree of life had recognized her great need.

Release her to me, Dimitri murmured softly. *I give thanks to you for holding her for me, but we need her back in our world.*

He didn't have the skill Skyler did when it came to communicating with all things earth, but he had sincerity. He opened himself up to attack from the greedy creatures waiting below in the darkness, crouched, just waiting for an unsuspecting soul to drift down, unaware of the danger lurking in the dark. He knew what was down there, but still, he wanted the tree of life to understand his great need.

The moment he opened his mind there in the nether world, he heard and felt the blast of greed and hatred coming at him from every direction. He remained where he was, his light surrounding Skyler's warmth, between the upper branches. Below him, he detected the sounds of the living dead clawing their way up the tree toward him.

He was *Hän ku pesäk kaikak*, and he would not falter. His spirit was bright, and he had newfound hope that his lifemate would not leave him. Tatijana, a Dragonseeker and sister-kin to Skyler, was above ground, guarding their bodies. He felt her strength and her brightness, that white-hot light of healing.

Skyler, sívamet, my heart and soul, come back to me. The worst is over. Let me help you return to the land of the living. He kept his voice calm, soothing, refusing to hurry her, or frighten her.

He had committed an unpardonable sin in possessing her body, but he felt no remorse. He had gone through the conversion, ensuring, if he could bring her back, that her Carpathian body waited and would heal naturally beneath the earth.

They were bound together, soul to soul. After what he had done, they would be bound mind to mind. She had trusted him, given her permission, but she hadn't known the consequences. He hadn't been able to give her up and he'd chosen for both of them. She would be as he was eventually—mixed blood—and their minds would be forever connected.

That should have been the worst of the sacrifices, but she would have to live with the knowledge of every single kill he'd ever made. The sorrow and guilt of hunting friends would weigh on an empath like Skyler. She would know his every dark secret, all those endless years after he had discovered he had a lifemate. He had fought the crouching darkness on each rising, but still, she would know how truly difficult it had been. He wouldn't be able to shield her from those terrible nights. Most lifemates left those memories alone; she wouldn't have that choice.

The tree vibrated, a subtle movement, and then shook a little harder as if attempting to dislodge her. He felt her warmth push against his light, and then into it. The moment they merged, he began the climb.

That's my girl. There's nothing to fear. Except perhaps an entire Lycan army surrounding them, but he refused to think about that. Tatijana's presence meant Fen was there. Fen would fight with his last breath to save them. He would have brought others with him.

He still felt Skyler's warmth and the small light that was her very essence flickered valiantly, but she needed blood and she needed to go to ground—if he could get her back into a body her spirit might not recognize after the conversion.

I don't know if I've ever told you how beautiful you are to me. Not just your looks, but what I see inside of you, and that was before I knew how courageous you were. You came for me, Skyler, and even when I was foolish and tried to turn you away, you refused to give up on us.

He wouldn't give up on her. He was prepared to do anything, fight any battle. No matter if the act was forbidden or not, if he could get her back, he would humble himself, put himself in any kind of jeopardy or fight any battle to save her.

Can you hear me, csitri? You cannot leave me. I have such need of you.

He felt no shame in pleading. She showed no outward signs of growing stronger. Her light was exactly the same, but it was there. She couldn't have lost her way in the other world as some souls had done, because she had been anchored to the top branches of the tree.

Dimitri didn't yet know if she had pleaded her cause and asked for aid, or if the tree recognized her as a daughter of the earth and had stepped in to save her. He wanted to believe, even in her dying moment, Skyler had thought to secure herself to those upper branches in the certain knowledge that he would come for her.

They floated together to the very surface. This was his moment. Could he bring her warm spirit and faltering light back into her body? He kept his movements gentle, his voice calm. He didn't want her to feel fear or experience any more trauma than she already had. If he could stay calm and instill his belief that both of them would be fine, she might take this transition as entirely natural and not try to retreat from him.

She had been more than aware of her body dying, of the pain of conversion, but she hadn't let go. She had stayed with him, clinging to life when it should have been impossible. He was beginning to realize, with Skyler, *all* things were possible.

I have always been secretly amused that others continually underestimated you, my love, he confessed, *but I have found these last few nights have taught me that even I underestimate you and your strength.*

For the first time, he felt the familiar stirring in his mind, that beloved touch that signaled the love of his life had ever so gently merged with him. How she found the strength when there was so little blood left in her body, he didn't know.

Dimitri.

His body came to life. His heart. His soul. That gentle touch, the brush of her voice across the scars in his mind held so much love he ached inside. She set up cravings with her soft gentle ways. Hunger. She found a well of tenderness in him that had been buried and forgotten for centuries.

You scared me, he admitted. *You can never do this again.*

She didn't reply in words, the effort to talk even telepathically was too much in her weakened state, but she stroked a caress over the sorrow and fear he'd been holding inside.

You must reenter your body, Skyler. It will be uncomfortable and there will be pain again, but not like we experienced before. He instilled absolute confidence in his voice, and kept it uppermost in his mind, although deep inside he was afraid she might balk.

There was a flutter against the walls of his mind, as gentle as the gossamer wings of a butterfly. *You?*

Every step of the way. I will hold you. You'll never be alone, not in that dark cold world or the one above where we face war and persecution.

She would know what he meant. If she chose to return to the other world, he would follow her. As much as he would love to retaliate against the Lycans for what they'd done to her, nothing was more important to him than Skyler.

She astonished him once again, her light glowing a little brighter, stretching more to finally touch his. He felt her immediately. She was there, her indomitable spirit, as determined as ever.

Again he took his time, uncaring that he was starving and that bringing her back from the land of the dead had taken its toll on him. He'd suffered every moment of the conversion right with her, yet now that she was alive and willing to return to her own body, the terrible exhaustion that had settled in him seemed to disappear.

His spirit escorted hers to her battered body. Skyler didn't hesitate as he expected, she simply united her spirit with her body, settling into her own skin with a small shiver. He stayed with her, afraid to leave her too soon. He'd been in three places, her body, his and the other world for far too long and was beginning to feel the effects of such a division.

I will not leave you, Dimitri, she reassured him.

He thought she whispered the words into his mind, but maybe he only heard what he wished. She was already fading, slipping into unconsciousness. Heart pounding hard, he checked her. Not death. She was ready to accept the healing earth.

He found himself back in his own body. Tatijana and Josef had removed the silver and the agonizing burn throughout his body was gone. He opened his eyes and looked around him, needing to see Skyler, needing to know he wasn't hallucinating, that she was really there and alive.

She looked so pale, so ravaged by the bullets, blood staining her clothing and even caught in her hair. But she was alive and she was beautiful. The soil beneath them had sunk, taking their bodies nearly a foot and a half down. Black loam, rich with minerals, had packed itself all around them, between their legs and even forming a thin blanket over them.

Again he heard the call of Mother Earth. He took a deep breath and turned his head, knowing Tatijana was close.

"You're back with us," she greeted. "You've accomplished what no other has done that I've heard of. You brought her back."

"It was a fight. She needs to go to ground."

"You both do. But first you'll need to feed."

He nodded. He knew she was right. Hunger beat at him now, stronger than ever. "Before anything else . . ." He looked around him, his gaze settling on Josef and Paul.

Paul lay on the ground, his expression set in lines of pain, but he made no sound. Josef sat close to him, and both were staring with apprehension at Skyler.

"She's alive," Dimitri announced. "Back with us, and I have you two to thank. You saved my life and then hers. I can never repay the great debt I owe you."

"She's alive?" Paul asked. "Really alive? She's not moving. She doesn't even look as if she's breathing."

"You've seen Carpathians slipping into rejuvenating sleep," Dimitri said. "I'll command her to sleep, ensure she doesn't wake until she's healed enough to get out of this place."

Paul pushed the hair back from his face and quickly averted his head, but not before Dimitri caught the sheen of tears.

"I didn't think it was possible," Josef admitted. His voice wobbled, but he refused to look away from Dimitri's penetrating gaze.

"You were the one who told me she wasn't dead," Dimitri reminded with a weary grin. "You said to go after her and I did."

"Yeah, I did, didn't I?" Josef said, a slow, answering grin pushing through the weight of his fear and sorrow. "But I honestly thought it was bull and you'd never be able to bring her back."

"It was all Skyler," Dimitri said. "She's strong. She found a way to stop herself, even in death, from moving too far away from me."

"Because she has such faith in you," Josef replied. He rubbed both hands over his face. "I never want to go through that again. Can you put her in a basement wrapped in Bubble Wrap so Paul and I don't have to worry about her anymore?"

"An excellent idea," Dimitri said.

Tatijana nudged him gently. "You need to feed and then go to ground. We'll be safe here for the time being. I checked carefully and there are no weak points that I can find."

Dimitri forced himself to move, to look around. The transparent structure allowed him to the see the Lycans, who appeared to be watching something other than the Carpathians. "Where's Fen?"

Tatijana put a restraining hand on his arm. Only then did he realize he had begun to struggle to his feet.

"Fen is backing Zev, trying to find answers. I'm only getting glimpses of what is happening. Sword fights, snipers, two Lycans battling for position of alpha in the pack, that sort of thing. I'd say he was busy," she replied.

Dimitri subsided, although he didn't like his brother out there alone with the Lycans. He had known many of them and liked them, but he didn't trust any of them anymore. "Did someone get word to Gregori that the prince may be in danger?"

"The moment Skyler died . . ." Tatijana broke off. "Everyone felt that terrible moment. She reached out to Francesca. Gregori will ensure the prince is safe."

Dimitri let out his breath. He couldn't think anymore. "Thank you for removing the silver from my body." He turned his head to include Josef. "Both of you."

Byron offered his wrist. "You'll need to be at full strength when Skyler wakes. We may have to fight our way out of here."

Dimitri took the offer, his hunger overcoming his need to see to everyone's safety. He couldn't do much in his weakened condition. He was careful not to take too much from Byron, no matter how tempting it was. He wanted the other males at full strength to make certain they could fight should the Lycans find a way in.

Vlad offered next. With the second feeding, Dimitri's body settled, the edge off just enough that he could gather Skyler into his arms, holding what appeared to be her lifeless body close. Tatijana blurred the background around them, making it impossible for prying eyes to see what he did next.

Waving his hand he opened the ground, taking Skyler deep, floating down into the very arms of Mother Earth. At once, even before he gave the command for Skyler to fall into the rejuvenating sleep of the Carpathians, the soil poured over them of its own accord, cradling them both in warm, loving arms.

Fen, Dimitri and Skyler are safe in the ground. Dawn will be breaking soon. We all have to follow them soon. Can you make it back to us? Tatijana asked. She kept the little catch out of her voice, the one that acknowledged she knew he probably wouldn't be with her throughout the day, but somewhere alone and in danger.

Zev's in trouble, Tatijana. The outer ring of Lycans have circled the inner ring. Those inside support Zev. The outer ring—and there are more of them—support Gunnolf. I think there's going to be a bloodbath here. I can't leave Zev to fight alone.

Don't get killed, Tatijana ordered.

Fen sent Tatijana reassurance, but he couldn't move from his position and he wanted Zev to answer him, to realize just how much trouble he was in. With an army of renegade Lycans surrounding the pack loyal to Zev, the situation looked grim for the elite hunter.

The sniper put his eye to the scope once more and Fen struck from behind, grasping his head and wrenching it around, breaking the neck. He plunged a silver stake through the heart, severed the head and left him there in the tree.

I can start picking them off, one by one, Zev, but there are a good number of them and we won't last forever.

The ferocious fight between Gunnolf and Zev continued. Gunnolf several times glanced up in the direction of the tree where the dead sniper was positioned, clearly expecting a shot to ring out. The large oaf of a Lycan maneuvering his way behind Zev had finally gotten himself in place. All Gunnolf had to do was drive Zev back and the other Lycan could kill him from behind.

Fen flinched when the two combatants hit the ground so hard it shook. They rolled, snarling and punching, tearing at each other. He cloaked his presence and used the doubled speed of both Carpathian and Lycan to cross the meadow and once again insert himself in the crowd.

Tatijana, this is going to go bad for Zev very fast. Those loyal to him are surrounded by Gunnolf's army.

What you need, wolf man, is a dragon in the sky.

True, but they have guns.

And we have shields.

The crowd pushed closer to the combatants, ringing the two males as they fought for supremacy. The great bulk of a Lycan surged forward with feigned eagerness. Up close, using his mixed-blood senses, Fen read *cold* and *calculating* in the closed-in energy field surrounding the assassin. This was a man used to committing assassinations. Killing Zev wasn't personal to him, but his job, a duty to perform, nothing else. He took pride in his work, and he wouldn't stop until Zev was dead.

Zev drove Gunnolf to the ground over and over, each time the other male tried to leap to his feet. The punches increased in strength each time Gunnolf refused to submit. Realizing he was in trouble, Gunnolf rolled away from Zev, attempting to conceal a small blade in his fist as he managed to get his feet under him in a crouch.

Those closest to him saw and reacted with a roar of rage. In a challenge fight, two males fought bare-handed. Gunnolf clearly wasn't following the rules. Zev feigned a kick at the knife hand and went in low, driving for Gunnolf's head. He locked his arm around the Lycan's neck and spun, bringing the head up over his shoulder behind him. Gunnolf hung there for a moment, but the crack was loud and his body stiffened and then went limp.

The crowd went silent as Zev dropped the lifeless body onto the ground. He palmed a silver stake and drove it down hard, directly through the heart of the fallen Lycan.

The crowd roared approval. Zev slowly straightened. As he did, the assassin made his move. He shuffled forward with others around him, gawking, seemingly trying to get a look at the dead body of Gunnolf. The moment he was close to Zev, his entire demeanor changed. There was nothing awkward about him. He was fast and smooth, keeping his knife low and covered with his fist, driving the poisoned blade straight at Zev's kidney.

Fen caught him from behind, twisted him around, his grip like steel, thumb digging into the pressure point of the wrist, exposing the knife and the assassin's intent. Zev spun around to face the killer. He caught the dagger as it fell from paralyzed fingers. Fen let the assassin go, and Zev stepped forward into the man's attack, plunging the silver blade into the heart.

A hot breath of fire swept over the crowd. Everyone looked up. There were three dragons in the sky, all circling around for a run at them. The lead dragon was blue, the neck elongated, stretched toward that outer circle of Lycans. Fire rained down, a steady stream that burned the fur on the Lycans' heads and shoulders.

Tatijana had learned from previous clashes just how high a wolf could jump. Her blue dragon was in the lead, staying high enough to keep out of harm's way, yet low enough to singe fur. The dragons circled the outer ring of Lycans, flames shooting down in long, steady streams. The Lycans broke formation, abandoning whatever plans they had to kill Zev's force.

The Lycans scattered, a few dropping to their knees to take aim at the impressive sight of dragons in the sky. They fired off several rounds, but the bullets seemed to bounce off the tough scales of the dragons. When the creatures flew over for another fiery pass, the rest of the Lycans took to the forest, sheltering beneath the canopy of the taller trees.

"I see you're still hanging around that woman," Zev observed. He hadn't moved a muscle when the dragons flew over, spraying the Lycan ranks with fire. "I can understand why you want to hang with her, but seriously, what does she see in you?"

Fen grinned at him. "I'm smart enough to always play the hero, unlike you, who seems to get into trouble every time you open your eyes."

"You like to play with fire, don't you?" Zev asked with a wry grin. He had warned Fen more than once that a relationship with a Carpathian woman was trouble—forbidden even. The council had decreed centuries earlier that all Lycans should avoid Carpathians so there was no chance of creating the dreaded *Sange rau*.

"Ha ha. You're very funny," Fen retorted. As far as Zev knew, Fen was Lycan. He might understand Fen's attraction to Tatijana, but he couldn't condone a union.

Zev nudged Gunnolf's body with the toe of his boot. "The really sad thing is, I liked him. I've known him for years." He looked up at Fen. "What the hell is going on?"

Fen nodded toward Gunnolf. "I'll ask him."

Zev shook his head. "It's too dangerous. I respect you as a fighter, Fen. I've told you that before. I can't understand why you're not running an elite pack, but questioning a dead Lycan, even for someone as strong as you, is not a good idea."

Fen shrugged. "One of us has to do it, and I'm more expendable than you are." And he had a lifemate, waiting to pull him back from the edge. It wouldn't be his first time extracting information from a dead Lycan. Zev *was* right, it had been dangerous, but Tatijana was powerful and she would never fail to pull him back. He had complete faith in her.

Zev shook his head and made a movement toward his lifeless opponent. Fen was there before him, grasping the head between his two hands. The Lycan became aware of him almost instantly and mentally fought him, desperate to protect his secret. Black hatred poured over and into Fen. Rage took hold, a violent, churning cauldron of such fury that Fen's body shook with it. The emotions of the dead wolf, still active in his brain, found a new home in Fen.

As if a great distance away, Fen heard Zev cursing, knew he'd drawn his sword and was close, very close. His hatred spread to the elite hunter like an infection. Why should he have to put up with the scout's orders? Why, each time Zev returned to the pack, did Gunnolf have to relinquish authority?

Zev was a traitor. He mingled with the Carpathians. He *danced* with one of them, clearly smitten. He'd allowed the woman to enter his mind, take his blood. Every member of the pack knew he was pining for her. He had even committed the biggest sin of all—he'd argued that there was a difference between Dimitri—their prisoner—and any other *Sange rau.*

Worse, Zev had sided with Dimitri and had even given him blood. The *Sange rau* should have died within three days. Everyone who had ever been sentenced to the *Moarta de argint* had succumbed to the pain and writhed and moved until the silver had managed to pierce their heart. Not once had there been a survivor beyond the third day, yet Dimitri had lasted over two weeks. Zev had to have been helping him.

The *Sange rau* was weak, dying. They had a chance to destroy the monster. It was the woman with him who had somehow, through a dark practice, managed to protect the abomination. Revulsion spread like cancer. A disgust and loathing like no other. They had the scent of her blood, it permeated the meadow and the very air itself. She had to die. Her very existence was an outrage to humanity. What if the *Sange rau* began breeding? They had to be stopped. It was a sacred mission.

Kill. Kill. Kill him. Kill her. They both have to die. Kill Zev. He should die with the monsters, the abomination. Kill them all. The chant was loud in his mind, echoing through his veins with a need and hunger that shook him.

Fen let the savage emotion wash through him, but he refused to stay there and wallow in it as Gunnolf wanted. The Lycan would trap him there or Fen would be forced to leave to prevent the intensity of the hatred and rage from consuming him.

The feelings of superiority helped. The emotion flooded his mind and Fen caught at the opinion and nurtured it. He was more than Gunnolf. More than Zev. He was Guardian, and this Lycan who wished to trap him for all time in the black mire of prejudice and hatred would not do so. Fen was too strong to be ensnared by the Lycan. Too intelligent.

He was ruthless, refusing to back down but searching through the memories to find a thread that would lead him back to Gunnolf's master. The Lycan reeked of fanaticism. His emotions were fiery, intense—and he believed in his cause with a single-minded purpose.

War. They had to wipe out the Carpathians to stop the spread of the mixed bloods. All Lycans who refused to join them, who frowned on the sacred code, would be wiped from the face of the earth as well. They were enemies of the great council—the great ones who had kept them alive and thriving for centuries. Those past moral compasses were slowly being forgotten or deliberately pushed aside by the new council who only wanted their own glory.

The zeal of devotion permeated every move and memory that Gunnolf had. It was difficult to find a single thread to get back to the one master who fed his extreme fervor. Fen couldn't stay much longer. The intolerance and radicalism was slowly eating at him, threatening to consume him in spite of his strength. He'd never encountered such vehemence.

It wasn't necessarily that Gunnolf was a bad man. He believed passionately that he was right. There was no other way, no other room for any other's beliefs. He would not only die for his cause, but would kill for it. Those who opposed him were the enemy and not fit to walk the same earth.

The vehemence and ardor of the fanatic turned everything to red and black. Emotions took hold, fighting to poison him, to spread that infection to every cell in his body.

Lifemate. The light to his darkness. All darkness. Nothing this ugly could ever touch something so bright. One word. One breath. That was all it took. He had complete faith in her to call him back from the brink of madness.

She was there instantly, pouring into his mind, lighting every dark place, pushing out the stench of fanaticism and hatred, replacing those intense, damaging emotions with her unconditional love.

He released Gunnolf's head, turning away, fighting down the terrible need to retch after being so consumed by the fervor of the Lycan's need to kill every living creature who did not believe as he did.

Zev swung the silver sword, slicing through the Lycan's neck, severing the head. There was a long moment of silence. "Was it worth it?" Zev asked quietly when Fen sank into the green grass.

At once Fen felt Mother Earth reaching for him, comforting him. He felt oily and dirty, shaking his head repeatedly to try to get Gunnolf's emotions out of his head. He swept his hand over his face and it came away bloody. Tiny beads of blood had pushed through his pores. Not a good thing. Lycans didn't sweat blood.

"You tell me," Fen managed to say. "This is all about the *Sange rau*. Gunnolf felt you were becoming too close to the Carpathian people and he had to act to save all Lycans from the damage that would do. The ultimate goal is to start a war between the two species. If they do that, then all Lycans would side with his faction—those who believe in the old ways—the strict code of morality—he used the term *sacred code*."

Zev sighed, wiped the blade clean and slipped the sword back into the scabbard before sinking rather abruptly into the deeper grass surrounding Fen. The laceration on his arm still bled, the wound all the way to the bone. "I'm going to pretend that I don't notice that the ground responds to you just as it does with Dimitri."

"Dimitri is my brother," Fen volunteered. He was through lying to Zev. They had a problem—a huge one. Either they were going to stop a war, or start one right there. "I was born Carpathian. I am *Hän ku pesäk kaikak*—Guardian of all."

"I'd like to say that comes as a huge surprise, but it doesn't. Tatijana is tied to you in some way?"

"She's my lifemate."

Zev's fingers played over the hilt of his sword. "I see. I'd cut off your head for you, but I'm too damned weak. You'll just have to wait for another day. How did you get this way, and when?"

"Over the centuries, it is easy to suffer severe wounds and need blood. Those I hunted with often gave me what I needed—and I did the same with them."

"That's why you were able to kill the *Sange rau*. You're more like they are."

Fen nodded. "Dimitri helped me. He saved both Gunnolf and Convel, but in doing so, they realized he was of mixed blood and they took him. Whoever is behind the movement to go back to this sacred code is the one trying to start a war between the two species. I couldn't stay in his mind long enough to get a name without risking infection."

Zev ripped a strip of cloth from his shirt and began to wrap it around his arm. "I've lost a lot of blood," he noted. "You may as well give me some. If I'm going to be strong enough in the future to hunt you down, I'll need to live through this."

"You risk becoming a mixed blood," Fen pointed out. "That's how Dimitri became a Guardian. There were times we hunted rogue packs and vampires together down through the ages. When wounded, we helped each other by giving blood."

"I fear it's a little too late to warn me," Zev said. He pushed a hand through his hair. "I became aware some time ago that there was something different gaining strength in me. I believe I have inadvertently become—or am becoming—the very thing I hunted for centuries."

Fen drew up his knees. The wound in Zev's arm had bled far too much. "I think Gunnolf used an anticoagulant on the blade of his dagger."

Zev nodded his agreement. "Lycans rejuvenate fast. At the very least, blood flow should have ceased. I'm bleeding out here." He gave an involuntary shiver, his body already growing cold. "Are you going to help or just sit there?"

"I'm calculating the odds that you might use one of the hundreds of weapons you've got on you, that you *didn't* use on Gunnolf, but should have." Fen's voice was thoughtful.

"I'm too damn tired to disarm myself so make up your mind," Zev said and lay back in the grass.

"Just know that hell is coming this way," Fen warned. "Your Lycans shot a young girl related to just about every powerful family that there is. Paul's family is every vampire's nightmare, and the boy was shot as well. Josef's family has already arrived, and when Dimitri rises again, he'll owe that boy. He'll hunt down every single Lycan who fired a weapon at those they perceive as children."

"I think you've more than conveyed the grave danger we're all in," Zev said dryly. He closed his eyes.

Fen sighed. "You know I'm mixed blood. I could call a Carpathian in to give you their blood. It might slow the process."

"Just give me your damned blood before I pass out."

"What a wuss," Fen said, matching the drollness in Zev's tone. He moved fast, though.

Zev was a man too valuable to be allowed to die. If he wasn't worried about the mixed blood then Fen knew the elite hunter was really in trouble. It would make sense, even if Zev knew he was close to the transformation, he would do everything he could to slow it down until the council ruled on the subject of the *Sange rau*—bad blood, versus the *Hän ku pesäk kaikak*—Guardian of all.

Fen tore at his wrist and pressed it to Zev's mouth. The danger in feeding a Lycan blood was they might become too fond of it. Lycans had forsaken the need for fresh blood and meat, embracing a civilized world, but it was impossible to tame a creature with a predatory nature. The savagery was there, lurking just beneath the surface, always threatening to overcome the hard-won shell of civilization.

Zev didn't seem to have any problems taking blood in the Carpathian manner. Fen knew that Tatijana had given Zev blood as well when he was gravely injured. More than once the Carpathians had donated their blood to keep this Lycan alive, but it wouldn't have been enough to cause the transformation. It was a slow process, happening over a long time of exposure, which meant more than once through the centuries, Zev had hunted with a Carpathian.

"You just want mixed blood because you took one look at a certain woman and all brain matter went dead," Fen accused.

Zev didn't open his eyes or stop feeding. *She did make an impression.*

12

The clash of swords rang throughout the room. Daciana and Makoce kept Rolf between them, while Lykaon and Arnau defended the other council members not—shockingly—from the Carpathians, but from other Lycans who suddenly turned on them.

They're trying to assassinate the council, Mikhail warned his warriors. *Choose your targets carefully.*

"Loyal Lycans," Rolf called out, "those loyal to the council, defend us, not from the Carpathians but from our kind."

Lucian cut down Lowell, the wolf who had tried to murder Francesca and Gabriel with one slice of his sword. Another Lycan stabbed a silver stake through the assassin's heart and sliced down with his sword to sever the head.

Gabriel thrust his lifemate to the back of the room, away from the skirmish. Zacarias leapt forward to close ranks, protecting the woman. He was everywhere, his expression never changing, reacting fast, so that it seemed each Lycan who cut down his own kind in an effort to get to a council member had to get through him or one of his brothers. Clearly, he directed his family, and they seemed to move together in a choreographed dance of death.

The Lycan faction that wanted the council dead were caught between their own kind and the Carpathians. Their bid to start a battle between species had failed when both sides kept a cool head and followed their leaders' orders.

"Lay down your weapons," Rolf commanded. "Your lives will be spared."

Not a single one of the Lycans who stood with Lowell and Varg obeyed; even knowing they would be killed, they increased their determination to get to a council member. Daciana took a vicious swipe across her stomach with a silver knife from Varg as he tried to get past her to Rolf. The sharp blade cut her open and the silver had to burn like an inferno, but she didn't flinch.

As the blade came at her a second time, she slammed her hand down on his wrist, sidestepping, trusting Makoce, her partner, to protect Rolf while she fought Varg. She knew him well, but he always had underestimated her. Lately, she'd noticed two of the elite hunters in their pack treating her just a little differently. Both Gunnolf and Convel had begun ignoring things she'd said, acting as if they hadn't heard her. They often walked away when she approached them.

Varg had the same attitude as Lowell. She should have brought the matter to Zev's attention, but she felt silly complaining. What had changed them? The differences had started long ago, but she hadn't really noticed until they'd become disdainful. They hadn't wanted her in their elite pack.

Using the Lycan's own momentum, she cut back with his wrist over his own shoulder, flipping Varg onto his back. He landed on the table of food Francesca had laid out for them and with a roar of rage, leapt up, throwing himself at Daciana. She had expected the move, counting on his new disdain of women fighters. She allowed him to slam her to the floor, his muzzle, as he transformed to half man and half wolf, snapping around her shoulder viciously.

In her fist she clenched a silver stake, aiming it upward. Varg's own body weight as well as the speed of his jump drove that spiraling stake straight through his heart. Her aim was perfect—as it always had been. She stared into his eyes, watching the life force fade. "That's right, hotshot. A *woman* defeated you. Go to hell thinking about that."

Zacarias pulled the body from her and extended his hand. She took it and leapt right back into the fray, leaving the Carpathian to slice off the head of the wolf.

The battle was over in a short space of time. A dozen Lycans lay dead on the floor. The Carpathian warriors stepped back, eyeing the remaining Lycans a little warily.

"I apologize for the behavior of my people," Rolf said, giving a formal bow. "We appreciate your help in dealing with the assassins. If you would excuse us, we will return to the inn. Our wounded need to be attended to, and the council members would like to make a few phone calls to see if we can get to the bottom of this treachery."

Mikhail swept his gaze over the remaining Lycans. If there was a faction of Lycans trying to start a war between the two species, he doubted if the twelve dead lying on the floor were all that remained.

This was a well-thought-out plot, Gregori, to make us look responsible.

I agree.

If the council members are assassinated on Carpathian soil there will be no explaining it to the remaining council members who elected to stay behind.

You and I both know the council is still not safe. Some of those conspiring against them are still alive. It would be ludicrous to believe all have been slain, Gregori pointed out.

"I mean no disrespect, Rolf," Mikhail continued aloud, "but I would prefer to send some of my men with you to ensure your safety."

Rolf gave a slight nod, indicating he wasn't opposed to the idea. He, like Mikhail and Gregori, had to have known that there were probably more assassins lurking among his guards, just waiting for an opportunity to kill him and the others.

Mikhail. Zacarias sent him a call along the common Carpathian path, which allowed Gregori to hear as well. *My family must set out now if we're going to make it to Paul before dawn. As it is, it will be close. Andre, Mataias, Lojos and Tomas have returned.*

Clearly, Zacarias was reminding him that there were others to take his family's place. Mikhail had known they would go. Still, it was troublesome. Zacarias was unpredictable. He wasn't a man to take prisoners or ask too many questions. If the Lycans provoked him, he would retaliate. There was no way to ask him to stay, not when Paul had been shot. Paul was his nephew, and no De La Cruz would leave a family member, especially a child, behind.

Mikhail had enough men to guard him and their women and children. He had no real excuse to keep the families of those that were in trouble in Russia with him. He knew Lucian and Gabriel Daratrazanoff would go as well. The combination of Zacarias, his brothers and the legendary twins was more than he would ever wish on his worst enemy.

Don't start a war, he cautioned. *The members of the council appear to have come here in good faith. Give us time to work this out.*

If a war has been started, Gabriel reminded him grimly, *the Lycans fired the first round.*

Emotions were high. There was no getting around that. He didn't know what he would have done had the Lycans attacked either of his children. He put his hand on Gabriel's shoulder. "Bring them home. All of them." He didn't care if Rolf and the other council members heard him. He wanted them to hear. They could see for themselves what his people were capable of, just by looking at them—seasoned, ancient warriors—every one of them. Let the council call their packs and warn them. There was no trap these men would be caught in.

He looked around him at the men and women. They were not volatile, or impatient. He couldn't even say that about Zacarias. They were steady, calm and deadly. *Do you understand what I'm saying? The children belong to all of us. Bring them home no matter the cost.*

The seven men looked at him, straight into his eyes—each one of them—and then nodded slowly. Mikhail lifted his hand. "Good journey and Godspeed."

Rolf shook his head with a soft sigh. "We have much to talk about."

Mikhail nodded. "We will talk, but our children must be brought home."

"Can you walk?" Fen asked Zev. He took a slow look around him. "Most of the Lycans have gone into the forest, or have retreated toward their camp, but a few remain. I believe those few are tasked with killing you. It seems you're an important man, Zev Hunter."

Zev didn't open his eyes, lying there in the tall grass, resting, waiting for his Lycan genes and the infusion of Carpathian blood to close the wound on his arm. He never took his hand from the hilt of his sword. "Being important has its drawbacks."

"Being the friend of an important man has its drawbacks," Fen said. He could feel the hair on the back of his neck raising. They were targets and the Lycans were armed with guns.

Tatijana, shield us. Zev has lost far too much blood. I need to bring him into the shelter.

You cannot. He is Lycan and no Lycan can pass.

It is the only way to save his life. He has Carpathian blood in him. How much I do not know, but he told me he feels the change already beginning.

It's a terrible risk.

Fen sighed. "You're really a pain in the ass, Zev, important or not. Here's where we stand. Tatijana is shielding us from bullets at the moment, but it won't last for long because dawn is breaking and we'll need to go to ground. You aren't safe with your Lycans without someone watching your back, until you're at full strength again, and even then, you're in danger."

"Is this going somewhere?" Zev asked, lifting his lashes enough to peer at Fen. "Because I figured that out all by myself."

"I can try taking you inside where no one can get to you, but if you don't have enough Carpathian blood, it won't work. We'll have to make a run for it and I'm not certain where to take you. I'll need to go to ground. Is there anyone you trust at this point? Trust them with your life?"

"They're in the Carpathian Mountains guarding the council. That's why they're there, because I trust them," Zev said. He tried sitting up, but a wave of weakness sent him back to the ground. "Get out of here, Fen. Go while you can."

Fen snorted his derision. "Tatijana's sister isn't here to see your heroics, so just stop. I'm going to try to bring you inside. You can rest and guard us while we sleep."

A faint grin softened the rough edges to Zev's face. "Now I see where this is going. I'm the one injured and you're going to bed expecting me to guard your sorry ass."

"That would be about right," Fen said with an answering grin that faded very quickly. "We have one fully human boy who would have to sit through the day alone. He's wounded, courageous and he'll stand, but the responsibility of guarding his father, uncle, my brother and Skyler as well as Tatijana and me, is a huge one for a kid."

Zev patted his sword. "No problem then. I can take on the entire Lycan world for you, with a kid no less, just so you can get your beauty sleep."

"My lifemate is Tatijana and you see what she looks like. I can't risk looking like I'm Dracula."

Zev laughed softly. "I don't know what that woman sees in you."

"Quite frankly, neither do I." Fen huffed out his breath. "You ready for this?"

"As ready as I'll ever be," Zev answered.

Once again he struggled to sit up. This time he made it. His face, weathered and tanned over the years, had gone pale. He looked as if he might be sick, but he forced himself to stay sitting upright, swaying a little.

"Give me a second and then we'll try standing."

"Once we're up, we've got to make it to the fortress," Fen cautioned. "Tatijana can only shield us from so many positions. If they put snipers in the trees . . ."

Zev nodded. "I feel them. They're surrounding us." He looked at Fen. "That's how I knew I was becoming something different. I felt the others sometimes when I shouldn't have. Lycans don't give off energy."

"They do, but they contain it," Fen corrected. "As your body becomes a Guardian, your senses grow even more acute."

If Zev was at the point where his awareness had grown to such an extent, it might be enough to allow him into Skyler's shelter. Weeks earlier they'd been in several battles together. Tatijana had given Zev blood. Other Carpathians had. It was possible those last infusions had pushed Zev into the actual transformation. No one really knew when it happened.

Going from Carpathian to Lycan was easier to know because the wolf was a dead giveaway. One slowly became aware of his presence. A Lycan already had the wolf in him. There was no way to realize what was happening until it was far too late. If Zev suspected he had become a mixed blood, he more than likely was.

Something smacked into the shield Tatijana had provided, a bullet splintering the transparent armor so that it spiderwebbed outward into a starburst pattern.

"I think we just ran out of time," Fen said. He leapt to his feet and reached down for Zev.

Zev was game, Fen had to hand it to him. He struggled up as Fen pulled him into a standing position.

"I'm good," Zev assured. "The dizziness is beginning to pass."

That was probably bull, but Fen wasn't about to argue. A second bullet joined the first, and then a volley rang out. He got his arm around Zev and they sprinted for the shelter. Fen heard the bullets hitting the shield from every direction. There had to be at least five shooters—all marksmen if the bullet patterns were anything to go by. Each would have been a hit in the head. Whoever was running Gunnolf's army had recruited some sharpshooters.

Once they reached the shelter wall, that rippling transparency that held out Lycans and bullets alike, Fen stepped back to allow Zev to go through first.

"What do I do?"

"You just walk through. If you make it, you're in, if not, I don't know what happens to you."

"You haven't been inside?"

"No, but Dimitri is in there and he's like us."

Zev took a deep breath, let it out and took a step. The wrench to his bones was horrendous, a twisting, yanking sensation ripping at him that drove the air from his lungs and seemed to pull apart muscle and tissue. His heart accelerated, beating so hard his chest hurt.

He would have pulled back but he knew Fen would stay with him, continuing to risk his life. They wouldn't stand a chance outside the fortress, either one of them. Not alone. He plowed forward while his cells screamed and his body felt torn into pieces.

Suddenly he was free of the sensation, falling to the ground, able to breathe again, his heart slowing to a more normal pace. He rolled over, coughing, pulling air into his burning lungs. He kept his gaze fixed on Fen. Fen had been mixed blood for centuries. He was truly half Lycan and half

Carpathian. There was no doubt in his mind that Fen experienced that same wrenching, tearing apart of his body when Fen fell to the ground beside him, breathing just as hard.

"Just who is this girl who managed to construct this thing?" Zev asked.

Fen would have laughed if he could get enough air to do so. His body still felt as if it had been jerked in a thousand different directions. How did one describe Skyler? "She looks like an innocent angel. That's how my brother describes her. Her name is Skyler."

Zev brought his hand to his forehead. "I met her. In the forest. She was lost, she said. She had a sprained ankle and couldn't find her way back to her camp."

Fen did laugh then. He couldn't help himself. "She totally suckered you."

"She's human."

"She's Skyler, Dimitri's lifemate. The Lycans took him, and she took him back."

Byron approached them with a hint of caution. He smiled, but his eyes were flat and cold. "Tatijana told me you were bringing him inside, that he was injured very badly. Does he need blood?"

"Yes," Fen said. "And I want Tatijana to take a look at his wound."

"I'm right here," Zev reminded. "I'm Zev. Zev Hunter. It seems my own people want me dead so Fen invited me inside."

"I'm Byron Justicano," Byron introduced himself. "Josef is my nephew. He and Paul helped Skyler rescue Dimitri."

"Brave kids," Zev said. He nodded toward Paul, who lifted a hand and gave him a faint grin. "Good actors, too. They fooled me." He huffed out his breath in disgust. "I carried that girl all the way back to her camp. She never gave herself away, not even for a second. I was suspicious, of course, because of the timing, but not of her, just that the camp was there when we'd made certain no one would be in the area."

Fen and Byron exchanged a small smile. It seemed it wasn't only the Carpathians who had underestimated Skyler, Josef and Paul.

"I'm sorry she's dead," Zev said. "She flung herself in front of Dimitri just as a dozen Lycans fired. Most of the Lycans obeyed when I told them to stand down, but Gunnolf's faction was determined to kill Dimitri. She just got in the way."

"She's not dead," Byron said.

Zev frowned and looked around him. The shelter had transparent walls and ceiling, he could see the occupants easily. Tatijana and another man seemed to be working on a younger man's wounds. He had spiked blue/black hair and was very pale. Paul lay on the ground close to him, looking back at him. But there were no others in the fortress besides Byron and Fen.

"Dimitri put her in the ground to heal," Fen explained.

"I thought she was human," Zev said, puzzled. "You are confusing me, and I'm already a little disoriented."

"She will rise fully Carpathian," Fen clarified. "Dimitri was able to save her."

"After seeing her wounds, I don't see how it was possible," Zev said. "Even from a distance, she looked dead or dying."

"Her father is Gabriel Daratrazanoff," Fen said. "Her adopted father."

Zev's breath caught in his throat. If it was possible for him to go any paler, he managed it. "The legend? Gabriel and Lucian? The twins? Every Lycan young or old has heard of them. I don't suppose there's any hope that they aren't heading this way, because where one is, so is the other."

"None at all," Fen said. "Gabriel and Lucian are hoping to make it before dawn."

Zev closed his eyes. "This is getting worse by the minute."

"I haven't told you the worst," Fen cautioned.

Zev groaned softly. "Just get it over with, Fen. What else?"

"Have you heard of a Carpathian by the name of Zacarias?"

Zev's eyes flew open. He even sat up again. "Are you kidding me? No Lycan goes near South America if they can help it. It's been done, but rarely. No one wants any part of him or his brothers. Of course we've heard of him. He's the boogeyman we scare our children with."

Fen indicated Paul with his thumb. "That's his nephew."

"Fen." Zev brushed his hand over his face. "How are we going to prevent a war? You know not every Lycan here at this camp is guilty. You know that. All of them, me included, were duped into thinking the council had sentenced Dimitri to death by silver. In a way it made sense, they could deny they had killed him because he would move continually until the silver reached his heart. Technically, they could claim he killed himself."

"That's bull," Fen snapped, his eyes beginning to glow. He even felt his teeth lengthen just a little.

Zev frowned at him. "Don't go vampire on me. I'm just explaining how it appeared from a Lycan point of view. I tried calling the council members but none of the phones worked. Looking back, Gunnolf and his followers must have been jamming the cell phones."

"You would have let him die," Fen accused. "My brother."

Zev nodded. "I thought about killing him myself, to stop his suffering," he admitted. "I have a sworn duty to uphold the rulings of the council whether I agree or not." He drummed his fingers on his leg. "Truthfully, I considered, for the first time in my very long existence, going against them. Not only was the ruling unjust, but it seemed suicidal. Council members were negotiating with Mikhail for an alliance—and they wanted it. They were in favor of it. Or most of them."

"Most?" Fen echoed.

"Majority rules on the council, and all Lycans abide by the laws. The alpha enforces the laws within individual packs, but no pack would ever go against a council ruling."

"I guess I should be glad you didn't kill him," Fen said.

"I would have asked him first. He lasted too long, so I figured he had a powerful reason for staying alive, one that transcended that kind of pain. He worked at remaining still, which meant he didn't want to die. I found traces of silver on the ground below him and realized he had to be pushing the silver out through his pores. He was completely wrapped in silver chain from head to toe, so that made no sense."

"Skyler," Fen said. "That girl—woman," he corrected.

"Who would have thought that innocent-looking child could possibly wreak such havoc and completely disrupt a takeover by some fanatical group within the Lycans?" Zev said.

"You do realize," Fen pointed out, "Gunnolf and Convel had to be working with someone else for a long time to put a takeover in place and when we stumbled across the same rogue pack heading for the Carpathian Mountains, we actually walked right into their opening move."

Zev nodded. He smiled up at Tatijana as she came to his side. "It's good to see you," he greeted her. "Thanks for saving us out there."

She smiled back at him and sank down into the grass, taking his arm to inspect the damage. "It's getting to be a habit. We can't have anyone killing you, Zev. My sister wouldn't be too pleased. She's hoping to get another dance with you sometime."

"She probably doesn't remember my name," Zev said. "But it's kind of you to say so."

Tatijana laughed. "Silly man. Your name is probably the only one she does remember. She's not very social."

Fen gave a small derisive snort. "The lengths you go to, getting yourself hurt just for a little female sympathy. You know, Tatijana, he really is far faster than he lets on and he could have prevented the knife from slicing him open. He was just hoping your sister would show up and kiss it all better."

Zev sent him a warning glare. "I'm still armed to the teeth, you bastard."

Tatijana shook her head, amusement in her eyes. "You two are awful." The smile suddenly faded from her eyes leaving her, serious-looking—and a little worried. "Zev, this cut is all the way to the bone. There is some kind of poison at work here I can barely detect. I can check it out if you allow me to, but I'll have to do so the Carpathian way."

Zev shrugged. "Apparently, I'm nearly half Carpathian already. I may as well learn how to do the healing the way you do. And it isn't like you haven't done it before."

Tatijana didn't wait, but shed her body, her spirit becoming white energy, moving into Zev to try to find the poisonous compound spreading through his system. A scratch along the bone from elbow to wrist showed where the slice had been. The tip of the blade had cut into the bone and she could see tiny, minute blisters, like little droplets all along the scratch. The globules clung to the bone, but spread along the scratch and beyond. The deadly beads crept their way up his arm, following the bone.

She had to eradicate every single tiny trace of that poison. More, throughout the tissue and muscles of his arm, she could see evidence of a blood thinner and anticoagulant. Gunnolf had been prepared to challenge Zev to a fight for pack leader and he'd come ready to murder him. As long as the thinner and anticoagulant saturated his arm, there would never be healing. They could give him blood over and over and it wouldn't matter.

She moved back into her own body, her eyes meeting her lifemate's, her expression grave. "Gunnolf planned to murder you, Zev. There are at least three compounds left behind in your system to kill you. Your Lycan blood is trying to regenerate tissue and muscle and your Carpathian blood is trying to remove the intruders, but you won't be able to do so on your own."

Fen reached out and took her hand, threading his fingers through hers. "We knew it was bad," he told her gently. "Nothing has stopped the bleeding. Can you get it out of him? I have some skills as well. Between the two of us, we should be able to clean him up."

"Vlad can give him blood," Byron said. "Once you stop the bleeding."

"I can, too," Paul volunteered.

"If he gives me blood, would I be considered part of Zacarias's family?" Zev asked. "That might be safer."

"I think Gabriel is going to be one who comes in like the avenger," Byron said. "I'm getting a few rumblings. Razvan, Skyler's birth father, is on his way with Ivory, his lifemate. They just reached out to me. None of them are happy about any of this. Razvan informed me that there was an assassination attempt on the members of the council."

Zev swore under his breath. "This is far worse than I thought. This isn't just happening here then. I was afraid of that. There are council members in a safe location as well. It's a precaution taken when there is danger to any of them. That way there is stability should any one of them die. There is always a continuity, older members with any necessary new members. Were any of them killed or injured? I sent my best people with them."

"Fortunately, cool heads prevailed," Byron informed him. "Razvan wasn't there when the assassins struck. Apparently, they tried to kill Gabriel and Francesca as they turned away. Zacarias stopped them, and both Mikhail and a senior member of the council persuaded the others to stand down after a brief but apparently ferocious battle. Twelve Lycans were killed, but they appeared to be for the other side, whatever that is."

Zev swore again. "I need to get there. If a single council member is murdered in the Carpathian Mountains, whoever is behind this has won." He half sat up as if he might go right then.

Fen held up a restraining hand. "Did you forget the poison? The anticoagulant? Were you planning on taking a body along with you to supply you with blood?"

Zev looked pained, rolling his eyes, shaking his head. "When did he get to be such a comedian, Tatijana?"

Tatijana pinned Fen with a glare, although amusement lurked in her eyes. "I have no idea, but you really are in trouble here. Sober up, wolf men, both of you, we have to get this arm taken care of." She looked over her shoulder. "Vlad, I'm going to need you. He's still losing too much blood."

"Did she just call us *wolf men*?" Zev asked, one eyebrow shooting up.

"Were lucky it wasn't wolf *boys*," Fen pointed out. "She throws that in upon occasion."

"Zev, lay back and just relax," Tatijana advised. "Fen and I are both going to work on you together." Her eyes met Fen's. "You go after the poison, and I'll work on the anticoagulant."

Fen nodded, knowing she was particularly worried about the wound. There was no keeping anything from Zev. He knew, probably because he'd been wounded a thousand times in battles. He was a wolf with a body that regenerated quickly. If his arm refused to stop bleeding and he felt weaker even after the infusion of blood, he would know.

Fen shed his body, becoming white, healing energy, his spirit traveling quickly into Zev. The blood of both Lycan and Carpathian was present, although the Lycan was still stronger. Probably, had they not given Zev so much blood over the last few battles, he would have gone several years without realizing he was slowly transforming.

He moved through the body, inspecting the bones for any trace of poison. Tatijana had provided a clear image in his mind, but already the tiny blisters were spreading from the arm to the shoulder and along the collarbone. He went to work extracting the poison, slowly driving it out of the body. Some of the venomous dots were so minute, it was difficult to spot them.

He felt Tatijana's presence, but only the heat of her energy, as she began her own work on separating the anticoagulant from the tissue and muscle surrounding the wound. Someone had worked on the formula to coat Gunnolf's knives and daggers, probably his sword. Fen should have thought to collect the weapons so they could find out exactly how it was done.

If the faction of Lycans who wanted war were using poisonous weapons, then the Carpathians and any allies had to quickly find a way to counteract the formula used. He pushed more of the beads from Zev's bone, driving the venom from Zev's body. There was no trace of silver in the poison that he could find, so he was positive a Lycan had worked out the compound. An enemy would have added that component as well, but a Lycan, even a treacherous one, would not want to get anywhere near silver.

He studied the line of drops. He'd seen something similar recently. Had a mage helped with the chemistry required? The idea of a mage and Lycan alliance was, frankly, quite terrifying. Once the crimes of Xavier, the high mage, were known throughout their world, most of the other mages had scattered, not wanting to be associated with him, but that didn't mean they weren't around. Xavier had exploited them and murdered them for his own experiments just as he had every other species. No one had been sacred to him—not even his own flesh and blood.

Fen had no idea of time passing as he meticulously removed every tiny drop of poison from Zev's body and then went back to work at healing from the inside out. Tatijana had already done her part and was working to repair the enormous slice as well. They finished together, and nearly fell into their own bodies.

"He needs blood," Tatijana told Vlad. "I'll give him more just before we go to ground."

"I want to make certain all of you understand that when you rise hungry tomorrow, and you will, especially after donating all this blood," Fen said, "that most likely anyone you come across will be Lycan. Ingesting their blood will eventually change you. Mikhail talked to all of you about the problems."

"He didn't talk to me," Zev said, and lifted his head to feed from Vlad's extended wrist.

"We don't have enough answers to all the questions we asked," Fen said honestly. "Like how a woman is affected, or a child, should we choose to have one. How a Carpathian can convert another. More, we continue to mutate the longer we live with such a mixture."

"You people should come with a warning label," Byron told Zev.

Zev flipped him off. Behind them, Paul snickered and Josef began to laugh. Flipping others off was not an accepted practice among the Carpathian ancients, or even those considered old, like Byron.

Byron stifled a grin and turned around with a sober, very serious expression. "Josef, I believe Tatijana told you to go to ground."

Tatijana stirred, and Josef quickly waved his hand to open the ground before she could reprimand him. He floated down and the rich soil quickly filled in over him, covering him completely.

Byron shook his head. "That boy is certainly courageous, but I have to tell you, Vlad, he's a handful."

"We never know what he's going to do or get into." Vlad sent Paul a quick frown over his shoulder. "We were happy when he was hanging out with Paul and Skyler because we thought—wrongly—that they were a good influence on him."

Paul sent him a smug smirk. "We pulled it off, though. All of us."

"I wouldn't look so happy," Vlad advised. "Your uncles are on their way. They'll be here before dawn."

The smile faded quickly from Paul's face. "Uncles? As in all of them? Rafael? Zacarias, too?"

Vlad nodded his head. "*All* of them," he confirmed.

Paul groaned, covered his face with his hands and lay back. "I wish I could go to ground. Maybe for twenty years or more. I don't think my sister is going to get me out of this one."

Zev politely thanked Vlad, trying hard not to laugh at the boy's dismay. The kid had fooled him and that wasn't an easy thing to do. "So it's you and me, kid," he said. "We'll be facing them together. The Lycan, who they blame for all of this, and you, because you outsmarted us all—even them."

"You might not want to mention that part," Paul said. "It isn't like they have the best sense of humor. I'm not certain I've ever actually seen Zacarias laugh. We might want to take our chances in the forest."

"You're surrounded by snipers," Fen pointed out. "That wouldn't be the best idea."

"Better a quick bullet than Zacarias tearing my head off and using it for some kind of macabre weapon, which he's quite capable of," Paul said.

"In the old days they used to cut off heads and put them up on spears to warn everyone what would happen to them if they angered the great lords," Fen said with a sly glance at Zev. He nudged him with his foot. "Your head would look mighty pretty perched up on top of a spear, staring into the woods as a warning to the Lycans who shot young Paul there."

"Fen!" Tatijana sounded shocked. "You're getting more bloodthirsty by the minute. Go to ground and behave yourself."

"He doesn't know the meaning of the word," Zev said, a little piously. "But if Paul's uncle does cut off my head, Fen, it will be up to you to keep him from starting a war. You'll have to talk sense into him."

Fen scowled at him. "I doubt anyone can do that, even me, and when my brother rises, it will take all of you to talk sense into me."

He couldn't quite suppress the rage that rose every now and then when he thought of his brother being tortured in the Lycan camp. He would never have found Dimitri in time to save him. If Skyler and Dimitri didn't have such an incredible, intense bond between them, his brother would have died an unspeakable death of sheer agony.

Zev's faint smile faded. "I *am* sorry, Fen."

Fen shrugged. He knew that Zev's years of service to the council had conditioned him to follow orders and carry out commands. He was the council's defense. Their eyes and ears. They trusted him implicitly, and he had earned that trust the hard way. He couldn't blame Zev. The elite hunter had even confessed to him that he'd considered going against the orders of the council, or even ending Dimitri's suffering himself by killing him.

"We're not at war yet," Fen reminded softly. "I find it difficult to understand how Dimitri could have been treated that way during wartime, let alone when we're at peace."

"I found it equally as hard to understand," Zev admitted. "I found myself realizing I couldn't uphold the council's rulings if I didn't believe they were just and fair." That realization had shaken the very foundation of his existence, his every belief.

Fen took a deep breath and let it out. "I'm sorry. None of this is your fault."

"Maybe. And maybe it is. I should have known something was very wrong when I couldn't reach the council for answers." Zev shook his head. He was tired. Exhausted actually. He wanted to close his eyes and go to sleep. "You don't have to stay up and keep me company. Paul and I will take turns keeping watch. You need sleep every bit as much as I do."

Fen looked over at Paul.

Paul nodded, looking far too old for his age. "No problem, we've got this," he agreed.

13

The sound of muted weeping filled his mind. Dimitri's eyes snapped open. He looked down at the woman in his arms. Skyler lay curled into him, looking smaller than ever. Tangled vines, bright in color, had wrapped them up in a cocooning blanket of living flora. Beneath the cover, both of them were naked, needing the soil to heal every wound. He caught glimpses of her body, white porcelain, marred now by several bullets tearing into her flesh.

Skyler's hand moved against his neck, the smallest of gestures, a mere brushing of her fingers, back and forth, betraying nerves.

Immediately he waved his hand and commanded the soil to open, to allow in air and the night. A cool breeze instantly fanned their faces. Overhead stars glittered and the moon glowed a soft yellow behind lazy clouds. He shielded them carefully from any eyes or ears, wrapping them in a warm cocoon of privacy.

He brushed back the hair from her face, removing all residue from both of them, while allowing the living blanket to remain. He wanted her to be comfortable with him, not aware both were naked beneath that twisting layer of vines.

"What is it, Skyler? Are you afraid?"

Her long lashes lifted and she looked up at him. The moment their eyes met, his heart leapt in his chest. She had always been stunningly beautiful to him. As she'd grown into a woman, her Dragonseeker blood became much more apparent. The heritage ran strong in her, giving her ever-changing eyes, dark now, with the tips of her lashes wet.

"I can't be afraid with your arms around me, Dimitri," she answered. She turned her face up into his neck, rubbing like a cat over his skin.

There was a little hitch to her voice that caught at him. "What then?" He lifted her chin with one finger and bent his head to kiss away the path of tears. "Why are you crying?" He trailed more kisses, featherlight, to the corner of her mouth.

He felt her tremble, the smallest of shivers, but she didn't pull away from him, rather she turned her face subtly so his next kiss brushed across her lips. "*Csitri*, we're safe now." He kissed her gently, demanding nothing. Asking for nothing. Simply telling her he loved her and holding her close were all that mattered in that moment.

Her lips curved into a faint smile beneath his. "We're safe as long as we stay here in the ground, my love. I believe my father and uncle are somewhere close."

"You have nothing to fear from your family, Skyler," Dimitri assured. "Without you, I would be dead. As my lifemate, you had every right to do what you did."

"I see. So if our daughter ever . . ."

"She would be locked in her room for the rest of her life," he interrupted. "Our child will be timid and want to cling to her parents."

She laughed, turning her face back up to his throat. Her soft lips brushed kisses over the three loops of burns circling around his throat and neck. Her tongue stroked caresses there, following the path of those silver chains. He knew why she'd awakened weeping. For him. Not for herself. She wept for him and the suffering he'd gone through.

He slid his hand into her hair, bunching the thick silken strands into his fist. "Beloved. It is done. We're both safe and together. Paul and Josef are alive and will heal nicely. Both will be heralded as heroes . . . well, after their families and Gabriel give them lectures and try to put the fear of death into them. Which won't work because they've already faced real death."

She laughed softly. "That's so true. Josef said he'd have to go to ground for a hundred years. But they came with me. Both of them. I have amazing friends." Her lips went back to feathering kisses in between the silken stroking of her tongue.

A rush of heat sent small flames flickering through his bloodstream. Every muscle tightened, became aware of the woman in his arms. *His* woman. With every movement, her bare skin brushed his intimately. He caught enticing glimpses of her breasts, the rose-tipped peaks and the rounded, very feminine curves.

They were bound now, soul to soul, and even a man as strong-willed as her legendary father could never separate them again. He didn't try to hide his body's reaction from her. He respected Skyler too much to pretend anything.

She lifted her head to look down at him, her dark eyes shimmering with ever-changing color. "I want you to want me, Dimitri."

He gave her a faint smile. "That's a good thing, Skyler," he assured her. "Because I do. It's natural to want to make love to the woman you're in love with."

"You'll need to be patient with me. I want you to teach me."

He framed her face with both hands. "It's okay to be afraid and to tell me when you are."

She nodded her head. "I know. I know you now. I know I'm safe with you." She leaned closer to him. "I missed you so much all the times you were gone. I have no idea when I began to really know I love you, but it's been a very long while now and growing stronger every moment."

"Thank you for coming to rescue me," he said simply, meaning it. She'd saved them both, giving them a chance at a life together. "You saved my life."

"I discovered, when I couldn't touch your mind with mine, that there was no Skyler without Dimitri." Her eyes went soft, that dove gray that he was especially fond of. "I suppose it was more of a selfish act than a heroic one, tracking you down."

He laughed softly. "Only you would think that."

The amusement faded from her eyes. "We need to find a place where we can be alone, Dimitri. I know I can do a better job of healing you, both inside and out, but not here. Not with the Lycans surrounding us and a mob of Carpathian hunters watching our every move."

"No one is watching us now, *sívamet*," he assured. "We're deep underground. Even should the Lycans crawl on the roof of the shelter above us and look down, they could not see us lying here. I have created a shield that no eyes can penetrate."

She collapsed against him, as if that small spurt of energy had gone and she was exhausted again. "I am trying not to blame all Lycans, Dimitri. Intellectually, I understand it was a few individuals, but I still want to kick them all."

Her confession made him laugh. "Kick them all?" he repeated. "You're priceless, *csitri*, you really are. I had something much more lethal in mind."

"Dimitri!" She turned her head up to look at him again. "How perfectly wonderful. You are capable of wanting revenge. I felt a bit guilty that I'm not a better person."

"I don't think you ever have to worry that you need to live up to me," he assured her. "I've got plenty of faults."

"Like?" she prompted.

He leaned in to kiss her. This time his mouth was firmer, a little more insistent. He stroked his tongue along the seam of her mouth and then traced her soft, full lips.

"I'm not telling you. You have to find those things out for yourself."

Skyler pressed her mouth to his, a soft little teasing kiss, brushing her lips back and forth over his, as if she was testing the sensation. Her tongue stroked over his lips, following his lead, tasting him a little tentatively, but growing bolder as she deepened the kiss.

His hand tightened in her hair, holding her still. She startled, a deer caught in a poacher's light, but she didn't pull away from him. Her eyes widened, went soft. That beautiful shade of gray, indicating she was relaxed and happy.

Loving with such intensity was terrifying—wonderful—but terrifying. He would never be the same. He would never have that perfect control of the emotionless warrior. He would forever need this small woman who held his life in the palm of her hand.

He took possession of that perfect mouth, so warm and soft and inviting.

His fist bunched in the thick silky strands of her hair, anchoring her to him, his first aggressive, controlling move, his first demand. He waited a heartbeat, giving her the chance to pull away, but she remained motionless, a small bird with a fluttering heart, holding still, waiting.

His mouth coaxed hers to open for him, more of a claim then he'd ever made on her before, more insistent. He counted his heartbeats this time, afraid she'd panic and pull away, but her trust in him overcame any fears she had and she opened her mouth to him. He took control, sweeping inside to claim her as a woman, a lover.

The rush was hot and instant, an electrical charge sizzling through his veins, snapping along his every nerve ending. Love for her encompassed him, infused into his very muscle and bone, so that his need of her, rising like a tidal wave, melded with desire. There would never be a way to separate the two emotions, that devastating urgent hunger for her, and the overwhelming love.

His brain threatened to short out. His heart raced, nearly burst in his chest. Every muscle hardened as blood rushed hotly to his groin. Her mouth was sweet, tangy and hot, a haven of pleasure he wanted to visit over and over. He tasted passion, not just his, but hers as well.

Her need met his. Rose with his. Matched his. Her mouth was untutored, and that made it all the sweeter for him. She wasn't hesitant, but maybe a little shy. Nevertheless, she followed his lead willingly, and when he touched her mind, there was no fear, only the need to give him the same pleasure he was giving her.

He kissed her over and over, allowing himself to drown in her passion, stealing her breath, giving her his. This soft, seemingly fragile woman had saved him with the core of steel running through her and the incredible feminine power she wielded. She had given him life once, a reason to live, and then a second time, when there was only agony and no reason to hope, she had come for him.

He lifted his head to look down at her, drawing air into his aching lungs. Skyler pulled back, looking at him with her enormous eyes, her lashes fluttering down to cover her expression, but not before he caught the stunned, dazed look. "Kissing is so amazing," she admitted, settling into his arms again. "I think I could get addicted to it quite easily."

"I am already addicted to kissing you," he said, his tone low. "So let's clarify, just in case we run into one of those not so nice things about my character. Kissing *me* is amazing. It would be very deadly for anyone else."

A little shiver went down Skyler's spine at his tone. He looked as calm and as familiar as ever—her perfect Dimitri—but there was something in the timbre of his voice and in his eyes that told her he was very serious.

"Silly man, who else would I be kissing?" Before he could answer, she laughed softly. "Except Paul and Josef and my family. They don't count."

Paul and Josef were her family. He'd accepted that a long time ago—and it hadn't been easy. Once he'd looked into her mind and really sorted out her emotions regarding both boys—no—men now, the relationship between them had never bothered him again. In fact, he'd grown quite fond of both, regarding them as she did—siblings more than friends.

"We need to feed," Dimitri said. "We're both weak."

She shuddered. "I don't think I could just creep up on someone and sink my teeth into their neck, Dimitri. It's not that I haven't thought about it a lot, and Josef gave me his blood several times, but to just take someone's blood that I don't know . . ."

"That's my job right now, not yours," Dimitri said. "I believe your father and uncle are waiting for you to rise so they can make certain you're alive and well. They'll give us blood. They're ancients and their blood is powerful. It will aid in healing. We'll both need to be strong in order to get out of here. The Lycans really do have us surrounded. I've scanned the forest and they're out there, waiting for all us to make a move."

Skyler stroked her fingers over the blanket of vines. "We're very lucky to have such help when we need it. Both of us were pretty banged up."

His heart contracted. He never wanted to relive those first few moments when she had flung her body in front of his to prevent the silver bullets from hitting him. His arms tightened around her, nearly crushing her, but she didn't struggle, just accepted his need to hold her close.

"Don't ever do that again, Skyler. Can you imagine what it was like for me thinking you were dead?"

She turned her head to look up at him. "Yes, Dimitri." Her voice was very firm. "I *can* imagine, seeing as how I did think it was possible you were dead."

"I'm sorry, *csitri*." He brushed another kiss over the top of her head. "I didn't want you to connect with me because I knew you'd feel my pain."

"Rather that than believe you were dead," she said very soberly. She waved her hand and the blanket over them retreated. "I know I have to face my father and his disappointment in me for lying to them. I'd rather just get it over with."

"You know I planned a wedding for you. A human one. The kind you talked about with your friends, with Gabriel walking you down the aisle. I wanted to bind you to me in front of them, and make that ritual special for you," Dimtri reiterated. "It was important to you to include your family and I did want that for you."

She got to her knees, wincing, as her body protested, telling her she wasn't anywhere near healed. Kneeling up beside him, she leaned over him, framing his face, her hair falling around her like a silken cape. "Our ritual was special to me. I asked you, Dimitri. It was important to me that we be bound together. You didn't dismiss me as a child. You listened to what I had to say. You told me your concerns and trusted me to listen to you. In the end, in spite of your reluctance, you did as I asked. That made our binding special for me."

He frowned at her. "Has it been difficult to have so many people telling you that you're too young for everything?"

She bent her head to his, brushing her mouth carefully over the chain loops burned into his forehead. "You have no idea how annoying it can be. Actually, it was Josef who made it easier for me. He finds it amusing that everyone around him dismisses him as a child. I developed a sense of humor about it—most of the time."

She frowned, studying the perfect image of a chain burned so deep into his skin. She brushed a fingertip over it, tracing the chain completely around his head in a circle. She could feel where the chain had burned into his skull.

I call to you, Mother, bring forth your might,
As I seal these paths that would bring pain and blight.
I call to aloe, so green and cool,
Bring forth your life's blood again to heal.
Each line I trace, may it fade day to day,
Taking all that causes pain away.

Her soft voice faded and she leaned forward to trail more kisses around the chain loops, and use the healing saliva as she traced the link with the tip of her tongue.

Dimitri found her ministrations not only soothing, and extremely intimate, but sexy as well. She had actually straddled his body, kneeling up, his hips between her thighs, her breasts pressed close to his face as she administered to him.

He brought his hands up to gently cup the soft weight of her breasts in his hands. He felt her quick intake of breath. She went still, but she didn't move. Her heart fluttered beneath his hand. She leaned in again, pressing her breasts deeper into his palms as she kissed his eyes and down his nose.

She took her time to find his mouth, using a tantalizing roundabout path that included his ears and his jaw before moving back to his lips. He brushed his thumb over her nipple. Featherlight. Immediately he felt her reaction, the shiver, the heat, the flush of her body, her startled eyes jumping to meet his gaze.

"Kiss me, *sívamet*. I want to get to know your body. I'm not asking anything of you, this is not the time or the place," he whispered, "but you are mine. This beautiful body is in my keeping. I need to see every wound. I need to know every curve. Everything that makes you gasp with pleasure and wince with fear."

Her eyes searched his for what seemed an eternity, although she hadn't stiffened or gone tense. She slowly linked her fingers at the nape of his neck and leaned forward to take possession of his mouth.

He kissed her deeply while sensations poured into him, igniting a flash fire in his every nerve ending. Kissing her over and over, wanting her lost in those same sensations, he began to explore her body with his hands. He mapped out every inch of her gently, the pads of his fingers going over her skin as if he was reading braille. The long line of her back. Her small rib cage. That tucked-in waist and those flaring hips. Her firm bottom that seemed to fit perfectly in his hands. Her thighs, and calves. Even her feet.

Dimitri took his time, exploring her body, careful not to make a single demand, simply familiarizing himself with her. Her breasts were very sensitive. She gasped each time he tugged or rolled her nipples. He licked at them, using a broad flat stroke of his tongue, as his hand slipped up her thigh to the growing heat between her legs.

She made a small sound that was somewhere between fear and excitement. He lifted his head to look into her eyes, keeping his hand pressed tight against her mound.

"Kiss me again," he whispered. "Just let yourself feel. I'm not going to do anything but learn your body."

She obeyed him instantly, finding his mouth again, kissing him a little frantically. He kept his hand still as he kissed her over and over waiting for her to relax into him again.

That's my girl, he whispered into her mind. *I meant what I said about taking your body into my keeping. You'll always be safe with me. Just let yourself feel, not think. You're with me, and I'll cherish and protect you for all time.*

He felt her settle, her body warm against his. The junction between her legs had grown hot and gone damp. He moved one finger in a slow, lazy circle, kissing her mouth and then her chin, down her throat, back to that soft swell of her breast. Every movement he made was gentle and nonthreatening, but designed to heighten her senses.

His tongue teased her left nipple, stroked and licked. His teeth grazed her and then he drew her nipple into the heat of his mouth. She gasped, arched, pushed deeper into him. At the same time, he pushed his finger into her tight, scorching hot sheath. Her muscles clamped down tightly around him, as if she grasped him with a tight fist. He nearly groaned aloud at the feel of her body's reaction to his small invasion.

You're all right. Just feel how good it feels when you're with someone who really loves you. You're my world. My everything. For me, you'll always be the most beautiful, desirable woman in the world. I love you and I love your body. I want to make you feel like this, but more.

I'm not certain I can take more. She sounded frightened.

What is it?

I feel a little out of control.

That's exactly what you should be feeling. When we do make love, csitri, we both will be a little out of control, but we'll be safe with each other.

Slowly, reluctantly, he withdrew his finger, took another gentle pull on her breast and then lifted his head. She was wide-eyed, a little dazed, her breathing just a bit ragged, and her body was totally flushed. He kissed her again, this time long and slow.

"You're so beautiful, Skyler. Just like this. I don't think there will ever come a day that I'll be able to resist you."

She wrapped her arms around his neck and held him close to her. "You surprise me all the time, Dimitri. You always seem to know exactly what to do. You make me feel beautiful and special." She paused, squirming a little.

"What is it, *sívamet*?" Dimitri coaxed gently. "We've always been able to tell each other everything."

"It's a little harder, face-to-face with no clothes on," she admitted. She pulled back just enough so their eyes could meet, blushing a deep shade of red. "I really wanted you. I was afraid, but I didn't want you to stop."

"I didn't want to stop either," he confessed, "but even though no one can see or hear us, I don't want half the Carpathian population around either."

"You even made me forget about them," Skyler acknowledged. "My mind took off and went somewhere else."

Dimitri laughed softly. "Lie back and let me take a look at these bullet holes. They're still pretty raw looking. Do you hurt?"

"A little," she conceded.

His hands were on her body, a little possessively, forcing her to lie back while he inspected the damage done to her. "These injuries are going to take some time to heal. Between getting shot and the conversion, I think your body needs to spend some time in the ground."

"But not here," Skyler said. "I don't know how long this shelter will last. I've never tried such a thing before. Tatijana might be able to tell us." She smoothed back his hair with loving fingers. "I'm not the only one who needs a lot more time to heal."

He brought her hand to the warmth of his mouth, kissing her knuckles tenderly. "I'm just fine. A little blood and I'll be up and running."

She rolled her eyes. "I see. That manly man thing you've mentioned in the past. I guess I just haven't gotten the concept. Worse, Paul and Josef now say the same thing."

He grinned. "See? Even they know."

Skyler shook her head. "I hate to burst your manly bubble, but they say it about themselves."

Dimitri did his best to look deflated, just to get a smile out of her. Tension was beginning to wear on her—the thought of facing her father and uncle. She was worried about her mother and younger sister as well.

"Let's go face the music and see if anyone has any ideas on where we can go and how we're going to get there," he suggested.

Skyler pressed her lips together and gave a small nod. "I'll need clothes."

"Have no worries, *sívamet*, I'll make certain everything is taken care of."

Dimitri clothed her in comfortable jeans and a soft, long-sleeved shirt. She kept shivering, although she could control her body's temperature. He took his time, braiding her hair by hand, giving her a little extra time to sort out in her mind what she was going to say to her father.

"I'll be right beside you," Dimitri assured her. "You know I would never allow anyone to get ugly with you."

"Gabriel isn't like that," Skyler said. "He'll be disappointed . . . not angry. I hated lying to my parents. They didn't deserve it, but I knew they would have tried to stop me." She turned her head to look over her shoulder at him as he tugged at her hair. "Nothing, *no one* could have stopped me, Dimitri."

He stroked his hand down her braid. "I know. Not even me. That's just one of the million reasons why I love you. You scare me to death with your courage, Skyler, you really do."

She smiled at him. "I told you, it wasn't courage, it was selfishness. I wasn't about to live without you."

She could turn him inside out without trying. His heart had gone into some ridiculous meltdown. She took the breath from his lungs, made his blood surge hotly and found a way to make him feel the most intense, overwhelming love he hadn't even known could exist.

There was nothing he could say to her, no words to express how, over the last three years, she had changed his life so completely. She'd given him purpose. Love. A reason to exist. She made every dark day he'd suffered over the centuries disappear. She made every brutal, ugly kill worthwhile.

Skyler. There was no other woman like her. A lump in his throat threatened to choke him. He forced air through his lungs. "Let's do this." His emotions were too raw, too intense. At moments like this one, he didn't trust himself to be alone with her. He wanted her to come to him gradually, to see that a physical relationship was simply another aspect of sharing their lives together. Body. Mind. Heart. Soul.

He hadn't considered that his gentle initiation would throw him into a firestorm of need or that every moment in her company would increase his love for her and only add fuel to that fire.

"You'll need clothes, too, my love," she pointed out gently, stroking her hand down his bare chest. "And don't think I'm not going to spend a very long time on these wounds of yours the moment we're alone and in a safer place."

The intimacy in her voice, that soft, almost husky note sent fingers of desire teasing down his spine, testing his control to his limits. He knew she would use her mouth on him, on each of those chain links from his neck to his ankles. His body shuddered with pleasure at the thought.

Dimitri waved his hand to don his own clothes, making certain both of them were immaculate as he wrapped his arm around her and floated them toward the opening above them.

He wasn't looking forward to facing her father either, but he wanted to see Fen. Fen had tried to be polite and not touch his mind, not interrupt his time with Skyler, but they'd always looked out for one another and Fen needed to see that Dimitri was alive and well.

Of course, he wasn't all that well. His insides felt raw and sore. He was far weaker than he'd imagined he'd be or he would have given Skyler blood. They both needed the safe haven she'd spoken of, a place to heal and be alone.

Gabriel and Lucian stood shoulder to shoulder some distance from where Skyler and Dimitri had rested in the ground. They seemed to be studying the western side of the forest carefully, but the moment the couple surfaced, they swung around, sensing their presence.

Gabriel immediately strode toward them, Lucian a step behind. Skyler started to run to her father, but it was impossible, she was too weak. She had to stand, waiting, Dimitri's arms holding her upright, for her father to reach her.

The moment he did, Skyler went into his arms. "I'm so sorry, Gabriel," she whispered. "I would never have put you and Francesca through such an ordeal if I felt I had any other choice."

Dimitri found her choice of words intriguing. He found himself admiring her all the more. He knew she was genuinely sorry for what her parents had gone through, thinking she was dead, but she was also taking a stand, signaling to her father that she was grown up and making her own decisions.

Gabriel's hard hold on her had to hurt, but she didn't wince or try to pull away. Her father kissed the top of her head. "We thought you were dead, Skyler. All of us. Everyone. Finding you alive is a miracle."

Lucian removed her gently from her father's grasp. "You scared the hell out of us, girl," he reprimanded. "Meaning no one can possibly get angry with you now that you're alive."

Skyler hugged her uncle. "That's a relief. I was worried I might be locked in my room for a millennium."

"Gabriel couldn't lock you in your room for an hour let alone a millennium," Lucian pointed out.

Even as her uncle teased her, the legendary warriors had their gaze on Dimitri. He didn't flinch. He'd never been a man to be intimidated, but he suddenly wished he was in a little better shape. He felt Fen come up on his right side. Big brother playing the badass. Fen could look intimidating when he wanted, and right now he was staring the twins down.

Skyler extracted herself from Lucian's arms and leaned into Dimitri, deliberately, he was certain. She kept her smile as she wrapped on arm around Dimitri's waist. He felt the slight trembling in her body.

"I asked Dimitri to claim me before I rescued him. I was afraid if I wasn't successful, he would die. I would have chosen to follow him and I would have been terrified without our souls being bound together." She looked her father in the eye when she told him.

Gabriel began to shake his head as she spoke.

Lucian put a hand on his shoulder. "It is done, brother. There is nothing to be done for it now. She's taken the matter out of all of our hands."

"He could have refused her." There was a warning in Gabriel's tone.

"Would you refuse your lifemate?" Lucian asked softly. "She was right to do as she did. Dimitri was in trouble and she went to him. She's his true lifemate, there's no denying it."

"There was every chance I wouldn't get to him in time," Skyler said. She reached out a hand to her father. "I can't live without him. You know what that's like. If something happened to Francesca . . ."

Gabriel shook his head again. "Don't say it. Don't think it."

"Daddy," Skyler said, for the first time sounding like a lost child. "I had no choice. You have to see that and understand."

Dimitri stirred, every protective instinct rising fast. His heart actually ached for her. Skyler needed reassurance from Gabriel. She had done the right thing. All of them knew it, but her father didn't want to concede that she was old enough to make her own decisions. He didn't want to let the child go and acknowledge that she was a woman.

Dimitri gathered her closer into his arms, sheltering her body against his. Going openly against Gabriel ran the danger of putting Skyler in the position of defending her father. Still . . . he wasn't about to allow anyone, even her father, to make her feel so terrible and guilty. Skyler had chosen to save her lifemate. She had been mortally wounded in the process and had undergone the conversion. She desperately needed her father to understand.

"No one else could find him," Fen said before Dimitri could speak. "Not even me. Whatever they have together is something very special."

It took a great deal of discipline for Dimitri to stand there silently and allow others to plead their case to Gabriel. He respected the legendary warrior, but he wasn't afraid of him, and he didn't feel he owed him an explanation. More, he wanted to lash out and tell the man to see Skyler for who she was, not the frightened child Gabriel had taken in, loved and nurtured.

The walls around them suddenly shimmered, nearly folding in themselves. The ground shivered under their feet and above them, the ceiling seemed to fall and then recoil back into place.

"We don't have much time," Tatijana said. "We have to leave tonight—soon."

Don't leave your daughter hurting when you know she did the right thing, Lucian advised his brother. *You should be proud of her. She did what no other could do.*

She's my baby. Our baby. Francesca's and mine. Our first. You know what her life was like. There was true pain in Gabriel's voice. *First I give Francesca the news that she lives, and I promised to bring her home, and now I must tell her she's gone for all time. We had so little time with her. I feel cheated.*

You feel fear for her. You cannot control her world or keep her out of harm's way. That's your fear, Gabriel. Every father must face it. Look at Dimitri. Really see him. You haven't even looked at him. What he went through—for her. To stay alive for her. What other man would suffer such a thing?

For the first time, Gabriel allowed himself to look at his son-in-law. His kin. Dimitri's forehead and neck had the links of chains burned into his skin, nearly to the bone. He could see one layer that had been wrapped around the forehead and three loops around his neck.

His entire body bears these marks. Tatijana and Fen told me that inside his body, every organ and bone was burned as well. He was starved for over two weeks—hung on meat hooks and swung from a tree. He stayed alive—for her. She would have followed him and he knew it, Lucian persisted. *This is an ancient hunter of exceptional skill. All know his reputation. Now you see not only his strength and determination, but his love for your daughter forever burned into his body for all to see.*

Gabriel brushed his hand over his face. He shook his head. He knew he was being unreasonable. Skyler was in good hands. Dimitri obviously loved her, it was there on his face. He might not be ready for Skyler to grow up, but somewhere along the line she'd done so, maturing into her own woman, gaining confidence and making her own decisions. He couldn't fault her for that. He knew, as a parent, it was the very thing he wanted for her.

He stepped up to the couple and clasped Dimitri's forearms, Skyler in between them. "Welcome, son. And thank you for saving her life. Few could have accomplished such a thing. Her spirit was so far from us, neither her mother nor I could find her."

Gabriel looked down at his daughter. "You made us very proud, Skyler. No one would ever have conceived that you, Paul and Josef could accomplish what all of us failed to do. Mikhail sent out search parties, but no one was able to find a hint of the trail."

Skyler circled his waist with her arms and laid her head on her father's chest, the tension slowly draining away. "I'm grateful you understand that I had to find him."

Gabriel kissed the top of her head. "I do." He glanced over his shoulder at the silent couple standing behind him. "I think there are others who wish to greet you and make certain you're alive and safe. They've gone hunting this morning and can provide both of you with blood."

Behind him, Skyler's birth father Razvan stood tall and straight. He'd been the most hated man besides his grandfather Xavier, before it came out that he was imprisoned as well and Xavier had used his body to commit unspeakable crimes. He was her father, yet he didn't know her. Razvan's blood, both Dragonseeker and mage, ran in her veins.

Skyler had inherited her concentrated power from this man. The woman beside him was Ivory, his lifemate, keeper of wolves. She stood beside Razvan, close to him, yet able to move easily and quickly should there be need to fight. Her wolves traveled like tattoos on her body, watching her back, and now half the pack guarded Razvan as well.

The two were considered skilled, dangerous fighters. They rarely were around other Carpathians, but hunted vampires relentlessly.

Skyler's hands tightened around Dimitri's. She'd always pushed aside this part of her life, unwilling to face it, subconsciously viewing Razvan as a participant in the evil Xavier had done. She'd been sold to a man, both her mother and she, by the high mage. That man had sold her to others for money.

"You don't have to," Dimitri said.

"No." She lifted her chin. "I do."

14

"It is best if we sit." Dimitri took charge. Skyler was swaying with weariness. He needed to sit as well. Both needed blood. "But Skyler wishes to greet her birth father."

Gabriel and Lucian stepped away to give Razvan and Ivory privacy, such as could be had in the close quarters of the transparent shelter.

Razvan crouched down in front of his daughter where Dimitri had helped her to sit in the grass. Ivory placed her hand firmly on his shoulder in support of whatever might happen.

"I was afraid the world had lost you," Razvan greeted.

"You came," Skyler said. "Even though we have barely talked, you still came."

"You are my daughter. I may not have had the pleasure of raising you, but you will always be my flesh and blood. No one will ever harm you and escape our punishment. We would hunt them to the ends of the earth."

Dimitri smiled up at Ivory in greeting. "Skyler has Razvan's fierce nature. She was quite willing to take on all the Lycans after seeing what they did to me."

The tension drained from Ivory's body and she smiled back at him. "We've come bearing a gift for you, for both of you, if you would accept it."

"Just coming is gift enough," Skyler said. She pushed back a few strands of hair that had escaped the thick braid. Her hand trembled.

"You need to feed," Razvan said. "Both of you."

"I'm not certain I can do it by myself yet," Skyler admitted, looking back at Dimitri.

"There's no need," Ivory said. "Razvan can aid you, and I'll give Dimitri blood. Later, the others can as well. At the moment, the De La Cruz brothers are hunting. They should be back very soon."

At Dimitri's alarmed look she smiled. "Discreetly. They said they'd be discreet." She extended her wrist toward Dimitri. "I offer freely."

Razvan didn't hesitate. He waved his hand toward Skyler to calm her, to distance her from what would take place. It would allow her to take his blood without real knowledge so she could take what she needed to survive. She had plenty of time to get used to taking her own food, but for now, to expedite her healing, it would be better to just allow her to feed without distress.

Skyler knew the moment Razvan's mind reached for hers and tried to take control. She'd always known when Josef or her parents had done so. She knew she needed to allow him to do so, to give her consent. Before, she never would have trusted someone mage born, not after what had happened to her, but this man had held out against impossible odds and he hadn't turned vampire or succumbed to the terrible temptation of power his grandfather had dangled in front of him. He had endured endless torture and had accepted the hatred of everyone who knew him with stoic resolve.

He was much like her beloved Dimitri. He didn't ask for understanding or plead his case. He simply accepted and walked away if shunned, but he would fight fiercely for those he loved. He was loyal and courageous and he could always be counted on.

She looked at the man who was her birth father for the first time through accepting eyes. She let go and allowed him entry into her mind. His touch was gentle, and it was over in an instant—she blinked and found herself stronger.

Dimitri had already politely closed the small wound on Ivory's wrist, giving her a slight bow from the waist, although they were seated in the grass.

"Thank you both," Dimitri said. "Your blood will aid in our healing."

Razvan smiled at the couple. "We did bring you a present of sorts, a gift to celebrate your becoming lifemates. We knew the moment we became aware Skyler still lived," he added by way of explanation. "Although, of course, it is a responsibility and therefore must be your choice to refuse or accept with no ill will on our part."

Dimitri and Skyler exchanged a long glance. Skyler's heart began to pound with excitement. Ivory and Razvan were considered eccentrics among the Carpathian people. More than anything, they loved wolves and ran with their own pack—not wholly animal and certainly not Lycan. These were wolves Ivory had accidently turned Carpathian. Such a thing was forbidden of course, but she'd taken responsibility for them and kept them in line.

Dimitri had spent centuries protecting wolves in the wild, advocating for them and providing land for them to hunt and live without fear of humans killing them. He had done so in the beginning to provide a sanctuary for his brother when he was injured in battle, but over the years, he'd purchased lands in various countries to provide safe preserves.

Ivory and Razvan would know how hard Dimitri fought for the wolves in the wild and they would know of all her studies, gearing her to aid him in his chosen fight. She held her breath, her eyes shining, she was sure, with her excitement. She just *knew*.

"We brought wolf pups. They were born nearly two years ago and are not from our pack. Our wolf pack found them, the adults had been torn apart, leaving the pups to starve. They were weak and we . . ." Ivory broke off and looked to Razvan for help.

"We saved them the only way we could. Our pack rarely asks for anything and we couldn't refuse them. The vampire mistook the pack for ours. We'd been hunting him for some time," Ivory continued. "I—we—felt responsible. We inadvertently led the vampire right to them. He wiped out the pack and slashed, but didn't kill the pups, leaving them as bait for us."

"I take it his plan didn't work out in his favor," Dimitri said, his voice going grim.

"No, he was brought to justice," Razvan assured. "And we acquired four more pups. A female and three males. We thought, under the circumstances, they would be best placed with you. As much as they're a part of our family now, we realized we couldn't allow our pack to get that large."

Skyler gripped Dimitri's hand. She was actually trembling with her excitement, hardly able to contain it.

"We thought the two of you would be perfect to care for them," Ivory confided. She rubbed her hand over her thigh restlessly.

Razvan reached over and placed his hand over Ivory's, stilling that small movement, comforting her. She was offering them part of her family, pups she'd raised, and loved.

Skyler could see the faint patchwork scars running through Ivory's skin. She was beautiful in spite of all those scars, radiant, knowing she had Razvan's unconditional love. Skyler looked at Dimitri, at the chain links burned into his skin. She would take away the blackness, and even out the pitting over time, but his scars would be there, his badges of courage, just as Ivory's were.

And she would love him. Nothing could ever change what she felt for Dimitri. The intense emotion for him would only grow with time—if that were possible.

"They're trained to adhere to our skin and watch our backs," Ivory explained. "They'll do the same for you. They just look like large, intricate human tattoos if anyone sees them."

"You have to allow them to hunt for food, but control what they choose to eat. And you absolutely have to be in control at all times," Razvan explained. "You can't allow them to run over you or you'll end up having to destroy them as you would a vampire."

Ivory nodded solemnly. "The two of you are the only ones we considered. Would you be interested? If you are, we can share information with you now and give you the pups when you're both feeling stronger. I'll train you, Skyler, to run them."

Skyler tried not to be disappointed. She wanted her own wolf pack that moment. She had always loved the idea of Ivory's famous wolf tattoos. *Dimitri?* She tried not to influence him. It was their decision together, not just hers. She knew he would listen with an open mind to her reasons and she wanted to be able to do the same for him.

His laughter was soft in her mind, filling her with an odd tingling sensation, with a small rush of heat. *Skyler.*

That was it. Her name. She sent him a look from under her lashes, one she usually reserved for Josef. *Are you mocking me?*

Teasing you. Just a little. We're getting the wolf pups. How could I possibly say no to a gift like that? You would never stop arguing with me.

Discussing. I was totally prepared to be reasonable and listen to you and then show you all the reasons you were absolutely wrong if you disagreed.

Dimitri burst out laughing. "Skyler Rose has a spine of steel. Yes. Yes with thanks. There are no words to express our appreciation of such a rare gift. We *both* want them."

Skyler leaned toward Ivory. "Thank you for the amazing offer to train me. I certainly accept. It would be an honor to get such an experience. I've always envied you for your wolves. They're so beautiful."

"But deadly," Ivory reminded. "They hunt the vampire with us. The pups have already hunted as well. Our adults share knowledge with them and they know what to do. You'll never be able to have a home in a city or even a town, not with your pack."

The shelter around them trembled. The western corner folded over. Once again the ground shifted beneath them.

"Our fortress is destabilizing rapidly," Dimitri said. "And the De La Cruz brothers have returned."

Skyler took a deep breath. "I'm not certain I can fix it. I can try, but . . ." She trailed off. She glanced over the other Carpathians, who had formed a loose circle and were discussing how to leave without starting a war. She could feel eyes watching them and she shivered, knowing they would have to leave their temporary sanctuary and once again face the Lycans.

"We should join the others," Razvan suggested. He reached out his hand to his daughter. "I know you've grown up with Gabriel and Francesca, and they're your parents. I would never want to take anything from them, but we do want you in our lives, Skyler."

"I love Gabriel and Francesca with all my heart," she admitted. "Without them, I wouldn't be here. They showed me what love was, what a relationship could be—should be. They also taught me that love is endless, that we have the capacity to love many people and it never takes away from those already in our lives."

She looked up at Dimitri and then made her confession in a little rush.

"When Tamara was born, I have to admit, I was a little afraid I'd be pushed aside. I wasn't Carpathian and I had a lot of problems, but that never happened. Tamara enhanced all of our lives, mine as well as Gabriel and Francesca's. Becoming closer to the two of you would never take anything away from Gabriel and Francesca."

"I would like that," Razvan said.

Skyler could still feel that little space between Ivory and everyone else but Razvan. She was very protective of her lifemate, used to others shunning him. Skyler leaned over to touch Ivory's hand, wanted to connect with her. "I feared my relationship with Razvan," she admitted, "not because I thought he was a criminal or horrible, but because he was mage. I didn't want to be mage born. The idea of that scared me to death."

Ivory frowned. "Why? Not every mage is out for power like Xavier. How could you know to fear mages?"

That was a good question. Skyler found herself matching Ivory's frown. Somewhere, deep inside, was a memory that slipped away faster than she could catch it. Her heart accelerated and she tasted fear in her mouth. She'd closed the door on that memory. Even cracking it open just an inch brought a terrible panic so that she could barely breathe.

Dimitri immediately wrapped his arm around her shoulders and drew her back against him. "You've embraced being mage. What could be so alarming that your body reacts with such anxiety when your mind is comfortable with the knowledge of who you are?"

"You don't have to remember," Razvan said. "Not for me."

"But Ivory's right. I spent my childhood in the human world. Granted, I was around monsters, but they were human monsters. How would I have developed a fear of mages? How would I have even heard of them? Even after Gabriel and Francesca adopted me, I was very sheltered for years. I certainly never ran across a mage."

"You've blocked something out," Ivory said. "Your reaction to your birth father wasn't normal. Most girls would have been curious, especially when he showed interest."

Skyler looked up at Dimitri. "I want to remember. I want to know. Can you find the memory for me?"

"If you want me to find it, Skyler," Dimitri assured. "I'll do it."

"I've faced every monster in my life. I can't imagine what's buried in my memories that would give me such an aversion to mages—to my own birth father. I've shared everything I can remember with you. I don't mind you knowing this, too."

Dimitri shook his head. Skyler was brave to allow him into her mind, exploring her memories when she knew what he would find. He knew about her past. He'd certainly shared dark nightmares with her. He'd seen the ugly things a sick individual could do to children—to her—but going into her memories and reliving such moments was an altogether different thing.

He didn't wait, preferring not to drag out her nervous tension. He wrapped his arms around her tightly, pulling her back against his chest, sheltering her protectively as he breathed her into his lungs. She opened her mind to him easily. He took the time to be astonished at how adept she was at merging with him. Their connection was so strong sometimes he couldn't tell where she started and he left off.

He sorted through her memories quickly, going to her childhood, trying not to see those nightmare times and the things done to her by depraved men. He had the urge to hunt them down, one at a time, and dispose of them.

I believe my uncle Lucian and my father have already done so, although I'm not supposed to know. There was humor in her voice.

He followed the memories down to her toddler years. There was her mother. She looked hauntingly like Skyler. A beautiful young girl, barely a woman herself. Her laughter was so like Skyler's. She sat beside her young daughter and absently began to make the rain dance, just by flicking her fingers toward the drops.

The two of them—mother and daughter—sat together very close, on a narrow plank with a single blanket which her mother had wrapped her child in to keep her warm. There were bars on the window and a chain around her mother's foot. Skyler's mother entertained her by creating music with the rain. She even whispered little rhymes to her daughter, helping the little fingers make the rain dance as well.

This, then, was where Skyler's gifts had begun to be so powerful. She'd been trained by the games her mother had played with her. Small insects suddenly poured into the room. Skyler stiffened, but she didn't cry. Her mother thrust her behind her, a finger to her lips.

"No matter what happens. Say nothing. Don't ever speak to him. Don't ever let on you can do anything at all extraordinary. Promise me. On my life, promise me."

The little toddler nodded her head solemnly.

A man burst into the room. Not Xavier, but someone Dimitri recognized from long ago, someone who seemed to lurk in the rooms where Xavier taught his classes to the more gifted. He strode into the room, lifted his hand and knocked Skyler's mother so hard she fell across the bed. He caught Skyler and dragged him to her.

"You little brat. This is the last time I come here. If you can't give him what he wants, you and your mother will be sold." He withdrew a knife.

Dimitri watched Skyler's mother, unable to bear seeing the toddler as the knife sliced through her little arm. She made no sound at all. Not one, as if she was mute. Skyler's mother tapped her thigh and danced her fingers toward the drops. She was the one to make a sound, drawing the mage's attention. When he turned, the drops of rain crept in through the bars on the windows and mingled with the blood seeping along Skyler's cut.

My mother saved me from Xavier, Skyler told him. *He didn't think the Dragonseeker blood in me was strong enough so he sold us. I didn't speak, so they thought me useless to them.*

Even as a toddler Skyler had impressive control. What baby wouldn't cry when an evil stranger cut across her arm with a knife? Dimitri wondered how that could be, but then when he went to examine the child, he realized her mother had taught her to retreat into a place in her mind no one could follow. It was how she kept her daughter safe.

"Who is that bad man?" Skyler asked her mother.

"He is mage, baby. Never go near a mage."

My mother warned me to keep me away from mages. That memory was so vivid when you pulled it up, yet I buried it deep. I want to remember everything I can about my mother. She pressed her head back against Dimitri. He made her feel safe when she looked into her memories. *Thank you.*

"Razvan, forgive me for asking," Skyler ventured, "but do you remember anything at all about my mother?"

He looked regretful. "Xavier possessed my body. I could see and hear what was taking place, but I couldn't interfere. I was pretty far gone by that time. Seeing what he was using my body for was worse than physical torture. I couldn't help the women he seduced. Of course he made certain they were fertile. I knew what was in store for them and their children, but I was completely helpless to stop it. Mostly the women ran together because, to stay sane, I tried to separate myself."

Skyler nodded. It was understandable, when terrible things were being done to her body, she had retreated into her mind in order to save her sanity, but still, she had wanted to know more about her mother. She retained glimpses of her, small little vignettes that at times she feared she'd made up.

Dimitri nuzzled the top of her head. *She was real. She loved and protected you as best she could. And then Gabriel and Francesca came into your life and now Razvan and Ivory. You are loved, csitri. Very loved.*

"One thing I do remember," Razvan said, "was how excited he was to find your mother. She was a powerful human psychic. Extremely powerful. He couldn't believe she was human. He said she was descended from the Incas and the line was extraordinary and very pure. He raged for months over the fact that the child produced was useless to him, and he wanted to punish your mother and you for disappointing him."

Skyler took a deep breath. Xavier had found a perfect punishment, selling them into the sex-trafficking world. She closed her eyes briefly, snuggling deeper against Dimitri. He felt solid, a wall of muscle and sinew, always to be counted on.

"Life certainly changes, doesn't it?" she asked her birth father. "One moment you feel there is no hope, no way out, and the next, the entire world opens up for you."

Razvan reached for Ivory's hand. "That is the truth, Skyler. You and your friends achieved the impossible rescuing Dimitri. If we manage to avoid a war with the Lycans, it will be a miracle—and due to you. Had he died, Mikhail would have had no forgiveness."

"I had no idea he sent out a rescue party," Skyler admitted.

"Although," Dimitri said, "you should have known Fen would come for me."

Skyler nodded. "But he would have been too late. You couldn't reach out to him." She traced the burn along his forehead, the links that had prevented him from telepathy—other than with her. She'd been lucky they had such a strong connection or she would have lost him. "I have good friends. Paul and Josef came with me without a thought for their own safety."

"*We* have good friends," Dimitri corrected. "I'll never forget what they did for us." He looked over at the two young men, sitting side by side in the circle of warriors discussing the upcoming escape from the collapsing shelter.

Josef looked happier than Dimitri had ever seen him. Josef hadn't expected any family members to come for him, and the fact that both his adopted father and uncle had come immediately had an impact on him. He'd run free, going his own way and often stirring up trouble with older Carpathians. It hadn't occurred to him that in spite of his differences, he was loved.

On the other hand, Paul had known the De La Cruz family would come if he got in trouble. They worked with him, teaching him how to fight vampires, working on the skills needed to run their impressive empires—many cattle ranches—in South America. They relied on him to keep his sister Ginny safe while they were in the ground. Paul was part of their lives and under their protection.

Dimitri sighed, looking at the grim faces of the Carpathians. They knew the little fortress was disintegrating, and the Lycans knew it as well. He, like the others, could feel eyes watching them. He could detect the wolves in the swaying branches of trees as well as the brush along the edges of the forest. He didn't see how they could avoid a fight.

"We should join the others," he said. "They're planning our escape out of here. Lycans are difficult in that they come at you as a pack and they're lightning fast. If we're supposed to avoid killing any of them, as Mikhail wishes, retreating without actually fighting is going to take a miracle."

Skyler leaned toward Ivory again. "I'm so excited and happy that you offered us such an amazing gift as the wolf pups. I really look forward to having them."

Ivory nodded. "Razvan and I discussed it for a long while. I knew better than to save them. We can't have Carpathian wolves running around without control, but it threw me back to the time when I returned from the hunt and found my pack annihilated by the vampire. For a few minutes there, I'm not certain I was entirely sane. I exchanged blood before I thought about what I was doing. Then I couldn't just leave them. Razvan was understanding and helped me with the conversion, but both of us knew, we couldn't keep that many wolves. Our pack is established. These four need their own."

Dimitri found himself smiling. His body hurt like hell and already, even with the transfusion of ancient Carpathian blood, he was exhausted, but the thought of the wolf pups being a permanent part of their lives was exciting.

"Do you think that with my mixed blood, my wolf so close at all times, such a part of me, that the pups will take to me?" he asked.

Skyler sobered. "I didn't think of that. We'll both be mixed blood at some point."

Ivory shook her head. "The wolf pups should be able to relate even faster to you both. They'll sense the wolf and accept you as alpha far more easily than we'd first anticipated. That acceptance is everything. The fact that you, Dimitri, knew so much about wolves influenced our decision. We are certain you could easily run a pack."

Dimitri tightened his arms around Skyler, feeling her joy. She needed joyful moments like this one and he knew it. She'd gone through far too much in a short period of time. She hadn't wavered for a moment in her determination, but still, the last few risings had been extremely difficult on both body and mind. The tremendous gift of the wolf pups had come at the most opportune time.

"Thank you both again," Dimitri said sincerely. "You found the perfect gift for the two of us and we're grateful. The moment we're healthy, we'll come to you."

"Just send word," Ivory said, with another quick glance toward Razvan, as if she in some way might offend him. Her privacy was legendary. Few, if any, knew the way to her home and clearly, even with them, she wanted to keep it that way.

Dimitri couldn't blame her. She'd been betrayed and chopped into pieces, and scattered across a meadow in the hopes the wolves would devour her. Ivory had risen stronger than ever, a fierce fighter, every bit as skilled as her male counterparts. Razvan had quickly caught up with her expertise and they had become the scourge of vampires. Even master vampires avoided them.

As the four of them rose, Dimitri and Skyler a little shakily, Skyler sent Gabriel a grateful look. *No father could be better than you, Gabriel. Thank you for bringing me peace with Razvan. You're such a generous man, and you taught me that trait. I hope to always make you proud to call me daughter.*

There's no need to fear I will ever be disappointed. I know the untruth you spoke to Francesca and me about your whereabouts and plans for your college vacation time weighs on you, but in truth, we let you down.

She went to protest, but he held up his hand, making room in the circle beside him. Skyler and Dimitri took their place next to him.

Even had you been too young to be claimed, it was already established that Dimitri was your lifemate. All of us knew it, yet we didn't give you the consideration to tell you what was happening. We treated you like a child and left you in the dark. That was our mistake and our fault. You have no reason to be guilty or ashamed. I thank the universe that you have such good friends in Paul and Josef.

Both Dimitri and Skyler thanked the universe for them as well. She smiled at the two of them, sitting in the warriors circle, suddenly being treated as men, although it was Zacarias De La Cruz everyone was listening to.

"The question is, how do we get everyone safely out of here?" Zacarias said. "We could fight our way out, and as a last resort, we will, but out of respect for Mikhail and what he's dealing with there, it would be best if we found a different way."

"Skyler and Dimitri need a safe resting place to heal," Gabriel added. "Both are still in poor shape." He sent an apologetic look toward his daughter.

The transparent walls around them suddenly rippled again. The ground shifted slightly.

Skyler nestled her hand inside of Dimitri's for comfort. She knew it wasn't her fault that the shelter was collapsing—it wasn't designed to last forever—but she was too weak to fix it.

Dimitri tightened his fingers around hers instantly and shifted his body, just a little to offer more protection. She leaned her head back against his shoulder. The Carpathians and Zev had been discussing various possibilities for some time. She thought by now, they would have figured something out.

"We've got enough of us here to slip out and pick them off one by one," Nicolas De La Cruz suggested. "They might feel our energy, but with a large electrical storm, we could easily slow them down and distract them. We know how they fight. We could take them."

"You can't kill every Lycan because you're angry at them," Zev protested.

"Why not?" Rafael demanded. "Making war on children makes them fair game as far as I'm concerned."

Paul and Josef exchanged a long look with Skyler. Josef's amusement was in his eyes, making the other two smile in spite of the circumstances. Although being invited to take part in the discussion, clearly they were still relegated, by some, to the "child" label.

Because they're solving this problem so peacefully and adult-like, Josef sent, his tone overflowing with laughter.

It was difficult to keep a straight face with Josef's sense of humor spilling over to them.

"I guess I'm their biggest problem," Paul confided in a loud whisper. "I can't shift."

"Neither can I at this point," Skyler said. "I can barely sit up anymore."

Her whispered words acted as some kind of a trigger for the conferring Carpathians. They all turned and looked at her.

She sank back against Dimitri again. He put both arms around her, caging her in—a small warning to the others that he was running out of patience with the arguing.

"I've got to get her out of here now," Dimitri decreed. "I don't care about retaliation, only making certain Skyler gets the care she needs."

"Let's just fly everyone out of here," Fen said. "There's no need to go to war with these people. We have a strong enough force to shield Paul, Zev and our wounded."

"We have a reason," Rafael declared.

Zev scowled and started to say something, but Fen shook his head in warning and cut him off before he could engage with Rafael, who clearly was upset over his nephew being shot multiple times.

"There's no way to tell who is with Gunnolf's faction and who stands with the council. We can't lump all Lycans together. Clearly, there's some internal war going on and whoever is behind the bid for power sees

Carpathians as a threat. Until we have a clear understanding of who our real enemy is, we can't risk injuring—or killing—an innocent."

"Fen's right," Zacarias agreed. His tone brooked no argument, and no one made one.

"Let's get it done then," Dimitri said. "We've got most of the night left."

"We can form the shield to allow the escape out of here"—Zacarias volunteered his brothers—"but we will retaliate if fired upon."

Zev shook his head. "I could try talking to them."

"At this point," Fen said, "most of the Lycans believe you are a traitor or have become the *Sange rau* and we're protecting you. Your council members, or most of them, are in the Carpathian Mountains. So is your pack. You'll do more good there. If we can get to the bottom of what's going on, we'll have a better chance to stop it."

Gabriel and Lucian looked at one another and gave a slow nod in perfect unison, as if they had one mind. They'd been battling together for centuries. Strategy was a way of life. Although retreating was abhorrent, sometimes they knew it was necessary.

"Lucian and I will lead us out," Gabriel said. "Razvan and Ivory can take up the rear. If Zacarias and his brothers shield us, that gives us Tatijana, Fen, Byron and Vlad to carry the wounded. We'll need one more carrier."

"I can fly myself out of here," Dimitri said. "I might be weak, but I'm not dead."

Gabriel shook his head. "I'm not willing to risk you, Dimitri. You've got my daughter's life in your hands. You've been tortured beyond all reason and shot as well. Your body needs recovery time."

"I can fly," Josef volunteered. "I brought Paul and Skyler here."

Zacarias swung around, his dark eyes steely and cold. "Riordan will take you. We will not risk you either."

Josef let out his breath and ducked his head. He hadn't expected Zacarias to take an interest in him, to even be on his radar. He was used to arguing with his adopted father and uncle, but Zacarias was on an entirely new level.

Man, how do you live with that? Josef asked Paul, but he was secretly pleased that Zacarias had even noticed him, let alone decreed one of the De La Cruz brothers would actually look after him.

He's cool, isn't he? Paul said.

Cool like a caged tiger, Josef replied. *He's a little bit terrifying.*

I know. But then you see him with Marguarita and he's all gooey and mushy with her.

"It's settled then," Gabriel continued as if he hadn't been interrupted. "Tatijana, you take Skyler and follow me out. Fen can take Dimitri. Riordan has Josef. Vlad will have Paul. Byron, will you take Zev?"

"Of course." He gave his nephew a warning glare. *Don't do anything crazy around the De La Cruz brothers.*

They know me through Paul, Josef assured, recognizing his uncle's gruff caution was more fear for him than embarrassment over something he might do. *But I want to get home as fast as possible. Skyler needs to heal and be safe.* His uncle knew he loved Skyler and that reassurance was the best that he could give.

"Zev will experience trouble getting through the wall," Fen cautioned. "It's difficult for me. I imagine it is for Dimitri as well. The more Lycan blood we have, the harder it is to get through."

Skyler nodded. "I designed it that way, so no Lycan could follow us inside. I counted on Dimitri's Carpathian blood to get him through, although I'll admit I was worried."

"Do you have any idea how extraordinary this is?" Gabriel asked, genuine admiration in his tone. "I'm so proud of you."

"I'm a little in awe of my sister-kin," Tatijana admitted.

"I can make it out," Zev assured. "I got in."

"But it hurts like hell," Fen pointed out. "And you're not anywhere near one hundred percent."

"I don't have to be one hundred percent to cling to a dragon's back," Zev pointed out with a wry grin.

"What about you, Dimitri?" Fen asked. "Do you think you can get through?"

"The wall is collapsing. I doubt if it's nearly as strong as it was. I'll get through. Like Zev, I don't think hanging onto a dragon is going to be harder than forcing myself through it like I had to earlier."

Gabriel turned to Vlad. "That leaves you with Paul. He has multiple wounds as you know and is still weak, although he refuses to admit it. One arm is nearly useless. I've given him blood along with both of you and Josef, but we didn't catch the fact that he had internal bleeding until this morning."

"That was my fault," Josef said. "I told Tatijana I'd healed his wounds from the inside. She was busy with Dimitri for the most part."

"It was a stupid nick," Paul said. "No big deal, and you were bleeding like from fifty places yourself, Josef."

The walls rippled again and this time part of the ceiling folded over. Along the western wall, the corner sagged.

"We're definitely running out of time," Lucian said. "We need to go now before the Lycans notice and get fired up."

Zacarias signaled to three of his brothers. Rafael nodded and chose the western wall, the fastest collapsing. He walked toward it casually, as if he didn't have a care in the world, or know that the Lycans stared back at him from the safety of the forest—or that the structure might fall in on itself and trap him. Nicolas took the eastern wall, striding toward it confidently. Manolito chose the north, leaving the southern entrance to Zacarias.

The brothers moved in perfect synchronization, slipping through the collapsing wall fast, hands up weaving a pattern in the air.

Gabriel didn't hesitate. He followed Zacarias out, his every sense on alert to the danger of the carriers flying the wounded back to the Carpathian Mountains. Tatijana shifted fast, extending her wing to Skyler. Dimitri helped his lifemate climb onto the blue dragon's back. Skyler took one last look at Dimitri and nodded her head.

Be right behind me. I have to be able to see you, she pleaded, suddenly afraid. She didn't want to be separated from him, not after all they'd gone through.

Fen will stay close to Tatijana to protect her, Dimitri assured. *I would never be far from you. Should something happen, I am quite capable of slipping off his back, shifting myself and coming for you. Have no fears. We'll travel far this night and rest at dawn.*

Tatijana rose fast, rushing the wall to break through. Skyler leaned low on the blue-spiked neck, looking back, her heart in her throat, watching for Dimitri. Fen was already in the air, crowding his lifemate with his dragon. Dimitri sat upright, no hands, a weapon at the ready.

To Skyler's horror, she saw a line of Lycans rushing from the forest straight at them as the wings of the dragon beat ferociously in order to gain height. She felt the blue dragon gather itself to take another impressive leap into the sky just as two incredibly fast Lycans flung themselves at her. Claws hooked into scales on either side of the dragon, and two more managed to fasten their claws into the softer underbelly in an attempt to drag the dragon from the sky.

15

Shots rang out as the next dragon emerged from the collapsing shelter. Riordan De La Cruz burst through the shelter wall with Josef on his back. Bullets whined through the air, the sounds reverberating through the night, but Zacarias and his brothers had constructed a shield around the materializing dragons. The bullets couldn't penetrate that safeguard. Unfortunately, the buffer was only so large, only keeping the dragons and their passengers safe as they left the collapsing shelter.

Vlad was next to appear, a great golden dragon winging its way clear of the disintegrating refuge with Paul on his back. Lycans poured into the clearing, realizing their long-range weapons did no good. Most were in Lycan form, half wolf, half man, taller and stronger and able to cover great distances in one leap.

The dragons necessarily had to come out low to the ground due to the structure falling in on itself. To gain altitude for such a large creature with the added weight of a passenger on its back, the dragon had to work immensely hard, wings straining to create enough lift for the jump.

Byron followed close behind Vlad, Zev on his back. The sight of the elite hunter with the Carpathians sent the Lycans into a frenzy of madness.

Most left Vlad's dragon alone to rush Byron, leaping at his sides, clawing and tearing, ripping at the wings in an effort to disable the creature so it couldn't fly. Several below it tore at the soft underbelly, ripping out chunks to bleed the dragon dry.

Razvan and Ivory stormed out of the shelter, two riders in the sky, shooting arrows simultaneously, aiming for arms and legs, wounding as many as possible, every bit as fast as the Lycans.

Byron's dragon faltered and went down, hitting with its nose first, skidding in the dirt and grass, leaving long, deep furrows behind.

Go, go. The rest of you, go, Zacarias ordered. *We'll get them free.*

Fen, I can't leave them, Dimitri said, putting his hand on the thick, spiked neck of Fen's dragon in order to leap free.

Neither can I. We're Hän ku pesäk kaikak. Let's go guard Byron and Zev. Just don't take any more hits. It really doesn't matter if these wolves know what we are at this point. Use your speed, Fen agreed, more because Dimitri was going back than anything else.

There was no stopping his brother when his sense of justice was crossed. Zev had fought battles with him, given him blood, and in spite of recent events, Dimitri regarded him as a friend. Byron was Carpathian. No warrior would leave another down.

Fen spun his dragon around, feeling the fire roaring in his belly, a rage that went deep after what these creatures had done to his brother. He thought he was past it, but seeing them tearing at Byron when the Carpathian hadn't even tried to defend himself, he found himself furious all over again, but in a cold rage, which didn't bode well.

He swore when the Lycans surrounded Byron's downed dragon, hooking their claws into him, preventing shifting. There were so many ripping and tearing at the body of the dragon, the arrows of the defenders seemed to make little difference. As fast as one fell, another took its place.

The Lycans had abandoned attempts at the other dragons and the rest were away safely. The pack concentrated their efforts on mutilating and killing the dragon in their possession. As Zev drew a silver sword in an effort to protect Byron, four large Lycans leapt on the dragon's back and pulled Zev to the ground.

Cursing, Fen redoubled his speed.

Wound them, Razvan insisted on the common Carpathian telepathic communication path. Clearly he was warning the De La Cruz brothers. *It isn't necessary to kill them.*

Drive them back away from Byron and Zev, Zacarias instructed. *Rafael, an arrow close to the heart can kill.*

Not these bastards, Rafael returned. *I didn't use silver. Although I will the next one.*

Fen banked his dragon, coming in hard, fire pouring from his mouth, engulfing the Lycans closest to the dragon on the ground, driving them away from their fallen comrades. Dimitri stood up on the dragon's back, balancing as Fen swept in low. Just before Fen was forced to pull up to avoid trees, Dimitri leapt from his back, right into the middle of the Lycans who had pulled Zev to the ground.

Dimitri ignored his protesting body, cutting through the crowd with astonishing speed, his silver sword stained and dripping with Lycan blood. He fought his way to Zev, yanking him up with one hand, going back-to-back with him. Zev was covered in blood and wounds, but he didn't hesitate to stand and fight with Dimitri.

Fen materialized beside them, so they formed a triangle of deadly fighters, moving toward the fallen dragon, cutting down everyone in their path.

Zacarias easily saw their plan. *Help clear the way, Razvan and Ivory. Make it too dangerous to stay between them and the dragon, Rafael; and Nicolas, take out the Lycans holding Byron to that form. Manolito and I will begin to clear another path to get out of here.*

"Are you all right?" Dimitri asked Zev when he sensed the other man falter for a moment.

"I'm alive, and that's all that counts." Zev's breath came in ragged gasps. He'd been injured, but Dimitri couldn't take the time to see how bad the wound or wounds were.

We need to see if we can find the divide between the factions, Fen suggested. *I can detect a faint difference in smell at times.*

Lycans conceal all odors when hunting, Zev reminded. His sword flashed as he whirled around two aggressive wolves wielding swords. He disarmed one and cut the arm off the other, returning to his position back-to-back with Dimitri.

Nevertheless, I can tell the difference, Fen said. *I can feel the energy leaking out of their shields as well.*

He drove three particularly large and hairy Lycans back from the fallen dragon. One actually had a chunk of dragon belly between his teeth.

Wait for it, Zev, Dimitri said, allowing his senses, growing so acute and sharp, to flare out, trying to find the differences Fen had detected. *He's going to start in any moment with how much more evolved he is than us.*

Two Lycans fell at his feet, both sprouting arrows. He nearly slipped in the blood surrounding Byron's dragon. The warriors in the sky were making the job easier, wounding every Lycan that dared to tear at the dragon.

With the addition of three deadly silver swords, the Lycans fell back, trying to drag their wounded with them.

I've got a shield up for you in case they try using guns again, Zacarias said. *This time the bullet will bounce off and return to the sender.* He sounded as low-key as ever. Nothing seemed to ruffle Zacarias.

We've got a few just below us, pulling out their rifles. Rafael's voice held a hint of satisfaction.

Dimitri, Zev and Fen reached the dragon, moving around it in a circle, making certain no Lycan remained.

You've got to shift, Byron, Dimitri insisted. *You can't pass out on us. We can't lug this form into the sky. It's dead weight. Shift and we'll get you out of here.*

They didn't have much time. The Lycans would rally and make another attack. A volley of shots rang out, bullets peppering the shield, head shots every one.

Military training for sure, Fen observed.

Screams and howls rose as the bullets found the shooters. Zacarias hadn't taken great care to ensure those firing didn't suffer permanent damage. He didn't much care, not with Byron nearly torn to pieces and three of his other men in harm's way.

Byron stirred inside the great dragon's body, groaning a little as his torn body refused to answer his demands. *Give me a minute.*

Zacarias was determined to buy him whatever time he needed. *Rafael, you and Nicolas take out the shooters, every last one of them. No kills if possible,* he tacked on. *The Lycan can regenerate limbs, so don't worry about being nice. And if you happen to get an inkling of the ones who shot Skyler, Paul and Josef, well, whatever happens to them, we won't shed any tears.*

Unleashing his two brothers on the shooters would most likely not have met with Mikhail's approval, but Zacarias knew them, knew their skill. They would make it so dangerous for any Lycan who dared raise a gun toward the Carpathians that few would try.

Nicolas in particular was adept at reading thoughts of various species. If he managed to find the original shooters, those men were definitely part of the group determined to assassinate the council members and start a war. He hadn't included those who shot Dimitri, mostly because he was a Carpathian warrior and considered fair game, but no one was going to shoot Paul and get away with it.

Zacarias was well aware he'd chosen the two most skilled and dangerous of his brothers to drive those with guns back. They knew to stay high, away from the Lycans. All of them shared the information Fen and Dimitri had provided the Carpathians with about the wolf packs and how they fought. He gave one more order to his brothers.

The moment you know for certain who the shooters are, I want to know.

It will be done, Rafael agreed. He was lifemate to Colby, Paul's sister, and she'd looked at him with tear-filled eyes, pleading with him to find Paul and bring him home. No one made his lifemate cry, or attempted to kill his young brother-in-law, without retaliation.

They had come to find and kill the shooters. They would do their best to follow Mikhail's orders and not start a war. They would avoid killing innocents if they could, wounding those they were unsure of whose side they were on, but once the guns had come out, those shooters had marked themselves.

As Byron managed to shift back into human form, another wave of Lycans erupted out of the ground where they'd dug, hidden, to get to their prey. Two caught at Byron's bloody body, dragging him back away from the three defenders while the other eight rushed the mixed bloods.

Dimitri leapt over the wall of Lycans, landing squarely over the top of Byron's body, straddling him, his sword cutting through one of the wolves trying to pull Byron away. At the same time, Dimitri leaned down, thrusting a silver dagger into Byron's fist, and yanked him up ruthlessly.

"Stay on your feet. No matter what, stay upright," he cautioned Byron, engaging in swordplay with the second, now frantic Lycan.

Byron was bleeding from a dozen or more wounds, some bone deep. He kept one hand over his belly, where the wolves had sought to eviscerate him as they were known to do.

Dimitri sliced through the Lycan's sword arm. The wolf screamed as his forearm, wrist and hand dropped to the ground. Dimitri dismissed him, swinging around to face the onslaught as five of his companions turned back to aid him. They swarmed Dimitri in an attempt to overpower and kill him.

Stay behind me, Byron, and keep an eye on the one-armed wolf. Keep in tight and move when I do.

Byron didn't answer. He'd lost far too much blood and was growing weak fast, but he refused to allow himself to slide into unconsciousness. He gripped the dagger and tried to tune himself to Dimitri's rhythm of fighting.

He was fast. Far faster than Byron had ever conceived of, even when he'd been warned about the mixed blood and their abilities. There was no possible way to keep up. More than anything he wanted to watch the deadly ballet between fighters. He couldn't feel any energy rising from any of the fighters, least of all Dimitri. He found himself anticipating the moves of the enemy, being guided by them rather than his defender as he tried to stay back-to-back with Dimitri. Dimitri's fast moves were entirely unpredictable.

Without warning, two more Lycans erupted almost at his feet. Byron thrust the dagger into the chest of the nearest one, sidestepping the knife coming at him from the Lycan's left hand. The second wolf had a sword and he swung it low, still half in the ground. Dimitri somehow sensed the two as they burst out of the ground, but still Byron heard Dimitri grunt and knew he'd taken a hit.

Dimitri swore softly under his breath as the tip of a sword caught him across the back of his calf. Fire burned through his skin and body as the silver penetrated. *You think I'd be used to it by now,* he said to his brother.

Get the hell out of there. Zacarias has created an opening for us. Razvan and Ivory will do a flyby and pick you and Byron up.

Screw that, Fen. Dimitri was not about to leave the other two on the ground, not with so many Lycans determined to kill them all.

Binding your lifemate hasn't improved your temper much, Fen noted. *I wasn't planning on hanging around. I'm not wounded in twenty-seven places, burned all to hell and back and playing the hero for my woman. I can grab Zev and go the moment you and Byron are safe.*

Dimitri parried two swords at once, riding them in a circle to the ground and then cutting deep into both Lycans' chests.

Not to mention those De La Cruz brothers are wreaking as much havoc as they dare. I don't think technically they've actually killed anyone, but they're ruthless as hell and definitely riding a thin edge. They plan to shield us as we take off. I can shift in the air. Zev's pretty adept at flight now.

That made more sense. Just this one time, Dimitri considered that it might be fun to be one of the De La Cruz brothers. They were a law unto themselves—or rather, their eldest brother. Every Carpathian alive knew one didn't cross Zacarias and come out of it unscathed.

I'm a little busy right now, Dimitri pointed out. *You two get out of here and we'll be behind you as soon as we can fight our way free.*

We're heading your way now.

As Fen and Zev began to move steadily toward Byron and Dimitri, there was a shift in their minds, a clear telepathic message of triumph.

We've found them, Nicolas said. *Seven shooters. All of them are feeling rather smug that they shot Skyler, Paul and Josef. They're even whispering about how the girl is the one to kill, that if they managed to kill her, the Carpathians would definitely go to war.*

They think Skyler is Sange rau because she was able to construct the shelter, Rafael added. *A hit has been put out on her and their top assassins have been sent to track and kill her, Dimitri, Fen and Zev.*

Dimitri's gut tightened. *Razvan, pick up Byron and get him somewhere you can close his wounds and give him blood.*

What the hell are you planning to do? Fen demanded. *Dimitri, have you lost your mind? You can't see yourself, but your skin is gray and drawn. You have to get out of here now before you collapse. You aren't fully healed and we haven't managed to replace the blood you lost.*

Dimitri was not a man who argued. Razvan swooped low, coming out of the sky fast, a streak of vapor, to materialize at the last moment and gather Byron up in his arms, taking him high before the Lycans even knew he was there.

Dimitri instantly shifted into tiny molecules impossible for a Lycan to latch on to. He shot through the trees, back into deeper forest, seeking the men Nicolas had found. They had started the fight between the species, just as they'd been ordered to do, but they weren't taking chances on getting hacked apart by the skilled warriors.

They'd done their job, stirring up the camp, poisoning minds against Zev, or at least raising doubts about him. They proclaimed the council was behind them and that Zev had done something to cut off all cell phone contact, leaving them isolated. They sent their pawns into the battlefield, right beside those who were still on the fence, or even loyal to the council.

Sitting up in the trees and watching the battle from a safe distance with night vision goggles, they acted as commentators at a sports event, even laughing when some of the council's loyal followers suffered amputations. The limbs would grow back, but still, the severe injuries would definitely make up the minds of those who hadn't fully believed them.

"This couldn't get any better," one of the Lycans stated. He had blond hair and considered himself quite handsome. He had believed in the sacred code, *all* of it, including the place of women in their society. Too long things had been influenced by human interaction. The old ways, the traditions and codes had long been forgotten. "We definitely managed to stir things up, even without Gunnolf."

Another nodded, peering through the branches to watch the chaos below. "They'll join us now. Half of them have been shot with arrows or hacked in two, just like Gunnolf predicted."

"Don't pat yourselves on the back yet," said a third. "Zev is charismatic. Everyone listens to him, including the council. He's got to die before he starts talking again."

"I haven't heard if we succeeded at the meeting, the talks for an alliance," another commented. "Keeping everyone from using their phones means we don't have the ability either. We can only hope they did their part and wiped out the council. The moment that news hits, everyone will take up arms against the Carpathians."

"Do you believe Zev is truly *Sange rau*? Or that the Carpathian prisoner was? If he was so powerful, why couldn't he free himself?"

"What difference does it make?" the blond snarled. "The woman is the one who freed him and set up that fortress we couldn't penetrate. If anyone's *Sange rau*, it's her. She used some kind of blood spell, I could smell her everywhere."

"Her name," Dimitri said, coming up behind him, "is Skyler." He plunged the silver stake straight through the blond Lycan's back so hard the tip came out through the wolf's chest. In one motion, Dimitri's sharp sword sliced through branch and neck so that the head tumbled to the ground below.

He whirled like a dancer, never actually placing his feet on the branches, but rather performed the brutal ballet there in the air, keeping the close quarters so that the Lycans were hampered by the branches and leaves. Even as they tried to scramble out of the trees, he cut down a second one, using his sword to sever the head from the neck.

"You could have waited," Rafael complained, driving a silver stake through the heart of the headless Lycan wedged in the tree. He whirled around in midair, using a silver knife to scoop out the heart of a third, dropping it in the crotch of the tree right in front of a shocked Lycan. He stabbed the knife through the center of the heart to nail it to the trunk and glided back to allow Dimitri's sword to send the head tumbling to the ground beside the other two.

One Lycan managed to extract himself from the branches. He leapt toward the ground, realizing, too late, that a third Carpathian stood waiting. The man was so still he could have been a part of the very landscape. When he moved, he flowed like water, striking so fast the Lycan was dead before he actually hit the ground, a silver stake in his heart and his head completely severed.

The three remaining conspirators pretended to surrender, fingers on the triggers of their weapons. "We haven't done anything to you," one pleaded, moving his head to the left to peer around the branch, trying to get a look at Dimitri. "We give up. You can have our weapons." Three swords and two knives were thrown to the ground below.

As the first of the trio bargained, the other two slipped their guns ever so quietly forward in an effort to find a target. One thought he saw a Carpathian for just a moment, and he nudged his companion and pointed to the brush below.

Behind them, Dimitri leaned down to whisper into their ears. "I can smell lies. And the three of you stink."

One whirled, firing as he did so, the gun exploding next to Dimitri's chest, but Dimitri's dagger had already gone deep, the blade finding a home in the liar's heart. The hand holding the gun stiffened and then went limp, the body sliding toward the ground, only to be caught in the lower branches where it lay sprawled out in a macabre manner.

Nicolas took the head, allowing it to drop to the ground with the others. With great contempt, he shoved the body out of the tree with the toe of his boot, so that it, too, landed in the mess that had been live Lycans only minutes earlier.

The two remaining wolves opened fire, shooting off round after round in all directions, desperate to kill their attackers. Unfortunately for them, the Carpathians had disappeared, and in the chaos of terror, the two Lycans left alive couldn't read the energy coming at them from all directions.

One clawed his way down the tree, shredding the bark, nearly sobbing. He landed in the middle of a puddle of blood and when he looked down, the eyes of his friends were staring accusingly at him.

"Don't leave me, Don," the other shouted. "We have to stick together. Wait for me."

The Lycan named Don didn't even look up at his companion, he ran for his life, the gun still clutched in his hand with his finger on the trigger, but he didn't even remember it was there. He had taken no more than five steps when he hit something sharp. Painful. He stopped abruptly, stood there swaying. The gun dropped from nerveless fingers.

Don looked down at his chest. A silver spiraling stake protruded. Shocked, he stared down, cupping his hands underneath it as if he could catch the blood pouring from around the wound. Twice he shook his head and then managed to look up. A tall man stood in front of him, one with terrible burns around his head and neck.

"You really shouldn't have shot her," Dimitri said dispassionately. "You were dead the minute the bullets left your gun. If I hadn't found you now, I would have hunted you down with the very last breath in my body." He lifted the silver sword and swung it, the movement graceful and deadly. Don's head rolled toward the others.

The Lycan left in the tree threw his gun down and tried to stand on trembling legs, raising both hands in the air. "You can't kill me. I'm a prisoner of war. You can't kill me."

"There is no war between our species," Nicolas said, his disembodied voice coming eerily out of the night.

"Unfortunately for you," Rafael added, projecting his voice from both above and below, "my brother doesn't believe in taking prisoners."

The Lycan leapt from the tree, clearing the branches, his arms flung out from his body as if he had wings. In midair, a silver sword appeared. There was no way to change his trajectory. He hit the tip of the sword with his chest, his momentum impaling him on the blade, right through his heart.

"Your brother doesn't believe in a lot of unnecessary talking either," Zacarias said, materializing behind the sword. He gave his brothers a dark scowl. "You do like your games." He withdrew the blade, severed the head with one stroke and wiped the blade on the body almost before it hit the ground.

Nicolas and Rafael exchanged a small secret smirk.

You've managed to draw a lot of attention, Fen said to his brother. *Get out of there.*

Zacarias looked up at the sky and immediately the clouds obeyed, churning black and blowing straight up. Lightning forked throughout a towering cloud. He directed the sizzling bolt into the middle of the pile of dead Lycans.

The flames leapt high, burning the bodies. Rafael left behind a message for the other Lycans. Traitors of the council, murderers of children. Brought to justice.

I'm not leaving you behind and Zev is losing the battle here with his numerous wounds. Get moving.

I'm on my way, Dimitri said placidly.

Fen might be his older brother, but Dimitri was an ancient warrior and had hunted vampires for centuries, mostly on his own. No matter how much he loved his brother, he went his own way and made up his own mind. These Lycans had been killers and they had dared to accost his lifemate. He wasn't about to let them live. Sooner or later he would have caught up with them. He was grateful they had been ferreted out by Zacarias and his brothers.

Who knew what more harm they would have done if they hadn't been destroyed?

He knew Fen was worried about him, but he refused to acknowledge that Fen had been right all along and his body wasn't yet up to bringing justice to anyone. He took to the air, heading back toward his brother. Razvan had made a clean getaway with Byron, yet Fen and Zev had refused to leave until Dimitri was safely away. Dimitri was fairly certain Zev was every bit as stubborn as his brother and neither was budging until they knew he was safe.

Rafael and Nicolas fell in behind him. Zacarias led the way. On some level Dimitri realized they were protecting him, flying in a formation that kept his battered body in the center of a triangle.

I'm waiting on you, Fen, he told his brother. *If you're having trouble and need a little help I'll circle back and save you as usual. Just say the word. I was just giving you a little time to work it out, but seriously, I can't have you holding everyone up.*

Dimitri had to keep the amusement out of his voice, and out of his mind as well. Laughing at Fen was a dangerous proposition.

Very funny. You're turning into a regular comedian. Have one of the De La Cruz brothers carry your sorry butt.

Dimitri knew he wasn't going to get away with laughing at his brother, but still, it felt good to be heading home, with Fen close by. He was free, the pain was slowly subsiding and Skyler was his for all eternity.

Moving through the night sky with the wind in his face and the stars glittering overhead had always been relaxing and peaceful. He didn't look at the battleground beneath him, strewn with wounded Lycans. He'd had enough of blood and death and pain—enough to last another lifetime. He was weary. Exhausted. Done with fighting for a while.

Where are you?

She reached for him immediately with her soothing touch as if she knew his weariness and exhaustion. She'd done so in the past. He remembered once when he'd spent months tracking a master vampire and witnessing the aftermath of the death and destruction the undead left in his wake, he'd been so sickened by the depravity he couldn't find solace or peace, even in the ground.

She had come to him then as she did now. Skyler. His miracle. She poured into his mind gently, with that slow, almost delicate touch he had grown so familiar with. She filled him, those dark places of death, the cracks that seemed impossible to mend, so many torn places inside of him caused by the numerous kills he'd made and the things he'd seen. Somehow, when she was there, when they merged like this, she managed to wipe it all out. Everything he'd seen and done was gone, replaced by warmth and love.

Safe. I'm following close, he assured her.

Dimitri, something's wrong. I feel it.

It's just the distance between us. I'm a little weak. He made the admission to her that he would never make to his brother. She was there with him, in his mind, she would know anyway. It was practically impossible to hide anything from one's lifemate, and his lifemate was especially sensitive.

It's not the distance. Something else. Something creeping up on you. It's close. Dangerous.

He'd put himself on autopilot, basically allowing Zacarias and his brothers to direct his flight, shielding them from any eyes that might see them while he kept his strength for the long way home. He took a quick look around. Fen, in the form of a dragon with Zev on his back, flew just to his left.

The De La Cruz brothers, like him, had chosen the form of birds, moving powerfully through the night sky. They were all on alert, but no one seemed unduly on edge.

He believed her. He had found, over the years, it paid to believe Skyler. He was a Guardian, a mixed blood, and he had special gifts. It was more than time to begin using the special abilities being the *Hän ku pesäk kaikak* gave him. The danger was in the feeling of superiority that crept in. He was stronger. Faster. His brain could solve problems at a tremendous rate of speed. One had to temper gifts with the inevitable price one paid for them.

His eyesight was especially keen. He took a long, slow look around, at the ground below him, to his right, his left, behind him and up ahead. His hearing was acute. He listened for any sound that might be out of place, a single note that might warn him of danger. His sense of smell was extremely sensitive, the combined wolf and Carpathian coming together to give him tremendous advantages if he just used them.

There was something. The faintest of ripples washed over him, an uneasiness that set in and held on, yet he couldn't identify the threat.

Fen. Reach out. There's something here. Something coming after us. Or we're heading toward it. Skyler feels it as well.

He knew his brother would take him seriously. They had battled together on and off for centuries. As much as Fen liked to pull rank as a big brother, he respected Dimitri's abilities and would never ignore a warning.

I feel it. But what? So subtle. What could be that subtle that none of us were aware of it? Fen asked.

The answer was clear to Dimitri—to both of them. *Sange rau. Whoever has orchestrated this war is using the Sange rau to assassinate those he wants out of his way.*

There were Bardolf and Abel. Fen named the two *Sange rau* they had defeated weeks earlier. The two had been sent to kill Mikhail Dubrinsky. *How could he control a mixed blood, a vampire at that. He has to be pretty powerful to do something like that.*

If he was Carpathian before he was Sange rau and we warn the others, he would hear, Dimitri pointed out.

Neither Fen nor Dimitri had ever exchanged blood with Zacarias or his brothers. They would have to use the common path—which would allow a Carpathian-born mixed blood to hear.

Skyler, can Paul reach out to his uncles? If so, have him convey the news that we are being pursued by an assassin. We're certain the assassin is Sange rau.

There was a brief silence, presumably while she conferred with Paul. *He has exchanged blood with Nicolas.*

Tell them to keep moving as if nothing has changed, but one will have to take Zev from Fen. I'm going to start dropping back just a little at a time, giving the impression I'm hurt and the flight is beginning to tell on me, Dimitri said.

You are hurt. Dimitri, you can't fight this monster, not in your condition, Skyler objected.

He laughed softly in his mind, reaching for her to surround her with love. *Csitri, I've got no intention of fighting him. I'll leave that to Fen. He needs to feel needed and I'd never take that away from him.*

For a moment he thought Skyler wouldn't catch on, but she did. *He's listening, isn't he? You're provoking your brother again.*

Of course I am.

Fen gave a little derisive snort. *He just can't handle that I'm better in a fight.*

Says you. As I recall, the last time, it was me saving your sorry butt, Dimitri pointed out.

You have to take this threat seriously, Skyler insisted, somewhere between laughter and exasperation.

No worries, sívamet. We've got this, Dimitri said with confidence.

He *was* confident. He'd survived the Lycans' worst torture and he had his lifemate. It didn't matter that his body was torn and exhausted, his mind was stronger than ever. His senses were rapidly developing.

You and I both know, the Sange rau will be difficult to kill, Fen cautioned on their private path of communication. *I know you're trying to keep Skyler from worrying, but don't get overconfident.*

In all the centuries we've been traveling, different continents even, how many times have either of us ever run across the Sange rau? Dimitri asked his brother.

I've seen four, counting Abel and Bardolf.

I've only come across Abel and Bardolf, and they were specifically sent to kill Mikhail, Dimitri said, waiting to let the implication sink in.

Dimitri knew the precise moment Paul conveyed the warning to Nicolas and Nicolas sent it to Zacarias. There was no change in them, but he *felt* the difference. He hoped their pursuer didn't as well. He faltered just a little, looked as if he tried to recover and slipped back, away from his protectors. Nicolas and Rafael in bird form flew past him, hesitated a moment and then continued on as if he'd told them to keep going.

Fen got the meaning fast. *Someone is creating them, using mixed blood to enhance them and using them as assassins. They aren't necessarily vampire.*

And they're probably newly made. Abel and Bardolf were most likely their most experienced and oldest. They would never send an amateur after the prince in our territory. Whoever is behind this is creating his own army of mixed bloods.

Dimitri allowed the body of his bird to dip a little, seeking a lower altitude, his wings beating double the time the others did, but not actually getting anywhere. The wind shifted just a little, blowing into him, making him falter more. He tried to redouble his efforts—the others seemed to be moving away from him faster—but he was too worn-out.

The large bird of prey—a bald eagle—seemed to come out of nowhere, dropping fast, talons extended, its beak a strange color. Dimitri shifted from an owl's body to that of the larger eagle, so fast it was impossible to detect the change until the other was nearly on top of him. Dimitri had just enough time to realize the talons and beak were silver weapons, designed to shred, stab and kill fast. He met the bird's talons with his own, locking them together so that they tumbled from the sky, end over end. Neither could shift, and the ground seemed to be rising fast to meet them.

The assassin tore at Dimitri's body, stabbing repeatedly in the chest, seeking the heart. He never heard or saw the attack from behind, Fen streaking through the sky, going for the kill. The *Sange rau* didn't even feel the stake going through his body to penetrate his heart. When Fen removed the head and the bird landed dead on the ground, Dimitri called down the lightning to burn it.

He sank into the soft soil, sitting abruptly, pushing both hands through his hair. There was blood on his chest, seeping from a dozen slashes and stabs.

"You know, Fen, I think I'll take that ride now," he said when Fen strode up to him.

16

On his last return home, Dimitri had taken up residence in the old family dwelling, deep in the forest where the wolves gave him warning if visitors came too close. He'd done a few modern repairs on it, but he wasn't in residence often. The outside stone was covered in moss, and trees and brush had grown so close they nearly covered the house. Thick vines wove around the stone columns that formed the verandah. The vines were so thick they'd nearly formed an impenetrable wall, yet there was an archway at the stairs as if it had been designed that way.

Beneath the stone building, deep underground, Dimitri and Skyler lay entwined together, their bodies slowly healing. Dimitri woke each rising and hunted, sustaining the two of them and then going back to ground to allow Mother Earth to rejuvenate them both.

He woke and lay listening to the beat of the earth's heart. Over time the rhythm had become reassuring, a constant, steady drumbeat he could always count on. It didn't matter where in the world he was, if he lay in the ground, it was there.

He opened the soil above their heads, staring at the underside of the house his parents had constructed so many centuries earlier. He had played in the room above them. He remembered the sound of his mother's laughter and the murmur of his father's voice. He realized he wanted to stay, to make this their home. It was deep enough in the forest to keep their wolf pack safe and yet still close enough to the other Carpathians that Skyler could have company whenever she wanted.

He leaned over her. He loved watching her as she slept. Skyler always looked peaceful now—so different from the nights he'd entered her room and found her tossing and turning caught in the throes of a hideous nightmare. Gently he brushed back silken strands of hair that had come loose from the braid he'd woven for her just the last rising.

Her lashes were long and feathery, dark, yet tipped with gold. He traced her high cheekbones with the pad of his finger, absorbing the satin-smooth skin. It had always annoyed her that she couldn't tan. Josef and Paul teased her mercilessly, throwing their hands over their eyes to accuse her of blinding them with her white stomach or legs depending on what she was wearing. If she was out in the sun at all, she burned a bright red, and then they called her "lobster girl."

Dimitri found himself smiling at the memory of the antics of her friends. "You make my life beautiful and full," he murmured aloud to her. *Wake, csitri. We have much to do. It's time to start our life.*

She stirred at his call, rolled in his arms and lifted her lashes. The impact of her eyes meeting his was physical, a low, wicked punch that drove the air from his lungs. She had her relaxed, happy color, the true dove gray that he loved beyond any other color.

"Good evening, *sívamet.* Are you feeling stronger?"

Skyler nodded and touched his face. "Much. I wouldn't mind exploring our home a little bit. I haven't really seen much of anything since we've been healing."

"I want you to hunt for food with me." It was the first time he'd asked her. He didn't push for an answer, knowing this would be one of the hardest concepts for her to accept.

Dimitri didn't mind supplying blood to her, but in the event they were ever in trouble, she needed to know how to hunt and that she could do it by herself. It was a natural part of being Carpathian. Skyler craved blood, but the thought of taking it from an unknowing source bothered her on a strictly human level.

There was a small silence. Skyler's hand had dropped to his chest and she smoothed over the chain burns there—absently—like she did each rising. "Okay."

His heart jumped. One little word. She accepted their way of life and trusted him to teach her the things necessary to survive. He knew this was a huge milestone for her.

"Afterward, I need to see Francesca."

He wanted her to himself. They'd spent several risings in the ground healing. Yes, he'd gotten to hold her, and even exchange blood with her, but the entire rest of the time, they'd both been beneath, sleeping the rejuvenating sleep of the Carpathians.

The time spent in the ground had been necessary—both of them were in bad shape when they'd arrived in the Carpathian Mountains. Skyler had barely enough time to hug her adopted mother before she collapsed. Unfortunately, that essential time spent in the soil meant they weren't able to really start their life together.

He held her while they slept, entwined together, skin to skin. He gave her blood and certainly there was intimacy in both, but he felt almost as if he was losing ground with her, that she'd taken a step back from him. She said little, and she seemed to prefer to spend the time in the ground, rather than face their life together.

"You've got that frown on your face again," Skyler said, and reached up to rub his lips as if she could remove it. "What's wrong? Don't you want me to go with you?"

His hands shaped her tucked-in waist as he helped her into a sitting position. "Of course I want you to go with me. We both needed healing, but at some point we've got to rebuild our strength. I want to show you so many things."

"And I want to learn. Specifically, shapeshifting," Skyler said. "And flying. And running with the wolves."

He couldn't help laughing. "In other words, everything."

She nodded, coming up on her knees to inspect the burns around his throat and forehead. His heart jumped. She had not leaned into him physically or touched his scars intimately since they'd arrived in the Carpathian Mountains. She'd definitely worked at healing them, but she had used more of a professional touch. The brushes of her fingers were far too intimate to him to ever be considered professional and both his body and heart responded to those caresses.

She murmured the words she chanted each time she carefully traced each chain loop surrounding his body.

I call to you, Mother, bring forth your might,
As I seal these paths that would bring pain and blight.
I call to aloe, so green and cool,
Bind with me now, become my tool.

Bring forth your life's blood again to heal,
Ease this suffering, these scars do steal.
Each line I trace, may it fade day to day,
Taking all that causes pain away.

He allowed himself to inhale her scent, to bring his hands up to her back and hold her, fingers splayed wide to take in as much of her bare skin as possible.

"You've been keeping things from me," Skyler said, leaning so close to him that the tips of her breasts grazed his chest as she ran soothing fingers into the deep indentations around his throat. "You've been worried about something. I've waited for you to tell me, but I figured rather than merging my mind with yours and prying, I'd just ask."

Dimitri took a breath and let it out. Her fingers stroked over his skin, her touch sending flames flickering through his bloodstream. He had dreamt of this, had wanted it, but knowing he couldn't act on the desire flooding his body made the moment bittersweet. She needed time, and he was determined to give it to her.

"You pulled away from me," he admitted starkly. "You've never done that before. I know everything that's transpired in the last few weeks has happened fast and you needed time to assimilate it all—especially becoming fully Carpathian."

It was more than that—she would eventually become as he was—*Hän ku pesäk kaikak.* There was no getting around it, not when they were lifemates and would never be able to resist the urge to exchange blood.

Skyler was silent a moment, turning his words over and over in her mind. She had to admit to herself she'd been nervous each rising. She felt safe, there in the ground, in her little cocoon, wrapped in Dimitri's arms.

Before, when he had come to her, sometimes several nights in a row, just to talk, they'd merged minds to do so, and she'd thought she knew him. He didn't hide anything from her, but she'd never really merged so deep with him that she saw beyond the darkness in him. It had grown like a cancer, spreading over his soul, always looking for a way in.

To save him, she had pushed beyond that crouching darkness. She saw every memory, every deed. She knew the dangers he'd faced without flinching, the centuries of loneliness he endured without dishonor, and she'd seen how patient he'd been, even while the darkness pushed at his soul. Then, he had saved her, possessing her body, taking control of her mind, merging them both so deeply that she relived those memories with him, not just observed them.

Every kill took something from him, leaving behind tears in the fabric of mind and soul, even after losing one's emotions. Bringing even the worst of criminals to justice was not without a price—and he'd paid often. The fissures and cracks had deepened, and that darkness had crept in, taking advantage at every turn.

She saw the thousands of physical wounds. He'd been alone, or he'd been with Fen, and sometimes, rarely, another hunter she didn't know. Mostly, he'd been alone. He'd lived lifetimes, through history, and he'd always been honorable, no matter the circumstances. He'd saved lives and never asked for anything for himself—except her. His lifemate. He'd held on, hoping someday he would find her.

"When I was trying to find you, Dimitri, I felt empowered. I felt as if I was a partner to you, someone who could give you every single thing you needed and deserved. I knew you needed me and I knew that I could be exactly what you needed." She sighed. "But then we came here to the Carpathian Mountains and I began to have doubts."

The pads of her fingers went still, remaining over the burns on his neck.

He found it amazing that in those raw indentations, he could feel the concentrated power of her healing ability, and yet she was expressing her reservations about whether or not she could be a partner to him.

A thousand arguments rose in his mind, but he stayed silent. She needed to be able to talk to him without misgivings that he might not really listen to her. As much as he wanted to reassure her, this was her moment, not his.

"I kept thinking, what have you really gotten in a lifemate? I've only lived nineteen years. I couldn't hope to know the things you know. How could I possibly match you intellectually? I'm smart, I know I am. I'm only nineteen, but I already have several degrees. Still, what I know about any one subject is a drop in the bucket compared to your knowledge."

Dimitri felt her fingers moving again, smoothing over the burns around his throat. She settled back on her heels and followed the chain links wrapped around his shoulders.

"I kept wondering, what exactly do I have to offer you?" Her gaze jumped to his and color flushed beneath her skin before her eyes went back to her work. "I'm afraid of physical contact—intimacy—you know that. It isn't news to you, but I just keep thinking I'm not bringing you anything at all. Not only do I not know the first thing about pleasing a partner, I find the entire idea repugnant." She paused. Took a breath. "Or I did."

He was grateful for that small admission. He knew, better than she did, that she was beginning to respond to him. She loved him, and her body had begun to respond to his touch. He felt it with every touch, every look. As they spent time together, he knew, if he was patient and careful, allowing her to take the lead, she would come to want his body as much as he wanted hers. It was another expression of love, she just had to come to realize that herself.

"I don't know the first thing about pleasing you, Dimitri, and that bothers me. I don't know how I'll react when you make love to me. What if I freak out?"

He wanted to assure her it wouldn't matter. They would stop until she was ready, but again he remained silent, waiting for her to tell him everything.

"I don't even have my virginity—that was lost long ago," she added sadly.

That was too much for him. He had to respond, but when he opened his mouth, she shook her hand and laid a finger across his lips.

"This is difficult for me. One of the things I valued most in our relationship was that we could talk about anything. My past, yours, sex, all of it. But we weren't face-to-face. We weren't skin to skin. I want to be as comfortable just like this as I was all those times we talked telepathically," she explained. "So I need to tell you this."

She linked her arms around his neck and leaned close again, using the healing saliva from her tongue to bathe the worst of the burns around his chest. He closed his eyes and just let himself feel her skin moving over his and the intimacy of her mouth against him. Her breasts tantalized him, swaying against him. His body was already hard, as it was nearly every moment around her, but he found the ability to feel anything at all was a miracle, let alone such intense desire.

His love for her was all encompassing; if that meant giving her time, he had all the time in the world, now that they were bound together. Whatever she needed, he would provide, and if that was time, it was a very small price to pay, in his mind, for her to be truly comfortable with him.

Skyler ran her hand down his chest, very lightly, just a brush really, but it set his blood on fire. Her palm brushed his thick cock. Again, it was the lightest of touches, but it sent a shock wave through him.

"I know you want me. How could I not? The crazy thing is, Dimitri, I need you to want me. I do. I need to know that you think I'm beautiful and desirable and even sexy. I dream of the time that I can touch you, and love you without reservation or hesitation."

Once again she sank back on her heels and looked at him with tears swimming in her eyes. He lifted her chin with his thumb and finger, waited until she lifted her long lashes before he leaned in to sip away her tears. Very gently he took her hand and formed it around his heavy erection. No doubt his size was intimidating when he was fully aroused, but she'd seen him naked several times now.

Her palm was warm as she curled it around his girth, her fingers one by one bending to make a fist, trying to close. He kept his hand over hers, light, so she could pull away the moment she needed to. Her heart beat so hard in her chest, he could almost see it beneath her pale skin.

He tapped his chest. "Feel my heart. Hear it. Follow the rhythm of mine."

The tip of her tongue moistened her lips, sending another rush of heat surging through his veins, straight to his groin. His cock jerked in reaction, grew hotter, swelling even more in her hand. Her thumb slid over the sensitive head, smearing the pearl of liquid. He knew she wasn't trying to tease him, she was trying to get to know his body, to feel comfortable with it, but her touch was killing him.

Her breathing turned ragged—small little gasps as if she couldn't get enough air. Her body flushed with color. He very gently placed his free hand over her heart, feeling it race beneath his palm.

"For me, you will always be sexy and desirable. Knowledge of technique or practiced art is never going to be sexy to me. The desire to give me pleasure, to please me in the same way I want to please you is what makes you sexy to me, *csitri.* I can feel that desire in you with every touch of your hand. Even now, your fingers stroke over my shaft instead of pulling away."

He stifled a groan of need. Her fingers brushed back and forth, but in that slow, leisurely way of hers, as if somehow she was imprinting the shape and feel of him into her very bones. She was naturally sensual. Given the right circumstances, she would grow in confidence and trust in herself and him, allowing that sensual part of her freedom.

He watched her take a breath, the action lifting her breasts temptingly. She didn't realize how intimate, how possessive her touch was. Long ago she had become his, her heart, her soul and her mind. She loved him with every fiber of her being. He belonged to her, body and soul, and she was very comfortable with him, even skin to skin, whether she knew it or not.

He uncurled her fingers one by one from around the thick length of his shaft, pulled her hand very gently back to his chest, and placed her fingertips in the bands of chain. He needed a respite almost as much as she did. His body was on fire. He needed just a few moments to breathe his way through the danger zone.

"You cannot disappoint me. You cannot. It is an impossibility."

"How do you know?" Skyler asked. "I feel like such a coward. There's more than just the physical relationship, Dimitri. Knowing the Carpathian ways and living them are two distinctly different things. When I first wake beneath the ground, I feel as if I'm buried alive. Intellectually, I know better. I know it's natural for us, but I can't control my reaction, that horrible moment when I feel I can't breathe and I'm being smothered."

"That is easily solved, Skyler. I can wake first and open the earth . . ."

"No. No. I don't want you to do everything for me. I refuse to be a burden to you. I want to be your partner. I need to come to terms with all of this."

He tugged her braid very gently. "*Sívamet*, it has been less than a week since your conversion. You were shot numerous times and died, were brought back to life. I am not expecting that you'll know everything and be comfortable with it. Isn't that too much to ask even of a woman as powerful as you?"

"No, not when I know what you've been through, what you sacrificed."

Dimitri brushed kisses along her temples, his heart nearly melting in that ridiculous way it had when she was concerned for him.

"I didn't do anything special, Skyler, although I'm grateful you think I did. Stop worrying so much about being young, or finding new things difficult. Carpathians age differently than humans. At fifty I might be considered your human age or Paul's human age. We don't mature fully until we've seen two centuries. After that, there is no real aging. Time goes by but we don't mark it with age. When one has such longevity, age ceases to mean anything. Humans mark time because they have a cycle of life and they become caught up in that and measure all things by it."

"I didn't think about that," Skyler admitted. "Francesca tried to explain it to me when I asked why Josef was treated like such a child when he's so brilliant. No one takes him seriously, but he actually is a real asset to the Carpathian community if they would just listen to him and utilize his talents."

"I think Josef will be seen in a different light after your daring rescue. Without the three of you, Skyler, you know I'd be dead. You proved yourself as well."

She sighed. "I don't know why I suddenly began feeling so inadequate, Dimitri. Just knowing the things you've had to face in your life . . . " She broke off again, shaking her head.

He shrugged his shoulders. Her fingers were already working their nightly magic, smoothing the burned flesh, easing the tight bands around his chest. The reminder of that agony of silver wrapped around his body like a boa constrictor would always be physically present. Skyler and Mother Earth did their best—and he was certain no skilled healer could do more—but the scars were too deep.

Sometimes, when he first woke, he could feel the bite of the silver burning into his skin, in a hundred places, surrounding his body, slowly, like a snake, penetrating his skin to slither inside him, burning long worm holes through every organ. He knew the memory would stay with him, century after century, right along with the scars.

"I told you everything, my love," she said. "What are you keeping from me?"

Her fingers traced the burns around his ribs. His left side in particular had been excruciatingly painful, digging deep until he was certain the chain had wrapped around bone, leaving its mark there.

He was branded forever by the Lycans. He was mixed blood, part of the Lycan world, yet half wolf and half Carpathian. Like Skyler with her mage blood, he would have to come to terms with what the Lycans did to him and how he felt about them.

"Mikhail wants me to go before the Lycan council and show them what was done to me."

Skyler frowned. Dimitri sounded as he always did—matter-of-fact, very steady and calm. But she *felt* a ripple beneath the surface. She was always tuned to him. He had become her world and she knew the very number of breaths he took at times.

She splayed her fingers over his belly, feeling the tension in him—not sexual as there had been only moments earlier. She felt humiliation and anger. Not anger. Rage. She took a breath, inhaling his scent, wrapping herself in him for a moment while she considered how to best come to his aid. She understood the way Ivory touched Razvan or stood close to him in moments of distress. She wanted to ease any burden, but wasn't certain how.

"You don't want them to see these scars?" she prompted. It would be easy enough to slip inside his mind and see for herself what battle he engaged in, but like Dimitri had done earlier with her, she wanted him to tell her himself—to trust his partner.

She loved touching him. It was that simple. Every stroke of her fingers along those terrible burns made her feel closer to him. She tried not to be intimate in her touch, but she couldn't help the possessive feeling she had when her fingers moved over his body. Dimitri belonged to her alone and so did his magnificent body.

Each time she found herself skin to skin with him, legs tangled together, his palm sometimes cupping her breast while they slept, her body reacted, coming to life when she'd thought that part of her would always be dead. She hadn't known she could want a man. She'd never felt that tension building in her, the electrical shock running from breast to thighs as fingers of desire pulsed through her, until Dimitri. Sometimes just his scent triggered her body's reaction.

She was terrified, and yet she was also equally as mesmerized by him. When she'd wrapped her fingers around his thick shaft, her first reaction had been panic, but Dimitri never forced anything on her—certainly not intimacy. She felt safe with him, safe to do some of the things she wanted to do—like explore his entire body. She didn't want to be a tease—she knew it was difficult for him, that she was lucky he had such control, but she had to know how she would react to him.

He'd felt so soft, like velvet over steel. So hot. Her body had become liquid, matching his heat, an urgent coiling need that burned through her body like wildfire. She had scared herself with a terrible hunger that seemed to come out of nowhere. But Dimitri steadied her. Always, she could count on him.

"I don't want anything whatsoever to do with them," Dimitri admitted. "Perhaps they didn't know what was happening. Maybe they really weren't the ones to sentence me to such a horrific death, but believe me, Skyler, when I say I planned out each of their deaths very carefully while I hung from hooks on that tree."

She felt the tremor going through his body beneath the palm of her hand. Not fear—definitely rage. She knelt up again and wrapped her arms around his neck, linking her fingers at his nape. She knew he would never pull away from her, never recoil. There was such freedom in that knowledge. She wanted the same for him. She wanted to give him that gift.

"Dimitri, those members of the Lycan council are nothing to us. Nothing. You survived the worst that they had. They couldn't defeat you. Standing in front of them is a slap in the face to them and their horrible medieval method of torture. Such a thing should be abolished." She leaned in to trail soft, butterfly kisses over his face until she reached his mouth.

His hands came up, sliding up her back. His arms wrapped her up tight as his mouth came down possessively on hers. She felt the aggression in his body and waited for the familiar panic, but his kiss was too enticing, sweeping her up like an avalanche of pure feeling, pure bliss. She loved his mouth and the way he kissed. She was learning how to respond, how to give him that same somersaulting stomach and send fire racing through his veins.

He pulled back just enough to rest his forehead against hers. "There aren't proper words in any language to tell you just how much I love you, Skyler."

"I feel the same way." She stroked his hair, fingers massaging his scalp. "You don't have to go, but if you do, I want to be there, too, standing next to you."

"I'll go. You're right about my presence being a slap in the face to them. Mikhail knows what he's doing. He's got the upper hand right now. He wants them to ban hunting Guardians, to acknowledge the difference between *Sange rau* and *Hän ku pesäk kaikak*. They assured him I was safe. When Mikhail brings me into that room, he'll know which ones—if any—are involved in this plan to turn Lycan and Carpathian against one another."

"What else? What else is bothering you?"

He sighed and straightened, dropping his arms. "You're so attuned to me sometimes it's scary, *sívamet*. In matters of your safety, I prefer to act rather than talk."

Skyler burst out laughing. "I know that feeling well."

He took her hand, giving her a dark scowl. "There's no more flinging your body in front of mine to take bullets or anything else."

She managed to look innocent. "Isn't that what you meant by action not words? Why are you worried about my safety when we're here, surrounded by Carpathians?"

"Because you left behind a blood trail," he said. "Any wolf worth his salt could follow it easily."

"That's true," she conceded. "Do you think one will be following us here?" She tried not to shiver, but it wasn't because she was worried about a

Lycan hunting her. Standing naked beside him was much more difficult than lying together or sitting. She felt vulnerable. "Teach me to put on clothes."

"Yes, I think one will be following you here. I like you naked. Are you certain you have to have clothes?" There was a little pained note to his voice.

Laughter bubbled up and she found herself relaxing again. "I suppose I could parade around in front of all those Lycans and Carpathians just like this, but there might be a bit of shocked protest from my parents—both sets of them. And," she added, "if I am going to be bare-butt naked, you have to be as well."

His laughter joined hers, and she was happy to hear how carefree he sounded. "I guess you're right. Sadly. I like looking at you. And if I walked around this way, I'd scare the children."

She immediately put a hand on his chest, running her palm down to his flat belly. "Don't do that, Dimitri. There's nothing wrong with the way you look. I've never seen a more beautiful man. These burns"—she traced one long loop with the pads of her fingers—"these are badges of your courage and mine. We overcame impossible odds."

He caught her fingertips and brought them to the warmth of his mouth, his teeth scraping gently back and forth. "You have a way of making me feel like a hero, *csitri*, a white knight from centuries gone by."

"That's what you'll always be to me, Dimitri," Skyler said. "That's how I've always seen you, and nothing has changed since we've been together."

He shook his head and kissed her knuckles. "Since clothes are so important to you, we'll start there with your first lesson. Everything starts in your mind, build the image of being clean and refreshed, as if you just stepped out of the shower."

Skyler was adept at using her mind. She was already more than capable and apparently far too good at it. She stood in front of him dripping wet. Small droplets of water fell all around them.

Laughing, she stood under the warm drops. "Dimitri, it's raining right here, under your big stone house and underground." She caught at his arm and tugged until he was standing under the shower as well.

"You have the concept," he said, amusement coiling in him like warm molasses. She changed his world just by being in it. He couldn't understand how she could ever doubt herself. She brought joy and happiness. She made him feel alive. He loved watching everything through her eyes. "Try again."

"Oh, you want more?"

The teasing note of challenge should have warned him. The shower increased, soaking him in a torrent while she stayed warm and dry in a little cocoon she had enveloped herself in.

He found himself really laughing, deep belly laughs, something he had never done in his life. Playing was a new experience as an adult. The house brought back memories of his childhood, but there had been no such antics until Skyler.

He caught her up in his arms, cradling her close to his chest for a moment before lifting her straight over his head as if she was his own personal umbrella. Her fancy little cocoon fell to pieces under the onslaught and her merriment.

Skyler let out a scream as the water went from warm to icy cold. "Okay, okay, I surrender."

Instantly the water stopped, and he set her on the ground. Skyler gave him a haughty look and swept her hand down her body, drying herself almost as adeptly as any Carpathian with a century or two on them could do.

"I think you know how to do this," he said.

"Once you told me *what* to do, I realized it was fairly easy. It's the details that can mix one up. You have to pay close attention to the smallest detail."

"That's right. After a few times, it will become second nature to you. You're both Dragonseeker and mage . . ."

"And becoming mixed blood like you," she asserted.

He nodded, frowning a little. "Eventually, yes. Your mind is already fully prepared to use images for dressing, shifting, or creating illusions such as eating or drinking around others not Carpathian."

She leaned into him, brushing at the frown on his lips. "Mixed blood is simply an enhancement, Dimitri. I've been in your mind, healed your body, I know what it's doing to you."

"But we don't know what it will do to you or our children should we have any," Dimitri pointed out. "I want to find a few answers before you're in too deep."

Skyler closed her eyes for a moment, choosing a comfortable outfit, this time, making certain she remembered every detail from the top of her head to her feet. "I'm already in too deep, my love. Stop worrying about things you have no control over. A very wise lifemate said that to me several years ago."

She turned in a circle, showing off the slim blue jeans, boots and soft flannel shirt. Her hair was in an intricate braid, hanging down her back. "What do you think? Ready to face hunting for my own food? Shifting? Standing before the Lycan council? Seeing my mother and father? Facing the prince?"

He took her hand as he donned his own clothes, going as casual as she had. They didn't need to go before the Lycan council in formal clothes. He was damned if he'd dress up for them. Evidently, his lifemate felt the same way.

"You look beautiful, Skyler. We'll hunt first." He felt her shudder and drew her in close, beneath his broad shoulder. He knew that taking blood from a stranger would be difficult for her. "You know you don't have to do this. I'm not altogether certain I even want you to. I find giving you blood and taking yours—erotic."

The low, sensual tone made her blush. "I do, too," she admitted. "It's very sexy and the pleasure is like nothing I've ever experienced." There was a question in her tone.

"It won't be that way with others," he said. "And if it were, I'd forbid you to take blood from anyone else." She laughed softly, but Dimitri could tell she knew he was serious.

They drifted up to the basement of the house, floating together. He had his arm around her waist, but she rose under her own power and he was immensely proud of her concentration. When they came to the ceiling above that that was the basement floor, they stopped.

"Think of mist. The way it looks, the feel and scent of it. Every component." He put the image in her mind, and watched her carefully as she examined every aspect of it. "Mist is more difficult than a lot of other forms because it appears so easy, but in fact, it has a distinct configuration. Mist and fog are both drops of water, clouds along the ground so to speak. Fog is denser. Mist travels as a rule close to the ground. Always remember you have to fit in with your surroundings. If you need mist or fog, you have to create the environment for it if it isn't already there."

Skyler nodded. She felt the first strange shifting in her body, as if she was falling apart, breaking into tiny molecules. She immediately plunged into Dimitri's mind—her safety net—but she kept going, trusting he would stop her if she did anything wrong.

Triumphantly, she found herself moving through the cracks as seemingly nothing more than tiny droplets of water, mist rising from the floor into the basement of the house.

Remember to visualize every single detail of your human form, including the clothes you wore. You can't leave out anything, so take your time. I'm right here with you.

She knew Dimitri was with her. He was the one believing in her, stepping back to allow her to do it on her own. She loved him all the more for understanding she needed to learn and she wanted to do each thing for herself if possible.

Her heart pounded. She could feel it. She heard the roaring of her blood in her ears, like the sound of thunder or a great waterfall, yet she had no body. It was strange and exhilarating. She couldn't let the wonder of it loosen her focus. She needed to put herself back together without losing any part of herself.

She was determined to be thorough, calling on the memory of her anatomy classes until she felt Dimitri's laughter.

If I had my boots on right now, I'd kick you. What am I doing wrong? You said thorough.

I should have known you'd take me literally. Your body is there waiting for you, whole and intact. Put that image in your mind. You'll come together, I promise. I just meant, don't forget your hair or fingernails.

I was thinking of more important body parts like ovaries.

I know you were.

Dimitri's laughter spilled into her mind. Everything in her responded to his merriment. She was having fun, and so was he. He didn't find it a tedious task teaching her things he'd known for centuries. He was enjoying the moments just as she was.

She took a deep breath with lungs that weren't there and shifted. She found herself standing on the floor of the basement with Dimitri looking down at her as if she were the greatest thing in the entire world. He picked her up and spun her around, leaving her breathless.

"You are amazing, *sívamet*. Perfectly amazing. I'm certain you'll have no trouble hunting."

17

Hunting. Just the word alone conjured up blood and death. Skyler had been a wildlife conservationist and advocate for most of her life. She didn't eat meat. She didn't believe in hunting unless one actually ate what they killed. The same with fishing. Killing for sport was abhorrent to her. Hunting sounded so . . . predatory.

Carpathians and Lycans, for that matter, are predators, Dimitri informed her.

He hadn't given her time to explore the house, something she was very eager to do. Instead, he had taken her quickly through the forest to the edge of the village. They waited in the shadows, staying very still, not moving or speaking, just absorbing the rhythm of the village at night.

She could hear the footsteps, feel the vibration through the soles of her boots—she had become that sensitive. She could hear murmured conversations from various houses and bars. If she actually tuned in to any one of them, she could hear exactly what they said.

Already hunger had taken hold of both of them. She could feel the deep need throbbing in her veins. The scent of animals and humans filled her lungs with every breath she drew. She knew where every single person on the street was in relationship to her. Her body had a stillness it never had, and her heart beat in anticipation of what was to come.

There was a kind of excitement and elation in hunting she hadn't anticipated. She actually could hear the ebb and flow of blood in the veins of those closest to her. Without thinking, she focused on one particularly strong beat. A male. She knew who he was, already tuning to him without conscious thought, as if her body knew exactly what to do. His footsteps were steady. He hadn't been drinking. She didn't want blood laced with alcohol.

What's happening to me? She reached out to Dimitri, both frightened and excited at the changes in her.

You are Carpathian. You are light to my darkness, but you are still a predator. You cannot live without sustaining yourself. You will walk up to him, smile, say hello, engage him in a short conversation as your mind tunes to his. When you feel his exact rhythm, you calm him, cloud his mind just long enough to take what you need from him.

Skyler frowned. *Like all of you have done for me. But I consented. I had knowledge.*

They cannot know. It isn't safe. Our species does not exist other than in myths and legends.

Skyler knew he was right. Carpathians, and even Lycans, who had integrated into human society, remained secretive. There were human societies that hunted "vampires," unable to distinguish between Carpathians and vampires, so they indiscriminately killed everyone, just as the Lycans did with the *Sange rau* and the *Hän ku pesäk kaikak.*

She took a deep breath. She'd agreed to this, and a huge part of her wanted to do it on her own, but taking blood from an unsuspecting person made her feel as if she was making the man her victim, and that didn't sit well with her.

You know you don't have to do this.

She shot Dimitri a quelling look. It was difficult enough to force herself to become a predator, let alone fighting the impulse to take the "out" he offered her.

Once you are absolutely certain you have him out of sight of any other and in a thrall, under your complete control, your body will know what to do. Take only what you need to survive and thrive. There is no need for more, although the impulse will be there just because your body craves blood. Use discipline. If you can't stop yourself, reach for me.

He would be monitoring her to ensure nothing went wrong, but he wanted to give her the opportunity to handle every aspect for herself. Children learned these lessons at an early age. She had been human and it could be more difficult.

Skyler moistened her lips and ran her tongue over her already sharpening teeth. She nodded and forced herself to take that first step out of the shadows. Once she managed that, she began to stroll toward her prey.

She was shocked at how quietly she walked, how she was so tuned to every heartbeat, every whisper of sound around her. Heat banded, changing her vision, so that she could see every artery and vein, the very heart of the man she approached.

Skyler flashed a smile. His head jerked up and he stopped in his tracks. A low growl came from out of the night, shocking her, shocking him. Instinctively he stepped closer, protectively to her.

"Good evening," she greeted, turning her head toward the sound.

Two red eyes stared back at her. Her heart stuttered for a moment. *Dimitri, you said this was necessary for me to learn.*

I didn't know how I would feel.

Stay in my mind so you know how I feel, not him. Carpathian women seem to mesmerize men fairly easily. He wasn't interested in the least until I smiled at him. In any case, he feels protective, not sexual.

Do not fool yourself, and don't let him touch you. I am disciplined, but find that perhaps I will need to work on control when other men desire you.

His unexpected reaction helped her to overcome her own nerves. She loved that Dimitri might have a small little weakness. It was so very human. Butterflies actually took flight in her stomach, wings fluttering against her abdomen. Her breasts tingled and she felt the heat rising between her legs, signaling her need of her lifemate. She was beginning to revel in her ability to want him. Each time it happened she felt more hopeful that she could meet his every need.

Stop! Stop thinking about sex when you're approaching another man and you're about to bite into his neck and take his blood.

The urgency in Dimitri's voice brought her up short. She touched his mind and found—chaos—a red, almost blinding rage that had nothing to do with enemies and everything to do with the poor innocent man she had selected as her first target.

She stepped back from him immediately and lifted her hand. "Have a good night."

"Wait. It isn't safe for you to walk alone right now," the man cautioned.

"My husband is waiting for me." She indicated just ahead of her. "Thank you for your concern though." She kept walking, moving quickly into the shadows, knowing Dimitri had moved to intercept her.

She walked right up to him, merging her mind more deeply with his. *Be calm, my love, this won't hurt a bit.*

She slid the buttons from the clasps, one by one, deliberately slow and sensuous. When his shirt fell open, she ran the palms of her hands up his belly to his chest.

There's nothing to fear. You're safe with me.

She bent her head and followed the path of her hands with her tongue, stopping for a moment to circle his belly button and trace the links of a few of the chains, as if she had gotten a little distracted by his body. She found the reassuring beat of his heart and the rhythm of his blood, surging so hotly in his veins, beckoning her.

Her teeth lengthened. She let need rise—the terrible, sweet hunger—until the feeling completely enveloped her. There was more than just the desire to feed. Her heart matched his, and she trailed kisses over the vein in his chest, over those heavy muscles that always intrigued her. Her tongue swirled and danced, stroked, and then she bit deep, finding the vein unerringly.

He gasped, threw his head back, one hand pressing her closer to him. There was no horror at what she was doing, only a rising urgency that had nothing to do with feeding. She wanted him with every breath that she took—wanted his body. She wanted him inside of her, possessing her, completing her.

His essence was addictive and so was the feeling rising just as sharp, just as terrible and just as sweet. Feeding from Dimitri was wholly erotic. She wanted to wrap her body around his, rub against him like an alley cat. She wanted his hands on her breasts and his fingers pressing into her body.

You must stop, sívamet, he cautioned.

His voice came from far off, barely heard through the roaring in her ears. She managed to obey, but only because it was Dimitri who commanded her. Pulling herself away from that erotic well was difficult, but she forced herself under control, sliding her tongue instinctively over the small wound in his chest.

She lifted her head to look at him, knowing her desire was there in her eyes. He had to feel the way her nipples had grown tight, peaking against him. He had to smell the welcoming hot spice spilling between her legs.

He framed her face and bent down to kiss her mouth. *Are you certain, csitri? Very certain?*

This seems to be a perfect night for teaching. We have this night for us. Let them all wait. We haven't asked for anything for ourselves, we should be able to have one night. She could barely breathe with wanting him. *Teach me what lovemaking is. I want to know everything.*

Wait one moment, Dimitri said. *I will feed quickly and we'll return to our home.*

And a bed. I want a bed.

His eyes glowed in the dark, moving over her possessively. Instead of frightening her, she felt excited. If she was completely honest with herself, there was a little trepidation, but that added to the thrill.

You will have your bed, avio päläfertiil.

Dimitri moved away from her. He was so skilled she couldn't really make out his image as he caught up with the man she had marked as her first prey. She blinked. Dimitri was on the man in half a second, wrapping them both in darkness, bending his head to the merchant's neck even as he shielded them from all eyes.

He was back to her almost immediately, in complete silence. He gathered her into his arms and took to the air, back into the forest, moving swiftly toward their stone house. When they'd walked through it, the house had been clean but mostly devoid of furniture. He'd removed the damp, musty smell and replaced it with a fresh, clean scent, but he hadn't had time to do much more.

Now he focused on the main bedroom, which was situated directly over the basement. There were numerous ways to get out of the room to safety should there ever be need. He put the bed in place with a thick mattress and soft sheets. Candles sprang up on the shelves and in the sconces, providing soft lighting.

As he took her through the house to get to the room, she looked around her, eyes wide. "We really need to work on the décor before we invite the neighbors," she told him.

"I wasn't planning on inviting anyone for a while," he confided, and kicked open the bedroom door. He carried her through to the bed. "You're certain, Skyler?" he asked again. "You don't have to do this for me."

"I'm doing it for both of us," Skyler said. "You ought to know me by now, Dimitri. I'm ready. Merge with me. See me the way I am right in this moment. I knew when I took your blood that this was the time for us, and I don't want to wait. I don't want to look back and realize that we missed our perfect moment."

Skyler looped her arm around his neck and reached up to kiss him. She didn't just kiss him, she devoured him, unafraid to show her demands. She loved his mouth. She loved the way he poured his passion into her and she caught fire.

He lowered her to the bed and she caught his open shirt in both hands and pulled him down with her.

"Before we do anything else," she whispered, "there's something I've needed to do, but I've not had the courage. Lie down for me and remove your clothes."

Dimitri did as she instructed, his eyes so intensely blue they could have been gemstones. He didn't take his gaze from her. "I'm removing your clothes as well," he told her. His voice had gone low and husky, need beginning to drive him. "Whatever you're about to do to me, you can do it naked. I might need a distraction."

"You're such a baby sometimes," she teased.

Skyler waited until Dimitri settled on the bed. He was a big man and he took up a lot of space, nearly the entire mattress. She studied his body for a long moment. His muscles were extremely defined, roped and fluid. His chest was deep, his waist narrow and his belly flat. Already his erection was heavy and full, long and thick, with desire for her. His long legs were very muscular.

From his neck down to his ankles, the loops of silver chain had been burned into his body. They went entirely around him, front to back. She had mostly tried to lessen the impact of the scars on his forehead and neck, but she had wanted to try something altogether different.

Slowly she slung one leg over his hips and straddled him, settling the heat between her legs directly over his erection. He sucked in his breath, but he didn't move, allowing her to continue.

"I've thought about this for the last five nights," she confided softly. "I'm Carpathian, a Dragonseeker and daughter of Mother Earth. I am Razvan's daughter, mage is in my blood. I learned from Francesca, one of our greatest healers. I will not let silver defeat me. What is it? A metal of the earth. The properties that burned you can be undone."

Dimitri opened his mouth, thinking to protest, wanting to complete the ritual of lifemates, but she leaned over him, her soft wet heat rubbing sensuously over his cock, robbing him of breath, of the ability to think, let alone speak.

Her tongue lapped at the chain burns high on his chest with her healing saliva. He heard her chant in his mind, a soft litany of words calling the tiny silver particles embedded in the burns to come forth, and take with them the damage they had caused.

I am Skyler, daughter of the Dragonseeker,
Great-granddaughter of the high mage,
I am Skyler, daughter of Mother Earth.
I call to thee, silver, let us break him from this cage.

Her voice rang with power, swelling in strength, not volume. She became commanding, a true child of both Dragonseeker and mage, as well as a child of the earth. Dimitri marveled at her poise and confidence, even as he tried to stay still beneath her ministrations.

You are silver, my beautiful brother,
But your beauty has been tainted by another.

You have been misled, you have been misguided,
I am calling to you, pleading, help me fight it.

The chant was in her mind. Her mouth moved over his skin, lapping gently, thoroughly, her fingers tracing ahead of her tongue. It was beyond sensuous, beyond anything he'd ever imagined. Skyler concentrated on healing him, but her body moved over his with such intimacy, her every touch mixed with passion and love for him.

Adoration, she murmured and stroked her tongue lower.

His cock jerked, as she slipped off of that intimate part of him to straddle his thighs. Her breasts pushed into his groin. He could feel the soft mounds and her erect nipples pressing into his center so that his heavy erection nestled in the heat between them.

I have adored you almost from the moment we met. You came into my life and there has been no other to fill those dark empty places. Only you, she whispered into his mind.

Her tongue continued to administer to his burns, following the chains lower and lower with those soft lapping velvet strokes until his heart nearly stopped beating in anticipation.

I call to my brother silver, let go,
Free yourself from this blessed soul.
Bring forth with you the damage to skin and bone,
My brother, give me aid, I cannot heal him alone.

Desire and love twined together until there was no separating the two. She used her devotion for Dimitri as well as her growing hunger for his body to chain the silver to her, to draw out the tiny particles, calling them to her, the worst of the burns adhering to the metal.

Her mouth moved lower, and a groan escaped him as her tongue lapped at the chain links across his shaft. Her tongue bathed him with soothing heat, her lips brushing kisses over him in between that soft stroking.

His lungs burned for air, but she didn't stop, moving even lower, to the chain marks around his hips and thighs. She was killing him with her healing, a slow, deliberate assault on his senses.

He knew she wanted to heal his scars, to ease that tightness in his body that refused to go away, but she could explore, she could taste him, get to know his body intimately, claim every square inch of him for her own, getting lost in the sensations rising between them—and not feel threatened. She was in her element healing him. She was in control.

Dimitri knew she was making her way to him the only way she knew how, and for him, her determination was not only beautiful, but sexy beyond description. She moved over him with care, every touch loving. He felt her love intertwining with her power to lift the rigid tight scars and draw out the tiny particles of silver left behind in skin and bone.

Her mouth moved over him in a kind of worship that left him mad with desire, and trembling with such a terrible love for her he felt the burn of tears behind his eyes.

Come to me, silver, I offer my skin,
Bring all the scars away from him.
Join with me, brother, drive out his pain,
So that only my warrior, my beloved, remains.

To his utter shock, the chains around him loosened noticeably. He hadn't realized he'd pushed pain to the back of his mind, accepting that it would be there for all eternity. He should have known she would find it there when she merged with him. It was impossible to hide anything from her. The pain eased and then slowly disappeared, leaving him lying beneath her, free of all silver, the chains only faint memories in his body.

Skyler sat up slowly, and at once he could see the burns covering her skin like a coat of armor. His heart jerked, his hands coming up to grip her arms. "What have you done?"

She shrugged, and the coat shimmied to the floor and disintegrated. "I've loved you the best way I know how." She smiled at him and brushed her hand over his flat stomach.

He rolled her over. "Then it's my turn, isn't it?"

Skyler lay sprawled beneath him, but he was very careful not to pin her down, or make her feel trapped. He caged her in with his arms, but made certain she had freedom of movement. She didn't flinch, but looked up at him, the love in her eyes wreaking havoc with his heart.

"I'm expecting great things, my love," she whispered softly, tracing his lips with her fingertip.

A slow smile curved his mouth. Amusement crept into his glacier-blue eyes. "I'll do my best not to disappoint."

He bent his head to fasten his mouth to hers. Tasting her. Savoring her. Loving her. She was a miracle of heat, of fire, pouring into him, cleansing him until he felt brand-new. He tasted her passion and knew he was addicted for life.

He kissed his way from her mouth to her chin, and then down her throat. He stroked one finger over her breast and felt her immediate response, a shiver of pleasure. Her hips moved subtly, a calling, a need.

He cupped her breast, his thumb sliding over her nipple, brushing gently at first, and then tugging and rolling, all the while watching her reaction. She shivered again, not pulling away, but rather pushing into his hand. Her breasts were definitely sensitive. Each touch sent a small rush of liquid fire dampening between her legs.

"You realize you have a fixation," she teased, her voice husky and a little ragged.

"Obsession," he corrected and lowered his mouth.

While he suckled, he flattened his tongue, stroking and teasing, even using the edge of his teeth. His fingers tugged and rolled the nipple of her other breast. He was very careful not to let his own desire get out of hand. From the moment he first saw her—touched her—inhaled her—he was lost and he knew it.

He wanted her with him every step of the way, her passion growing until it matched his—until she got to that euphoria of pure feeling and let herself go completely. Skyler needed to be comfortable with him and trust him. No matter how aroused she was, there would be moments she would panic, and she had to know he was capable of hearing, even perceiving those moments before she did and stopping immediately if necessary.

He lifted his head from the sweet temptation of her curves and kissed her again, long and slow. Their world was about love and he wanted to wrap her in it. He had enough love for her to hold her for eternity and he wanted her to feel that always.

He lowered his head again to the sweet curve of her breasts, licking over the tempting pulse just along the swell that led to the valley, using the edge of his teeth, letting her feel the sensation. Her heart accelerated. Her hips moved again, urgency beginning to grow in her. He bit deep. She gasped. Arched. The bite of pain burst through her. Merged as he was with her, he felt that erotic bite spread like a firestorm through her body.

Her arms came up to circle his head, fingers fisting in his hair. She cried out as he began to draw her life's blood from her body, merging them further, his hands once more at her breasts. She was his, this beautiful body, soft and warm and so responsive. Once she made up her mind, she gave of herself so freely, putting herself in his hands, trusting him. Her trust humbled him.

He lifted his head, watching the twin ruby beads began to flow over the slope of her breast. He chased them, drew them into his mouth and then closed those small wounds. He'd left his mark on her, and he found it pleased him.

He kissed his way down her flat stomach, taking his time, tracing each rib with his tongue, his hands exploring and shaping. Her breath came in ragged little gasps and she made a soft sound that sounded like his name, a chanting barely heard, but music nonetheless. His tongue dipped into her belly button and his hands slipped lower to cup her bottom.

Skyler's hands went to his hair, bunched there. Her body writhed under his now. Her skin was hot, glowing. "Dimitri?" Her voice trembled, and in her mind he could feel the skittering of fear. But this time, she wasn't afraid of her own reaction, or that he might hurt her; the pleasure engulfed her, threatened her control and she hadn't expected that.

"I've got you. Just let yourself feel. You're safe with me."

Her eyes met his, searching. He looked at her steadily, letting her see he would always be there to catch her. She let her breath out and nodded, lying back again, but her fists remained in his hair as if she anchored herself there.

He kissed her belly button and continued his leisurely exploring, running his tongue along her hipbones, and then over to the dragon, the mark of the

Dragonseeker, much like a tattoo, very faint just over her ovary. He spent time there, lapping at it, tracing it, nuzzling her over and over. His hand went to her thigh, parting her legs, letting her feel the cool air on her hot, wet entrance.

So much heat. He was drawn there, his mouth moving lower until he could catch drops of nectar. Her taste was addictive and he found he couldn't stop. He lifted her hips to his mouth, pressing deep, his tongue pushing into that little tight flower, drawing out as much liquid as he could get. She gasped and cried out, thrashing again.

Dimitri lifted his head to look at her. He knew his eyes glowed with the heat of a predator. There was no way to hide what he was from her, but she was safe with him. "Let me," he said softly. "Give yourself to me. All of you. You belong to me, *csitri*, you know you do. Let me have you."

She nodded, but she looked frightened. "It's too much. The sensation. As if I might fly apart and never be me again."

Deliberately, watching her eyes, he swiped his tongue through her soft folds, circled her most sensitive bud and then stabbed deep again. Tremors wracked her body, but her gaze didn't falter. He saw fear, but he saw trust. His heart leapt and his cock jerked. He was already caught between the intensity of love and urgent need for her body. The two were woven so tightly together he couldn't separate them.

He began to devour her, driving her up that high cliff and stopping just before she tumbled over. Again and again. He needed to hear her soft little cries. He wanted to feel her fingers clamped in his hair, or her nails digging into his shoulders. Her cries were music to him, a symphony of desire, the notes so sweet he was nearly as addicted to that as he was to her taste.

Skyler crammed a fist in her mouth as fiery need licked over her skin. She had expected pain and degradation, not his worshiping her body as she had his. Her breathing came in harsh gasps, and she couldn't stop writhing, no matter how hard she tried. She felt as if Dimitri's passion and love were destroying her, tearing down fear and shame and forging her into a strong, sensual woman.

She heard herself chanting his name and she couldn't stop. He was her talisman, her anchor, her very strength. He lapped at the hot nectar spilling from her body, his tongue licking and stabbing deep, moving in torturous slow circles, driving her insane as tension built and built, stretching her out on a rack of pleasure.

Her head thrashed back and forth. Tremors ran down her thighs. Her breasts burned and ached for him. Deep inside, she coiled tighter and tighter, desperate for release. She whimpered. Sobbed. Pleaded with him. She needed him inside of her, to sate the all-encompassing hunger. She felt as if she was soaring out of control. She was skating the edge of panic, only her trust in him keeping her from fighting. She was afraid of burning up from the inside out, fragmenting into tiny pieces, or going insane from sheer pleasure.

He lifted his head when she cried out, her hips bucking, as she pleaded with him. He knelt up slowly between her thighs. He looked . . . intimidating. He was a big man and the thought of him fitting inside her was daunting, but she was too far gone to care. She needed him. Desperately. She wanted him. More than anything she wanted to be fully his.

You are mine.

Her eyes met his. His had gone nearly all wolf, the glowing predatory, focused stare that should have terrified her, but kept her steady and sane. *She* terrified herself, never Dimitri. No matter what face he wore, he was hers. She moistened her lips, her heart pounding.

His hands were big as they ran up her thighs, and then slowly back toward her heated center. The head of his cock lodged at her entrance, pressing hotly into her. Her heart pounded so loud she feared it would burst from her chest.

"I take into my keeping your body." His voice was rough with need.

His expression was sin itself, so sensual her body flooded with more welcoming heat. He inched into her, stretching her impossibly. Her gaze jumped to the junction where their bodies met. Her body struggled against the invasion, reluctantly giving way for him, strangling his thick shaft as it moved deeper inside of her.

He was everywhere, surrounding her. In her mind. Her heart. Her soul. And now, at last he was in her body, making them truly one. Another sob escaped. Tears ran down her face. He was in her mind, so he would know she wanted him just like this. It was all too perfect, too overwhelming and too good.

"Take a breath," he ordered roughly. "Relax for me."

She was used to doing as he said and she did both. He drove deep, burying himself to the hilt, so deep she thought he might have lodged in her stomach. She heard her own cry as her tight inner muscles gripped him nearly to the point of strangulation. The bite of pain as he stretched her only added to the erotic pleasure pulsing through her body, coming in waves now, from thigh to breast.

Dimitri blanketed her body with his, bracing his arms at her shoulders. His hips took up a fast, hard tempo that kept her breath rushing from her burning lungs. He moved in her with deep harsh strokes that drove her higher and higher, always up toward that impossible cliff. The pace was furious, his body a piston, moving harder and deeper, over and over, so that shocks of pleasure coursed through her.

Dimitri's relentless, surging hips drove into her again and again, his hunger nearly insatiable. He felt as if flames licked at him, all over his body. His cock felt as though it was held tight in a fist of fiery, living silk. He was drowning in her. He never wanted it to end. He had known they were meant for one another, but her body was exquisite, made for him, the perfect fit.

She felt small and soft, her skin melting under him. Her ragged breathing and breathy chants interspersed with sobs and pleading only added to the sheer pleasure coursing through his veins. She had changed him for all time. She moved him, took him to places he never thought he could ever go.

Hunger was a monster that clawed and raged. It had been with him since he'd laid eyes on his lifemate, heard her speak and knew she was the one. It had torn at him every rising, yet even in his most savage moment, love tempered his touch. He kept his mind in hers, wanting her pleasure above all else, above his own.

She had given herself to him, body and soul, placing her absolute trust in him, a priceless gift he would treasure above all else. Her body was flushed, her eyes glazed, her hips bucked under his assault, but with every surge of his hips, every gasp she drew, there was pleasure streaking through her—through him.

He set a wild pace, and she followed. He knew she would. He had sensed the building passion in her, and no matter how fragile she was, she had a core of solid steel. She was determined to match him. His control slipped even more.

Tell me you want this, sívamet. Tell me I can lose myself in you.

His love for her was ferocious, consuming them both, and his discipline was fast dissolving before the urgency of his need.

Always, my love. Anything.

He closed his eyes briefly for a moment, listening to her voice. There was no hesitation, but there was that little edge of trepidation. She wasn't afraid of him, only of the rising pleasure, rolling over her in waves now and the tightening coil of tension in her body, begging for release. She meant what she said, giving herself generously, wanted—no—needing to be what he needed.

He penetrated deep, allowing the fire pouring over him to take him to another place. The breath hissed out of him as he reared back and plunged deep. With every furious stroke, her body surrounded his, tight and hot, stroking and squeezing. Her strangled moans and gasping chant added to his pleasure, and filled him with the most protective of instincts.

Her head tossed back and forth, her body flushed, her breasts swaying temptingly as her hips rose to meet his. She was beautiful, with her eyes slightly glazed and the shock on her face. The little sounds she made resonated right through his cock adding to the fire that only seemed to grow hotter and hotter.

He was close, the power in his body coiling tighter and tighter, ready for release, but he refused to allow the pleasure to end. He gathered her hips tightly, holding her still, pushing them both into another realm where the exquisite pleasure skated close to pain.

Skyler could feel the thickness and length of him driving into her, stretching her, forcing her tight body to allow his invasion. She was so hot and slick, surrounding him with fire. The erotic tension winding so tight in her refused to release, refused to give her the time to catch her breath.

Skyler felt her body melting around his, and she cried his name, gripping his shoulders as the tension coiled so tight the edges of mind began to blur, to go dark. It was too much for her, too perfectly beautiful and too terribly frightening. She was losing herself in him, in pleasure, in their bodies coming together in a frenzy of heat and fire.

"Stay with me, *sívamet*," he whispered roughly, his mouth moving over her neck, teeth nipping and scraping. "Soar with me."

As always, just the sound of his voice calmed her, and she let go, knowing he would catch her, that he would keep her safe. Her body gripped his so tightly that she heard his roar of release and felt the hot spurts of seed filling her. Wave after wave rocked her body, but his arms were around her, holding her tight. She felt the ripples in her stomach, down her thighs, up to her breasts. Thunder roared in her ears. Her body clamped down hard, like a vise, around his while wave after wave of pleasure tore through her.

Skyler buried her face against his shoulder, gasping for breath, aftershocks rocking her, nearly as strong as the orgasm that had taken her over. He rolled them both over so they were on their sides, still locked together. She could feel his struggle for every breath. A fine sheen of sweat dampened his body. Even his long hair was damp.

She nuzzled his shoulder, pressing kisses along his collarbone. They were a tangle of legs and thighs, and she never wanted to untangle. He pulsed and throbbed inside of her. When he could move, it was toward her breast, and she changed position slightly to give him better access. The movement caused another rogue wave to burst through her body.

He licked at her nipple and then caught it gently between his teeth, tugging and then suckling strongly, bringing her fully into the heat of his mouth. His arm went around her, hand sliding down her back to her bottom. She had never realized just how sensitive the nerves were there. His every touch sent another spasm of pleasure through her core.

They lay together in silence while their hearts slowed down and their bodies cooled—a little. She had to admit to herself she loved his hands and mouth on her.

When he finally lifted his head to look down at her, his body slowly, reluctantly leaving hers, she had the urge to stop him. His eyes were so blue, so brilliant, and he looked at her with so much love, she wanted to cry. He was the true miracle, no matter what he thought, and she was determined to make him happy she was his lifemate.

"*Csitri*, I doubt I will ever be able to show you your true worth," he told her softly. "You don't understand what you mean to me."

There were no words to explain to him what a miracle he was. He had given her the gift of making love, something she had been absolutely certain she'd never have in her life. More, she could lie next to him, completely naked and vulnerable and feel as if she was the safest woman in the world. She *wanted* to be naked beside him. She wanted him to touch her whenever he needed or—or simply desired. She loved stroking her fingers down his shaft just to feel him tremble at her touch. Who would ever have thought she would have a man such as Dimitri love her?

"I'll understand how much I mean to you someday, probably a long time from now," she said, "but it really doesn't matter right at this moment. All that matters to me is that you gave me this incredible gift. I love you all the more for it."

18

"The council members are inside," Fen greeted them. "Waiting." He pinned his brother with an appraising eye.

"They've been waiting the last six nights," Zev added. "We thought for certain you would be here last night."

Skyler blushed and glanced up at Dimitri's impassive face. Clearly, he couldn't care less that he'd kept the council waiting. They hadn't left the bed the night before. Dimitri had taught her all kinds of intriguing things she would much rather be doing than standing before the Lycan council with the prince looking on.

She had made certain that Dimitri looked exactly as he had before she'd healed him the night before. She wanted the Lycans to see the evidence of their medieval tortures. She slipped her hand into Dimitri's for comfort. She didn't especially want to see any of these people.

At once she had his undivided attention. *What is it, csitri?*

One word from her and they would turn and walk away. Dimitri wouldn't care what others thought of him. He never had. He was a man who went his own way. It was tempting to use that power she knew she had, but it was wrong. This meeting was important. She took a deep breath and let it out.

I'm just steeling myself to meet the prince again. Well, because she wasn't going to lie to him, *that and seeing these Lycans.*

Zev is Lycan and he's a good man.

She gave a little indelicate sniff of disdain. *Maybe he is, but he didn't save you when he should have.*

Dimitri's amusement filled her mind. *Why, Skyler Rose. You carry a grudge.*

So true. She stared at the tree nearest the elite hunter.

Above his head, a hive rocked and bees came pouring out.

I believe in revenge, she added complacently.

Fen flung his hands into the air, building a shield fast to keep them all from being stung by the angry bees. It took him a couple of moments to notice not a single bee came near any of them but Zev. He glared at his brother.

"I didn't do it," Dimitri proclaimed.

Skyler put on her most innocent face. "Nature is so unpredictable."

"Isn't it?" Fen said wryly. "Is it safe to let you inside?"

Skyler shrugged, unrepentant. "Only if those inside didn't issue a death by silver order on my lifemate."

Zev burst out laughing. "Lord, Dimitri, you have your hands full."

Dimitri tightened his fingers around Skyler's, bringing her hand to his chest, right over his heart. "I'm well aware of that. She's Dragonseeker. I would expect nothing less."

"Related to Tatijana and Branislava?" Zev asked, interest creeping into his tone.

Fen groaned. "Give it up, Zev. Seriously, you're like a wolf with a bone."

"I just asked if she's related," Zev pointed out. "And if you keep it up, we're going to be crossing swords."

Fen laughed. "I'm not drawing my sword around you. We could use lightning bolts."

Zev's eyebrow shot up. "I haven't quite mastered that yet, but I might ask Skyler for lessons in keeping bees."

"I'm still angry with you," Skyler said. "So any spell I give you could backfire."

"Well, at least you warned me," Zev said. "I understand why you're angry with me. *I'm* angry with me right now. I don't understand completely yet what is happening with my people. None of us understand. The council members swear they didn't issue the order for *Moarta de argint*, in fact, they claim just the opposite—that Dimitri was to be kept safe at all times."

"Why weren't you with him?" Skyler asked. "If you're the one trusted by the council, why wouldn't they have you guarding a prisoner so important?"

"I was taken behind his back," Dimitri explained, his voice gentle. "Fen and I were fighting the *Sange rau*. Zev and his hunters were with the prince, fighting off the rogue pack. The two men who grabbed me were from Zev's pack, but they should have been with those guarding Mikhail."

"Dimitri and I had gone off on our own without letting Zev know what we were doing," Fen clarified. "At the time he wasn't aware we both were of mixed blood, and we wanted to keep it that way for obvious reasons."

"Fen also figured we had the best chance of defeating the *Sange rau*," Dimitri added. "With our mixed blood we were both faster and better equipped to deal with one. Fen had more experience than anyone else."

"How did those two hunters come to be in the same place?" Skyler asked. "If no one knew where you went, how did they? Was it coincidence?"

"I don't believe in coincidence," Zev said.

For the first time, his voice made Skyler shiver. Her gaze jumped to his face. He was a man who had seen battle often. She could see danger stamped in him, the predator close to the surface, but she'd also experienced his kindness.

"Neither do I," Dimitri agreed. "If there had been time, I would have known something was wrong, but everything happened so fast. Fen was in trouble and the two hunters were as well. I didn't stop to think, I just reacted. Had I asked myself that question, how did they find us, I wouldn't have been knocked over the head and taken prisoner."

Fen lifted an eyebrow. "And then your lady wouldn't have come running to bail your butt out of trouble."

Dimitri pressed her hand tighter against his heart. *You are worth every link of those silver chains burning into my flesh night and day*, he whispered into her mind, meaning it.

Skyler stepped closer to him, slipping beneath his shoulder. *You could be just a little crazy thinking like that, I must ask the healer to take a look at you.*

She couldn't help the little flare of excitement at his compliment. He had a way of always making her feel special. "Are Gabriel and Francesca inside?" she asked aloud.

"Not yet," Fen answered. "Gabriel and your uncle Lucian are out with a few others patrolling, making certain we aren't going to get any uninvited guests."

Dimitri's gaze met his brother's over Skyler's head. *You know if the assassins come for us, they will most likely go undetected by any patrol.*

Fen inclined his head. *It's true, but we're still looking. Gabriel and Lucian are very good at sensing the enemy, and they have a better chance than most. Zev and I are taking turns scouting around. He's really adept at finding tracks, much better even than I am. I'm learning quite a bit from him.*

It's been six days, nearly a week, plenty of time for an assassin to follow a blood trail, Dimitri pointed out.

Skyler cleared her throat. "Really, it isn't necessary to try to protect me from your fears for me, either of you. All of you are in as much danger as I am."

"Maybe," Dimitri conceded, bringing her fingers to his mouth. "But they considered you a sorceress of some sort, perhaps a female *Sange rau* capable of populating the earth with your children. I think you and Zev are in the most danger."

Zev grinned at her. "You aren't the only one who despises me."

She sighed, giving him a pained look. "Well that just changes things," she said in mock disgust. "Now I have to be on your side."

"We'd better go in before Gregori comes out here," Fen said. "And if you're wondering where that threat came from, he just sent me a solemn oath that he'd be out here in two seconds if we didn't move it."

Zev and Dimitri both exchanged a long look and shrugged their shoulders as if Gregori's threat mattered little to them—and it most likely didn't. Still, Dimitri placed his hand on Skyler's back lightly, guiding her, maintaining contact with her at all times. They followed Fen inside with Zev bringing up the rear. She realized that with Fen in front of them and Zev behind them, their escort was really protecting them from any unforeseen trouble.

The meeting room was spacious, with plenty of seating and tables set up with food and drink along the walls for the Lycans. Each council member had his own pack and therefore, his own elite guards. Over all of the elite guards were Zev and his pack. He answered to the entire council and when there was trouble within an elite pack, he was the one sent to make it right. If he showed up, the situation was considered dire—and it would get fixed one way or the other.

Skyler hadn't known Zev was so well respected, but even the council members treated him with deference, much like the respect afforded to Gregori. The council members averted their eyes from Dimitri as he walked Skyler straight over to the prince. He didn't look at anyone else in the room, but she did, wanting to see reactions.

Most of the Lycans in the room seemed horrified by the sight of the survivor of the *Moarta de argint*. She noted two men who seemed fascinated by the scars and more than a little satisfied. Several others nodded, as if they agreed with the torture. But . . .

The council member just to the left of the man in the center, she sent to Dimitri, including Fen in her observation. *Check him out.*

The man hadn't so much as looked up. He appeared to be looking at text messages on his phone, rather than being interested in the Carpathian prisoner whose treatment at the hands of the Lycans had nearly started a war.

Can you see what he's doing? she asked.

Playing with his phone, Fen said. *Some people can't handle scars and burns. It makes them uncomfortable.*

Dimitri greeted the prince with a warrior's forearm clasp as Mikhail did the same with him. *Except, Fen, he doesn't look uncomfortable. He looks smug.* "It is good to see you, Mikhail," he said aloud. "I trust Raven and your son are well."

"Very well, thank you," Mikhail answered and turned to look at Skyler with his piercing dark eyes. "We owe you, Paul and Josef a debt of gratitude. Fen tells me had you not found Dimitri, he wouldn't have survived. Our rescuers would have been too late."

Up so close to Mikhail, his power and presence were intimidating, although she could see kindness in his face. "I'm fortunate that we have a strong bond and I was able to find him."

"She put a tracking device in my pocket," Zev said. "She's a clever woman."

There was admiration in his voice, surprising Skyler. She hadn't expected that from Zev. He clearly didn't hold any grudges.

Mikhail's eyebrow shot up. "She did?"

Zev nodded. "I never suspected a thing. She was smooth, so smooth I'm certain she could easily live the life of a successful pickpocket if she chooses to. She has that innocent face, and no one would ever suspect her."

Skyler smiled at him. "That was the plan."

"So simple," Mikhail mused. "It's a good lesson for us all. Sometimes the simplest plan is far better than all the intrigue in the world." His eyes met Dimitri's. "I would like to introduce you to the Lycan council members. If you don't mind answering their questions, it would perhaps help us put pieces of the puzzle together. You were in the Lycan camp two weeks."

"Over two weeks," Skyler clarified. She couldn't suppress the little bite to her voice. She didn't care if she was talking to the prince. Dimitri had suffered at the hands of the Lycans, and he would have been dead if he'd had to wait for the Carpathians to rescue him.

Dimitri took her hand, threading his fingers gently through hers. *This is not his fault, sívamet. Perhaps it is not the fault of these men on the council either. Fen and others were sent out on my trail, but they couldn't find tracks.* He brushed his mouth across her knuckles. *Only you managed to reach me in spite of the silver cutting me off from everyone else.*

Mollified, Skyler nodded to let him know she understood. She went to step back, tugging at her hand, but Dimitri refused to release her.

Dimitri glided with the prince across the room to the Lycan council table, taking her with him. Dimitri moved in absolute silence, his body fluid, shoulders straight and his head high. The blackened scars were vivid, circling his forehead and throat. He wore a white shirt, opened to the waist, allowing everyone to see the bands of blackened scars around his body.

A hush fell over the room as he approached the table of council members. Three of the four men rose to their feet as he neared them, and the last one did a little reluctantly and only because one of the other council members glared at him.

"Rolf, Lyall, Randall, Arno, this is Dimitri. He may be able to tell us a lot more about what happened in the Lycan camp," Mikhail introduced them.

Skyler had never been prouder of Dimitri. He gave the council members a courtly bow. He looked very old world and elegant, a man of great courtesy and courage. There was a subtle aura given off by him, and judging by the way the council's guards came to attention, she wasn't the only one who felt it. She didn't know if it was in the way he moved, the fluid, silent glide that told anyone watching he was dangerous, or rather the elusive scent of the predator clinging to him, that put everyone on alert.

She watched Rolf, the eldest of the group, hold out his hand to Dimitri, apologizing on behalf of the Lycan people for what the Carpathian warrior had endured at their hands. He promised Dimitri they would find those responsible and punish them. The ring of honesty was in his voice, and Skyler found herself believing him.

Randall was a frightening bear of a man. Had she met him in the forest rather than Zev, she would have run for her life. He had a booming voice that echoed through the room when he spoke, adding his apologies to those of Rolf. She stood just a little behind Dimitri, his body partially shielding her from the Lycans, but to his bodyguards' dismay, Randall stepped out from behind the table and came around to stand in front of Dimitri.

"Is this the young woman who saved your life?" He didn't wait for Dimitri to answer, but leaned down to take her hand.

Dimitri's hand got there first, deflecting the Lycan away from Skyler, his body suddenly solidly between the two. Randall's bodyguards sprang forward the moment Dimitri touched Randall. As the Lycans put their hands on their weapons, Fen and several other Carpathians moved into position to protect the couple. Gregori glided very subtly, positioning himself just a little in front of the prince.

The tension in the room rose to a screaming point. Zev stepped between the two species, his hand in the air. Skyler hadn't even seen him move, but his presence seemed to calm everyone.

"In the Carpathian culture, other men rarely touch one's lifemate," he explained quietly, addressing Randall as if the others weren't rattling their weapons. He sounded as if he was merely passing on information, not stopping a battle. "Skyler is Dimitri's lifemate. As you know, she nearly died, and you can understand he is quite protective of her."

Skyler admired his voice, low, smooth, calming. It was a gift, a rare one, but powerful. He could calm a crowd with that voice and he did so easily.

"I apologize," Randall said to Dimitri. "I had no idea. Is talking to her forbidden as well?"

His booming voice rang through the room, making Skyler wince. She felt as if she'd been reduced to a schoolgirl, a small child who needed parental permission before speaking with an important adult.

What are you doing? She hissed the question to Dimitri, a little shocked at his behavior. *I thought we came here to stop a war, not start one.*

It was an automatic reaction. I don't like men I don't know or trust in such close proximity to you.

Then I shouldn't have come. You should have told me.

His self-derisive amusement slipped into her mind. *I had no idea I would have such a reaction. Apparently, there are things I have to learn about myself.*

It was impossible for Skyler to be angry with Dimitri. He had a strong protective instinct and a wicked sense of humor that was always going to get him out of trouble with her.

She stepped around Dimitri. "Of course it isn't forbidden to talk to me, or any other woman for that matter. I think everyone is a little on edge after what happened." She smiled at the shaggy, very large Lycan and held out her hand.

Randall glanced at Dimitri, who remained impassive. He looked relaxed, but Skyler, so tuned to her lifemate, felt his body coil, ready to strike.

The Lycan took her hand in his enormous one, completely engulfing hers. "We've heard a lot about you," Randall said. "You're quite a legend already. I trust you're recovering from your injuries?"

Skyler nodded. "Dimitri took great care to see to my recovery. We're sorry we kept you waiting, but the wounds were . . . severe."

For her, everything about Randall rang true—what one saw was what one got. She glanced at her lifemate.

He isn't a deceptive man and I doubt if he would lie about ordering death by silver. Had he done so, he would have owned up to it. If he believes in something, he's not the kind of man to hide his opinion.

You got all that from holding his hand?

Skyler pressed her lips together tightly to keep from laughing. *You're in a foul mood.*

You've got a wolf slobbering all over your hand. These wolf men are charmers and I don't trust any of them, especially the one holding your hand, further than I can throw them.

Her eyebrow shot up. Dimitri was teasing, but there was just that little bit of truth in his tone as well. *That would be pretty far. I've seen you in action.*

A second council member came out from around the table to join them. This was Lyall, the man who hadn't seemed at all interested in seeing what the Lycans had done to their prisoner. She was surprised that he came up to them, introducing himself to Dimitri and reiterating how sorry they all were for what had taken place.

She stepped back again, just a little, knowing it would make Dimitri more comfortable. The moment she did, both Zev and Fen moved subtly, coming in from either side so that she was hemmed in, although it didn't really look that way.

She kept the frown off her face and watched Dimitri talking with Lyall and the last of the council members, a man by the name of Arno. He was friendly, but openly wary of Dimitri. In the end, after Dimitri told his story to them, it was Arno who asked the most questions, and the majority of the questions seemed to be about being a mixed blood rather than who had been Dimitri's worst tormentors.

He wants the alliance with Carpathians, but he doesn't believe in distinguishing between Sange rau and the Hän ku pesäk kaikak, Skyler pointed out to Dimitri.

Rolf seemed to grow impatient with Arno's questions. "This is becoming tedious, Arno," he interrupted. "It's important to find out who is behind this treachery. In case you've forgotten, it was not only Dimitri who was targeted for death; we were as well." He looked around the room. "Mikhail, if you don't mind me saying so, I think we should clear this room. Tempers seem to run hot the more of us there are."

"I agree," Mikhail said.

Skyler *felt* his relief rather than heard it in his voice. She was more than happy to exit the room and find her adopted mother, but as she turned to go with Dimitri, both Mikhail and Rolf stopped them.

"If you don't mind," Mikhail said, "we'd prefer that you two, as well as Fen and Zev, stay just a while longer to help us."

Dimitri took a deep breath. Their eyes met. He inclined his head. *You don't have to stay, csitri. I can do this alone and you can visit with Francesca.* He had spoken to her on the common Carpathian path, not their private one, indicating to Mikhail that if she wanted to leave, Dimitri would insist on it.

She sent Dimitri a reassuring smile. *I wouldn't mind hearing what they have to say. Sometimes I know when someone is lying. I might catch that vibe and we'll know if someone here really is behind this conspiracy.*

I'm not certain it is a conspiracy, not in the way you mean, Zev chimed in thoughtfully, shocking Skyler.

She hadn't realized he was able to speak telepathically to all Carpathians, but she should have. He had been inside the shelter she'd created, and only those with Carpathian blood could pass the shield. In order for him to cross that barrier, he had to be fairly advanced as a mixed blood.

"We'll stay," Dimitri said aloud.

They waited until most of the Lycan and Carpathian guards left the room. Dimitri took a careful look around the room. It appeared to be nearly empty. The four council members remained, each with two guards. He recognized Daciana and Makoce from Zev's elite pack. Both had stayed behind with Rolf. Each of the other council members also retained two guards.

Mikhail had Gregori and his brother Jacques with him. Dimitri knew better. Gregori would never allow the prince in a room where the other faction had more men. He found himself uneasy, but couldn't put his finger on why.

Rolf and the other council members seemed sincere in wanting to talk about the issue of the *Sange rau* and whether or not any mixed blood should be hunted and killed regardless of whether or not they had done harm to anyone.

Fen. This time he used the private connection he had with his brother.

I've been feeling uneasy for some time.

Yet no one else does, Dimitri pointed out. *Not even Mikhail.*

If there is danger close by, no doubt, it is either a few of the Lycans who just left, or we've got a Sange rau close.

They use sniper rifles, Fen. These are trained assassins coming after us.

Gregori waved his hand and a large round table appeared in the center of the room. "I suggest you all sit down, gentlemen."

They won't be able to get a shot through the windows, Fen said. *Gregori has already thought of nearly any kind of attack that could take place. This room is sealed. Even the Lycans who left cannot get back in without Gregori allowing it.*

Dimitri toed a chair around, straddling it, uncaring what the Lycans thought of his actions. He pulled Skyler's chair closer to him. Knowing he could shield her from any trouble made him feel a little better, although he was still very uneasy. Fen toed the chair on the other side of Skyler around and straddled it as well. Both were in a position to move fast if they needed to.

The council members and Mikhail took their places. Only Zev sat at the table, while the Lycans guarding the council lined up with their backs to the walls.

Again Dimitri took a long slow look around the room. Gregori was standing within striking distance of Mikhail, but there were others. He found himself focusing on the wall where all the Lycans had draped themselves. Of course that wall had been left temptingly blank, perfect for the councils' guards to wait for their council members.

There were at least four Carpathian warriors somewhere on that wall, a part of it, knots in the wood, perhaps a tiny insect, and each would have already chosen their targets.

Lojos, Tomas and Mataias, he guessed. *And the ghost. Andre's here as well, isn't he?*

Fen sent him a little grin and inclined his head very subtly. *They wouldn't miss the party.*

"At the risk of offending Dimitri," Arno began, "I believe very strongly that the things we've been taught since practically the very beginning of our existence, that mixed blood is far too dangerous to be tolerated, are sacred. We can't abandon the very code we live by because a few of the *Sange rau* have not yet turned rogue."

Mikhail leaned forward, his eyes meeting Arno's. "We've come together to discuss this subject and we want to hear all opinions. This sacred code is something that has been in your culture for centuries and shouldn't be so easily discarded. We have to examine what we know now, versus what those who put the code into existence knew in their time. Knowledge is power, and hopefully, over the centuries, we've managed to gain more awareness, understanding, comprehension and information."

"Our experience with this issue clearly has been different than yours," Rolf said. "Our packs were destroyed. No one was spared. We nearly were extinct thanks to the *Sange rau*."

Mikhail nodded. "It is easy to understand why your ancestors laid down such extreme rules, but you are sitting at this table with one of our most skilled ancient hunters. Dimitri has defended Lycan, Carpathian and humans alike for centuries. He has hunted and killed both the vampire and rogue wolves and has done so with honor for centuries. Clearly, he is no threat to the Lycans, and in fact, is an asset."

Arno shook his head. "There is no guarantee that he will continue to be so. Again, Dimitri, I must apologize for speaking as if you aren't sitting right here, but these things must be said."

Beneath the table, Skyler put her hand on his thigh. He felt her trembling. Keeping his face expressionless, he placed his hand gently over hers. *The things he is saying have no impact on me one way or the other,* he assured her. *Fen and Zev are also as I am, of mixed blood. This council member isn't stupid. He knows that because we're lifemates, we exchange blood, and eventually you will become like me.*

He might not know that.

He knows. Just as Randall knew not to touch you earlier. Zev would have given them every detail about our culture possibly before they ever came here. They would have researched carefully and consulted with those who have known Carpathians. These council members have been around a long time, Skyler. Believe me, they act as ambassadors and they don't make mistakes in protocol. Zev took the blame by pretending he hadn't passed on the information about lifemates, but Randall knew.

"I have no problem with you speaking your mind, sir," Dimitri said politely. "Hearing truth is always preferable to lies."

Are you saying that shaggy old bear of a Lycan deliberately made me feel like a schoolgirl in front of all the Lycans?

Dimitri didn't dare answer that, not when Skyler had a bit of a fiery temper. He took another look around the room just to assure himself there was no beehive clinging to the rafters.

Randall reached for his glass of water, and raised it to his mouth. Without warning the glass slipped out of his hands, dumping the water down the front of him. The amount of liquid pouring into his lap seemed to exceed the size of the glass.

At once Randall's bodyguards sprang to help, handing him napkins and small towels from the table of food. The council members were not as polite, laughing and teasing Randall good-naturedly about his big hands and how he couldn't even hold a glass of water. Randall took it all in stride, grinning at his friends and shrugging his shoulders.

Lycans can detect energy when Carpathians use spells, Zev warned, frowning at Skyler. *These men are used to deference.*

Skyler raised her eyebrow, looking more innocent than ever. Dimitri kept his face impassive, controlling his amusement.

Are you accusing me of causing an accident? Did you feel energy coming from me? She managed to sound as blameless as she appeared.

Dimitri waited for the merriment to die down. "I have a lifemate. It is impossible for me to turn vampire. In order for me to become the *Sange rau* you fear I would have to choose to give up my soul. There is no way for that to happen."

Mikhail nodded. "Carpathian males who have lived too long and have not found a lifemate are in danger of turning vampire, but no man with a lifemate could do that," he reiterated. "There is a difference between a *Hän ku pesäk kaikak* and the *Sange rau.* All Lycans do not become rogues. All Carpathians do not become vampire. All mixed bloods do not become *Sange rau.*"

Arno frowned back at them. "Carpathian hunters can kill the vampire. Elite hunters can kill the rogue packs. Neither can kill the *Sange rau*. Better to exterminate them than to take the chance that they will wipe out all of us."

Skyler's fingernails dug into his thigh, but she didn't speak or retaliate. It was the first truly insulting thing Arno had said. Up to that point he had been polite and even friendly. Dimitri suspected his beliefs ran as deep as did his prejudice.

"I would prefer not to be exterminated," Dimitri said. "I am a man, not an insect."

"A very dangerous man," Arno pointed out. "Your lifemate nearly died. I know because we were in this room when your prince and her mother believed her dead. It nearly started a war right here. Suppose she had died?" he challenged. "Without a lifemate, you could turn, isn't that correct?"

Dimitri shrugged his shoulders. "Lifemates follow one another into the next life."

"In every case? Always?" Arno continued to push his point.

"Not always," Dimitri conceded, "but it is rare not to do so."

"We've studied your culture." Lyall took up the argument. "We know that when a mate dies, madness grips the male. How would this affect the mixed blood? Wouldn't he be more likely to choose the way of the vampire rather than lose his life?"

"It isn't about losing one's life," Dimitri answered. "As a Carpathian, as a lifemate, our first duty is to see to the health and happiness of our mate. She wouldn't die of sickness. That would be impossible. She wouldn't die in an accident. She would have to be targeted—murdered." His eyes met Lyall's. "Then choosing life over death would be about revenge."

The word *revenge* hung in the air between them.

Mikhail sighed. *You could have chosen your words more carefully, Dimitri.*

I am no politician, Mikhail. If they have studied our culture, they know that by sentencing me to death, they would also be sentencing my lifemate as well. They sit across from Skyler and calmly discuss exterminating us. Both of us. Do you think I will allow any of these men to harm my lifemate?

For the first time he felt the impact of Mikhail's rage. It hit like a solid body blow, mean and wicked. *Do you think that I would? That any Carpathian would? There is no chance that we would ever agree to what they are proposing. There is, however, a small chance that they will see things our way.*

Dimitri took a deep breath. Mikhail was right. It wasn't that Dimitri couldn't be objective, he just thought sitting there was a waste of time.

Trying to change centuries of prejudice seemed impossible to him. Arno had almost a religious fervor to him when he forgot to be a polite council member and began to heat up over a subject that clearly he felt passionate about.

Forgive me, Mikhail. I see that you have had to walk a fine line in spite of what you would like to say to these people.

It was Rolf who broke the silence. "I can understand how one would want revenge, Dimitri. If my wife was murdered, I would hunt down the one who killed her and, God forgive me, I am certain I would kill him. I am Lycan, not human, and my instincts as a predator would likely overcome all civilization."

Dimitri nodded. "Seeing Skyler dead, or at least believing she was, it was a very dark moment for me, but I would not let her go into another life without me by her side. I would leave the hunt to her father and uncle." He looked at Arno. "I am *Hän ku pesäk kaikak* and I have never failed my people or dishonored myself or my family. Duty and honor have been ingrained in me since I was a child, centuries ago. I can only tell you, I serve as a Guardian, not a predator on the people I protect."

"It is easy enough to pass judgment on the mythical *Sange rau* when few in our lifetime have ever seen his destruction," Randall said. "It is an altogether different thing when we have Dimitri and his lifemate sitting across the table from us. Clearly he poses no threat to us."

"Now," Arno said. *"Now* he poses no threat. We don't know what he will do in the future, and what if they breed?"

The word *breed* was said with such repugnance and loathing, Dimitri gripped Skyler's hand tightly, warning her not to speak. This was Mikhail's territory, not his. Fen and Zev were both silent, but they exchanged a long look.

Dimitri was grateful that the council members weren't aware both Fen and Zev were of mixed blood. They had been targeted by assassins, not for their blood, but because whoever wanted the war between the two species saw them as threats to his plans.

"That was rude, Arno," Rolf said quietly. "Extremely rude. Skyler, please accept my apologies on behalf of all Lycans." He pinned the council member with a frown. "We are sworn to put all prejudices aside and judge fairly. You swore that, although you were a member of the Sacred Circle, you could accept the changes modern society brought." Rolf indicated Daciana. "She is one of our best elite hunters, yet her skills would be denied to us if the members of the Sacred Circle had their way. You helped pass the law allowing her to serve. We came here with open minds, prepared to change our law if it was warranted."

"I know. I know." Arno shoved both hands through the thick pelt of hair on his head. "Women hunted before the sacred code was put in place. A precedent had already been set," he defended. "The sacred code was written after the *Sange rau* decimated our people. We needed the women home. Now, it isn't as crucial."

"That's understandable." Mikhail sought to bring the rising tension down. "We lost our women as well, and most of them do not hunt. We prefer them to remain safe. A few go out with their lifemates, but we're still rebuilding and we debate the issue often."

Arno sent him a grateful look. "Forgive me, Skyler and Dimitri. I struggle with my beliefs. Sometimes they don't make sense and I fight all the harder for them."

He sounded genuinely upset, a man who definitely wanted to do the right thing, but was caught in a war between past and present.

His beliefs are strong, anchored in centuries of reinforcement. He believes very strongly that every mixed blood poses a threat to his species and shouldn't—no, can't *be tolerated,* Dimitri observed, using the common Carpathian path.

He is not alone in that belief, Zev said. *All members of the Sacred Circle believe as he does, and they are not only great in number, but loud about it. Arno is one of their highest-ranking members and speaks regularly on the sanctity of their code. He is probably one of their biggest recruiters. He's a good speaker and feels passionate about his subject.*

Could he be the man targeting the council members for death on our soil? Mikhail asked.

Zev sighed. *I would never have believed such a thing of him. He's always been a good man, but now . . .* He trailed off. *Gunnolf and Convel were both members of the Sacred Circle, but I never thought they would betray us, or betray our pack.*

Rolf shook his head. "We're all tired. Perhaps we should adjourn until tomorrow night. Dimitri has given us much to think about."

Lyall glanced at his watch. "It is late," he agreed.

Arno checked his cell phone. "Later than I thought. I believe it would be best to adjourn also. I need to put things in perspective."

The council members rose, as did the Carpathians.

"Before you leave," Zev said, "we need to make absolutely certain all of you are safe."

19

Fen, Zev and Dimitri stepped outside to scan the area around them. Both still had an uneasy feeling that signaled danger—and it was much stronger in the open air—yet neither could get a direction or a scent.

Fen swore softly. "We seem to go from one bad situation into another," he said. "I have a really bad feeling."

Zev took a slow, careful look around. "What do you want to do? Keep them all inside while we scout around?"

Dimitri's first impulse was to say yes, but something made him hesitate. His gut churned and knots formed in his belly.

"We're sitting ducks out here if they have sniper rifles," Zev pointed out.

"Dimitri?" Fen said. His brother knew him and waited for Dimitri's assessment.

"That's exactly what they would expect us to do," Dimitri said. "Every hair on my body is raised. I think we've got snipers staring at us through scopes right now, but they're waiting to pull the trigger. Why?"

"Why haven't you thrown up a shield?" Zev asked. "I don't like the idea of being shot in the head."

"The moment we do something like that, it will tip them off that we're on to them," Fen explained.

Even as Fen uttered the words, a voice burst through their minds. Mikhail. *Gabriel and Lucian are under attack. Lycans are pouring into the village. All warriors are needed. Every woman who can fight must do so. Defend the humans in the village and keep our children safe.*

A chill went down Dimitri's spine. This was a serious, coordinated attack on both Carpathians and the council. "Fen, put up the shield. If they shoot us, for certain, Mikhail and Gregori will keep the council in that room in order to protect them, but I think the trap is there."

A bullet whined through the air even as he spoke. It crashed into a transparent wall, so that a crack appeared first and then spiderwebbed out, revealing the shield Fen had raised instantly. Two more bullets were fired in rapid succession, both hitting in the exact spot the first had. A third bullet fired almost simultaneously hit a quarter inch from the hole.

"He's good," Fen commented. "And he must have been waiting for the Lycans to attack the village."

"There're two of them," Zev said. "One, for certain, is Hemming. He's been in the military all his life as a sniper. The council uses him when necessary. No one can shoot like he can. He's also a member of the Sacred Circle."

Dimitri swore as a fourth slug hit the small hole precisely where the other two bullets had. This time, the bullet nearly penetrated the shield. "Inside. There has to be a traitor inside, one of the elite guards." He turned to race back inside.

Fen swore as well. "He's right, otherwise they would have shot us the moment we stepped outside. The snipers gave him time to get close to the council members as everyone stood up to say their good-byes." He followed his brother. "They were just waiting for the Lycans to attack as well."

Zev took off after them, just as another bullet whined past his ear. He ducked as he ran for the shelter of the building.

Dimitri burst into the room, his gaze going to Skyler like a magnet. She was talking to Rolf and Daciana, laughing at something the elite hunter had said. Her eyes jumped to his face, the smile fading immediately as she recognized something was wrong. Daciana did as well, quickly catching Rolf's arm and thrusting him back against the wall. Her partner, Makoce, was there, using his body as a shield.

Dimitri hastily scanned the room, looking for a betraying "tell" that might give him a hint where the danger would come from. *Gregori, get the prince out of here. I don't care how much he protests, but go to vapor and leave fast. He isn't safe here.* Above all else, their prince had to survive.

Gregori didn't hesitate or argue with Mikhail. He shifted, his hand on Mikhail's arm, shoving the image of mist into his mind so that his body began to shift almost before he was aware.

We're leaving now, Gregori informed his charge.

Mikhail completed the shift, although the look on his face told Dimitri that Gregori was in for a rough ride once they were alone. Gregori could handle it; he'd been the prince's primary guardian almost from the moment the two of them were born.

Just as Dimitri took to the air to get to Skyler's side, one of Arno's elite guards stepped into her so that she stumbled back with a small cry, her hands going up to protect herself from the dagger in his palm. Before the guard could shove the blade deep, something caught his wrist.

The ghost. Andre was there before Dimitri, dropping down out of sight, shifting at the last moment to emerge between Skyler and the guard, his fist circling the guard's wrist. He turned the silver dagger back on the guard, shoving it deep just below the Lycan's heart.

Dimitri caught Skyler and yanked her back away from the Lycans. There was nowhere he felt she was safe, not inside that room, or outside of it.

"They have snipers outside," Zev informed his hunters. "At least two, and one of them is Hemming."

Fen inhaled sharply. Dimitri followed suit. If it was possible for a mixed blood to go pale, they both did. The distinct odor of C-4 drifted to them.

Fen waved his hand and opened the ground, tearing easily through the floor to the dirt below them. "Get in, all of you." *Zev, there's a bomb.* He used the Carpathian common path, warning all the warriors to get out quickly or use the ground for shelter.

"Daciana, move it," Zev called. He rushed to Lyall, gripping his arm, dragging him way from his guards. "Get underground now."

Daciana and Makoce both caught Rolf between them and dove for the opening. Zev managed to shove Lyall down as well. Randall took matters into his own hands while his guards debated whether or not it was a Carpathian trap. He jumped inside the hole as well. Zev went back for Arno.

Dimitri all but threw Skyler down, his body over hers as the world above them exploded. He covered her head, murmuring soothing words as the ground shook. She felt small and vulnerable beneath him, causing every protective instinct he had to rage. He'd had enough of playing politics. More than enough. He was an ancient Carpathian hunter, and it was time to hunt.

He raised his head. Several of the elite hunters had followed the council members into the ground. Fen had raised a protective shield over their heads and debris from the room, dirt and rocks covered that shield above their heads. In the meeting room, dust swirled in the air, so dense it was impossible to see much else over their heads.

He sensed movement and spun around, coming to his feet, a raging tornado, ready to do battle. The second Lycan who had guarded Arno was in the shelter, although his partner wasn't. He had climbed to his feet, his hand slipping inside his jacket. He pulled out a gun and in one smooth motion, turned and aimed it at Lyall's head.

The council member's eyes went wide with shock. The guard took another step forward, lifting his aim just past Lyall's head to center on Rolf. Daciana threw herself in front of the council member as the guard squeezed the trigger. Dimitri was on the guard even as he fired, leaping over everyone to tackle him, taking him down hard.

The guard shoved his gun into Dimitri's stomach and pulled the trigger rapidly, but nothing happened, only the sound of the wolf desperately attempting to fire off a volley of rounds.

Dimitri had jammed the weapon. He let his wolf surge to the surface, Lycan against Lycan. They rolled together, a twister of thrashing bodies, teeth, claws, snarls and growls. Dimitri was enormously strong, and each time the Lycan tried to bring up the gun, Dimitri slammed his wrist over and over into the ground.

The Lycan howled as his bones snapped, then fragmented and then pulverized. Dimitri was relentless, determined not to kill him, but keep him alive for questioning. If he had been sentenced to death by silver, he couldn't imagine what fate a traitor attempting to assassinate council members might receive.

Makoce and Rolf both bent over Daciana, attempting to stop the flow of blood.

"I wouldn't advise moving," Fen warned the other Lycan guards. "I'm certain most of you genuinely are here to protect your council members, but at this point, any one of you who makes a sudden move is going to be dealt with harshly. Just sit down slowly and keep your hands away from your weapons."

Most obeyed, but Lyall's elite guards looked as if they might challenge him.

"In case you believe that you're faster than me, I'll warn you right now, you aren't and I'm not in a mood to play games. I'll put you down hard and fast."

Lyall glared at his guards. "Don't be ridiculous. Do you want to get yourselves killed? Sit down and do what he says."

A little reluctantly, the remaining guards sank to the ground. Fen trusted Andre to watch them. He had the reputation for being fast and as merciless as any Carpathian could get.

"We need to aid those caught in the explosion," Rolf said, looking at Fen over his shoulder. "And Daciana needs help. This wound is . . . severe."

Skyler slipped past Andre's restraining hand, although he paced beside her, keeping his body between her and the rest of the sitting guards. She crouched down beside Rolf. "Let me see." Very gently she lifted Rolf's hand. At once blood spurted. "Keep your hand there, press hard. I'll see what I can do."

"I will watch over you, little sister," Andre assured.

Skyler shed her body and became white-hot healing energy. She had to stop the flow of blood or there would be no regeneration for Daciana.

"I don't want to move too fast until we know exactly what is happening above us," Fen told the council members. "We've got two snipers, both skilled and trained in the military. Zev, Dimitri and I believe they are *Sange rau*. You and I both know any hunter, elite or ancient, going up against them will not win the battle."

The Lycan guard fighting with Dimitri attempted to shift to his half man, half wolf form, but Dimitri was too fast, using the speed of the *Hän ku pesäk kaikak*. He slammed his elbow repeatedly into the Lycan's face. The wolf's head fell back, eyes rolling in his head.

"Catch," Makoce tossed a pair of handcuffs through the air.

Dimitri remembered to coat his hands at the last moment, realizing the cuffs were silver. Uncaring that the traitor's arm and wrist were broken, he held him down with one knee pressed tightly into the small of his back.

The Lycan snarled and raged, howled in pain and fought to free himself. Dimitri pulled both arms behind him, slamming the handcuffs tightly around the wolf's wrist. The assassin let out a high-pitched scream.

Fen reached for Zev, afraid they had lost him in the explosion. *Are you alive? Come on, man, give me something.*

There was a moment of silence. Fen counted his own heartbeats, waiting for Zev to answer. He felt a faint stirring in his mind and relief flooded him.

I'm in a little trouble, Fen, Zev admitted. *I've got a piece of table through me and I'm not going to lie, it hurts like hell. If I pull it out, I'll bleed out before you can get to me.*

Well, I guess you'd better not be foolish enough to pull it out then, because I'd be royally pissed off if you died. What were you doing? Fen cautiously moved part of the shield above their heads. Debris fell into the hole. *Playing hero again? Did you fling your body over the council member while his bodyguards were down here trying to kill us?*

Something like that. I can't tell if Arno's alive or not. He isn't moving. I can't even feel him breathing. But then I can't exactly get off of him either. I'm probably smothering him. There was a faint note of humor in Zev's voice in spite of the pain.

"Skyler, I'm going to need your skills as a healer," Fen announced. "It might be ugly up there, but I have no choice. Zev's in trouble."

Skyler came back into her own body, swaying with weakness, answering the urgent call in Fen's voice. She had managed to repair most of the damage to Daciana's body. "She needs blood," she announced.

Andre helped her to stand. *You need blood, too, little sister,* he said. *Allow me to shield you while you take what you need.*

Skyler knew she would never be able to help Zev if she wasn't strong enough. Healing took a tremendous amount of energy, but she'd never fed by herself before, not unless it was from Dimitri, and he'd reacted very strongly to her taking blood from another male.

He's right, sívamet, he has asked my permission and I gave it. I will need all my energy to battle the Sange rau, Dimitri encouraged. *If you feel you cannot, I'll help you.*

Skyler was well past being reluctant to feed, especially under the circumstances. She felt the urgency of Fen's request. He would never put her in harm's way unless the situation was dire. Worse, she actually liked Zev. She might still be a little angry with him, but it was impossible not to respect him.

It is given freely. Andre shielded her from the sight of the Lycans as he offered his wrist.

Thank you, Andre. I accept your offering. She took his hand and sank her teeth into his vein.

Fen looked across the small shelter to his brother. "You'll have to keep them off our backs. I'll join you as fast as I can. They'll be coming to inspect the damage."

"By them," Randall said, "you mean the snipers, the *Sange rau*." He made it a statement.

"I'll go with you," Makoce volunteered. "You can't face two of them alone."

Dimitri shook his head. "You're one of few we trust. We need you here, protecting the rest of the council members."

"Are you ready, Skyler?" Fen demanded.

She closed the small wound in Andre's wrist. "Yes."

"Andre, I'll need you here to make certain no one else decides to kill off the council members while we're out of the way," Fen said. "I can send a couple of others down to help you."

Andre raised an eyebrow, but didn't reply.

Dimitri stepped over the handcuffed assassin and followed Fen and Skyler up to the ground above them. The meeting hall was mostly rubble. Two bodies lay ripped apart a few feet from the entrance to the shelter, as if they'd been running for safety. Skyler coughed and covered her mouth and nose. Floating particles of wood, dirt and stone turned the air in what was left of the room to a thick, gray ash.

Fen rushed around the bodies toward the far wall where he spotted Zev's leg sticking out from under what appeared to be scrap wood. The table was shredded, great jagged splinters of wood as thick as a man's arm pointed to the ceiling like spears.

Skyler's heart accelerated, slamming hard against her chest when she saw Fen stop, his hands around one of the spears. Breaking into a run, she flashed by the dead bodies without looking at them and found herself kneeling beside Zev, shoving one fist into her mouth to keep from sobbing.

She was a healer and all they had, but she was no miracle worker. Zev's body lay sprawled over Arno. The elite hunter had wrapped his arms around the council member, protecting him from the flying wood. He must have tried to use the tables as a shield, knocking them over to their sides, both men diving behind them.

Arno turned his head cautiously toward them as Skyler knelt beside him. "Is he alive? I can't tell but I've been afraid to move, afraid I'd make it worse."

Blood from Zev's wound coated Arno's back, but otherwise, he appeared unhurt. Skyler glanced up at Fen's grim face. "Barely," she answered.

"I'm going to slip you out from under him," Fen told Arno. "Slide sideways and try not to bump him."

I can't do this alone. I'll need help, Skyler said. *I'm calling Tatijana and Branislava. I've warned them about the danger of the two snipers. They know to come in without form.*

She glanced around the room. Fen would have to help Dimitri. He couldn't possibly fight two *Sange rau* alone. The prince had to be guarded, and someone had to get the remaining council members and Daciana to safety. Still . . .

"I know you need the warriors, Fen, but I'll need a couple for blood. Can you pull back Lucian and Gabriel from what they're doing?"

"I doubt it, but I'll try."

"I can give him blood," Arno volunteered. "What the hell is going on?"

"Lycans have attacked us from nearly every direction," Fen told him. "With them are the snipers we believe are *Sange rau*. Both of your elite guards tried to kill council members."

"Fen, hurry," Skyler hissed. They couldn't worry about what was going on politically or outside the shredded walls of the building, not if they were going to save Zev's life.

Fen nodded curtly and sent a cushion of air between Zev and Arno, lifting the body away from the council member without jarring it. Arno shifted his weight carefully, easing out from under the floating, wounded, elite hunter. As soon as he was clear, he scrambled back on all fours, his face a mask of concern.

The moment he saw the large stake going through Zev's body, he turned white, his eyes going wide with shock. "He can't possibly be alive," he said.

Zev's eyelashes fluttered but didn't lift. "I'm alive," he whispered, his voice hoarse with pain. "I'm just not certain I want to be."

Tatijana and Branislava materialized on either side of Skyler. Tatijana gently touched Skyler in sympathy as they assessed the situation.

"One of us will have to hold him to us," Tatijana said.

"I can try," Skyler agreed reluctantly. "I've got a connection with him."

"I'll do it," Branislava announced. She leaned over Zev and took his hand gently. *You remember me, right, Zev? We danced together. It was a beautiful moment in my life and I'll treasure it always. We shared blood to bond and to be able to speak telepathically. Allow me to bind your spirit to mine. I'll keep you safe while my sister and Skyler heal you.*

I remember you. Zev's spirit was already fading, slipping away from them, as his life's blood drained out on the floor. The shock to his body was tremendous. *My beautiful dream lady.*

Branislava reached for his spirit, that fading light, and surrounded it with her own. Her spirit was strong and bright and she corralled the flickering insubstantial spirit that remained of Zev so that the two spirits melded together. She wove her light through his to bind him to her.

We can make our own dream right here, together, while they work on your body. You won't have to feel it or think of what they're doing, only stay here with me. Stay with me.

Skyler looked at Fen, her heart pounding nearly out of control, her mouth dry. She had Tatijana beside her and that gave her courage, but she knew they all believed she was a great healer. She didn't have the experience, or the training. They were on their own. A coordinated attack on the Carpathians required every warrior and woman to defend their homeland.

She took one breath and nodded her head. "Do it," she said.

Fen pulled the stake from Zev's body. Blood gushed. Tatijana was ready with her hands, pressing them deeply into the wound, light bursting out from under her palms. Skyler shed her body and entered Zev's, working fast to repair the damage.

The stake had torn through layers of muscle and organ. There were splinters throughout the wound and the tip had actually penetrated through Zev's abdomen, as well as crashing through two ribs. How he managed to stay alive, she had no idea. For a moment she hesitated, not knowing where to start. His body was a mess.

Dimitri. He had been with her all along, merged deep, so much a part of her. His belief in her always gave her confidence and she needed that now.

Save his life, Dimitri said. *It's what you were born to do. Save him, csitri. He is needed in this world.*

Just the sound of his voice soothed her, righted her world, and she began, choosing the edges of the great hole to start closing that terrible gap.

Dimitri let go of the merge he'd been holding with his lifemate. She had her work to do and he had his. He couldn't think of anything else but finding and destroying the two snipers with their long list of targets to assassinate. It wouldn't be intelligent to divide himself when he was hunting anything as deadly as the *Sange rau.*

Staying in the form of dust particles, he started his search at the bullet hole in the shattered shield Fen had thrown up to protect them. Taking his time, using the patience of a Carpathian hunter, he traced the trajectory of the bullet across a fifty-foot open space back toward the village.

He was unhappy with the direction. The thought of the *Sange rau* loose in the village with unsuspecting humans was frightening. Lycan soldiers attacked the Carpathians where they found them, but they seemed to be avoiding killing the humans in the village as far as he could tell.

It was obvious to him that the Carpathians had learned from their earlier encounter with a rogue pack that fighting one-on-one would do no good with Lycans. The warriors had formed their own packs, Lucian and Gabriel directing them, and they were meeting the wolves on equal terms.

The skies roiled with clouds. Thunder rolled and boomed. Bolts of lightning flashed from ground to sky and back down. The sound of gunfire and screams of pain filled the night. The scent of blood was heavy in the air. War.

Dimitri felt an overwhelming sadness steal over him. He had seen too much death. Too many shattered lives. Over what? The blood that ran in his veins? This kind of violence, the treachery involved in conspiring to murder the council members who had come to try to form an alliance with another species, was abhorrent to him.

He kept moving through the houses and shops, until he came to the rooftop of the church. There was a kind of irony in the fact that the sniper had chosen a place of peace, of worship, to attempt to commit murder.

There were no casings left on the roof, but Dimitri was *Hän ku pesäk kaikak*, and even though the sniper was *Sange rau*, he was newly made. The wolf in their assailant was very strong and Dimitri caught the scent stamped into the roof. Once he had the actual scent markers of the sniper, he could follow the trail much easier.

This one had slipped down the side of the building and had mingled with the people running to barricade themselves in their homes or shops. He avoided the Lycans as well as the Carpathians, using buildings for cover. That alone told Dimitri the *Sange rau* was newly made. He didn't have the first clue about what a Carpathian could or couldn't do. He was using his Lycan senses and military training to get him through the village without being seen.

He had another target. That was the only answer as to why the sniper was circling back around toward the rubble of a building. He didn't attempt to join in the fighting, or help the other Lycans out in any way. They probably didn't even know he was there.

Fen, he's coming back around toward you. I think this is the one Zev called Hemming. He's very good, but he has no clue what a Carpathian is or what he can do. All of his training is military or Lycan. If he is a true mixed blood, how can that be?

That's a good question. Do you have any idea where the second sniper is?

I traced a bullet path to the rooftop of the church, but only one had been there. You'll have to use the same method I did. This one must have a target or targets still inside the building. He's absolutely relentless and determined. Nothing is slowing him down or deterring him, Dimitri replied.

Fen swore. *Zev is in bad shape. We haven't moved the council members because we have no idea if any of the other guards are planning to make a move against them. Skyler, Tatijana and Branislava can't leave, not until they lose the battle for Zev's life, or heal him enough to put him in the ground. That leaves the second sniper anywhere, capable of doing damage to anyone.*

Dimitri hissed out his irritation. *We'll have to trust that Gregori can do his job, if the prince is a primary target. We have to go after this one. He's too close to our women and the council.*

I'll warn those here. Keep closing in on him.

I am. Fen, is it even possible for Zev to go to ground?

There was a long silence. Fen sighed. *I don't know, Dimitri. At this point, I don't think any of us know what's really possible or what isn't.*

Dimitri increased his speed, following the scent of the *Sange rau.* He doubted the vapor trail speeding through the air would draw attention, not when those on the ground were trying to save themselves. The fighting was more sporadic now. Bodies lay on the ground, most with severed heads and stakes through the heart. If there were any dead or dying Carpathian warriors, Dimitri didn't see them.

Lucian and Gabriel were skilled at warfare. They had engaged in a thousand battles over the centuries and few were better strategists. The moment they knew Lycans had taken Dimitri and then later, when Skyler was thought to have died, they had acquired every bit of information possible on how Lycans conducted warfare, from early centuries to modern times. They were more than prepared to meet them in battle.

Telepathy helped as well. The Carpathians were able to speak to one another mind to mind. They kept in constant communication, relaying information from one part of the village to another. So far, Dimitri hadn't heard that the prince's home had been attacked.

Dimitri slipped around the corner of the building closest to the meeting hall that had been destroyed. The sniper was just ahead of him, creeping stealthily through the rubble to gain the wall that was partially down. The wall had holes blown out of it. The roof had collapsed and a good portion of the wall itself had crumbled from the force of the blast.

Hemming didn't go to one of the holes to peer through as Dimitri expected him to do. Instead, the sniper leapt up to one of the remaining larger pieces of the wall itself. He crouched low, his case with his equipment in his hand. The smooth jump onto such a precarious structure warned Dimitri not to underestimate the wolf.

The low murmur of voices chanting the Carpathian healing ritual reached him. He could hear even the warriors in the midst of battle, chanting with the women and children. They had banded together to try to save Zev, a warrior all of them respected. They considered him one of them, and losing a single Carpathian, whether mixed blood or no, was unacceptable.

Those inside were busy attempting to save a life, while the sniper outside was setting up to murder them. Hemming crouched low and leapt once again, landing nimbly on the roof. For a moment it looked as if the roof might collapse under his weight, but the rubble held together in spite of the damage.

Dimitri slipped up behind the sniper as he bent to open his case. When he materialized directly behind the *Sange rau*, he set one foot down for an anchor as he caught the wolf's head in his hands, whirling around to pull the head over his shoulder in an impossible position.

The roof shifted out from under him, throwing him off balance just as a shot rang out. Dimitri's heart jerked in his chest. This man was not Hemming. He should have known the newly made *Sange rau* was bait to draw him out. It had been far too easy to track him.

Dimitri leapt into the air, still holding the wolf in an unbreakable lock, deliberately hitting the roof hard as he landed, snapping the sniper's neck and going straight through the flimsy roof. He landed on the floor in the middle of debris and rubble, the sniper cushioning his fall. Palming a silver stake, he slammed it through the chest of the assassin and leapt away from the body.

As he did so, a second bullet whined passed his ear and lodged in the far wall. "Stay down," he cautioned.

The three women and Arno paid no attention to him, their entire concentration on the man lying in front of them.

Fen, he's on me and the women are in here with Zev. I'm going to get out of here, show myself for a moment to make certain he targets me and not them. This has to be the real Hemming, the one Zev spoke of who was such a tremendous marksman. The other was bait.

And now you're making yourself bait.

It's a decent plan. Are you on him yet?

Not until he fires again.

Dimitri hissed a curse out between clenched teeth. He risked another run, streaking past the fallen sniper, slashing down with his silver sword to sever the head from the body as he ran. He made it to the hole in the wall, and instead of going through it, as the assassin would expect, he leapt back through the hole in the roof and sprinted for the other side.

A succession of bullets followed him, one smacking into the tree trunk on the other side of the meeting hall, head level. He zigzagged, and then dropped low, shifting as he did so. If Fen couldn't find the bastard after that, he was going to do it himself.

Fighting had died down in the streets. He saw a few bodies as he sped away from the meeting hall, trying to trace back the last bullet that had been fired. He didn't use vapor—the *Sange rau* would be expecting it.

He isn't vampire, Dimitri informed Fen. *How can he be Sange rau basically committing murder, if he isn't rogue or vampire?*

Whoever is behind this has built himself an army and they're fanatical. Hemming is either a mercenary, or he believes what he's doing is right. I'm coming around downwind of him. He's packing up his rifle to make a run for it. I'm not close enough to stop him yet.

Deliberately, Dimitri shifted, moving stealthily through the buildings, giving the sniper just a glimpse or two of him, enough to make him hesitate leaving. If he had a mission to fulfill and he had been trained in the military, he wouldn't stop until he'd managed to kill his target.

He's buying into it, Dimitri, be careful. He's intelligent. If you overplay your hand, he'll know we're on to him.

I'm going to give him a shadow to fixate on and then I'll swing around and come in from the other side.

Dimitri projected his shadow on the shop closest to where he had revealed himself to the sniper. The shadow crouched low, keeping within darker shadows as much as possible as it wove in and out of the buildings, moving toward the church. Once he knew his shadow clone appeared realistic, but stayed where the sniper could only catch glimpses of it, he began to circle around to close in on Hemming from the side opposite Fen.

He's settled back on the roof and is hunting you, Fen reported. *I'm in position and staying still. I don't want to spook him.*

Pack hunting was new to most Carpathians, but Dimitri and Fen had used the tactics of the Lycans often over the last few centuries. They worked well together. There was little difference between hunting the vampire and hunting the *Sange rau*—not now when they were evenly matched in speed, intelligence and skill.

Dimitri closed in from the other side and signaled that he was ready. They had to be fast, stripping Hemming of his rifle and any other gun quickly. He, no doubt, was deadly with them.

Fen struck from the left, streaking fast, keeping his energy contained, slamming into Hemming, rolling him out of the tree and riding his body down, so that when they hit the ground he could slam the stake into the assassin's heart.

Hemming was struck so hard he dropped the rifle, but as they fell and Fen's legs clamped around him, he drew his own dagger and stabbed Fen's thigh. He was fast, piercing flesh and muscle three times before they hit the ground. Fen didn't flinch, ignoring the wounds, waiting his moment. He slammed the stake into Hemming's chest as they landed in the dirt, using the momentum from the fall and the unforgiving ground to ensure he struck deep enough. Hemming had been thrashing so much, the stake cut through the edge of his heart, but failed to pierce the center.

The breath was driven from their lungs, but Hemming retained possession of his dagger. He rolled, slicing at Fen's chest and throat in desperation, trying to pull the silver stake from his body as he did so. Before he could rise, Dimitri was there, silver sword flashing. He severed the head and Fen jerked the stake free and slammed it home again, this time penetrating the heart all the way through.

The two of them sat in the dirt beside the body, trying to get their breathing under control. "We're getting better at this," Fen said.

Dimitri surveyed the damage to his brother. "I can see that." He pushed his hand through his hair before kneeling up to stop the flow of blood leaking from the wounds on Fen's thigh. "He had military training, Fen, but wasn't like us. He didn't have centuries of growing as a mixed blood. Where are they coming from?"

Fen sighed. "We've got one of them alive. The council members and Mikhail will question him. I did notice that he had a small tattoo on his wrist, an intricate kind of tribal design, in a circle. Arno has that same tattoo."

Dimitri pulled back the sleeves of the sniper. "He's got it as well. So do most of the dead Lycans I encountered in the street."

"So if someone wants to kill all of the mixed bloods, why are they using them to aid their cause?" Fen asked. "The deeper we get into this puzzle, the less any of it makes sense."

"I'm at a loss for an explanation," Dimitri admitted. "But that symbol they all wear means something."

"We'll have to ask Zev what it means." Fen took a deep breath. "If he lives. They're still fighting for him."

"Let's go help," Dimitri said. "I reached out to Gabriel and Lucian, and they have everything under control and we're not needed right now. They'll do cleanup and burn any bodies."

Fen nodded and accepted his brother's help rising. "Andre, Tomas, Lojos and Mataias took the remaining council members back to the inn. Mikhail and Gregori are sorting all that out. We just have to make certain Zev survives."

Dimitri and Fen made their way back to the rubble that was the meeting hall. Skyler and Tatijana had taken turns working inside Zev's body. Arno had given blood more than once and clearly was dizzy, lying down beside Zev's body.

Skyler looked so pale Dimitri rushed to her side, wrapping his arm around her and immediately offering her blood. The energy it took to heal such a severe wound required a tremendous supply of life-giving blood.

Zev needs blood much worse than I do. Arno couldn't keep up and both Tatijana and I have had to work to clean and close this terrible hole in his body. The stake went through numerous organs, Skyler reported to both of them.

Fen immediately dropped down beside his lifemate. "I can give him blood."

Tatijana glanced at him, taking in the sight of his wounds. She sighed but said nothing as he tore a laceration in his wrist and held it over Zev's lips to drip the ancient blood into his mouth. Zev didn't respond and the drops ran down to his jaw.

Zev, you must take this offering of blood, Branislava called to him. *Allow Fen, your brother-kin, to give to you what you need.*

Zev heard that angelic voice, but he didn't respond. He heard the call and answer chant, the swelling volume of voices, so many warriors and women and even children, attempting to draw him back.

Yes, come back.

That voice was a melody, a sweet, soft melody playing through his mind as elusive as the wind. He knew he should recognize it, but he was tired and trying to work puzzles out was too difficult. *I am weary of this life. I have lived far too long. War and killing have become all that is left to me.* Letting go would be so much easier than facing the pain of his horrendous wounds and the endless loneliness that would follow. He had done his duty a million times over. What was really left for a man such as him?

Stay. We are bound together, you and I. Our spirits are woven together. There was no other way to save your life. If you go, you take me with you.

That made no sense to him. He was bound to no one, forever alone. The blood dripping into his mouth became bothersome. He licked at the drops to remove them. The taste burst through his system, a rush of adrenaline. *Fen*. Fen was there. Of course.

The adrenaline allowed him to identify that soft melodic voice. Branislava, the woman he couldn't get out of his mind. He didn't ever get involved with a woman. His lifestyle forbade such a thing. No one had ever intrigued him or had drawn him the way she had. She was off-limits and yet, he couldn't get her out of his head.

I'm dreaming. That was the only answer, and men like him didn't dream of beautiful women weaving their spirit with his in order to fight for his life. No one would do that. No one. The risk was far too great.

Stay with me. Take the blood Fen offers. It is ancient Carpathian blood. It is the blood of the Lycan. We will go together to the ground, allowing the earth to heal you. You will not be alone. I have tied my fate to yours.

She made the revelation so simply as if what she had done was nothing.

He knew better. Zev pushed aside weariness and forced his body to respond to Fen's offer. He couldn't do less for a woman who offered her life for his. He wasn't a coward and he wasn't afraid of pain. He would *not* allow an innocent to die simply because it was a difficult road to travel back to life.

His entire lifetime had been a fight. He wouldn't lose this one.

20

Skyler ran into her mother's arms, hugging her tightly. "I missed you so much, Francesca. I'm sorry I caused you such worry."

"You scared us to death," Francesca admitted, tears welling up in her eyes. "If it wasn't for Gabriel, I would have . . ." She broke off and shook her head. "I never want to go through that again. Thank God, your connection with Dimitri was so strong he was able to pull you back. Do you realize how far gone you were? Neither Gabriel nor I could reach you."

Skyler hugged her again hard. "I did try to hold on, when I realized I was slipping away so fast, I knew he would come for me. I anchored myself as best I could, but it was so cold and I was so lost, I was terrified I couldn't hold on long enough."

It had been her absolute belief that Dimitri would find her that allowed her, even as her spirit slipped away from her dying body, to withstand the icy cold and dark. It had been terrifying in that other place, the flicker of life in her drawing the attention of those crouched in the darkness, waiting for a new soul to steal.

Francesca drew back to look her over carefully. "I inspected you when they flew you back here, although you probably don't remember much. You were exhausted, needed blood, rest and healing. How are you feeling?"

"I feel fine," Skyler assured. "Fully healed. I couldn't wait to see you, but Mikhail wanted Dimitri to talk to the council members first."

"I heard." Francesca gave her a faint smile. "Were you able to keep your temper while they talked as if Dimitri was a bug to be squashed?"

"You mean *exterminated*," Skyler corrected with a faint grin. "I didn't blow the place up, that was someone else."

They walked together out into the meadow, crossing a field of wildflowers. "He's good for you," Francesca observed. "You're confident and happy."

"I'm so in love with him," Skyler confessed. "More even than I thought possible."

"We should have seen that you were grown-up," Francesca admitted. "Neither of us could bear the thought of you going away from us so soon. It was selfish, but you're our first and we've always been a bit overprotective."

"I understand. I *hated* lying to you. It was truly the worst feeling in the world, but no one would give me any information on where he was or what they were doing to save him."

"That was wrong as well. We knew you were his lifemate," Francesca said. They reached the center of the meadow where the flowers grew in abundance. Francesca sank down into the middle of the fragrant wildflowers. "As his lifemate you should have been kept informed at all times."

"Still," Skyler sat beside her adopted mother, "I might not have gone off on my own to rescue him, and he wouldn't have lived. Fate seems to have a funny way of making things right."

Francesca smiled at her. "You came to us and made our lives so full, Skyler. Never think that I don't feel love just as fiercely for you as I do for Tamara. We *chose* you. I think you were always meant to be ours."

"I think so, too," Skyler said. She was a silent a moment and then reached for Francesca's hand. "You know what Dimitri is, a mixed blood, the very thing that caused all this fighting."

"The *Hän ku pesäk kaikak*," Francesca said firmly. "He may have been the catalyst, but he wasn't the cause. This type of warfare had to be planned a long time in advance. Our enemies had no way of knowing that Dimitri was *Hän ku pesäk kaikak*, let alone that he would fall into their hands. They used him as their excuse to start their war."

Skyler nodded. "The thing is, we don't know what having mixed blood might do to a child. MaryAnn and Manolito haven't gotten pregnant. Tatijana is like me, not yet there, but both of us will be someday. It may be that we can't have children."

Francesca was her usual thoughtful self. She didn't jump in to reassure Skyler, but thought it over in her mind. "There are two ways for you and Tatijana to look at this. You could try to get pregnant now, before you have enough of the Lycan blood to fully transform you, or you can wait and see. There is no sense in worrying about something you have no control over."

"I just thought . . ." Skyler trailed off and reached out to grasp a flower stem, pulling the flower to her so she could smell the perfumed center.

"What?"

"The flowers up in the mountains, the Night Star flower, do you think the ceremony helps beyond fertility? Do you think it actually prevents miscarriages?"

"I know that it enhances one's addiction—for lack of a better word—for the taste and scent of one's lifemate. The flower ritual seems to create a tight sexual bond between lifemates, but as to whether or not it helps keep a child alive, no one honestly knows yet."

"But Gregori and Savannah and Mikhail and Raven didn't actually undergo the ceremony, and their babies have survived."

"So has Shea and Jacques's little boy. Tamara survived. Corrine and Dayan's little Jennifer is doing well and she had a very scary start," Francesca said. "None of them even knew about the fertility ceremony."

"Did you know about it?" Skyler asked.

"I'd heard of the ceremony, but of course I'd never witnessed it," Francesca admitted. "Why are you so worried about having a child, Skyler? You and Dimitri are just starting your lives. You'll know eventually because, truly, you have all the time in the world. There is no ticking biological clock for you. You're Carpathian."

Skyler plucked at the hem of her jacket. "Maybe that's true, but what if the clock is ticking? What if I can't have children because I'll be a mixed blood? Josef had to convert me," she confessed in a little rush.

"Because Dimitri had to hold you to earth."

Skyler shook her head. "Not just that. He was afraid to convert me. No woman has gone through the conversion as a mixed blood."

"MaryAnn . . ."

"Was already Lycan," Skyler finished. "Her body refused the total conversion. She retained her wolf. The two bloodlines coexist in her, just as it does in Fen and Dimitri." She bit her lip and looked at her mother. "I knew everything, every concern Dimitri had when I asked him to convert me. And I accept it, if we can't have children, I really do. Dimitri is my everything, but I did always picture us having children."

Francesca stroked caresses over Skyler's hair. "Don't give up on the idea. And you need to talk to Dimitri about your fears."

"I don't want to make him feel bad, it's not like he can do anything about it. This mixed blood thing isn't anyone's fault. It started centuries ago when he would fight vampires, need blood and there you go. He is what he is, and I'll be the same." She shook her head. "I guess I had all these fantasies in my head about my little house and my children and you and Gabriel coming to see us. It's silly."

"It isn't silly. You have a house you and Dimitri will fix up into a beautiful home," Francesca pointed out. "Whether you have children or not, we'll come to see you. Skyler, it's okay to be worried or upset, even when you have a lifemate. It's a natural part of life. Dimitri is there for you to talk to. If children are important to you, he'll find a way to make it happen."

Skyler nodded. "I know he will. I just needed my mom for a minute to tell me everything is going to be okay."

"It will be," Francesca assured. She looked around the meadow. "Look how beautiful the night is, honey. Who would have thought that only two days ago men were killing one another?"

"Does anyone know why yet?"

Francesca shook her head. "I'm sure they all thought they had good reason. The Lycan council is staying to try to work the alliance out with Mikhail. They've sent for their own packs, ones they believe they can trust." She hugged Skyler again. "You saved Zev's life, Sky. It was an impossible wound to heal, but you saved his life."

Skyler shook her head. "I had a lot of help. Tatijana and I played tag team. When one got too drained the other went in. The Carpathian people came through for us in spite of the battle going on, and Branislava"—she shook her head—"I don't even know what she did."

"She's with him now, in the ground," Francesca asked.

Skyler nodded. "I think everyone fears if Zev wakes he'll think we buried him alive. He's Lycan more than Carpathian, at least in his mind. I know what it feels like to think you're buried beneath the earth and can't get out." She shuddered and wrapped her arms around herself.

"Maybe your father and I did you a disservice by allowing you to remain human."

Skyler sent her mother a smile. "No, I think you raised me exactly right. Dimitri's teaching me everything I need to know, and Ivory's been helping me as well. She and Razvan have offered us wolf pups. We're both very excited to be able to have them and become a pack with them."

Francesca's eyes widened. "How amazing. Ivory and Razvan are very . . . elusive. I'm glad he's reaching out to you and sharing your life a little more."

"It was me more than him that kept a distance," Skyler admitted. "The idea of having mage blood was repugnant to me, until I needed it. Suddenly I was more than grateful to have it. I realized the blood and lineage had nothing to do with whether or not I chose to use my gifts for good or evil. That is my choice and my responsibility."

Francesca smiled at her. "I'm so very proud of you. The things you've accomplished already are far beyond your years. Dimitri is lucky to have you."

"I'm lucky to have him. He's so good to me and patient. He never once pushed me for anything. He just was this constant in my life. A rock. Always there, expecting nothing from me. How could I not fall in love with him?"

Francesca took her hand. "I think the flower ceremony would be good for you, Skyler. Are you able to be with him intimately without panicking?"

Skyler nodded. She had become used to the open way of Carpathian communication and even with her mother, or maybe because she'd always talked things over with Francesca, talking about making love to Dimitri didn't embarrass her. "So far, so good. He's very gentle with me and patient. I love him all the more for that."

Francesca nodded. "I'm grateful he's your lifemate. He is a good man and a fierce warrior. He'll protect you always. It's nice to know he's so capable. Gabriel was telling me that just last rising." She suddenly lifted her head. "Oh, dear. I do believe your friends have tracked you down, Skyler. I love them dearly, but tonight their exuberance will be just a little too much for me."

Skyler gripped her hand, suddenly comprehending. Francesca was very pale, and she hadn't come to help save Zev, although she was a tremendous healer. "You're pregnant, aren't you? You didn't want to tell me because of this silly worry of mine."

Francesca leaned over to kiss her on the cheek. "Yes, I'm pregnant. With all this going on, the fighting, the scare with you, I've been a little exhausted. Gabriel wants us to go home so I can rest, but he's needed here and I don't want to leave until I know you're safe."

"Mom, you should have told me right away, instead of letting me go on and on about whether or not I could have a baby. You have to know I'm so excited and happy for you and Gabriel—for us all. I love babies. Tamara is the cutest, best sister in the world. Have you told her yet?"

Francesca shook her head. "We thought it best to see if I carry. You know it's always so scary during the pregnancy."

Skyler frowned. "Have you had trouble?"

"Just a little bit, while I was traveling. I've been spending most of my time with Sara. She's on bed rest so we've kept things as quiet as possible with everything going on. She's very near term while I'm just starting out."

Skyler let her breath out. She could hear Josef and Paul running across the field toward them, Paul whooping enthusiastically and Josef playing leapfrog over him.

"Francesca, let Gabriel take you home. Have him call in Darius and Julian." Darius was Gabriel's younger brother. "They'll come. You know they will. They can take his place. I'll be fine. I've got tons of protection. I can't turn around without stumbling over Carpathian men, watching that no assassin creeps out of the woodwork to do me in."

Francesca sighed, her fingers once more stroking lovingly through Skyler's hair. "If we go, you know Lucian and Jaxon will go with us. Lucian still watches over Gabriel like a hawk. Gabriel thinks it's funny."

"Go, Mom," Skyler encouraged. "Mikhail would tell them all to take you home." She leaned over and kissed her mother.

"You're on some kind of a hit list."

"Go. Really. I'd be on that list whether you were here or not. I'd rather know that you and the baby are out of harm's way and that you have a good chance to carry this little life to term. If it comes to me never being able to have a baby, I'll have my sisters and brothers." She hugged Francesca hard. "Go home for me, Mom."

Pounding footsteps announced the arrival of Paul and Josef.

Francesca smiled at Skyler. "That's my cue. I'll talk to Gabriel. I know Ivory and Razvan are staying close to watch over you."

"Aww, Mrs. D.!" Josef skidded to a halt and bowed low, sweeping a jaunty black fedora from his head. "Have no worries about young Skyler Rose. I'm here to save the day."

"Thank you, Josef. Now that I know she's safe, I'll go find my lifemate. Hi, Paul. It's so good to see you again. The two of you take good care of my girl."

Paul threw his arm around Skyler's neck and pretended to strangle her. "She's safe with us," he growled in a threatening manner, winking at Francesca.

Skyler ducked her shoulder and threw him in a smooth, rolling move. Paul somersaulted and landed on his feet.

"I see that you boys have this under control," Francesca said. She blew a kiss to her daughter and was gone, shifting into vapor and streaming away.

"Nice move, hotshot," Paul said admiringly. "I let you show off for your mother."

Skyler laughed. "You're the one who taught me that move so don't pout." She flung her arms around him and kissed his cheek. "How are you feeling? You're the only one of us who couldn't go into the ground to heal properly."

Josef snorted. "Don't go giving him any sympathy. He's been basking in it ever since he arrived here. He's got that sister of his and four aunts to fuss over him as well as his uncles, who don't dare give him the lecture he so richly deserves because they'll face the wrath of their lifemates. He's milking it."

Paul's grin turned a little sheepish. "There could be some truth in that. Better to have them all fuss over me than Zacarias and Rafael boxing my ears or something equally as nasty."

"Now *he* has a point," Skyler said. "I'd take the sympathy over those two, or any of the De La Cruz brothers for that matter, lecturing me."

"And you didn't fare so bad either, my man." Paul poked Josef in the ribs. "Don't think I didn't notice you basking a little yourself."

Josef smirked. "My mom and my aunt did a little fussing, I'll admit. And Byron and Vlad aren't nearly as intense as Zacarias and Rafael. It was kind of nice being spoiled after I thought I might get flayed alive over our little adventure."

"We did the right thing," Skyler said, sobering. "Thank you both. Without you, Dimitri would have died. There's no question about that. I couldn't have gone after Dimitri alone, and you both came through for me when I needed you most. I'll never forget it."

"We made a pact a long time ago to stick together," Josef said. "That's forever for me."

Paul nodded. "I'm in. I might not have forever like the two of you, but . . ."

"I'll convert you myself," Josef said. "Of course you have to be converted. Why wouldn't you? You have enough Carpathian blood in you to be Carpathian."

Paul shrugged. "I'm not certain my psychic gifts are strong enough to allow me to survive the conversion. Ginny's might be, but we don't know. I would never take chances with her, and neither would Colby, so we're just waiting to see what happens in the future."

"You're psychic enough," Josef declared.

"What's it like, Skyler? Going through the conversion? It looked horrible. I was terrified for you."

"She was dead," Josef said. "She probably doesn't remember it."

Knots formed in Skyler's stomach. She remembered every convulsion, that endless wave of pain that tore through her body, destroying everything human and reshaping to give birth to Carpathian. "I remember," she admitted in a low voice.

She shivered, her body cold, reacting to the memory. She couldn't imagine how anyone would go through it without help. Dimitri had taken the brunt of the conversion by taking over her body and riding it out, shielding her as much as he could from the pain wracking her physical body.

Do you have need of me?

Dimitri. The moment he poured into her mind, filling her with warmth and love, she felt different. Unafraid. *Paul asked me about the conversion. I remember the pain. And you. You shielding me. What you did was extraordinary.*

What I did was possess your body. It is forbidden.

I gave you permission and that makes it different. I don't think I ever thanked you. What you did was save my life and take away pain. I love you more than anything, Dimitri. In that moment, she wanted to reach out and touch him, to stroke her fingers down his beloved face and trace every line and scar.

I will leave this meeting with the prince and the others if you wish me to come to you.

Skyler found herself smiling. He would, too. He would just walk out of an important meeting with the prince to see to her every need or desire. She wrapped her arms around herself and hugged hard. Sometimes she couldn't believe she was so lucky.

I can visit with Josef and Paul while you work. I know that meeting is important.

We have to devise a plan to protect the council members during the day while we're underground. At this point, no one is certain which Lycans can be trusted. Two council members and a good third of the remaining Lycans have the same little tattoo that was on the assassins.

Did Arno's guard say anything yet? she asked hopefully. Dimitri had made certain he would remain alive so they could question him.

There was a small silence. Skyler's heart jumped. *Just tell me.*

He's been murdered. At first we believed he'd committed suicide, but we discovered a small needle mark in his neck. Someone poisoned him.

Skyler closed her eyes briefly. *Then you know for certain at least one more of the elite guards is dangerous to us all.*

Or a council member. We can't rule them out. Arno was pretty outspoken against anyone with mixed blood. In fact, he was passionate about his beliefs.

He worked hard to help save Zev's life.

He doesn't know Zev is mixed blood. Dimitri flooded her with warmth again. *Have fun with Paul and Josef. I'll meet you at home shortly.*

The low sensual tone moved through her body like thick molasses. The man could make her want him just by looking at her let alone talking in that smooth, sexy voice.

Josef groaned aloud. "Stop talking to that man of yours and ignoring us. You've got your goofy face on."

Laughing, she nudged him with the toe of her boot. "I don't have a goofy face."

"You go all moony and dreamy," Josef accused. "It's sick."

"It's a sickness all right," Paul teased. He clasped his hands to his chest over his heart and fell backward in the grass. "Oh, Dimitri, you make me swoon."

"I'm *so* telling him you said that, Paul." Skyler gave him a hard punch in the thigh, hoping to give him a dead leg. "He'll be delighted to know you swoon over him."

"He's so manly and everything," Josef added.

"Ow!" Paul rubbed his thigh, glaring at her. "I've been shot, woman. Have some respect for my still healing wounds."

Josef rolled his eyes. "There he goes, looking for feminine sympathy, reminding everyone very subtly he's heroic."

Skyler gave a little derisive snort. "He's barking up the wrong tree if he expects sympathy from me. I was there, remember, Paul? Didn't you get shot in the butt?"

Josef and Skyler burst into a riot of laughter.

Paul glared at them. "I did *not* get shot in the butt as you well know. Fat lot of good you two are. I've got to milk this thing as long as I can. Having you two howling like hyenas isn't going to serve my cause one little bit."

"He's got a point," Josef said. "We are his best friends. We really should help him out. Zacarias and Rafael are on his butt all the time now."

"And Colby is actually supervising a 'healthy' diet for me." Paul gave a little groan. "I'm a grown man and you'd think, just because I got shot, I've reverted to being a toddler in her eyes. I actually had to sneak out to find you, Skyler. That's how close a watch they have on me."

"Poor Paul, to have to put up with all those people loving you and taking care of you," Skyler teased. "It makes me so sad for you."

Paul scowled at her. "All right, I give up." He held up his hands in surrender. "I'm getting no sympathy from this crowd."

"We could compare scars," Josef offered. "That might make you feel better. I've only got a couple." He sounded disappointed.

"Naw. Skyler would win that round," Paul said. "They riddled her with bullets. They only winged me six times."

Skyler shuddered. "Don't say 'riddled.' You both are a little out there, you know that? Who wants to get shot and compare scars?"

Josef's eyebrows shot up. "You know, woman, you just don't get it. Number one reason—chicks. Chicks love guys with heroic scars."

Paul nodded in agreement. "Totally."

Skyler shook her head. "The two of you are sad, sad, sad. You shouldn't need gimmicks to get girls."

"Are you kidding, Skyler?" Paul said. "We use whatever we can. Look at Dimitri. He suffered death by silver, valiantly staying alive, and did it work for him? In the end, he got the girl."

Laughter bubbled over. "He already *had* the girl. He didn't need to get hung on hooks with silver winding through his body just to impress me. I was already impressed. And that should teach you both something."

Josef and Paul looked at one another. "That you're easy?" Josef asked.

Skyler smacked him on the back of his head. "Those bullets are nothing compared to what I'm going to do to you."

"Simmer down, little sister," Josef said. "And spill your secret, because you have one and we want to know all about it."

Skyler tried her most innocent face, widening her eyes and looking very sober. "Whatever are you talking about?"

"*Whatever* is the word," Paul said. "I knew it. You're hiding something. You've been going off with Ivory and Razvan for hours the past couple of nights."

"He is my birth father. I'm getting to know him," Skyler defended.

"In those fancy hunting clothes of yours?" Josef asked.

"You've been spying," Skyler accused.

"Trying to spy," Paul corrected without even a small hint of remorse. "Seriously, those two were on us in a second, and even Dimitri looked intimidating when they sent us home."

Skyler scowled. "Clearly, I have a lot to learn if all three of them knew you were following us and they caught you, sent you away and never even let on. I wasn't even suspicious." She glared at them. "But I should have been. You two are awful."

"Awful good," Paul quipped. "Come on, what's the secret."

"We're getting our own pack," Skyler said. "That is, if I can master the techniques and get the hunting part down. Dimitri has no problem, but I'm always messing up."

Josef whistled. "Totally cool. A wolf pack. I always thought Ivory was the coolest of the cool, but now you're just plain ice."

Coming from Josef that was a huge compliment. Skyler laughed. "In the middle of this horrible stuff happening around and to us, I still feel I'm the luckiest girl in the world. I've got Dimitri, the two best friends ever and now Ivory and Razvan are giving us wolves to care for."

"It's a lifetime commitment, isn't it?" Paul said. "Don't the wolves have to be part of your family?"

Skyler nodded. "We have to be as committed and as devoted to them as they are to us."

"I have to agree with Josef," Paul said, "you're just plain ice."

Dimitri emerged out of thin air, startling all three of them. "Are you two gentlemen being good to my lady?"

"You mean, strangling me, putting me in head locks, and teasing me unmercifully? If so, then yes, they're being ultra-good to me," Skyler said, flinging herself into his arms. Just fitting her body against his made her feel sheltered and safe. "I missed you."

Josef groaned. "Here it comes. She'd got that goofy face again. That's our cue to leave."

"Run like a rabbit now that Dimitri's here." She began to hum an old song Francesca always sang when Skyler was younger. "My boyfriend's back . . . "

"I'm retreating gracefully," Josef said. "It's the only gentlemanly thing to do when you've got that silly look."

"I've got to agree with my bro," Paul said. "You do look a little smitten."

They each waved and began to trot back toward the village. Skyler let them get nearly to safety and then she retaliated by sending a gust of wind blowing a mini-tornado of leaves and debris around them. Twigs and moss covered both, even sticking on the spikes in Josef's hair.

"You just *had* to show off, didn't you?" Josef called. He spit moss out of his mouth.

"You are such a little believer in revenge," Dimitri accused and turned her in his arms so that he could look down at her face. "A beautiful one, but I am beginning to think your 'angel' title might have to be changed."

"Since you never actually called me angel," Skyler said, "I'm not offended."

"Let's hope I never offend you," Dimitri said. "Those who do, don't fare very well."

She smoothed the lines in his face with her finger. "Have you heard how Zev and Branislava are doing?"

"Fen, Tatijana and I have taken turns giving them blood. Zev, so far, is only responsive when Bronnie pushes him to accept the blood. He hasn't really regained consciousness. Tatijana is worried about her sister. To hold him to us, she wove her spirit through his. Whatever his fate is, so is hers."

"Why would she do that?" Skyler asked. "He's a virtual stranger."

Dimitri shrugged. "Healers heal anyway they can. All of us have gone too far at times to save someone—even strangers. Look at Ivory. She knew she shouldn't save those wolf pups, but she couldn't stop herself."

He gathered Skyler up and took her into the air. She loved flying, by herself or with him, it didn't matter. Just the wonder of moving across a night sky, whether clouds had gathered or the stars were out in force, didn't matter. The feeling was the most amazing thing. The wind in her face, the butterflies in the stomach, and the view, was so different from the one below.

As they moved through the trees into denser forest, she began to open the buttons of Dimitri's shirt one by one, until his bare chest was exposed. Circling his neck with her arms, she leaned into him to trace the heavy muscles with her tongue. The scars were there, but no longer rigid, raw or discolored. The chain links were mere white lines, faded now. She knew she would never be able to make them disappear altogether, but she always traced the patterns over his body, delighting in the way he came to such glorious life under her ministrations.

"Take me to the fertility flower field, Dimitri," she whispered. "Make love to me there. It isn't so much that I might or might not get pregnant, but I've heard the flowers enhance the sexual need for one another. I never want to let you down. Not ever."

He switched directions. "Nothing you do would let me down. When we make love, it's always beautiful. If there's ever a problem, we'll stop and talk it out."

Skyler laid her head against his chest, listening to the steady beat of his heart. "I want more for us. I want wild, crazy sex sometimes. Not just for you, Dimitri, but for me. Sometimes when we're making love, I see those images in your mind, or maybe they're in mine and I want that for us as well as what we have now, but honestly, I'm scared at the same time."

"We have all the time in the world for wild and crazy sex, Skyler," he said gently. Once again they were out in the open air, making their way up the mountain. "Give yourself time. Sex is all about trust with us. The more you trust me, the more you know absolutely that you're safe with me, the better it will be and the more things we can do together."

"I do trust you implicitly," she said. "I can't imagine a situation where I wouldn't."

"What if I were to blindfold you? Would you be able to handle that?"

The field of flowers below them was beautiful, like a thousand glittering stars staring up at them, rather than looking down on them. Skyler's breath caught in her throat. Her heart gave a wild jump and then settled, following the steady rhythm of his. A million butterflies took wing in her stomach, but her breasts tingled, her nipples growing hard and she felt the familiar rush of damp heat gathering between her legs.

"I wouldn't mind trying," she said, fear skittering down her spine even as every nerve ending in her body came alive.

He put her down in the very center of the field, stripping her clothes from her with a simple wave of his hand. The night air teased her skin, playing over her like a million fingers, caressing and stroking until she trembled with desire.

"I love looking at you," Dimitri told her. "You're so beautiful." He turned his finger in a small circle, and she spun slowly around for him. "Let your hair down, *sívamet*."

Obediently, Skyler lifted her arms up, the action lifting her breasts. The coolness of the night air and that simple act of stretching upward sent a small rush of liquid heat pulsing between her legs. He didn't have to actually touch her to make her body want his. The glacier-blue of his eyes turning cobalt with intense desire was enough.

She let the thick silken mass of hair fall down her back. Already it was banding with color, giving away her stark hunger and need for him. He was fully dressed, his eyes dark with a mixture of love and lust, a sinful stamp of pure sensuality on his face.

Around her the fragrance of the flowers began to take on his scent. The smell was intoxicating and potent. Her mouth watered. The tip of her tongue licked at her lips. She could taste him already, that addictive, masculine, foresty—*warrior* flavor she craved. It was stamped into his skin, there in his kiss, his blood and the male essence of his body.

He leaned down and chose a bloom, offering it to her with both palms open. As he did, he shed his clothes, standing tall in the midst of the field of beautiful flowers. He looked magnificent to her, very male, already hard and thick and eager for her attention.

"Sometimes my slumber is disturbed when images arouse me, taking hold of my body, setting my imagination and hunger free, all the things I want to do with you, Skyler, all the things I want to show you that will bring us so much pleasure."

The sound of his voice, so smoky and sensual, an instrument of velvet playing over her body like the touch of fingers, like the cool of the night, wreaked havoc with her nerve endings. It took a moment to tear her gaze from his impressive erection to inspect the blossom. The Night Star flower seemed to have an impressive erection of its own.

Skyler found herself blushing. The ovary was a deep crimson red, with two striped filaments, but the stigma had color infusing her entire body because clearly it was shaped exactly like Dimitri's heavy erection. There were even thin white bands as if the stigma had been scarred as he'd been.

"Use your tongue, *csitri*, the way you would on me." His voice went low. Sexy. Mesmerizing.

Her gaze jumped to his. She lowered her head to the open petals, still looking at him, her tongue stroking along that long, bulbous head and thick shaft. She licked under the head and down the sides, curling her tongue, pretending it was him. Wanting it to be him. Sharing with him that she wanted it to be him and not a flower.

The taste was all Dimitri—his mouth, his blood, even his skin. It was addictive, that spicy, vivid flavor that burst through her body and sent blood surging through her veins.

His eyes darkened more, the hunger building in them. His shaft thickened, the girth enlarging impossibly, the head leaking small drops of nectar. She licked her lips, craving more.

Dimitri held out his hand, palm up, for the blossom. She gave it to him a little reluctantly. Still holding her gaze, he lapped at the honeyed liquid along the filaments and ovaries of the flower.

21

Skyler's entire body went hot, tension coiling tight. She nearly groaned with wanting him. Everything about him was sexy, but watching him devour the nectar as if it was her feminine cream he was consuming made her go a little weak.

"Kneel back on your heels, *sívamet*, your thighs open for me," he instructed. His voice went a little rough.

Her heart jumped and more liquid spilled between her legs. Keeping her gaze on his, she slowly sank down in front of him. The ground was covered in soft petals, cushioning her. He put the blossom right at the junction between her legs, so that the open petal caught any liquid spilling from her body.

Her heart pounded as his fingers brushed across her thighs. As he straightened, standing very close to her, her face was almost level with his erection. All she would have to do was kneel up. Her mouth watered, craved more of his taste.

"*Tied vagyok.* Yours I am, *csitri*," he said softly, his gaze growing even hotter. She couldn't look away from him. "*Sívamet andam.* My heart I give you. *Te avio päläfertiilam.* You are my lifemate." He put his hand on top of her head. "Do you understand, Skyler? I'll always be yours. This body, this heart, my soul, belongs to you."

She nodded. She *did* know. He always made her feel as if she was the most important woman in the world to him and everything he was, belonged to her.

"Bring the flower to my cock, and hold it there while you repeat the same words back to me." His voice dropped another octave and she shivered with anticipation.

Cupping the blossom in her open palms, she inhaled his scent deeply as she slowly knelt up. Keeping her eyes on his, she brought the flower beneath his heavy sac, so that his balls rested inside the open petals. Leaning forward she took a long, slow lick up the shaft, over the head seeking more of his addicting taste.

His hands caught the back of her head, fingers fisting in her hair. "Say the words back to me, *sívamet*."

His scent was heady, all around her, as hundreds of blossoms in the field took on his fresh, masculine aroma.

"*Tied vagyok*. Yours I am," she whispered, and opened her mouth to draw that large, glistening head into her mouth. She suckled strong, pulling out more nectar. He shuddered, his strong thighs bunching with tension. She slowly drew back, licking down the shaft. "*Sívamet andam*. My heart I give you." Her tongue danced underneath the very sensitive head and then licked all the way down to the base, until she could sip at the nectar in the flower and stroke her tongue over the velvet flesh nestled there.

"Skyler." He hissed out her name, his voice edged with tight control.

She smiled. "*Te avio päläfertiilam*. You are my lifemate." She kept her gaze steady on his, wanting him to see she meant every word. "I belong to you, Dimitri, all of me, heart and soul. This body is yours as well. I know I'm safe with you."

He had earned her trust over several years. She knew with an absolute certainty she wanted their relationship to progress. If at any time she was afraid, she knew he would stop instantly. That knowledge gave her more freedom than anything else ever could.

"If we weren't already lifemates, I would braid your hair with the smaller flowers and stems, but because you are, you feed me the petals and I'll feed you and the ritual will be complete." When she started to rise, he kept his hand on her shoulder, holding her there.

Skyler smiled up at him, pulled the flower to her and once again licked along the stigma before pulling a petal free. He bent down to reach her hand, taking the petal with his teeth. As he did so he fed her one. She wasn't surprised that it was velvety soft and bursting with the taste of him.

When the petals were consumed he slipped a blindfold of soft petals woven together around her head, the fragrance heady with passion. The world went completely dark. Her heart jumped, but again she felt a coiling tightness building in her deepest core. The wind caressed her body and teased her hair. There was a small silence and then his hand stroked through her hair, down to her shoulder and lower, until he cupped her breast. Deprived of sight, every nerve ending was heightened. Her entire body shuddered with need.

"Do you want to try this? You don't have to."

Her body pulsed for his. She could barely breathe with the hunger for him coursing through her. She would do anything for him, try anything, but more, she wanted to do it for herself. She wanted to prove to herself she could trust him no matter what and feel only pleasure in everything they did.

She nodded. To steady herself, she reached out and found his thigh. The moment she touched him, the trembling lessened.

"Feel the wind on you. Feel the way your hair falls so soft and sensual down your back and slides over your skin."

His voice was commanding. Mesmerizing. She shivered again. Fear? Excitement? Anticipation? Her core was on fire, a melting liquid heat that demanded fulfillment. Her mouth watered for him. She'd been so close to her goal, wanting to give him the same kind of pleasure he gave her. He knew her body, every square inch of her and she had been too shy to make her own demands of his.

She had caught some of the erotic images in his head and she wanted to be all those things for him. Right now, kneeling on the soft petals unable to see, the cool night air playing over her body so that she was acutely aware of her breath, her every movement, she found herself growing even more slick and hot.

Silence stretched. She could hear the creak of tree branches around the meadow as the wind played in the leaves. It whispered over the flowers and insects droned. Several frogs called in the distance, and she even caught the sound of running water. She didn't move, waiting for him. Her breath came and went, but she remained silent, her heart pounding.

She nearly jumped out of her skin when he caressed her right breast with one large hand. His fingers settled around her nipple, the tug more insistent than he'd ever used before. An electrical shock ran straight from her nipple to her core. She gasped, her lips parting, a rush of air escaping. She smelled his spicy scent and then he rubbed nectar across her lips.

"Open your mouth for me, *sívamet*."

At last. She would truly feel as if she was his. As if he belonged to her. She felt the lash of heat against her mouth and her hands moved up to cup his sac.

"Place both hands on my thighs," he instructed. His voice sounded a little rough, a little hoarse.

Her sheath clenched, melted, dripped wild honey, calling to him. He sounded so sexy. She *felt* sexy. Through her palms she could feel the slight shudder of pleasure that ran through his body as she licked at the drops of pearl liquid, with that addictive, rare taste. She opened her mouth and allowed him to push inside. The taste she craved so desperately exploded against her tongue and burst through her mouth. Without thinking she suckled, flattening her tongue, wanting to feel pleasure blossoming through his mind. She surrounded him with warmth, enfolded him with love.

She reveled in his groans, in the way his thigh muscles twitched and danced under her fingers. She found herself happy, enjoying the moment, feeling sexy and strong, her mouth tight and hot around him, worshiping him, showing him her love, claiming his body for her own.

He began to move with small, deeper thrusts. Her newfound courage faltered, a small schism of fear skittering down her spine. She was helpless there, blind and unable to stop him if he choked her. A million nightmares rose out of nowhere, flooding her mind, driving out everything around her until she felt rough hands and loud voices, slaps and kicks. Just that fast, her world went from bliss to panic.

Before she could react, his hands were gentle on her head, fingers massaging the tension from her. "You're safe, here with me, and nothing, no one, can ever harm you again. You aren't really blind at all, *csitri*. You're in my mind and you can see and feel what I do. See how beautiful you look to me. Feel what you do to me, the pleasure you brought to me."

His soft whisper calmed her as nothing else could. Behind the mask of petals, she closed her eyes and inhaled his scent. That male fragrance, so familiar to her, was as reassuring as his voice. Her heart continued to pound, but she didn't lift her hands to remove the mask of petals.

"It's still there, Dimitri," she whispered, wanting to cry. "It's never going to go away."

"Of course not, *sívamet*," he replied, his voice so tender, her eyes did burn. He removed the mask of petals and gently brought her to her feet. "Your past, like mine, shaped who you are now. That steel running down your spine, that incredible will and determination that allows you to do things no one expects—those attributes came from your past. It's part of you."

"A nightmare." She laid her head on his chest for comfort, feeling she'd failed both of them. "My childhood was a nightmare."

Instantly his arms swept around her, holding her tight to him, surrounding her with his strength and love. "Nothing in our future changes our past. You know that, Skyler. You've always known it. We talked of this moment happening. There is no right or wrong. No failure. We both expected it to happen. It is. That's all."

She let herself find a small smile. "Talking about it and having it happen are two different things, Dimitri. I wanted to please you."

"You did please me."

"I wanted to show trust. How could I be feeling happy, enjoying giving you pleasure and have my past creep into our private moment?" She looked up at him, unable to prevent the tears from swimming in her eyes. "I *do* trust you."

That was the worst of it. She had let both of them down. How could she think Dimitri would ever harm her?

"You didn't think I would harm you, Skyler," Dimitri said, gathering her into his arms. He lifted her, cradling her trembling body close to his chest. "I wasn't there in that moment."

Her heart jumped. She gave a little shattered cry and buried her face against his neck. He *hadn't* been with her. She'd lost him and panicked. Just that one act of aggression on his part and instead of feeling his familiar form—in a field of flowers holding his scent—her past still had such a powerful grip on her that she'd lost the man she loved more than anything. That seemed so much worse.

"I want to go home," she whispered, feeling defeated.

It was as if those men, those terrible monsters from her childhood, had defeated her. They'd won. She'd let them come between her and Dimitri.

To her astonishment, Dimitri put her feet back on the ground. "You are home, Skyler. Wherever I am, is home. There is no more comfort in that house than there is here with me. No one has defeated you—or us. It is impossible unless we allow it."

There was steel in his voice, and the butterflies in her stomach took flight. She threaded her fingers through his to gain courage. "I'm sorry, I didn't mean to hurt you."

He sighed. "*Csitri*, you're hurting yourself, not me. Why are you so upset over something we knew would happen?"

"I didn't really think it would," she confessed, more to herself than to him. "Not once I committed to you. Every time we've made love it's been so perfect. I honestly thought I could do anything because I *do* trust you, Dimitri."

"You *can* do anything," he replied. "What happened here is nothing at all. It will happen again and again at unexpected times and it's perfectly all right. This is not a defeat. It isn't a failure. It simply is."

Skyler swallowed hard. Allowing his wisdom to sink past hurt was difficult, but his calm logic was difficult to ignore. He wasn't upset with her.

She moved in his mind and all she could find was his love for her and the memories they'd made in the field. She could see the image of herself before him with the petals wrapped around her head, covering her eyes, kneeling in the field of flowers. She did look beautiful and sexy. Her body stirred all over again.

"I don't know why I lost you." That was the real problem. How could she have let him go out of her mind for even a moment? That was all it had taken, and she had allowed the monsters in.

"When we make love, the chemistry is very intense and powerful between us," he said. He stroked a finger over her breast and watched her shiver. "The slightest touch and our bodies respond. That's how it's supposed to be, Skyler. Sometimes, when we're really enjoying what we're doing, we get lost in the act of it, in the doing. It feels good, so how could we not?"

"So I was thinking of myself, not you?" She tried to puzzle it out in her mind.

For months, long before she had committed to him, she'd thought about whether or not she'd be able to perform oral sex when the very idea of it terrified her. Whether she would like it. How to do it—could she actually please him.

She had loved giving him so much pleasure. At the same time, it had brought her pleasure. The field of flowers with his scent, the mask of soft petals, even kneeling before him with her hands on his thighs, feeling that heavy erection against her face, her mouth. All of it was sexy and wonderful. She *had* gotten lost in the moment, her own body on fire.

He shook his head. "You were definitely thinking of me, *sívamet*. Had another man crept into your mind I would have banished him immediately. I have always touched you gently. Reverently. Even when I become a little aggressive, you can feel my love in the way I touch you."

She frowned. She hadn't considered that, but it was true. She loved it when he was aggressive, but he was there in her mind, holding her to him. She had always felt surrounded, even protected by his love.

"Shift, Skyler. Let's take to the sky. We can circle around together above the trees and head home. I want you to feel who you are. What you are. Carpathian. A formidable being without me. You have never needed me to be strong. In your own right, you wield more power than most. You are not insignificant or weak. You are Skyler. Dragonseeker. Mage. And most of all, that elusive mother of yours we know so little about, provided you with an indomitable spirit. That is your true self. We all have monsters in our past. We shrug them off as no consequences because we will never allow them to devour us."

Tears burned in her eyes again. She turned away from him and spread her arms, calling to the bird in her mind to come forth. A night owl, one that would take her soaring through the sky. Feathers burst through her skin and for a moment the world around her shimmered into strange colors and then she was in the sky.

She was lucky to have Dimitri. He saw her worth when she couldn't. He held the way he saw her out to her, that strong love he felt, giving it to her like a gift to wrap around her when she couldn't find her own way.

It was impossible to cry, not for joy or for their lost moment, while she was in the form of an owl. Instead, they flew together over the meadow of flowers. Above them was a canopy of white stars and below them there was that same sight, hundreds of stars looking up at them. It was a beautiful sight, and one she knew few would ever see.

I love you, Dimitri. And I loved the ritual we performed tonight. I loved seeing myself through your eyes. And I loved giving you pleasure the way I did.

I was the one on the receiving end, csitri, so I will admit to you, it was a wonderful evening for me as well.

She took a breath and let her failure go. If Dimitri didn't see it that way, then she wouldn't either. She had panicked. It was simply a fact, and it probably would happen again. She knew it would take a long time for her to accept those moments in the matter-of-fact way Dimitri did, but someday, maybe a century or two away, she would.

She dropped down into the canopy of the forest, flying lower through the branches, playing a little, as she had to maneuver through the openings between boughs.

Don't get carried away, he cautioned, the male owl shadowing her flight.

She changed direction abruptly, dropping out from under the male, swooping through a narrow opening to glide low over the grass growing on the forest floor.

She was Carpathian. She embraced the fact that she could fly like this, that she could see the world through the eyes of an owl.

If you were blindfolded, csitri, you could still see through the eyes of the one you merge with. It is well within your power.

Of course that had been the lesson all along. Dimitri had told her, but she'd been too upset with herself to listen to him. He had found another way and simply waited until she realized what she should have known all along.

She'd been merged with Dimitri. When they made love, he always merged with her. She knew it was not only for their heightened awareness of one another's needs and pleasure, but to protect her. All she had to do was reach out to him and she could have been in complete control.

I will remember. She made the vow more for herself than for him.

Dimitri was—well—Dimitri. He never seemed ruffled or annoyed or angry at her over anything, least of all lovemaking. He hadn't expected her to come to him and offer herself and he really took everything they did together as a miracle.

Let me show you what you gave to me, this great gift of love I will treasure always.

She flew just beneath him, heading for their home. She could see the structure in the distance, nestled in the trees. One by one they had gone through the rooms in the old stone house and remade them to their liking. There was a fire already roaring in the fireplace. Of course there would be. Dimitri saw to details.

He was always there for her, her steady rock. No matter what happened, she could count on him. She felt a burst of pure joy. Nightmares didn't have a chance against a man like Dimitri. He could say all he wanted that she was strong without him—and maybe that was the truth—but she was better with him. Always. Forever.

Show me, my love.

The images slipped into her mind unfiltered. With them came his feelings. The absolute ecstasy of her tight hot mouth surrounding him like a velvet fist, sending fire dancing through his groin, down his thighs and up into his belly. *She* had done that.

The sight of her, so trusting, that blindfold of petals, her hands on his thighs, her complete gift of herself, it had all combined together to make him lose his control and get lost in the feeling of bliss she created, that paradise he'd slipped into.

Your trust is your absolute gift to me, Skyler. Not the way you make me feel. You put on a blindfold in the middle of a field and gave yourself to me. Look what memories I have. I'll cherish them for all time.

Show me the moment I panicked. I want to feel what you felt. That was all important. She needed to know if she'd ruined that beautiful memory for him.

Dimitri didn't hesitate. The intensity of his hunger for her overwhelmed her, that need surging through his veins, centering in his groin, a roaring firestorm building hot and fast. She found herself caught up in the heat, her own body coiling with sexual tension, hunger for him moving through her even deep within the body of the owl.

She felt that first flicker of uncertainty moving through his mind. Skyler. His world. Instantly the focus went from what he was feeling to her. His mind completely and utterly focused on her. There was no thought for him or his building desire, no regret, no anger, nothing but the need to made certain she was all right.

You are my life. Your happiness is placed above my own always. Just as you trust me to do these things for you, I know that you will do them for me.

The little owl came to rest on the wide stone railing around the verandah, spreading her wings and flapping them before she shifted back to her human form. She stood on the broad, stone rail, holding her arms out to the night. She didn't bother with clothes, their home was far from any others, and she had scanned the area around them just as Dimitri had taught her.

The male owl landed on the stone floor of the porch, shifting fast, so fast she barely caught the change as she turned to face him.

"How do you do that?" she asked, swinging around to face him. "Shifting is way cool, but I really have to think about what I'm doing."

His hands closed around her waist and he lifted her off the railing to set her on the stone flooring of the porch. "I've had centuries to practice."

"You say that so casually," Skyler said. "Centuries. I'm still thinking in terms of years. My next birthday."

He brushed a kiss on top of her head, and then threaded his fingers through hers, tugging her closer to him until she felt heat radiating off his body. "Eventually time passing means nothing at all."

"I guess. I suppose if I thought in terms of years, you'd be old and decrepit," she teased.

"Fortunately for me, we don't age past a certain point," he said with a small grin. He reached around her and opened the door as if he was human.

Again she realized he did little things to make her comfortable that she hadn't even considered. The house itself was for someone human. He'd modernized it and included even a kitchen, so anyone coming to visit would think they were just like everyone else. She knew that would be his explanation, but she had actually gone to the refrigerator several times and opened it, looked in and examined the food he changed nightly in it. It was a human habit and one that would take time to overcome.

"What do you miss most?" he asked.

"You mean food? Chocolate." She laughed softly. "Most women love chocolate, Dimitri, and I have to admit, I'm one of them."

"What does it taste like?" he asked.

She frowned. She'd never really thought about it. "It's hard to explain."

"Don't explain it, *csitri*, you're Carpathian. Bring the memory into your mind and then transfer it to me."

Skyler nodded, squeezing his hand. It was always the little things she had to remember to do. She knew she'd get used to doing them, but still, there were so many details. She pulled up her best memory of chocolate. She'd been in the college library studying for hours, forgetting she was hungry, and her aunt Jaxon, Lucian's lifemate, had come to see her.

The visit was unexpected, but welcome. Seeing a familiar face made her happy. Jaxon, like Skyler, had been human and she knew what long hours were. She'd brought dark chocolate, an entire bar, with her. Skyler had sat there talking to her for a long time, enjoying every moment while the chocolate melted in her mouth.

She had savored that bar, eating one small square at a time over the next week. Each time she ate one of the pieces, it conjured up her visit from Jaxon and she'd been happy all over again. She loved college, but she missed her family and somehow that small gift had made her feel very loved.

The taste of the chocolate poured into her mind and into her mouth. She turned to Dimitri, circling his neck with her arms and pressing her body tightly against his. She lifted her face to his in invitation.

Dimitri bent his head to hers, his blue eyes going dark, setting off the butterflies and causing her sheath to clench hotly. She brushed her lips featherlight over his.

"You let it melt in your mouth," she advised softly.

Her fingers bunched in the hair at the nape of his neck, as she felt his tongue trace along the seam of her lips. She opened her mouth to him, allowing his tongue to sweep inside. Along with the taste of dark chocolate, she held the feeling she got, the joy that bar had brought to her uppermost in her mind, sharing that as well.

His arms went around her, pulling her close, imprinting her soft body onto his. She felt his groin stirring against her stomach, already full and hard. His mouth was hot, his skin radiating heat. He kissed her thoroughly, over and over, robbing her of breath first, and then her ability to think.

Chocolate is very tasty, he agreed.

Mmm, yes, she said. *But so are you.*

I'm taking you into the bedroom.

You must be reading my mind.

She kept her eyes closed because he didn't end the kiss. She felt herself floating, but then his kisses tended to make her feel that way as a rule anyway. His teeth nibbled at her lip.

He placed her gently in the middle of the bed on her hands and knees. Skyler opened her eyes slowly. The room was lit only with the soft light of flickering candles. The scent was a spicy cinnamon. Mirrors surrounded them, as if the walls had been constructed of them, as if the ceiling had been.

"You're so beautiful," he murmured. "I wanted to look at your face when I make love to you in this position."

There was something very decadent about kneeling on a bed perfectly naked, her hair falling around her, her breasts swaying gently, her hips moving seductively—and she couldn't stop them—in invitation. Flames seemed to burn between her legs, and even the cool night air couldn't put out the fire.

He knelt behind her, his fingers dancing up her inner thighs, to that waiting heat to slide inside, testing her readiness. Now the images weren't just decadent, they were erotic. Her eyes met his in the mirror.

Already her breath came in ragged gasps as anticipation made her tremble. He pressed his fingers deeper.

"I love how you get so wet for me, *sívamet*. No matter how many times I reach for you, you are always ready for me."

"Because you drive me crazy," she admitted softly. "I love your body. Just looking at you can make me want you. And then there's the sound of your voice. Hearing you can do it, too. If you touch me, or kiss me or take my blood, I'm completely lost."

It was the truth and she wasn't in the least ashamed to admit it.

She felt the hot head of his erection press tightly into her entrance. He always felt too large for her initially. Her body seemed to resist his invasion, even when she was so eager for him to be inside of her. His hands went to her hips, fingers anchoring there. Her heart beat hard as he waited. Heat coiled. She felt her slickness bathe him, her muscles clenching, desperate to draw him in.

He surged forward, filling her, driving through tight muscle, deeper and deeper until he seemed to lodge in her very womb. She screamed as lightning streaked through her, white-hot, fiery, sending flames from her thighs to her belly and up to her breasts.

Dimitri sank deep, watching her face, watching her eyes glaze as he drove into her again and again, setting a wicked pace. He was aggressive and rough, wanting her to see that she wasn't afraid of that side of their lovemaking. *Anything* could trigger her panic. It would never matter. They would accept it and move on.

Her eyes met his in the mirror. She was so beautiful, he wanted to weep with joy. With every thrust, her breasts swayed and her head thrashed. Her mouth opened as she panted. She pushed back into him, taking him as deep as she could, matching his rhythm and riding him all the way, no matter how strong or hard each thrust was.

He began to lose himself in the beauty and fire of their passion. Control began to slip. There was always that moment of danger, when she realized he abandoned all constraints and just allowed himself to give himself over to the pleasure.

She surrounded him with scorching hot heat. Her muscles were a tight vise, the friction exquisite. She took him to places he hadn't known existed, her sheath a fist of velvet, squeezing and massaging until he knew he wouldn't last.

Every muscle in his body seemed to contract. Coil with tension. With anticipation. He watched the color on her body, the flush of red, the telltale little pleas escaping as she pushed back frantically, her own release building and building.

So beautiful, he whispered.

She gasped as her body clamped down hard on his. He felt the first wave like a tsunami ripping through her, taking him with her. She screamed out his name as wave after wave followed, her clenching muscles milking him dry.

Skyler collapsed forward on the bed, gasping for air. Dimitri blanketed her body, falling with her, his arms caging her in. They were still locked together, hearts pounding and lungs burning. When he managed to pull in some air, he let his body disengage from hers, and rolled to his side so that he wouldn't crush her with his weight.

It took him a few more minutes to wave away the mirrors, stop the roaring fire and get rid of most of the candles.

"Do you think we can just sleep here?" Skyler asked. "I don't want to move."

He laughed softly. "We never sleep where we can be found. You know that."

"What are safeguards for?"

He cupped her breast in his palm and locked one leg over her thigh. "It is never safe to sleep where we can be found," he repeated. "Even with safeguards."

She turned her head to look at him over her shoulder. "Can the *Sange rau* stay out during daylight hours?"

He frowned, nuzzling her neck. "So far, no. *Sange rau* is rogue wolf and vampire. A rogue wolf can walk in daylight of course, but a vampire cannot. Fen says he can be out in the sun longer than he's ever managed it, but he still burns if he stays too long. I was out in the sun when hanging in the trees. Fortunately, the sun never really penetrated the canopy and fell across my body, but I still blistered. Had I been fully Carpathian that may have killed me. I don't know. Our Carpathian blood will always be Carpathian blood and the Lycan blood will always be Lycan. It's our ability to utilize the gifts of both species that seems to increase. With that may come the ability to walk in the afternoon sun, but it's too soon to predict that."

"Were you listening to Arno's voice when he talked about mixed bloods?" Skyler asked, turning over to face him.

His fingers traced her frown. "Yes."

"Not just his words, but the passion and loathing in his voice? He's a good man, Dimitri. He thinks of himself as a good man. He tries to do his best, tries to do the right thing, and yet he was so adamant that anyone with mixed blood needed to be exterminated. He believes that, deep down in his heart and soul. He even recognizes the difference between *Sange rau* and *Hän ku pesäk kaikak* but he wants them all dead."

Her distress ate at him. He stroked back the wild mess of hair. He liked her hair messy. She looked as if she'd just thoroughly been made love to. "I know, *csitri*. Don't let it get to you. We have no control over others. If we're lucky, maybe in time just being around us, he'll feel differently. The council members have voted to stay to attempt to come to some agreement. I believe a couple of the others have opted to come as well, although I don't know that for certain."

"He really worked hard to save Zev's life. He knew Carpathians were giving him blood, but he didn't object or try to stop us." Skyler bit her lower lip. "Right then, he was so torn. Zev saved his life. Had he not covered Arno's body with his own, Arno would be dead. Zev should have been. Fortunately he had enough Carpathian blood mixing with his Lycan blood that he held out until help came."

Dimitri leaned forward and kissed the tip of her nose. "In the form of my amazing and talented lifemate. From what Fen and Tatijana told me, you were incredible."

"It took all of us, but it certainly has made me curious to know more about my birth mother. I feel her sometimes, guiding me when I lose my way healing someone. She's a force inside of me, unexpected and rare, but she sometimes comes to me. I can't remember her healing people, but I dream of it sometimes. I think it's possible I was there with her when she helped others. I had to be very young, maybe a toddler, and she showed me what she was doing."

"I could find those memories for you," Dimitri offered.

Skyler squirmed uncomfortably. He knew everything about her past, the fact that as a child she'd been sold to men, but he would have to get past those memories to find the ones of her mother. As much as she wanted to know as much as possible about her birth mother, she wasn't ready for him to replay those monstrous memories.

"Sometime. When things aren't happening so fast for me," Skyler said. "There have been so many changes, and sometimes I feel overwhelmed. I know everything could blow up any moment between Lycan and Carpathian and the thought terrifies me. I'm still getting used to being fully Carpathian and learning everything that goes with that." She smiled at him. "And there's you. The love of my life. The intensity of *us* is a little disconcerting at times."

He gathered her up, nuzzling the top of her head. "Dawn is breaking and you need sleep. We've got another big day ahead of us. Ivory and Razvan want us training hard all day, every day so that the pups accept us."

"When they first called them pups, I thought they would be little things, but they're huge," Skyler said.

"Do they intimidate you?"

She shook her head. "Not anymore. When I first saw them, they did. I think they accepted me because I must have some of Razvan in me. They certainly recognized the alpha wolf in you right away."

He growled in her ear as he opened the floor and floated down to the basement. "Of course they did."

"Very funny. I don't find you intimidating either." She sniffed for emphasis.

He laughed. "After watching Ivory show you how to use the crossbow and throwing wedges she has, I think I'm becoming a little intimidated by you."

She grinned at him. "I am getting good at it. I actually love it. Especially the wolves. In my wildest dreams I never thought I'd have my own wolf pack like Ivory and Razvan do."

They both dissolved and slipped through the cracks in the stone floor to the ground below. Dimitri opened that for them as well. Skyler was too excited by the prospect of renewing her training with the wolves the following evening to have her usual brief moment of fear as they floated into the rich, welcoming soil.

Dimitri wrapped her in his arms, as he did each dawn, holding her close, commanding her to sleep before he settled the earth over them and secured their safeguards for the coming day.

22

Mist rolled in, long white fingers stretching through the forest and curling around thick tree trunks. The dense vapor muffled sound and lent an eerie quality to the woods. Out of that heavy fog stepped a woman. She went still, nearly blending into her background. Very slowly, she crouched low to place her hand on the forest floor, feeling the very heartbeat of the earth, checking for information, for sounds or vibrations of an enemy.

She was small, her long blond hair woven into a thick, intricate braid that reached her waist. She wore black pants that rode low on her hips and were tucked securely into black boots. Her sleeveless vest left her midriff bare. The vest had three sets of steel buckles with tiny crosses embedded in the metal, looking ornamental on the squares.

She carried a crossbow in one hand, a silver sword hung on her left hip and a knife on her right. A quiver of arrows was slung across one shoulder, some tipped in silver. Down both legs of her trousers were loops containing many sharp-bladed weapons. A low-slung holster on her hip housed a pistol as well as rows of very small, flat but extremely sharp arrowheads.

She was patient, taking her time, her palm flat on the ground, absorbing the news of the night. It was cold, but she didn't feel the chill in the air, or the mist as it gathered around her. She closed her eyes briefly, allowing her senses to see for her. Very slowly she rose, turning to her left. There, where the fog was most dense, where the trees were the thickest, her quarry lay in wait to ambush her.

She seemed to glide over the forest floor. Even the brush parted for her so that there was no whisper of movement as she made her way cautiously toward that thick stand of trees. As she approached, she felt the first stirring on her back, a small brush of fur, warning her.

Elation swept through Skyler. She continued forward a few more feet and then whipped around, her fingers already pulling the arrowheads free and snapping them with tremendous strength as she ran toward the grotesque vampire emerging from the trunk of a twisted dead fir tree. Though dead, the tree shuddered and shook as it expelled the foul creature from its depths.

Six arrowheads went up his leg, lodging deep, the formula coating them preventing the vampire from shifting into another form. She ran forward with her sword. His torso and head disappeared as did his feet, lost in the thick fog. Only one of the vampire's legs remained behind, a strange, almost laughable sight.

Cursing in a very unladylike manner, Skyler halted her attack. "I can't believe I made such a stupid mistake."

The leg disappeared as if it had never been. Ivory and Razvan materialized in front of her. Dimitri wrapped a comforting arm around her.

"You listened to your wolves," Ivory said. "But the arrows have to go from belly to shoulder if you want to be able to take the heart."

Skyler couldn't help but smile. "Frost warned me. I was so proud of him. I actually knew it was him and not Moonglow. I can tell the difference between them now."

Frost had a beautiful silver coat, thick and unusual, tipped in white so that he appeared to be covered in frost. The lone female was a beautiful specimen, her pelt so silver she glowed like the moon. Ivory had named her Moonglow, but most of the time they called her Moon. Both rode on her back as tattoos, so that she had eyes and ears on both sides and behind her, aiding her on the hunt.

She was grateful the four pups had accepted Dimitri and her as their pack leaders, the alphas they looked to. She knew it was Dimitri's calm, decisive manner and firm leadership that had captured the pups' attention, but she was getting better every single day.

Shadow was darker, a thick pelt of nearly black fur, tipped in gray so that he could slide through the darkness without detection, and he was definitely an alpha. He adhered to Dimitri's back along with Sonnet, the wolf with the most surprising voice. He was large and a stealthy hunter, working closely with Shadow to bring down game.

"Did Moon give you any indication there was a threat to you?" Ivory asked.

Skyler sighed. "If she did, I didn't feel it. I think she's still in a snit because I tried carrying them as a fur coat earlier. When I shrugged it off and tried to throw it out smoothly to allow them to go free, instead of the coat sailing through the air flat, the pelt was bunched up and she got tangled. She let me know she wasn't happy."

Ivory shook her head, covering her smile with one hand. "I had so much trouble with the coat," she admitted. "It isn't easy to learn all of the different weapons, as well as how to hunt with the wolves. The movement on your skin has to be subtle. You never want anyone to know your wolves are the real deal."

Skyler nodded. Ivory had so much to teach her.

Us, Dimitri corrected. *I'm learning, too.*

You're so good at everything. I feel like the dunce in class. I'm used to being the top student.

Dimitri burst out laughing. Both Ivory and Razvan raised eyebrows.

"I'm sulking because I'm not at the top of my class," Skyler confessed with a wry grin. "Dimitri thinks that's very funny. I really want to be able to do this."

Ivory smiled at her, touching her arm briefly. "The most difficult task has already been completed. The wolves had to accept you. You will have to find another female for Shadow. Little Moon is his sister, and she doesn't have an alpha bone in her body."

"Actually Shadow will find her in time," Razvan said. "When he does, you'll know, and you'll have to train her as well."

"They need to be worked with every day," Ivory cautioned. "A pack is cohesive and successful as long as they have good leaders. You have to hunt with them when they go after game. Direct and help them. That's part of being alpha."

Skyler ducked her head. She didn't mind hunting and killing vampires, but it was difficult for her to hunt live animals even though she knew the wolves needed to eat. She was working hard to overcome that squeamish feeling in the pit of her stomach each time they took the wolves out to hunt.

More and more, she wanted to spend time learning to use her weapons and the wolves for hunting vampire, not game. She was determined to be an asset to Dimitri. If it took centuries of practice she was going to make certain she was the best so he didn't have to worry.

"I'll always worry when you're in danger," Dimitri said aloud.

"Not if I get really good at this."

"Even then," he assured. "But I'm very proud of you, Skyler. You've come a long way in this last week."

"Ivory is one of the best hunters we have," Razvan said, "but as her lifemate, I worry. That's not something that will go away. You're improving every time we go out."

Skyler sent him a smile of thanks. "I'm not very good with a crossbow yet," she admitted. "And I'll need to be if I'm going to be of any use on a hunt."

Dimitri winced a little at that. She planned to hunt vampire with him, just as Ivory and Razvan did together. The idea still didn't sit well with him, although she learned fast and the wolves would give them an edge. He had to admit that she'd been a huge asset when she'd rescued him. Without her, he'd be dead. She didn't panic and she was methodical.

Skyler sent him a long look from under her lashes. He knew that look. He found himself giving her a sheepish smile. "You've already wrapped me around your little finger, *sívamet*, I can't deny you anything. But you will wait to hunt until we all think you're ready. All three of us, not you."

Skyler resisted rolling her eyes. Razvan would side with Dimitri, saying just a little longer before she could hunt with him, but Ivory . . . She smiled at the woman who was fast becoming a close friend and ally. Ivory would advocate for her, but only if she worked hard and learned the lessons necessary to become an asset to Dimitri.

"I know I can't possibly learn every weapon in a few weeks, but eventually I will."

"You can't just know how to use them," Ivory said. "You have to have it be second nature to you. Vampires use all kinds of tricks, illusions and deadly poisons, not to mention their own weapons, when you hunt them. You can't hesitate when you go in for the kill. We'll keep working on your training until we know for certain you're capable of destroying the undead."

"I know you don't like to hunt game," Razvan added, "but that, more than anything, will help you adapt to hunting with the wolves. Your speed, stealth and ability to read the animals will improve fast."

"You need to create a home for the wolves so that they're with you all the time," Ivory added. "Your house will serve you well, but they'll need to know they can lie by the fire while you're moving around the other rooms. When you go to ground, they'll want to go to ground with you. Never forget they're Carpathian and need the rejuvenating soil just as you do."

Skyler reached out her hand to Dimitri. Immediately his fingers closed around hers and she felt the warmth of his love enfolding her like a blanket. More, the wolves felt it as well. Already, she was tuning to them, sharing her mind with them, as Dimitri did so naturally. They seemed to snuggle closer to her, brushing against her back in affection before settling.

She knew they had difficult times ahead. A war with an unknown enemy was brewing and her people had to be protected. She wanted to be able to fight if necessary, to protect those she loved. The wolves gave her added confidence.

"The tattoos suit the two of you," Razvan said. "I would never have thought those scars would diminish in the way they have, Dimitri. I can barely see evidence of them, only faint white circles. On your back, the fur of your wolves just blends seamlessly."

Dimitri tugged until Skyler was beneath the protection of his shoulder. "Skyler has skills beyond anything I've ever seen."

A flash of pride lit Razvan's eyes. "We were all amazed that she was able to save Zev. Has anyone heard how he's doing?"

Dimitri shook his head. "He's still hanging on, thankfully. Branislava has woven her spirit to his and holds him to this world. Fen says they aren't out of the woods yet, but he has taken blood each time they've gone to feed them both."

Razvan's breath hissed out and Ivory moved closer to him, simply touching his arm in a silent gesture of comfort, reminding Dimitri that Tatijana and Branislava were Razvan's aunts. They'd all three been prisoners together in the ice fortress where Xavier had ruled and carried on his malicious experiments.

"Bronnie barely had surfaced again before she did this," Razvan said. "I hadn't even seen her." There was quiet acceptance in his voice, learned no doubt from centuries of torture and having to accept things outside of his control, no matter how distressing.

"Bronnie knew what she was doing," Skyler explained. "There was no other way to save him. His wound was so bad, fatal, however you want to put it. It took all three of us working for what seemed hours to mend him from the inside out. Had Bronnie not woven her spirit to his, and locked him to her, he would have drifted away."

"I don't understand," Razvan said. "A spirit can be surrounded and held, why would she have to tie her fate to his?"

Ivory took his hand. "He would have chosen to leave us," she said softly. "But his instincts to protect others are very strong in him. She knew that, didn't she, Skyler?"

Skyler nodded. "We all saw it in him. He's deadly and scary when you first get inside his head, but then you find his first instinct is to defend and shield others. By weaving her spirit through his, Bronnie took away his choice to leave. He would take her with him if he did, and that is something almost beyond Zev's capability."

"Unless the wound kills him," Razvan said.

Skyler nodded. "There's always that. But I go nightly to work on him, and Mother Earth has accepted him as her son. She works harder than I do to attempt to save him. I think he's getting better. A wound like his is such a trauma to the body. It takes time."

"He's Lycan," Dimitri added. "Lycans regenerate faster than most, and because he's now mixed blood, that should give him added strength and speed to recover."

Razvan nodded, his gaze on his daughter's face. "Thank you. I know what you did was extremely difficult, no matter how many times you say you had help. The toll it took on you showed for many days after. If Bronnie lives, it is due to your continued healing of Zev's wounds."

Color rose in Skyler's face and she moved closer to Dimitri. She was very glad she finally had a relationship with her birth father and that she could do something to make him proud of her.

"Are you ready for another run at this?" Ivory asked. "This time you should hunt together and when you find your prey, release the wolves and coordinate the attack on the vampire with your pack to give them hunting experience with the undead."

Skyler's heart jumped with pure joy. "I'm ready." She looked to Dimitri.

He leaned down, uncaring of their audience, and found her mouth with his. He took his time kissing her, allowing himself to get lost in her for just a moment. He lifted his head, his eyes dark with desire. Very slowly he smiled down at her. "Let's do this then."

Skyler went up on her tiptoes and kissed him back. "I'm with you." She always would be. Right there, by his side.

Keep reading for an excerpt from the next exciting Carpathian novel by Christine Feehan

DARK BLOOD

Available September 2014 from Piatkus!

Sound came to him first. A low drumming beat growing louder. Zev Hunter felt the vibration of that rhythmic booming throughout his entire body. It hurt. Each separate beat seemed to echo through his flesh and bone, reverberating through his tissue and cells, jarring him until he thought he might shake apart.

He didn't move. It was too much of an effort even to open his eyes and figure out what that disturbing, insistent call was—or why it wouldn't go away. If he opened his eyes he would *have* to move, and that would hurt like hell. If he stayed very still, he could keep the pain at bay, even though he felt as if he were floating in a sea of agony.

He lay there for a long time, his mind wandering to a place of peace. He knew the way there now, a small oasis in a world of excruciating pain. He found the wide, cool pool of blue inviting water, the wind touching the surface so that ripples danced. The surrounding forest was lush and green, the trees tall, trunks wide. A small waterfall trickled down the rocks to the pool, the sound soothing.

Zev waited, holding his breath. She always came when he was there, moving slowly out of the trees into the clearing. She wore a long dress and a cape of blue velvet, the hood over her long hair so that he only caught glimpses of her face. The dress clung to her figure, her full breasts and small waist, the corset top emphasizing every curve. The skirt of the dress was full, falling over her hips to the ground.

She was the most beautiful woman he'd ever seen. Her body was graceful, fluid, an ethereal, elusive woman who always beckoned to him with a soft smile and a small hand gesture. He wanted to follow her into the cool forest—he was Lycan, the wolf that lived inside of him preferred the forest to the open—but he couldn't move, not even for her.

He stayed where he was and simply drank her in. He wasn't a man clever words came easily to, so he said nothing at all. She never approached him, never closed the distance between them, but somehow, it never mattered. She was there. He wasn't alone. He found that as long as she was close to him, the terrible pain eased.

For the first time though, something disturbed his peaceful place. The booming beat found him, so loud now that the ground lifted and fell with an ominous, troubling thump. The water rippled again, but this time he knew it wasn't the wind causing the water to ring from the middle of the pool outward. The drumbeat throbbed through the earth, jarring not only his body but everything else.

The trees felt it. He heard the sap running deep in the trunk and branches. Leaves fluttered wildly as if answering the deep booming call. The sound of water grew louder, no longer a soft trickling over rocks, not a steady drip, but a rush that swelled with the same ebb and flow as the sap in the trees. Like veins and arteries flowing beneath the very earth surrounding him, making its way toward every living thing.

You hear it now.

She spoke for the first time. Her voice was soft and melodious, not carried on the wind, but rather on breath. One moment she was on the other side of that small pool of water, and the next she was sinking down into the tall grass, leaning over him, close to him, her lips nearly skimming his.

He could taste cinnamon. Spice. Honey. All of it on her breath. Or was it her skin? His Lycan senses, usually so good at scent, seemed confused. Her lashes were incredibly long and very dark, surrounding her emerald eyes. A true emerald. So green they were startling. He'd seen those eyes before. There was no mistaking them. Her bow of a mouth was a man's perfect fantasy, her lips full and naturally red.

The booming continued, a steady, insistent beat. He felt it through his back and legs, a jarring pulse that refused to leave him alone. Through his skin, he seemed to follow the path of water running beneath him, bringing life-giving nutrients.

You feel it, don't you? she insisted softly.

He couldn't look away. Her gaze held his captive. He wasn't the kind of man to allow anything or anyone to ensnare him. He forced his head to work—that first movement that he knew would cost him dearly. He nodded. He waited for the pain to rip him apart, but aside from a little burst through his neck and temples that quickly subsided, the expected agony never came.

What is it?

He frowned, concentrating. The sound continued without a break, so steady, so strong and rhythmic, he would have said it was a heart, but the sound was too deep and too loud. Still, it was a pulse that called to him just as it called to the trees and grass as if they were all tied together. The trees. The grass. The water. The woman. And him.

You know what it is.

Zev didn't want to tell her. If he said the words, he would have to face his life again. A cold, utterly lonely existence of blood and death. He was an elite hunter, a dealer of death to rogue packs—Lycans turned werewolves and preying on mankind—and he was damned good at his job.

The booming grew louder, more insistent, a dark heralding of life. There was nowhere to hide from it. Nowhere to run even if he could run. He knew exactly what it was now. He knew where the sound originated as it spread out from a center deep beneath him.

Tell me, Hän ku pesäk kaikak, what is it you hear?

The melodic notes of her voice drifted through his pores and found their way into his body. He could feel the soft musical sound wrapping itself around his heart and sinking into his bones. Her breath teased his face, warm and soft and so fresh, like the gentlest of breezes fanning his warm skin. His lungs seemed to follow the rhythm of hers, almost as if she breathed for him, not just with him.

Hän ku pesäk kaikak. Where had he heard that before? She called him that as if she expected him to know what it meant, but it was in a language he was certain he didn't speak—and he knew he spoke many.

The drumbeat sounded louder, closer, as if he were surrounded on all sides by many drums keeping the exact beat, but he knew that wasn't so. The pounding pulse came from below him—and it was summoning him.

There was no way to ignore it, no matter how much he wanted to. He knew now that it wouldn't stop, not ever, not unless he answered the call.

It is the heartbeat of the earth itself.

She smiled and her emerald eyes seemed to take on the multifaceted cut of the gems he'd seen adorning women, although a thousand times more brilliant.

She nodded her head very slowly. *At long last you are truly back with us. Mother Earth has called to you. You are being summoned to the warrior's council. It is a great honor.*

Whispers drifted through his mind like fingers of fog. He couldn't seem to retain actual words, but male voices rose and fell all around him, as if he were surrounded. The sensation of heat hit him. Real heat. Choking. Burning. His lungs refused to work, to pull in much-needed air. When he tried to open his eyes, nothing happened. He was locked in his mind far from whatever was happening to his body.

The woman leaned closer, her lips brushing against his. His heart stuttered. She barely touched him, feather light, but it was the most intimate sensation he'd ever experienced. Her mouth was exquisite. Perfection. A fantasy. Her lips moved over his again, soft and warm, melting into him. She breathed into his mouth, a soft airy breath of clean, fresh air. Once again he tasted her. Cinnamon. Spice. Honey.

Breathe, Zev. You are both Lycan and Carpathian and you can breathe anywhere when you choose. Just breathe.

He was not *Sange rau.*

No, not Sange rau, you are Hän ku pesäk kaikak. You are a Guardian.

The breath she had exchanged with him continued to move through his body. He could almost track its progress as if that precious air was a stream of white finding its way through a maze until it filled his lungs. He actually felt her breath enter his lungs, inflating them.

I'm not dreaming, am I?

She smiled at him. A man might kill for one of her smiles.

No, Zev, you're not dreaming. You are in the sacred cave of warriors. Mother Earth called the ancients to witness your rebirth.

He had no idea what she was talking about, but things were beginning to come back to him. *Sange rau* was a combination of rogue wolf and vampire blood mixed together. *Hän ku pesäk kaikak* was Lycan and Carpathian blood mixed. He wasn't certain what or where the sacred caves of warriors was and he didn't like the word *rebirth*.

Why can't I move?

You are coming to life. You have been locked away from us for some time.

Not from you.

She had been with him while he was locked in that dark place of pain and madness. If there was one thing he knew for absolute certain, it was that she had been there. He couldn't move on, because he hadn't been able to leave her.

He remembered that voice, soft and pleading. *Stay. Stay with me.* Her voice had locked them both in a sea of agony that seemed endless.

Not endless. You are awakening.

He might be waking, but the pain was still there. He took a moment to let himself absorb it. She was correct, the pain was subsiding to a tolerable level, but the heat surrounding him was burning his body. Without the air she'd given him, he would be choking, strangling, desperate.

Think what body temperature you wish. You are Carpathian. Embrace who you are.

Her voice never changed. She didn't seem impatient with his lack of knowledge. Before, when she was a distance from him, she hadn't been aloof, she simply waited. Now she felt different, as if she expected something from him.

What the hell? If she said to think about a different body temperature other than the one burning his flesh from his bones, he could give her that. He chose a normal temperature and held that in his mind. She spoke to him without words, telepathically, so she must be able to see he was doing as she asked.

At once, the burning sensation ceased to be. He took a gasping breath.

Heat filled his lungs, but there was air as well. He knew her. Only one woman could speak to him as she did. Mind to mind. He knew her now. How could he have ever forgotten who she was?

Branislava.

How had she gotten trapped with him in such a terrible place? He sent up a small prayer of thanks that he hadn't left her there. *She* had been the one to whisper to him. *Stay. Stay with me.* He should have recognized her voice, a soft sweet melody that was forever stamped into his bones.

You recognize me. She smiled at him again and he felt her fingers brush along his jaw and then go up to his forehead, brushing back strands of hair falling into his face.

Her touch brought pleasure, not pain. A small electrical current ran from his forehead down to his belly, tightening his muscles. The current went lower, coiling heat in his groin. He could feel something besides pain and, wouldn't you know it would be desire?

It seemed absurd to him that he hadn't known all along who she was. She was the *one* woman. The *only* woman. *The* woman. He'd known women, of course. He'd lived too long not to. He was a hunter, an elite hunter, and he was never in one place long. He didn't form attachments. Women didn't rob him of breath or put him under spells. He didn't think about them night and day. Or fantasize. Or want one for his own.

Until her. Branislava. She wasn't Lycan. She didn't talk much. She looked like an angel and moved like a temptress. Her voice beckoned like a siren's call. She had looked at him with those unusual eyes and smiled with that perfect mouth, inciting all sorts of erotic fantasies. When they danced, just that one unforgettable time, her body had fit into his, melted into his, until she was imprinted there for all time, into his skin, into his bones.

Every single rule he'd ever made about women in the long years he had lived had been broken with her. She'd robbed him of breath. Put him under her spell. He thought of her day and night and fantasized far too much. He wanted her in every way possible. Her body. Her heart. Her mind. Her soul. He wanted her all for himself.

How did you get here? In this place?

It alarmed him that he might have somehow dragged her down into that sea of agony because he'd been so enamored with her. Could a man do that? Want a woman so much that when he died, he took her with him? The idea was appalling. He'd lived honorably, at least he'd tried to, and he'd never hurt a woman who hadn't been a murdering rogue. The idea that he might have taken *this* woman into hell with him was disturbing on every level.

I chose to come with you, she replied, as if it was the most normal thing in the world. *Our spirits are woven together. Our fate is entwined.*

I don't understand.

You were dying and there was no other way to save your life. You are precious to us all, a man of honor, of great skill.

Zev frowned. That made no sense. He had no family. He had his pack, but two of his pack members, friends for so many long years, had betrayed and tried to murder him. He was mixed blood now and few of his kind would accept him.

Us all? he echoed. *Who would that be?*

Do you hear them calling to you?

Zev stayed very still, tuning his acute hearing to get past the heartbeat of the earth, the flow of water beneath him, reaching for the distant voices. Men's voices. They seemed to be all around him. Some chanted to him in an ancient language while others throat-chanted as the monks from long ago had done. Each separate word or note vibrated through him, just as the heartbeat of the earth had.

They summoned him just as the earth had. It was time. He couldn't find any more excuses and it seemed no one was going to let him vegetate right where he was. He forced himself to open his eyes.

He was underground in a cave. That much was evident immediately. There was heat and humidity surrounding him, although he didn't feel hot. It was more that he saw it, those bands of heat undulating throughout the immense chamber.

Great stalactites hung from the high ceiling. They were enormous formations, great long rows of teeth of various sizes. Stalagmites rose from the floor with wide bases. Colors wound around the columns from the flaring bases to the pointed tips. The floor was worn smooth with centuries of feet walking on it.

Zev recognized that he was deep beneath the earth. The chamber, although enormous, felt hallowed to him. He lay in the earth itself, his body covered by rich black loam. Minerals sparkled in the blanket of dirt over him. Hundreds of candles were lit, high up on the walls of the chamber, illuminating the cavern, casting flicking lights across the stalagmites, bringing the muted color to life.

His heart began to pound in alarm. He had no idea where he was or how he got there. He turned his head and instantly his body settled. She was there, sitting beside him. Branislava. She was truly as beautiful as he remembered her. Her skin was pale and flawless. Her lashes were just as long, her lips as perfect as in his dream. Only her clothes were different.

He was afraid if he spoke aloud she would disappear. She looked as ethereal as ever, a creature from long ago, not meant for the world he resided in. The chanting swelled in volume and he reached for her hand, threading his fingers tightly through hers before he turned his head to try to find the source—or sources—of that summons.

There were several men in the room, all warriors with faces that had seen too many battles. He felt comfortable with them, a part of them, as if, in that sacred chamber, they were a brotherhood. He knew their faces, although most he'd never met, but he knew the caliber of men they were.

He recognized four men he knew well although it felt as if a hundred years had passed since he'd seen them. Fenris Dalka was there. He should have known he would be. Fen was his friend, if someone like him could have friends. Beside him was Dimitri Tirunul, Fen's brother, and that too wasn't surprising. The brothers were close. Their last name was different only because Fen had taken the last name of a Lycan in order to better fit in during his years with them.

Two figures stood over another hole in the ground where a man lay looking around him just as Zev was. The man, in what could have been an open grave, looked pale and worn, as if he'd been through hell and had come out the other side. Zev wondered idly if he looked the same way. It took a few moments before he recognized Gary Jansen. Gary was human and he'd waded through rogue wolves to get to Zev during a particularly fierce battle. Zev was very happy to see him alive.

He was familiar with Gregori Daratrazanoff. Usually Gregori wasn't far from his prince, but he hovered close to the man who struggled to sit up. Gregori immediately reached down and gently helped Gary into a sitting position. The man on the other side of the "grave" had the same look as Gregori. This had to be another Daratrazanoff.

On the other side of Gregori, a short distance from him, stood two of the De La Cruz brothers, Zacarias and Manolito, both of whom he knew and who had joined with him in a battle of some kind. The actual facts were still a little fuzzy. A third man stood between them.

In the center of the room were several smaller columns made of crystals forming a circle around a bloodred formation with what looked to be a razor-sharp tip. Standing beside it was Mikhail Dubrinsky, prince of the Carpathian people. He spoke very low, but his voice carried through the chamber with great authority.

Mikhail spoke in an ancient language, the ritual words to call to their long-gone ancestors. *"Veri isäakank—veri ekäakank."*

To his absolute shock and astonishment, Zev understood the words. Blood of our fathers—blood of our brothers. He knew that was the literal translation, but the language was an ancient one, not of the Lycans. He had been born Lycan. He had heard the language spoken by Carpathians down through the centuries but he shouldn't have understood the words so clearly.

"Veri olen elid."

Blood is life. Zev's breath caught in his throat. He *understood*. He spoke many languages, but this was so ancient he couldn't have ever learned it. Why was he understanding it now? Nothing made sense, although his mind wasn't quite as foggy as it had been.

Branislava tightened her fingers around his. He turned his head and looked at her. She was so beautiful she took his breath away. Her eyes were on his face and he felt her gaze penetrating deep. Too deep. She was already branded in his mind. She was coming far too close to his heart.

"Andak veri-elidet Karpatiiakank, és wäke-sarna ku meke arwa-arvo, irgalom, hän ku agba, és wäke kutni, ku manaak verival," Mikhail continued. The power of his voice rang through the chamber, raw and elemental, bringing Zev's attention back to him.

Zev interpreted the words. "We offer that life to our people with a blood sworn vow of honor, mercy, integrity and endurance."

What did that mean? This was a ritual—a ceremony that he felt part of—even though he didn't know what exactly was going on. The appearance of Fen and Dimitri was reassuring to him. The longer he was awake, the more his mind cleared. The two were of mixed blood, although both had been born Carpathian.

Mikhail dropped his palm over the very sharp tip of the dark red column. At once the crystals went from dark red to crimson, as if Mikhail's blood had brought them to life.

"Verink sokta; verink kaŋa terád." Mikhail's voice swelled with power.

Zev saw sparks light up the room. He frowned over the words Mikhail had uttered. "Our blood mingles and calls to you." He was mingling his blood with someone of power, that much was obvious from the way the columns throughout the room began to come alive. Several gave off glowing colors, although still very muted.

"Akasz énak ku kaŋa és juttasz kuntatak it."

Zev interpreted again as the columns began to hum. "Heed our summons and join with us now." The columns throughout the room rocked, the multicolored crystals illuminating, throwing vivid, bright colors across the ceiling and over the walls of the chamber. The colors were so dazzling, Zev had to shade his sensitive eyes.

Crimson, emerald, a beautiful sapphire, the colors took on the strange phenomenon of the northern lights. The humming grew louder and he realized each took on a different note, a different pitch, the tone perfect to his ear. He hadn't noticed that the columns appeared to be totems with faces of warriors carved into the mineral, but now they came to life, the color adding expression and character.

Zev let out his breath slowly. These warriors were long dead. He was in a cave of the dead and Mikhail had summoned the ancient warriors to him for some purpose. Zev had a very bad feeling that he was part of that purpose.

"Ete tekaik, saγeak ekäakanket. Čač3katlanak med, kutenken hank ekäakank tasa."

Zev swallowed hard when he translated. "We have brought before you our brothers, not born to us, but brothers just the same."

Zev had been born Lycan and he'd served his people for many long years as an elite hunter who traveled the world seeking out and destroying rogue wolves who preyed on mankind. He was one of the few Lycans who could hunt alone and be comfortable and confident doing so. Still, he was Lycan and he would always have the need to be part of a pack.

His own kind despised those of mixed blood. It mattered little that he became mixed blood giving service to his people. He'd been wounded in hundreds of battles and had lost far too much blood. Carpathian warriors had more than once come to his aid as they had done this last time.

Zev looked up to find Fen on one side of him and Dimitri on the other. The two De La Cruz brothers stood with the stranger between them.

Gregori and his brother stood on either side Gary, who now was getting to his feet with Gregori's help. Zev took a breath. He would not be the only man sitting on his ass while the others stood. He was getting up or would die trying.

Zev let go of his lifeline, and the moment he did nearly panicked—another thing men like him didn't do. He didn't want her to disappear. His eyes met hers. *Don't you leave me.*

She gave him a smile that could allow a man to live for the rest of his existence on fantasies. *We are tied together, Zev. Where you go, I go. Only the ancients can undo a weave of the spirits.*

Is that what this is about? He wasn't certain he wanted to continue if it was.

Not even the prince can ask for such a release. Only me. Or you.

She gave him the information, but he had the feeling she was a little reluctant. That suited him just fine. He wasn't willing to relinquish his bond with her just yet.

Fen, I don't have a stitch on and I want to stand up. I'm not going to lie in this grave like a baby. For the first time he realized he was absolutely naked and Branislava had been beside him the entire time holding his hand; even when his body had stirred to life she hadn't run from him.

At once he was clean, and clothed in soft trousers and an immaculate white shirt. He struggled to get to his feet. Fen and Dimitri both reached for him at the same time, preventing him from falling on his face and making a fool of himself. His legs were rubber, refusing to work properly. For a Lycan that was embarrassing, but for an elite hunter it was absolutely humiliating.

Mikhail looked over at him and nodded his approval, or maybe it was relief at him being alive. Zev wasn't certain yet if he was relieved or not.

"Aka sarnamad, en Karpatiiakak. Saγeak kontaket ŋamaŋak tekaiked. Tajnak aka-arvonk és arwa-arvonk."

"Hear me, great ones. We bring these men to you, warriors all, deserving of our respect and honor." Zev translated the words carefully twice, just to make certain he was correctly interpreting the prince's discourse with the ancient warriors.

Gary, standing between the two Daratrazanoff brothers, straightened his shoulders as if feeling eyes on him. Zev was fairly certain that somehow, those spirits of the dead were watching all of them, perhaps judging their worth. Colors swirled into various hues and the notes blended together as if the ancient warriors questioned the prince.

"Gregori, és Darius katak Daratrazanoffak. Kontak ŋamaŋak sarnanak hän agba nókunta ekäankal, Gary Jansen, hän ku olenot küm, kutenken olen it Karpatii. Hän pohoopa kuš Karpatiikuntanak, partiolenaka és kontaka. Saγeak hänet ete tekaik."

"Gregori and Darius of the great house of Daratrazanoff claim kinship with our brother, Gary Jansen, once human, now one of us. He has served our people tirelessly both in research and in battle. We bring him before you."

Zev knew that aside from actually fighting alongside the Carpathians, Gary had done a tremendous amount of work for the Carpathians, and had lived among them for several years. It was obvious that every Carpathian in the chamber afforded him great respect, as did Zev. Gary had fought both valiantly and selflessly.

"Zacarias és Manolito katak De La Cruzak, käktä enä wäkeva kontak. Kontak ŋamaŋak sarnanak hän agba nókunta ekäankal, Luiz Silva, hän ku olenot jaquár, kutenken olen it Karpatii. Luiz mänet en elidaket, kor3nat elidaket avio päläfertiilakjakak. Saγeak hänet ete tekaik."

"Zacarias and Manolito from the house of De La Cruz, two of our mightiest warriors claim kinship with our brother, Luiz Silva, once jaguar, now Carpathian. Luiz saved the lives of two of their lifemates. We bring him before you."

Zev knew nothing of Luiz, but he had to admire anyone who could stand with Zacarias De La Cruz claiming kinship. Zacarias was not known for his kindness. Luiz had to be a great warrior to run with that family of Carpathians.

"Fen és Dimitri arwa-arvodkatak Tirunulak sarnanak hän agba nókunta ekäankal, Zev Hunter, hän ku olenot Susiküm, kutenken olen it Karpatii. Torot päläpälä Karpatiikuntankal és piwtät és piwtä mekeni sarna kunta jotkan Susikümkunta és Karpatiikunta. Saγeak hänet ete tekaik."

"Fen and Dimitri from the noble house of Tirunul claim kinship with our brother, Zev Hunter, once Lycan, now Carpathian. He has fought side by side with our people and has sought to bring an alliance between Lycan and Carpathian. He is of mixed blood like those who claim kinship. We bring him before you."

There was no mistaking the translation. Mikhail had definitely called his name and indicated that Fen and Dimitri claimed brotherhood with him. He certainly had enough of their blood in him to be a brother.

The humming grew in volume and Mikhail nodded several times before turning to Gary. "Is it your wish to become fully a brother?"

Gary nodded without hesitation. Zev was fairly certain that, like him, Gary hadn't been prepped ahead of time. The answer had to come from within at the precise moment of the acting. There was no prepping. He didn't know what his own answer would be.

Gregori and Darius, with Gary between them, approached the crystal column, now swirling a dull red. Gregori dropped his hand, palm down, over the tip of the formation, allowing his blood to flow over that of the prince's.

"Place your hand over the sacred bloodstone and allow your blood to mingle with that of the ancients and that of your brothers," Mikhail instructed.

Gary moved forward slowly, his feet following the path so many warriors had walked before him. He placed his hand over the sharp tip and allowed his palm to drop. His blood ran down the crystal column, mixing with Gregori's.

Darius glided just behind him in the same silent, deadly way of his brother, and when Gary stepped back, Darius placed his palm over the tip of the bloodstone, allowing his blood to mingle with Mikhail's, Gregori's, Gary's and the ancient warriors who had gone before.

The hum grew louder, filling the chamber. Colors swirled, this time taking on hues of blue, green and purple.

Gary gave a little gasp and went silent, nodding his head as if he heard something Zev couldn't. Within minutes he stepped back and glanced over to the prince.

"It is done," Mikhail affirmed. "So be it."

The humming ceased, all those beautiful notes that created a melody of words only the prince could understand. The chamber went silent. Zev became aware of his heart beating too fast. He consciously took a breath and let it out. The tension and sense of anticipation grew.

"Is it your wish, Luiz, to become fully a brother?" Mikhail asked.

Zev took a long look at Zacarias and Manolito. The De La Cruz brothers were rather infamous. Taking on their family as kin would be daunting. Only a very confident and strong man would ever agree.

Luiz inclined his head and walked to the crystal bloodstone on his own, Zacarias and Monolito behind him. Clearly Luiz had not been wounded. He was physically fit and moved with the flow of a jungle cat.

Zacarias pierced his palm first, allowing his blood to flow down the stone, joining with the ancient warriors. At once the hum began, a low call of greeting, of recognition and honor. Colors swirled around the room as if the ancients knew Zacarias and his legendary reputation. They seemed to greet him as an old friend. There was no doubt in Zev's mind that the ancient warriors were paying tribute to Zacarias. Many had probably known him.

When the humming died down, Luiz stepped close to the stone and pierced his palm, his blood flowing into that of the eldest De La Cruz. Manolito came next and did the same so that the blood of all three mingled with that of the ancient warriors.

At once the humming of approval began again and the great columns of both stalagmites and stalactites banded with colors of white and yellow and bright red.

Luiz stood silent, very still, much as Gary had before him, and just as Gary, Luiz nodded his head several times. He looked up at Zacarias and Monolito and smiled for the first time.

"It is done," Mikhail murmured in a low tone of power that seemed to fill the chamber. "So be it."

Zev's mouth went dry. His heart began to pound. He felt tension gather low in his belly, great knots forming that he couldn't prevent. There was acceptance here—but there could also be rejection. He wasn't born Carpathian, but Fen and Dimitri were offering him so much more than that—they stood for him. Called him brother. If these ancient warriors accepted him, he would be truly both Carpathian and Lycan. He would have a pack of his own again. He would belong somewhere.

The feeling in the great chamber was very somber. The eloquence of the long dead slowly faded and he knew it was time. He had no idea what he would do when asked. None. He wasn't even certain his legs would carry him the distance, and he wasn't going to be carried to the bloodstone.

"Is it your wish, Zev, to become fully a brother?" Mikhail asked.

He felt the weight of every stare. Warriors all. Good men who knew battle. Men he respected. His feet wanted to move forward. He wanted to be a part of them. He was physically still very weak. What if he didn't measure up in their eyes?

You aren't weak, Zev. There is nothing weak about you.

Her voice moved through him like a breath of fresh air. He hadn't realized he was holding his breath until she spoke so intimately to him. He let it out, braced himself and made his first move. Fen and Dimitri stayed close, not just to walk him to the bloodstone, but to make absolutely certain he didn't fall on his face. Still, he was determined it wouldn't happen.

With every step he took on that worn stone floor he seemed to absorb the ancients who had gone before him. Their wisdom. Their technique in battle. Their great determination and sense of honor and duty. He felt information gathering in his mind, yet he couldn't quite process it. It was a great gift, but he couldn't access the data, and that left him even more concerned that he might be rejected. Somewhere, sometime, long ago, he felt he'd been in this sacred chamber. The longer he was in it, the more familiar to him it felt.

As he approached the crystal column, his heart accelerated even more. He felt sheer raw power emanating from the bloodstone. The formation pulsed with power, and each time it did, color banded, ropes of various shades of red, blood he knew had been collected from all the great warriors who were long gone from the Carpathian world, yet who, through the prince, could still aid their people. Mikhail understood their voices through those perfectly pitched notes.

Fen dropped his palm over the tip of the stalagmite. His blood ran down the sacred stone. The colors changed instantly, swirling with deep purple and dark red. He stepped back to allow Zev to approach the column.

Zev wasn't going to draw it out. Either they accepted him or they didn't. In his life, he couldn't remember a single time when he cared what others thought of him, but here, in the sacred chamber of warriors, he found it mattered much more than he wanted to admit. He dropped his palm over the sharp tip so that it pierced his skin and blood flowed over Fen's, mingling with the one who would be his brother, and with the great warriors of the past.

His soul stretched to meet those who had gone before. He was surrounded, filled with camaraderie, with acceptance, with belonging. His community dated back to ancient times, and those warriors of old called out to him in greeting. As they did, the flood of information through his brain, adhering to his memories, was both astonishing and overwhelming.

Zev was a man who observed every detail of his surroundings. It was one of the characteristics that had allowed him to become an elite hunter. Now, everything seemed even sharper and more vivid to him. Every warrior's heart in the chamber from ancient to modern times matched the drumming of the earth's heart. Blood ebbed and flowed in their veins, matching the flow of the ancients' blood within the crystal, but also the ebb and flow of water throughout their earth.

Dimitri dropped his palm over the crystal and, at once, Zev felt the mingling of their blood, the kinship that ran deeper than friendship. His history and their history became one, stretching back to ancient times. Information was cumulative, amassing in his mind at a rapid rate. With it came the heavy responsibility of his kind.

The humming grew loud, and he recognized now what those notes meant—approval, acceptance without reserve. Colors swirled and banded throughout the room. Those ancient warriors recognized him, recognized his bloodline, not just the blood of Fen and Dimitri who claimed kinship, but his own, born of a union not all Lycan.

Bur tule ekämet kuntamak. The voices of the ancestors filled his mind with greetings. Well met, brother-kin. *Eläsz jeläbam ainaak.* Long may you live in the light.

Zev had no knowledge of his lineage being anything but pure Lycan. His mother had died long before he had memory of her. Why would these warriors claim kinship with him through his own bloodline and not Fen and Dimitri's? That made no sense to him.

Our lives are tied together by our blood. They spoke to him in their own ancient language and he had no trouble translating it, as if the language had always been a part of him and he had just needed the ancients to bridge some gap in his memory for it all to unfold.

I don't understand. That was an understatement. He was more confused than ever.

Everything, including one's lifemate, is determined by the blood flowing in our veins. Your blood is Dark blood. You now are of mixed blood, but you are one of us. You are kont o sívanak.

Strong heart, heart of a warrior. It was a tribute, but it didn't tell him what he needed to know.

Who was my mother? That was the question he needed answered. If Carpathian blood already flowed in his veins, how was it he hadn't known?

Your mother's mother was fully Carpathian. Lycans killed her for being Sange rau. Her daughter, your mother, was raised wholly Lycan. She mated with a Lycan, and gave birth to you, a Dark blood. You are kunta.

Family, he interpreted. From what bloodline? How? Zev knew he was taking far longer than either Gary or Luiz had, but he didn't want to leave this source of information. His father never once let on that there was any Carpathian blood in their family. Had he known? Had his mother even known? If his grandmother had been murdered by the Lycans for her mixed blood, no one would ever admit that his mother had been the child of a mixed blood. The family would have hidden her from the others. Most likely her father had left his pack and found another one to protect her.

The humming began to fade and Zev found himself reaching out, needing more.

Wait. Who was she?

It is there, in your memories, everything you need, everything you are. Blood calls to blood and you are whole again. The humming faded away.

"It is done," Mikhail said formally. "So be it."

Appendix I

Carpathian Healing Chants

To rightly understand Carpathian healing chants, background is required in several areas:

1. The Carpathian view on healing
2. The Lesser Healing Chant of the Carpathians
3. The Great Healing Chant of the Carpathians
4. Carpathian musical aesthetics
5. Lullaby
6. Song to Heal the Earth
7. Carpathian chanting technique

1. THE CARPATHIAN VIEW ON HEALING

The Carpathians are a nomadic people whose geographic origins can be traced back to at least as far as the Southern Ural Mountains (near the steppes of modern-day Kazakhstan), on the border between Europe and Asia. (For this reason, modern-day linguists call their language "proto-Uralic," without knowing that this is the language of the Carpathians.) Unlike most nomadic peoples, the wandering of the Carpathians was not due to the need to find new grazing lands as the seasons and climate shifted, or the search for better trade. Instead, the Carpathians' movements were driven by a great purpose: to find a land that would have the right earth, a soil with the kind of richness that would greatly enhance their rejuvenative powers.

Over the centuries, they migrated westward (some six thousand years ago), until they at last found their perfect homeland—their *susu*—in the Carpathian Mountains, whose long arc cradled the lush plains of the kingdom of Hungary. (The kingdom of Hungary flourished for over a millennium—making Hungarian the dominant language of the Carpathian Basin—until the kingdom's lands were split among several countries after World War I: Austria, Czechoslovakia, Romania, Yugoslavia and modern Hungary.)

Other peoples from the Southern Urals (who shared the Carpathian language, but were not Carpathians) migrated in different directions. Some ended up in Finland, which accounts for why the modern Hungarian and Finnish languages are among the contemporary descendents of the ancient Carpathian language. Even though they are tied forever to their chosen Carpathian homeland, the wandering of the Carpathians

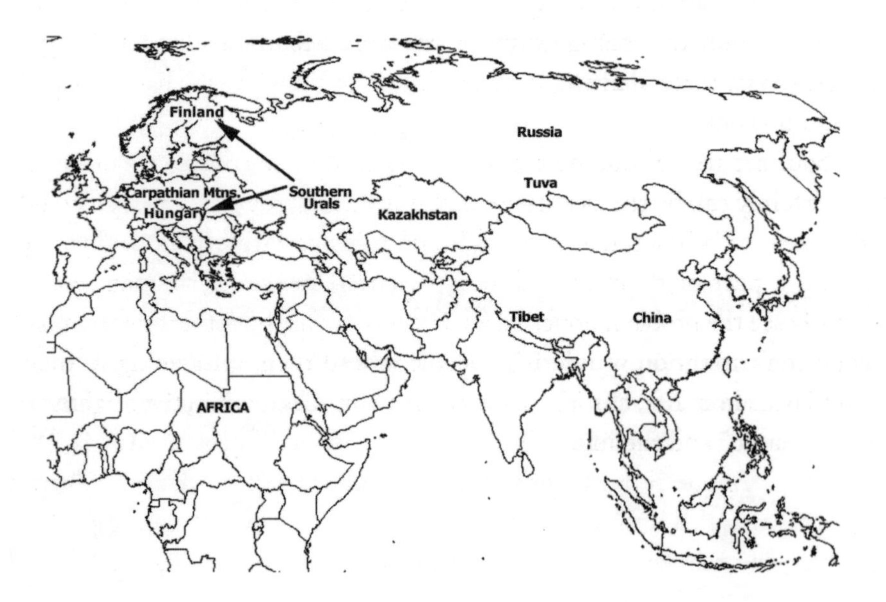

continues as they search the world for the answers that will enable them to bear and raise their offspring without difficulty.

Because of their geographic origins, the Carpathian views on healing share much with the larger Eurasian shamanistic tradition. Probably the closest modern representative of that tradition is based in Tuva (and is referred to as "Tuvinian Shamanism")—see the map on the previous page.

The Eurasian shamanistic tradition—from the Carpathians to the Siberian shamans—held that illness originated in the human soul, and only later manifested as various physical conditions. Therefore, shamanistic healing, while not neglecting the body, focused on the soul and its healing. The most profound illnesses were understood to be caused by "soul departure," where all or some part of the sick person's soul has wandered away from the body (into the nether realms), or has been captured or possessed by an evil spirit, or both.

The Carpathians belong to this greater Eurasian shamanistic tradition and share its viewpoints. While the Carpathians themselves did not succumb to illness, Carpathian healers understood that the most profound wounds were also accompanied by a similar "soul departure."

Upon reaching the diagnosis of "soul departure," the healer-shaman is then required to make a spiritual journey into the netherworlds to recover the soul. The shaman may have to overcome tremendous challenges along the way, particularly fighting the demon or vampire who has possessed his friend's soul.

"Soul departure" doesn't require a person to be unconscious (although that certainly can be the case as well). It was understood that a person could still appear to be conscious, even talk and interact with others, and yet be missing a part of their soul. The experienced healer or shaman would instantly see the problem nonetheless, in subtle signs that others might miss: the person's attention wandering every now and then, a lessening in their enthusiasm about life, chronic depression, a diminishment in the brightness of their "aura," and the like.

2. THE LESSER HEALING CHANT OF THE CARPATHIANS

***Kepä Sarna Pus* (The Lesser Healing Chant)** is used for wounds that are merely physical in nature. The Carpathian healer leaves his body and enters the wounded Carpathian's body to heal great mortal wounds from the inside out using pure energy. He proclaims, "I offer freely my life for your life," as he gives his blood to the injured Carpathian. Because the Carpathians are of the earth and bound to the soil, they are healed by the soil of their homeland. Their saliva is also often used for its rejuvenative powers.

It is also very common for the Carpathian chants (both the Lesser and the Great) to be accompanied by the use of healing herbs, aromas from Carpathian candles and crystals. The crystals (when combined with the Carpathians' empathic, psychic connection to the entire universe) are used to gather positive energy from their surroundings, which then is used to accelerate the healing. Caves are sometimes used as the setting for the healing.

The Lesser Healing Chant was used by Vikirnoff Von Shrieder and Colby Jansen to heal Rafael De La Cruz, whose heart had been ripped out by a vampire as described in *Dark Secret*.

Kepä Sarna Pus (The Lesser Healing Chant)

The same chant is used for all physical wounds. "Sívadaba" ["into your heart"] would be changed to refer to whatever part of the body is wounded.

Kuńasz, nélkül sívdobbanás, nélkül fesztelen löyly.
You lie as if asleep, without beat of heart, without airy breath.

Ot élidamet andam szabadon élidadért.
I offer freely my life for your life.

O jelä sielam jõrem ot ainamet és soŋe ot élidadet.
My spirit of light forgets my body and enters your body.

O jelä sielam pukta kinn minden szelemeket belső.
My spirit of light sends all the dark spirits within fleeing without.

Pajńak o susu hanyet és o nyelv nyálamet sívadaba.
I press the earth of our homeland and the spit of my tongue into your heart.

Vii, o verim soŋe o verid andam.
At last, I give you my blood for your blood.

To hear this chant, visit: http://www.christinefeehan.com/members/.

3. THE GREAT HEALING CHANT OF THE CARPATHIANS

The most well-known—and most dramatic—of the Carpathian healing chants was ***En Sarna Pus*** **(The Great Healing Chant)**. This chant was reserved for recovering the wounded or unconscious Carpathian's soul.

Typically a group of men would form a circle around the sick Carpathian (to "encircle him with our care and compassion") and begin the chant. The shaman or healer or leader is the prime actor in this healing ceremony. It is he who will actually make the spiritual journey into the netherworld, aided by his clanspeople. Their purpose is to ecstatically dance, sing, drum and chant, all the while visualizing (through the words of the chant) the journey itself—every step of it, over and over again—to the point where the shaman, in trance, leaves his body, and makes that very journey. (Indeed, the word "ecstasy" is from the Latin *ex statis*, which literally means "out of the body.")

One advantage that the Carpathian healer has over many other shamans is his telepathic link to his lost brother. Most shamans must wander in the dark of the nether realms in search of their lost brother. But the Carpathian healer directly "hears" in his mind the voice of his lost brother calling to him, and can thus "zero in" on his soul like a homing beacon. For this reason, Carpathian healing tends to have a higher success rate than most other traditions of this sort.

Something of the geography of the "other world" is useful for us to examine, in order to fully understand the words of the Great Carpathian Healing Chant. A reference is made to the "Great Tree" (in Carpathian: *En*

Puwe). Many ancient traditions, including the Carpathian tradition, understood the worlds—the heaven worlds, our world and the nether realms—to be "hung" upon a great pole, or axis, or tree. Here on earth, we are positioned halfway up this tree, on one of its branches. Hence many ancient texts often referred to the material world as "middle earth": midway between heaven and hell. Climbing the tree would lead one to the heaven worlds. Descending the tree to its roots would lead to the nether realms. The shaman was necessarily a master of movement up and down the Great Tree, sometimes moving unaided, and sometimes assisted by (or even mounted upon the back of) an animal spirit guide. In various traditions, this Great Tree was known variously as the *axis mundi* (the "axis of the worlds"), Ygddrasil (in Norse mythology), Mount Meru (the sacred world mountain of Tibetan tradition), etc. The Christian cosmos, with its heaven, purgatory/earth and hell, is also worth comparing. It is even given a similar topography in Dante's *Divine Comedy*: Dante is led on a journey first to hell, at the center of the earth; then upward to Mount Purgatory, which sits on the earth's surface directly opposite Jerusalem; then farther upward first to Eden, the earthly paradise, at the summit of Mount Purgatory; and then upward at last to heaven.

In the shamanistic tradition, it was understood that the small always reflects the large; the personal always reflects the cosmic. A movement in the greater dimensions of the cosmos also coincides with an internal movement. For example, the *axis mundi* of the cosmos also corresponds to the spinal column of the individual. Journeys up and down the *axis mundi* often coincided with the movement of natural and spiritual energies (sometimes called *kundalini* or *shakti*) in the spinal column of the shaman or mystic.

En Sarna Pus (The Great Healing Chant)

In this chant, ekä ("brother") would be replaced by "sister," "father," "mother," depending on the person to be healed.

Ot ekäm ainajanak hany, jama.
My brother's body is a lump of earth, close to death.

Me, ot ekäm kuntajanak, pirädak ekäm, gond és irgalom türe.
We, the clan of my brother, encircle him with our care and compassion.

O pus wäkenkek, ot oma śarnank, és ot pus fünk, álnak ekäm ainajanak, pitänak ekäm ainajanak elävä.
Our healing energies, ancient words of magic and healing herbs bless my brother's body, keep it alive.

Ot ekäm sielanak pälä. Ot omboće päläja juta alatt o jüti, kinta, és szelemek lamtijaknak.
But my brother's soul is only half. His other half wanders in the netherworld.

Ot en mekem ŋamaŋ: kulkedak otti ot ekäm omboće päläjanak.
My great deed is this: I travel to find my brother's other half.

Rekatüre, saradak, tappadak, odam, kaŋa o numa waram, és avaa owe o lewl mahoz.
We dance, we chant, we dream ecstatically, to call my spirit bird, and to open the door to the other world.

Ntak o numa waram, és mozdulak, jomadak.
I mount my spirit bird and we begin to move, we are under way.

Piwtädak ot En Puwe tyvinak, ećidak alatt o jüti, kinta, és szelemek lamtijaknak.
Following the trunk of the Great Tree, we fall into the netherworld.

Fázak, fázak nó o śaro.
It is cold, very cold.

Juttadak ot ekäm o akarataban, o sívaban és o sielaban.
My brother and I are linked in mind, heart and soul.

Ot ekäm sielanak kaŋa engem.
My brother's soul calls to me.

Kuledak és piwtädak ot ekäm.
I hear and follow his track.

Saγedak és tuledak ot ekäm kulyanak.
Encounter I the demon who is devouring my brother's soul.

Nenäm ćoro, o kuly torodak.
In anger, I fight the demon.

O kuly pél engem.
He is afraid of me.

Lejkkadak o kaŋka salamaval.
I strike his throat with a lightning bolt.

Molodak ot ainaja komakamal.
I break his body with my bare hands.

Toja és molanâ.
He is bent over, and falls apart.

Hän ćaδa.
He runs away.

Manedak ot ekäm sielanak.
I rescue my brother's soul.

Alədak ot ekam sielanak o komamban.
I lift my brother's soul in the hollow of my hand.

Aləmam ot ekam numa waramra.
I lift him onto my spirit bird.

Piwtädak ot En Puwe tyvijanak és saγedak jälleen ot elävä ainak majaknak.
Following up the Great Tree, we return to the land of the living.

Ot ekäm elä jälleen.
My brother lives again.

Ot ekäm weńća jälleen.
He is complete again.

To hear this chant, visit: http://www.christinefeehan.com/members/.

4. CARPATHIAN MUSICAL AESTHETICS

In the sung Carpathian pieces (such as the "Lullaby" and the "Song to Heal the Earth"), you'll hear elements that are shared by many of the musical traditions in the Uralic geographical region, some of which still exist—from Eastern European (Bulgarian, Romanian, Hungarian, Croatian, etc.) to Romany ("gypsy"). Some of these elements include:

- the rapid alternation between major and minor modalities, including a sudden switch (called a "Picardy third") from minor to major to end a piece or section (as at the end of the "Lullaby")
- the use of close (tight) harmonies
- the use of *ritardi* (slowing down the piece) and *crescendi* (swelling in volume) for brief periods
- the use of *glissandi* (slides) in the singing tradition
- the use of trills in the singing tradition (as in the final invocation of the "Song to Heal the Earth")—similar to Celtic, a singing tradition more familiar to many of us
- the use of parallel fifths (as in the final invocation of the "Song to Heal the Earth")
- controlled use of dissonance
- "call and response" chanting (typical of many of the world's chanting traditions)

- extending the length of a musical line (by adding a couple of bars) to heighten dramatic effect
- and many more

"Lullaby" and "Song to Heal the Earth" illustrate two rather different forms of Carpathian music (a quiet, intimate piece and an energetic ensemble piece)—but whatever the form, Carpathian music is full of feeling.

5. LULLABY

This song is sung by women while the child is still in the womb or when the threat of a miscarriage is apparent. The baby can hear the song while inside the mother, and the mother can connect with the child telepathically as well. The lullaby is meant to reassure the child, to encourage the baby to hold on, to stay—to reassure the child that he or she will be protected by love even from inside until birth. The last line literally means that the mother's love will protect her child until the child is born ("rise").

Musically, the Carpathian "Lullaby" is in three-quarter time ("waltz time"), as are a significant portion of the world's various traditional lullabies (perhaps the most famous of which is "Brahms' Lullaby"). The arrangement for solo voice is the original context: a mother singing to her child, unaccompanied. The arrangement for chorus and violin ensemble illustrates how musical even the simplest Carpathian pieces often are, and how easily they lend themselves to contemporary instrumental or orchestral arrangements. (A wide range of contemporary composers, including Dvořák and Smetana, have taken advantage of a similar discovery, working other traditional Eastern European music into their symphonic poems.)

Odam-Sarna Kondak (Lullaby)

Tumtesz o wäke ku pitasz belső.
Feel the strength you hold inside.

Hiszasz sívadet. Én olenam gæidnod.
Trust your heart. I'll be your guide.

Sas csecsemõm, kuńasz.
Hush my baby, close your eyes.

Rauho joŋe ted.
Peace will come to you.

Tumtesz o sívdobbanás ku olen lamt3ad belső.
Feel the rhythm deep inside.

Gond-kumpadek ku kim te.
Waves of love that cover you.

Pesänak te, asti o jüti, kidüsz.
Protect, until the night you rise.

To hear this song, visit: http://www.christinefeehan.com/members/.

6. SONG TO HEAL THE EARTH

This is the earth-healing song that is used by the Carpathian women to heal soil filled with various toxins. The women take a position on four sides and call to the universe to draw on the healing energy with love and respect. The soil of the earth is their resting place, the place where they rejuvenate, and they must make it safe not only for themselves but for their unborn children as well as their men and living children. This is a beautiful ritual performed by the women together, raising their voices in harmony and calling on the earth's minerals and healing properties to come forth and help them save their children. They literally dance and sing to heal the earth in a ceremony as old as their species. The dance and notes of the song are adjusted according to the toxins felt through the healer's bare feet. The feet are placed in a certain pattern and the hands gracefully weave a healing spell while the dance is performed. They must be especially careful when the soil is prepared for babies. This is a ceremony of love and healing.

Musically, the ritual is divided into several sections:

- **First verse**: A "call and response" section, where the chant leader sings the "call" solo, and then some or all of the women sing the "response" in the close harmony style typical of the Carpathian musical tradition. The repeated response—*Ai Emä Maγe*—is an invocation of the source of power for the healing ritual: "Oh, Mother Nature."
- **First chorus**: This section is filled with clapping, dancing, ancient horns and other means used to invoke and heighten the energies upon which the ritual is drawing.
- **Second verse**
- **Second chorus**
- **Closing invocation:** In this closing part, two song leaders, in close harmony, take all the energy gathered by the earlier portions of the song/ritual and focus it entirely on the healing purpose.

What you will be listening to are brief tastes of what would typically be a significantly longer ritual, in which the verse and chorus parts are developed and repeated many times, to be closed by a single rendition of the final invocation.

Sarna Pusm O Maγet (Song to Heal the Earth)

First verse
Ai Emä Maγe,
Oh, Mother Nature,

Me sívadbin lańaak.
We are your beloved daughters.

Me tappadak, me pusmak o maγet.
We dance to heal the earth.

Me sarnadak, me pusmak o ɦanyet.
We sing to heal the earth.

Sielanket jutta tedet it,
We join with you now,

Sívank és akaratank és sielank juttanak.
Our hearts and minds and spirits become one.

Second verse
Ai Emä maγe,
Oh, Mother Nature,

Me sívadbin lańaak.
We are your beloved daughters.

Me andak arwadet emänked és me kaŋank o
We pay homage to our mother and call upon the

Pōɦi és Lōuna, Ida és Lääs.
North and South, East and West.

Pide és aldyn és myös belső.
Above and below and within as well.

Gondank o maγenak pusm ɦän ku olen jama.
Our love of the land heals that which is in need.

Juttanak teval it,
We join with you now,

Maγe maγeval.
Earth to earth.

O pirä elidak weńća.
The circle of life is complete.

To hear this chant, visit christinefeehan.com/members/.

7. CARPATHIAN CHANTING TECHNIQUE

As with their healing techniques, the actual "chanting technique" of the Carpathians has much in common with the other shamanistic traditions of the Central Asian steppes. The primary mode of chanting was throat chanting using overtones. Modern examples of this manner of singing can still be found in the Mongolian, Tuvan and Tibetan traditions. You can find an audio example of the Gyuto Tibetan Buddhist monks engaged in throat chanting at: christinefeehan.com/carpathian_chanting/.

As with Tuva, note on the map the geographical proximity of Tibet to Kazakhstan and the Southern Urals.

The beginning part of the Tibetan chant emphasizes synchronizing all the voices around a single tone, aimed at healing a particular "chakra" of the body. This is fairly typical of the Gyuto throat-chanting tradition, but it is not a significant part of the Carpathian tradition. Nonetheless, it serves as an interesting contrast.

The part of the Gyuto chanting example that is most similar to the Carpathian style of chanting is the midsection, where the men are chanting the words together with great force. The purpose here is not to generate a "healing tone" that will affect a particular "chakra," but rather to generate as much power as possible for initiating the "out of body" travel, and for fighting the demonic forces that the healer/traveler must face and overcome.

The songs of the Carpathian women (illustrated by their "Lullaby" and their "Song to Heal the Earth") are part of the same ancient musical and healing tradition as the Lesser and Great Healing Chants of the warrior males. You can hear some of the same instruments in both the male warriors' healing chants and the women's "Song to Heal the Earth." Also, they share the common purpose of generating and directing power. However, the women's songs are distinctively feminine in character. One immediately noticeable difference is that, while the men speak their words in the manner of a chant, the women sing songs with melodies and harmonies, softening the overall performance. A feminine, nurturing quality is especially evident in the "Lullaby."

APPENDIX 2

The Carpathian Language

Like all human languages, the language of the Carpathians contains the richness and nuance that can only come from a long history of use. At best we can only touch on some of the main features of the language in this brief appendix:

1. The history of the Carpathian language
2. Carpathian grammar and other characteristics of the language
3. Examples of the Carpathian language (including The Ritual Words and The Warrior's Chant)
4. A much-abridged Carpathian dictionary

1. THE HISTORY OF THE CARPATHIAN LANGUAGE

The Carpathian language of today is essentially identical to the Carpathian language of thousands of years ago. A "dead" language like the Latin of two thousand years ago has evolved into a significantly different modern language (Italian) because of countless generations of speakers and great historical fluctuations. In contrast, many of the speakers of Carpathian from thousands of years ago are still alive. Their presence—

coupled with the deliberate isolation of the Carpathians from the other major forces of change in the world—has acted (and continues to act) as a stabilizing force that has preserved the integrity of the language over the centuries. Carpathian culture has also acted as a stabilizing force. For instance, the Ritual Words, the various healing chants (see Appendix 1), and other cultural artifacts have been passed down through the centuries with great fidelity.

One small exception should be noted: the splintering of the Carpathians into separate geographic regions has led to some minor dialectization. However the telepathic link among all Carpathians (as well as each Carpathian's regular return to his or her homeland) has ensured that the differences among dialects are relatively superficial (e.g., small numbers of new words, minor differences in pronunciation, etc.), since the deeper, internal language of mind-forms has remained the same because of continuous use across space and time.

The Carpathian language was (and still is) the proto-language for the Uralic (or Finno-Ugrian) family of languages. Today, the Uralic languages are spoken in northern, eastern and central Europe and in Siberia. More than twenty-three million people in the world speak languages that can trace their ancestry to Carpathian. Magyar or Hungarian (about fourteen million speakers), Finnish (about five million speakers) and Estonian (about one million speakers) are the three major contemporary descendents of this proto-language. The only factor that unites the more than twenty languages in the Uralic family is that their ancestry can be traced back to a common proto-language—Carpathian—that split (starting some six thousand years ago) into the various languages in the Uralic family. In the same way, European languages such as English and French belong to the better-known Indo-European family and also evolved from a common proto-language ancestor (a different one from Carpathian).

The following table provides a sense for some of the similarities in the language family.

Note: The Finnic/Carpathian "k" shows up often as Hungarian "h." Similarly, the Finnic/Carpathian "p" often corresponds to the Hungarian "f."

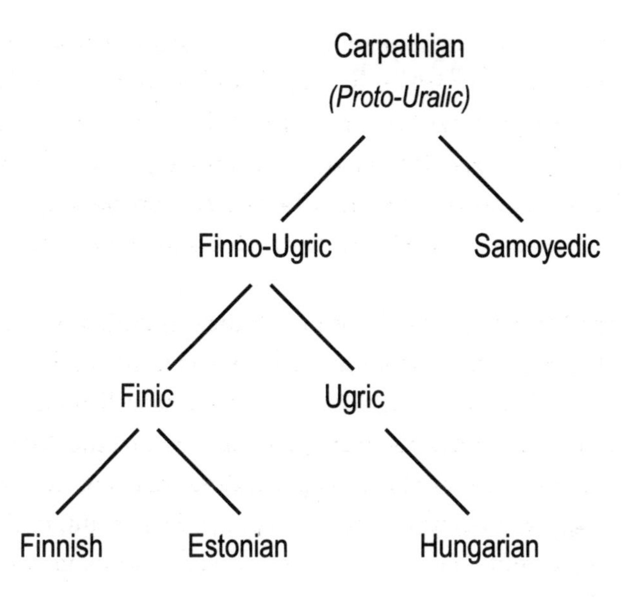

Carpathian *(proto-Uralic)*	**Finnish** *(Suomi)*	**Hungarian** *(Magyar)*
elä—live	*elä*—live	*él*—live
elid—life	*elinikä*—life	*élet*—life
pesä—nest	*pesä*—nest	*fészek*—nest
kola—die	*kuole*—die	*hal*—die
pälä—half, side	*pieltä*—tilt, tip to the side	*fél, fele*—fellow human, friend (half; one side of two) *feleség*—wife
and—give	*anta, antaa*—give	*ad*—give
koje—husband, man	*koira*—dog, the male (of animals)	*here*—drone, testicle
wäke—power	*väki*—folks, people, men; force	*vall-vel*—with (instrumental suffix)
	väkevä—powerful, strong	*vele*—with him/her/it
wete—water	*vesi*—water	*viz*—water

2. CARPATHIAN GRAMMAR AND OTHER CHARACTERISTICS OF THE LANGUAGE

Idioms. As both an ancient language and a language of an earth people, Carpathian is more inclined toward use of idioms constructed from concrete, "earthy" terms, rather than abstractions. For instance, our modern abstraction "to cherish" is expressed more concretely in Carpathian as "to hold in one's heart"; the "netherworld" is, in Carpathian, "the land of night, fog and ghosts"; etc.

Word order. The order of words in a sentence is determined not by syntactic roles (like subject, verb and object) but rather by pragmatic, discourse-driven factors. Examples: *"Tied vagyok."* ("Yours am I."); *"Sívamet andam."* ("My heart I give you.")

Agglutination. The Carpathian language is agglutinative; that is, longer words are constructed from smaller components. An agglutinating language uses suffixes or prefixes whose meaning is generally unique, and which are concatenated one after another without overlap. In Carpathian, words typically consist of a stem that is followed by one or more suffixes. For example, *"sívambam"* derives from the stem *"sív"* ("heart") followed by *"am"* ("my," making it "my heart"), followed by *"bam"* ("in," making it "in my heart"). As you might imagine, agglutination in Carpathian can sometimes produce very long words, or words that are very difficult to pronounce. Vowels often get inserted between suffixes to prevent too many consonants from appearing in a row (which can make the word unpronounceable).

Noun cases. Like all languages, Carpathian has many noun cases; the same noun will be "spelled" differently depending on its role in the sentence. Some of the noun cases include: nominative (when the noun is the subject of the sentence), accusative (when the noun is a direct object of the verb), dative (indirect object), genitive (or possessive), instrumental, final, supressive, inessive, elative, terminative and delative.

We will use the possessive (or genitive) case as an example, to illustrate how all noun cases in Carpathian involve adding standard suffixes to the noun stems. Thus expressing possession in Carpathian—"my lifemate," "your lifemate," "his lifemate," "her lifemate," etc.—involves adding a particular suffix (such as "*-am*") to the noun stem ("*päläfertiil*"), to produce the possessive ("*päläfertiilam*"—"my lifemate"). Which suffix to use depends upon which person ("my," "your," "his," etc.) and whether the noun ends in a consonant or a vowel. The table below shows the suffixes for singular nouns only (not plural), and also shows the similarity to the suffixes used in contemporary Hungarian. (Hungarian is actually a little more complex, in that it also requires "vowel rhyming": which suffix to use also depends on the last vowel in the noun; hence the multiple choices in the cells below, where Carpathian only has a single choice.)

	Carpathian (proto-Uralic)		Contemporary Hungarian	
person	**noun ends in vowel**	**noun ends in consonant**	**noun ends in vowel**	**noun ends in consonant**
1st singular (my)	-m	-am	-m	-om, -em, -öm
2nd singular (your)	-d	-ad	-d	-od, -ed, -öd
3rd singular (his, her, its)	-ja	-a	-ja/-je	-a, -e
1st plural (our)	-nk	-ank	-nk	-unk, -ünk
2nd plural (your)	-tak	-atak	-tok, -tek, -tök	-otok, -etek, -ötök
3rd plural (their)	-jak	-ak	-juk, -jük	-uk, -ük

Note: As mentioned earlier, vowels often get inserted between the word and its suffix so as to prevent too many consonants from appearing in a row (which would produce unpronounceable words). For example, in the table on the previous page, all nouns that end in a consonant are followed by suffixes beginning with "a."

Verb conjugation. Like its modern descendents (such as Finnish and Hungarian), Carpathian has many verb tenses, far too many to describe here. We will just focus on the conjugation of the present tense. Again, we will place contemporary Hungarian side by side with the Carpathian, because of the marked similarity of the two.

As with the possessive case for nouns, the conjugation of verbs is done by adding a suffix onto the verb stem:

Person	Carpathian (proto-Uralic)	Contemporary Hungarian
1st (I give)	-am (andam), -ak	-ok, -ek, -ök
2nd singular (you give)	-sz (andsz)	-sz
3rd singular (he/she/it gives)	— (and)	—
1st plural (we give)	-ak (andak)	-unk, -ünk
2nd plural (you give)	-tak (andtak)	-tok, -tek, -tök
3rd plural (they give)	-nak (andnak)	-nak, -nek

As with all languages, there are many "irregular verbs" in Carpathian that don't exactly fit this pattern. But the above table is still a useful guideline for most verbs.

3. EXAMPLES OF THE CARPATHIAN LANGUAGE

Here are some brief examples of conversational Carpathian, used in the Dark books. We include the literal translation in square brackets. It is interestingly different from the most appropriate English translation.

Susu.
I am home.
["home/birthplace." "I am" is understood, as is often the case in Carpathian.]

Möért?
What for?

csitri
little one
["little slip of a thing," "little slip of a girl"]

ainaak enyém
forever mine

ainaak sívamet jutta
forever mine (another form)
["forever to-my-heart connected/fixed"]

sívamet
my love
["of-my-heart," "to-my-heart"]

Tet vigyázam.
I love you.
["you-love-I"]

***Sarna Rituaali* (The Ritual Words)** is a longer example, and an example of chanted rather than conversational Carpathian. Note the recurring use of "*andam*" ("I give"), to give the chant musicality and force through repetition.

***Sarna Rituaali* (The Ritual Words)**

Te avio päläfertiilam.
You are my lifemate.

Éntölam kuulua, avio päläfertiilam.
I claim you as my lifemate.

Ted kuuluak, kacad, kojed.
I belong to you.

Élidamet andam.
I offer my life for you.

Pesämet andam.
I give you my protection.

Uskolfertiilamet andam.
I give you my allegiance.

Sívamet andam.
I give you my heart.

Sielamet andam.
I give you my soul.

Ainamet andam.
I give you my body.

Sívamet kuuluak kaik että a ted.
I take into my keeping the same that is yours.

Ainaak olenszal sívambin.
Your life will be cherished by me for all my time.

Te élidet ainaak pide minan.
Your life will be placed above my own for all time.

Te avio päläfertiilam.
You are my lifemate.

Ainaak sívamet jutta oleny.
You are bound to me for all eternity.

Ainaak terád vigyázak.
You are always in my care.

To hear these words pronounced (and for more about Carpathian pronunciation altogether), please visit: http://www.christinefeehan.com/members/.

***Sarna Kontakawk* (The Warriors' Chant)** is another longer example of the Carpathian language. The warriors' council takes place deep beneath the earth in a chamber of crystals with magma far below that, so the steam is natural and the wisdom of their ancestors is clear and focused. This is a sacred place where they bloodswear to their prince and people and affirm their code of honor as warriors and brothers. It is also where battle strategies are born and all dissension is discussed as well as any concerns the warriors have that they wish to bring to the Council and open for discussion.

***Sarna Kontakawk* (The Warriors' Chant)**

Veri isäakank—veri ekäakank.
Blood of our fathers—blood of our brothers.

Veri olen elid.
Blood is life.

Andak veri-elidet Karpatiiakank, és wäke-sarna ku meke arwa-arvo, irgalom, hän ku agba, és wäke kutni, ku manaak verival.
We offer that life to our people with a bloodsworn vow of honor, mercy, integrity and endurance.

Verink sokta; verink kaŋa terád.
Our blood mingles and calls to you.

Akasz énak ku kaŋa és juttasz kuntatak it.
Heed our summons and join with us now.

To hear these words pronounced (and for more about Carpathian pronunciation altogether), please visit christinefeehan.com/members/.

See **Appendix 1** for Carpathian healing chants, including the *Kepä Sarna Pus* (The Lesser Healing Chant), the *En Sarna Pus* (The Great Healing Chant), the *Odam-Sarna Kondak* (Lullaby) and the *Sarna Pusm O Maγ et* (Song to Heal the Earth).

4. A MUCH-ABRIDGED CARPATHIAN DICTIONARY

This very much abridged Carpathian dictionary contains most of the Carpathian words used in these Dark books. Of course, a full Carpathian dictionary would be as large as the usual dictionary for an entire language (typically more than a hundred thousand words).

Note: The Carpathian nouns and verbs below are word stems. They generally do not appear in their isolated, "stem" form, as below. Instead, they usually appear with suffixes (e.g., "*andam*"—"*I give*," rather than just the root, "*and*").

a—verb negation (*prefix*); not (*adverb*).
agba—to be seemly or proper.
ai—oh.
aina—body.
ainaak—forever.
O ainaak jelä peje emnimet ŋamaŋ—Sun scorch that woman forever (*Carpathian swear words*).
ainaakfél—old friend.
ak—suffix added after a noun ending in a consonant to make it plural.
aka—to give heed; to hearken; to listen.
akarat—mind; will.
ál—to bless; to attach to.

alatt—through.

aldyn—under; underneath.

alə—to lift; to raise.

alte—to bless; to curse.

and—to give.

and sielet, arwa-arvomet, és jelämet, kuulua huvémet ku feaj és ködet ainaak—to trade soul, honor and salvation, for momentary pleasure and endless damnation.

andasz éntölem irgalomet!—have mercy!

arvo—value; price (*noun*).

arwa—praise (*noun*).

arwa-arvo—honor (*noun*).

arwa-arvo olen gæidnod, ekäm—honor guide you, my brother (*greeting*).

arwa-arvo olen isäntä, ekäm—honor keep you, my brother (*greeting*).

arwa-arvo pile sívadet—may honor light your heart (*greeting*).

arwa-arvod mäne me ködak—may your honor hold back the dark (*greeting*).

aššа—no (*before a noun*); not (*with a verb that is not in the imperative*); not (*with an adjective*).

aššatotello—disobedient.

asti—until.

avaa—to open.

avio—wedded.

avio päläfertiil—lifemate.

avoi—uncover; show; reveal.

belső—within; inside.

bur—good; well.

bur tule ekämet kuntamak—well met brother-kin (*greeting*).

ćaδa—to flee; to run; to escape.

ćoro—to flow; to run like rain.

csecsemõ—baby (*noun*).

csitri—little one (*female*).

diutal—triumph; victory.

ećі—to fall.

ek—suffix added after a noun ending in a consonant to make it plural.

ekä—brother.
ekäm—my brother.
elä—to live.
eläsz arwa-arvoval—may you live with honor (*greeting*).
eläsz jeläbam ainaak—long may you live in the light (*greeting*).
elävä—alive.
elävä ainak majaknak—land of the living.
elid—life.
emä—mother (*noun*).
Emä Maγe—Mother Nature.
emäen—grandmother.
embε—if, when.
embε karmasz—please.
emni—wife; woman.
emnim—my wife; my woman.
emni hän ku köd alte—cursed woman.
emni kuŋenak ku aššatotello—disobedient lunatic.
én—I.
en—great, many, big.
én jutta félet és ekämet—I greet a friend and brother (*greeting*).
én maγenak—I am of the earth.
én oma maγeka—I am as old as time *(literally: as old as the earth).*
En Puwe—The Great Tree. Related to the legends of Ygddrasil, the axis mundi, Mount Meru, heaven and hell, etc.
engem—of me.
és—and.
ete—before; in front.
että—that.
fáz—to feel cold or chilly.
fél—fellow, friend.
fél ku kuuluaak sívam belső—beloved.
fél ku vigyázak—dear one.
feldolgaz—prepare.
fertiil—fertile one.
fesztelen—airy.

fü—herbs; grass.
gæidno—road, way.
gond—care; worry; love (*noun*).
hän—he; she; it.
hän agba—it is so.
hän ku—prefix: one who; that which.
hän ku agba—truth.
hän ku kaśwa o numamet—sky-owner.
hän ku kuulua sívamet—keeper of my heart.
hän ku lejkka wäke-sarnat—traitor.
hän ku meke pirämet—defender.
hän ku pesä—protector.
hän ku piwtä—predator; hunter; tracker.
hän ku vie elidet—vampire (*literally: thief of life*).
hän ku vigyáz sielamet—keeper of my soul.
hän ku vigyáz sívamet és sielamet—keeper of my heart and soul.
hän ku saa kuć3aket—star-reacher.
hän ku tappa—killer; violent person (*noun*). deadly; violent (*adj.*).
hän ku tuulmahl elidet—vampire (*literally: life-stealer*).
Hän sívamak—Beloved.
hany—clod; lump of earth.
hisz—to believe; to trust.
ho—how.
ida—east.
igazág—justice.
irgalom—compassion; pity; mercy.
isä—father (*noun*).
isäntä—master of the house.
it—now.
jälleen—again.
jama—to be sick, infected, wounded, or dying; to be near death.
jelä—sunlight; day, sun; light.
jelä keje terád—light sear you (*Carpathian swear words*).
o jelä peje terád—sun scorch you (*Carpathian swear words*).
o jelä peje emnimet—sun scorch the woman. (*Carpathian swear words*).

o jelä peje terád, emni—sun scorch you, woman. (*Carpathian swear words*).
o jelä peje kaik hänkanak—sun scorch them all. (*Carpathian swear words*).
o jelä sielamak—light of my soul.
joma—to be under way; to go.
joηe—to come; to return.
joηesz arwa-arvoval—return with honor (*greeting*).
jŏrem—to forget; to lose one's way; to make a mistake.
juo—to drink.
juosz és eläsz—drink and live (*greeting*).
juosz és olen ainaak sielamet jutta—drink and become one with me (*greeting*).
juta—to go; to wander.
jüti—night; evening.
jutta—connected; fixed (*adj.*). to connect; to fix; to bind (*verb*).
k—suffix added after a noun ending in a vowel to make it plural.
kaca—male lover.
kadi—judge.
kaik—all.
kaŋa—to call; to invite; to request; to beg.
kaŋk—windpipe; Adam's apple; throat.
kać3—gift.
kaδa—to abandon; to leave; to remain.
kaδa wäkeva óv o köd—stand fast against the dark (*greeting*).
kalma—corpse; death; grave.
karma—want.
Karpatii—Carpathian.
Karpatii ku köd—liar.
käsi—hand (*noun*).
kaśwa—to own.
keje—to cook; to burn; to sear.
kepä—lesser, small, easy, few.
kessa—cat.
kessa ku toro—wildcat.

kessake—little cat.
kidü—to wake up; to arise (*intransitive verb*).
kim—to cover an entire object with some sort of covering.
kinn—out; outdoors; outside; without.
kinta—fog, mist, smoke.
kislány—little girl.
kislány kuŋenak—little lunatic.
kislány kuŋenak minan—my little lunatic.
köd—fog; mist; darkness; evil (*noun*); foggy, dark; evil (*adj.*).
köd elävä és köd nime kutni nimet—evil lives and has a name.
köd alte hän—darkness curse it (*Carpathian swear words*).
o köd belső—darkness take it (*Carpathian swear words*).
köd jutasz belső—shadow take you (*Carpathian swear words*).
koje—man; husband; drone.
kola—to die.
kolasz arwa-arvoval—may you die with honor (*greeting*).
koma—empty hand; bare hand; palm of the hand; hollow of the hand.
kond—all of a family's or clan's children.
kont—warrior.
kont o sívanak—strong heart (*literally: heart of the warrior*).
ku—who; which; that.
kuć3—star.
kuć3ak!—stars! (*exclamation*).
kuja—day, sun.
kuŋe—moon; month.
kule—to hear.
kulke—to go or to travel (on land or water).
kulkesz arwa-arvoval, ekäm—walk with honor, my brother (*greeting*).
kulkesz arwaval—joηesz arwa arvoval—go with glory—return with honor (*greeting*).
kuly—intestinal worm; tapeworm; demon who possesses and devours souls.
kumpa—wave (*noun*).
kuńa—to lie as if asleep; to close or cover the eyes in a game of hide-and-seek; to die.

kunta—band, clan, tribe, family.
kutenken—however.
kuras—sword; large knife.
kure—bind; tie.
kutni—to be able to bear, carry, endure, stand, or take.
kutnisz ainaak—long may you endure (*greeting*).
kuulua—to belong; to hold.
lääs—west.
lamti (*or* **lamt3)**—lowland; meadow; deep; depth.
lamti ból jüti, kinta, ja szelem—the netherworld (*literally: the meadow of night, mists, and ghosts*).
lańa—daughter.
lejkka—crack, fissure, split (*noun*). To cut; to hit; to strike forcefully (*verb*).
lewl—spirit (*noun*).
lewl ma—the other world (*literally: spirit land*). *Lewl ma* includes *lamti ból jüti, kinta, ja szelem*: the netherworld, but also includes the worlds higher up *En Puwe*, the Great Tree.
liha—flesh.
lõuna—south.
löyly—breath; steam (*related to lewl: spirit*).
ma—land; forest.
magköszun—thank.
mana—to abuse; to curse; to ruin.
mäne—to rescue; to save.
maγe—land; earth; territory; place; nature.
me—we.
meke—deed; work (*noun*). To do; to make; to work (*verb*).
mića—beautiful.
mića emni kuŋenak minan—my beautiful lunatic.
minan—mine; my own (*endearment*).
minden—every, all (*adj.*).
möért?—what for? (*exclamation*).
molanâ—to crumble; to fall apart.
molo—to crush; to break into bits.
mozdul—to begin to move, to enter into movement.

muonì—appoint; order; prescribe; command.
muonìak te avoisz te—I command you to reveal yourself.
musta—memory.
myös—also.
nä—for.
nâbbŏ—so, then.
ŋamaŋ—this; this one here; that; that one there.
nautish—to enjoy.
nélkül—without.
nenä—anger.
ńiŋ3—worm; maggot.
nó—like; in the same way as; as.
numa—god; sky; top; upper part; highest (*related to the English word: numinous*).
numatorkuld—thunder *(literally: sky struggle)*.
nyál—saliva; spit (*related to nyelv: tongue*).
nyelv—tongue.
odam—to dream; to sleep.
odam-sarna kondak—lullaby (*literally: sleep-song of children*).
olen—to be.
oma—old; ancient; last; previous.
omas—stand.
omboće—other; second (*adj.*).
o—the (*used before a noun beginning with a consonant*).
ot—the (*used before a noun beginning with a vowel*).
otti—to look; to see; to find.
óv—to protect against.
owe—door.
pä̦ämoro—aim; target.
pajna—to press.
pälä—half; side.
päläfertiil—mate or wife.
palj3—more.
peje—to burn.
peje terád—get burned (*Carpathian swear words*).

pél—to be afraid; to be scared of.

pesä (n.)—nest (*literal*); protection (*figurative*).

pesä (v.)—nest (*literal*); protect (*figurative*).

pesäd te engemal—you are safe with me.

pesäsz jeläbam ainaak—long may you stay in the light (*greeting*).

pide—above.

pile—to ignite; to light up.

pirä—circle; ring (*noun*). to surround; to enclose (*verb*).

piros—red.

pitä—to keep; to hold; to have; to possess.

pitäam mustaakad sielpesäambam—I hold your memories safe in my soul.

pitäsz baszú, piwtäsz igazáget—no vengeance, only justice.

piwtä—to follow; to follow the track of game; to hunt; to prey upon.

poår—bit; piece.

põhi—north.

pukta—to drive away; to persecute; to put to flight.

pus—healthy; healing.

pusm—to be restored to health.

puwe—tree; wood.

rambsolg—slave.

rauho—peace.

reka—ecstasy; trance.

rituaali—ritual.

sa—sinew; tendon; cord.

sa4—to call; to name.

saa—arrive, come; become; get, receive.

saasz hän ku andam szabadon—take what I freely offer.

salama—lightning; lightning bolt.

sarna—words; speech; magic incantation (*noun*). To chant; to sing; to celebrate (*verb*).

sarna kontakawk—warriors' chant.

śaro—frozen snow.

sas—shoosh (*to a child or baby*).

saɣe—to arrive; to come; to reach.

siel—soul.
sieljelä isäntä—purity of soul triumphs.
sisar—sister.
sív—heart.
sív pide köd—love transcends evil.
sívad olen wäkeva, hän ku piwtä—may your heart stay strong, hunter (*greeting*).
sívamet—my heart.
sívam és sielam—my heart and soul.
sívdobbanás—heartbeat (*literal*); rhythm (*figurative*).
sokta—to mix; to stir around.
soŋe—to enter; to penetrate; to compensate; to replace.
susu—home; birthplace (*noun*). At home (*adv.*).
szabadon—freely.
szelem—ghost.
taka—behind; beyond.
tappa—to dance; to stamp with the feet; to kill.
te—you.
Te kalma, te jama ńiŋ3kval, te apitäsz arwa-arvo—You are nothing but a walking maggot-infected corpse, without honor.
Te magköszunam nä ŋamaŋ kać3 taka arvo—Thank you for this gift beyond price.
ted—yours.
terád keje—get scorched (*Carpathian swear words*).
tõd—to know.
Tõdak pitäsz wäke bekimet mekesz kaiket—I know you have the courage to face anything.
tõdhän—knowledge.
tõdhän lõ kuraset agbapäämoroam—knowledge flies the sword true to its aim.
toja—to bend; to bow; to break.
toro—to fight; to quarrel.
torosz wäkeval—fight fiercely (*greeting*).
totello—obey.
tsak—only.

tuhanos—thousand.
tuhanos löylyak türelamak saγe diutalet—a thousand patient breaths bring victory.
tule—to meet; to come.
tumte—to feel; to touch; to touch upon.
türe—full, satiated, accomplished.
türelam—patience.
türelam agba kontsalamaval—patience is the warrior's true weapon.
tyvi—stem; base; trunk.
uskol—faithful.
uskolfertiil—allegiance; loyalty.
varolind—dangerous.
veri—blood.
veri-elidet—blood-life.
veri ekäakank—blood of our brothers.
veri isäakank—blood of our fathers.
veri olen piros, ekäm—literally: blood be red, my brother; figuratively: find your lifemate (*greeting*).
veriak ot en Karpatiiak—by the blood of the Prince (*literally: by the blood of the great Carpathian; Carpathian swear words*).
veridet peje—may your blood burn (*Carpathian swear words*).
vigyáz—to love; to care for; to take care of.
vii—last; at last; finally.
wäke—power; strength.
wäke beki—strength; courage.
wäke kaδa—steadfastness.
wäke kutni—endurance.
wäke-sarna—vow; curse; blessing (*literally: power words*).
wäkeva—powerful.
wara—bird; crow.
weńća—complete; whole.
wete—water (*noun*).